'And how do you spend
Rutherford leaned forwa
your little bit for the wa
Amused by his conde
she said. 'I work for the

It was true. It just happened that the Inter-Services Research Bureau was the innocuous-sounding cover name for the highly secret Special Operations Executive.

Not surprisingly Greville Rutherford had never heard of it. For a second he looked blank. 'Secretarial, is it?'

'That's right,' Helen agreed. 'They don't trust us girls to do much more than that.'

He laughed delightedly. 'I should think not.' Then he frowned at Louise. 'That's what you ought to be doing, Louise, something gentle and ladylike, not grubbing about in some factory getting grease under your nails.' Looking back at Helen, he smiled, clearly pleased to be able to use her as an example to his errant daughter.

Helen returned his smile sweetly and wondered vaguely what he would say if she told him the truth, that her 'gentle and ladylike' work actually involved providing background intelligence briefings to secret agents going into occupied France to sabotage and kill, that she rather relished the dirty undercover world of secrets and danger, that it had in fact crossed her mind to volunteer for undercover work in France herself …

Educated in Oxford, Thame and at L.S.E., Helen Carey has had a variety of jobs including waitress, tour guide, oil trader and management course tutor. Now working as a freelance training consultant and writer, she divides her time between her home overlooking Clapham Common and a cottage in West Wales overlooking the Irish Sea.

By the same author

Lavender Road
Some Sunny Day

HELEN CAREY

On a Wing and a Prayer

ORION

An Orion Paperback
First published in Great Britain by Orion in 1997
This paperback edition published in 1998 by
Orion Books Ltd,
Orion House, 5 Upper St Martin's Lane,
London WC2H 9EA

A CIP catalogue record for this book
is available from the British Library.

Typeset by Deltatype Ltd, Birkenhead, Merseyside
Printed and bound in Great Britain by
Clays Ltd, St Ives plc.

In Memory of
Sally Wood

Prologue

October 1941

'So.' Angus McNaughton closed the interview room door, nodded at the military police corporal waiting outside, then glanced at his assistant as they began to walk away down the long, grey-walled War Office passage. 'What do you think, Helen? A possibility?'

Helen de Burrel glanced back at the unmarked door. 'He speaks very good French,' she said.

'But?'

Helen hesitated, surprised by the question. When Angus McNaughton had become her boss two months ago, he had made it quite clear that her role at selection interviews was to assess the candidate's language capability, nothing more. Nevertheless, in the face of his query, she felt obliged to state her reservations. 'There was something about him,' she said. 'He didn't seem to have quite the grounding of the others I have seen.'

Angus laughed. 'You mean he wasn't public school? Well, we can't all be out of the top drawer, Helen. So long as he's got guts and balls he'll make a good agent.'

Refusing to react to his deliberate taunt, Helen thought of the number of men with guts and balls the Special Operations Executive had sent to France. Some were already dead, tortured to death or shot by Gestapo firing squads; others, perhaps understandably, had gone over to the Germans and, even as they spoke, were causing immeasurable damage to the fragile Resistance networks. 'Surely they need more than that?' she asked. 'An integrity? Patriotism? A real courage?'

'Courage is a funny thing,' Angus said. 'The oddest people have it and the oddest people don't. It's not a quality you can measure. It's only when the chips are really down that you know whether you've got it or not. That's why we've toughened up the training programme. It's not infallible but it sorts the men from the boys.'

As they took the taxi back to the SOE building in Baker Street, Angus drew out a cigarette from his silver cigarette case and then hesitated, half offering her the case. 'You don't, do you?'

'No, thank you.'

He snapped the case shut. 'No vices, eh? Always immaculately dressed. Always polite. Competent. Diligent. Beautiful. How do you do it, Helen? Does it come with the title?'

The title. Lady Helen de Burrel. Lady. Just four meagre letters, but however much she tried to ignore them, in other people's eyes they inevitably set her apart. 'You make me sound very boring,' she said.

'On the contrary.' He opened the taxi door and stood back to let her out. 'I find you fascinating. You have worked for me for two months now and I have yet to find one single flaw.' As he ushered her into the discreetly anonymous building, he glanced at her with a faintly mocking smile. 'Tell me, you can trust me. Do you have any?'

Helen was about to make a joky reply when she heard the telephone ringing in her office.

'Helen? It's Louise. You haven't forgotten, have you? Only you said you'd be here early enough to help me decide what to wear.'

'Oh gosh,' Helen said. 'Louise, I'm awfully sorry. It's been a busy day. I promise I'll be there within the hour.'

Putting down the phone, she glanced at her watch and at Angus McNaughton who was standing in her doorway.

'There's a flaw,' she said lightly. 'I'd forgotten that I was to have dinner with one of my best friends. She's got a new boyfriend and she wants some moral support when she introduces him to her father.'

'Important stuff indeed,' Angus McNaughton said. He scooped his notes off her desk. 'These can keep for tomorrow. Far be it from me to interfere with the love lives of London's young ladies.'

Helen met his sarcasm with an easy smile but deep down she was annoyed. Whatever she did, however hard she tried to be efficient and competent, somehow Angus McNaughton always contrived to make her feel like a brainless little deb. It was particularly annoying considering that her previous boss, the Canadian Ward Frazer, had treated her so much as an equal. Someone he could trust. But now, unfortunately, Ward Frazer was locked up in a German prisoner-of-war camp.

With a deep sigh, Helen sat back in her chair and longed for the means to prove herself. So far everything had always come so easy. Even driving an ambulance at the beginning of the war had been surprisingly painless. She wished that at least once in her life she had really had to struggle. Like Ward Frazer's wife Katy had struggled to get her father's pub going again when it was bombed to rubble; even as Louise Rutherford had struggled to overcome the injury she received when Balham Tube station collapsed on top of her after a direct hit by the Luftwaffe.

Checking Angus was out of earshot, she lifted the telephone and gave a Mayfair number. 'Mrs Ford, I'm sorry to ring so late. I wonder if you could ask Nancy to put out my blue Chanel dress for this evening. Yes, the silk one. It might need pressing ... Thank you so much.'

Part One

Chapter One

'Goodness me, is that the best you can do?' Celia Rutherford eyed her daughter's flower arrangement with dismay as she brought the napkins into the dining-room. 'We didn't spend all that money on Lucie Clayton's just to have you shove half a dozen stems in a vase, you know. I do hope this factory war work you insist on doing isn't making you lose your feminine touch.'

Smarting, Louise snatched the flowers out of the vase and began arranging them all over again. She knew her mother would tell Jack that she had done the flowers, and the only thing worse than having Jack think that all she was interested in was flower arranging, was for him to notice that she had done them badly.

Catching sight of the clock she grabbed a white, late autumn rose and pricked herself on the stem. Feeling ridiculously close to tears, she sucked her finger and tried to steady herself. Panicking would only make things worse. If they could be worse.

She had only met Jack three times. Once at a private party at the Grosvenor when she hadn't been able to dance because of her injured hip, once at the reopening of the pub in Lavender Road when he had turned up unexpectedly and found her tipsy and sweaty from helping clear up the glasses, and once when he had taken her to the theatre to see Noël Coward's *Blithe Spirit* and she had been so tongue-tied afterwards that she couldn't think of one intelligent thing to say about the play.

It wasn't a good start, which made the success of tonight so very important. Because Louise had already decided that Sub-Lieutenant Jack Delmaine was going to be her salvation. He didn't know it yet, of course, but all her hopes rested on him. All her hopes of getting away from the stiff, disapproving formality of her parents' house. All her hopes of making an enviably successful marriage.

Jack was the perfect man for her. There was no doubt about it. Handsome in his own way with sandy hair, a scattering of freckles and wonderful blue eyes crinkled at the corners from staring out at the horizon for submarines or whatever naval officers stared at, Jack Delmaine was a man any girl would be proud of. He was charming, kind and well spoken.

Best of all he seemed to be keen on her. Really keen. Keen enough to face a dinner with her autocratic father and tweedy mother. Louise closed her eyes for a second. Thank God she had had the brainwave of asking Helen de Burrel to come as well. Her parents approved of Helen. Being a lady helped of course, particularly with her father, and Helen, as well as being blonde and coolly beautiful, always knew what to say. She could certainly be relied on to smooth over any awkward silences.

As the clock chimed, Louise looked up in horror. Seven o'clock and Helen still wasn't here. In sudden panic, frantically scooping up the trimmings and fallen petals, Louise realised she was going to have to decide for herself what to wear.

Lowering her menu reluctantly, Joyce Carter racked her brain for something to say to break the uneasy silence. With most men you could ask about their jobs or their business, but with a pawnbroker it didn't seem quite the thing somehow. The weather was a possibility, she supposed, or the war, but both of those were gloomy and depressing at the moment and she felt a lighter subject would be more appropriate. She was just about to ask if he often ate out in fancy restaurants like this, when Mr Lorenz leaned forward courteously.

'Have you chosen?'

'What? Oh.' Joyce grabbed the menu again and studied it nervously. It was all very well this going-out-to-dinner lark, but how was she meant to know what to pick? She couldn't understand half of it anyway. There were French words scattered in among the English ones and the only thing she really fancied was grilled pilchards and she could just as well have them at home. Not that she normally had them grilled. Generally she mashed them up with a fork and spread them on bread for the boys' tea. The older two, Pete and Bob, weren't fussed about pilchards but young Mick had been particularly partial to them.

She wondered suddenly how Mick was getting on in the merchant marine. She had had one short note, a scruffy bit of paper saying he was going to America. America. Clumsy, cocky young Mick. It seemed incredible. Mick on a boat. Mick in America. She wondered what trouble he would manage to cause there. Then she felt a stab of remorse. Mick wasn't all bad. He'd done her a good turn before he left by bubbling his father to the coppers.

Joyce felt the sweat prickle in her armpits as she relived that wonderful moment when Stanley had been led away in handcuffs. She still could hardly believe it. Nor the subsequent relief when she heard that this time he'd gone down for two years. Two years.

To her dismay, she felt a lump of emotion in her throat and swallowed hard. It was ridiculous to want to cry, but she just couldn't help it. Stanley had been gone well over a month now and she still wasn't used to it. She still felt tense when she woke up, she still jumped nervously when she heard a step behind her. Sometimes, until she remembered, she even felt that hard ball of fear in her stomach. And then, when she did remember that she was safe, she wanted to cry.

Aware suddenly of a polite cough, she looked up blankly

to find a waiter standing by the table expectantly. 'Has madam decided?'

Joyce frowned. A Frenchie, she reckoned. She wasn't much of a one for foreigners, with their smarmy accents and condescending smiles. In any case, the bloody French were the last people on earth who should be condescending just now. As far as she could see they'd handed their whole country over to Hitler on a plate and offered him a glass of wine to be going on with and all. 'Yes,' she said, pointing at the menu. 'I'll have them pilchards.'

'And to follow?'

'What?'

'The pilchards are an *hors d'oeuvre*, madam.'

Feeling a faint sense of panic creeping over her, Joyce glanced helplessly at her dining companion.

'What would you like for your main course, Mrs Carter?' Mr Lorenz asked gently. 'After the pilchards.'

Joyce blinked. Was she meant to have two things? In some desperation she stared at the menu again. 'I'll have the cod,' she said. Cod was all right, although cream sauce sounded a bit dodgy. She would have preferred it in batter.

'Pilchards followed by cod,' the waiter said with a slight sneer and she knew immediately that she had made the wrong choice.

Wishing she was at home with a nice Marmite sandwich and a cup of tea, she heard Lorenz order soup and a lamb stew and wondered why she hadn't chosen those. She was about to check her menu again when the waiter flicked it out of her hand and left her staring across the table into the pawnbroker's soft dark eyes.

He leaned forward slightly. 'Are you feeling all right, Mrs Carter?'

'Oh yes,' she said. 'Yes. I'm fine.' But she could feel herself flushing. 'It's ... just that I'm not used to restaurants.'

Mr Lorenz looked concerned. 'Perhaps you would have preferred to go to the cinema?'

'No, no, this is all right,' Joyce mumbled, feeling ungrateful. She looked rather wildly around the elegant restaurant with its flickering candles and white tablecloths. 'It's very nice.'

After all, he hadn't had to ask her out. He was only being kind. Same as he'd been kind earlier in the year when he'd slipped her a couple of Guinnesses to keep her going over a bad patch. He wasn't to know she'd feel all at sea. Awkward and embarrassed and wanting to cry. He wasn't to know that it was too soon. That all she wanted just now was to be left alone. Left alone to come to terms with the fact that she had her own life again and wasn't going to be beaten up every time she put a foot wrong.

Biting her lip she sat back in her chair and smoothed the napkin on her lap. She couldn't go on like this. She was going to have to make conversation. But what about? It had to be something impersonal, something safe. She sighed. It was going to have to be the war after all.

Fixing a smile on her lips she took a deep breath and looked up at Lorenz determinedly. 'Have you seen the paper today? It doesn't look as though them poor Russians are going to last out much longer.'

'It was Clapham Common Northside you wanted, wasn't it?' the taxi driver shouted over his shoulder as he threaded his way through the blacked-out Victorian terraces that lined the steep hill on the south side of the river.

'That's right,' Helen said. 'Cedars House. On the corner of Lavender Road.'

'All these blinking roads look the same to me,' he grumbled. 'And the houses and all.'

Helen glanced at the delicate gold watch on her wrist. Seven thirty. Louise would kill her. 'This one doesn't look the same,' she said. 'I've been there once before. It's quite a big place,' she said. 'White, I think.'

She was right. It was a large, white, flat-fronted

Georgian house set back in a short drive and overlooking the wide open expanse of Clapham Common. It wasn't as large or as elegant of course as her own father's house, nor did it have such a prestigious address, but it was definitely a step up from the shabby slate-roofed terraces behind it, and made Helen feel that the Rutherford & Berry brewery which Louise's father owned and ran must be quite a lucrative business.

Indoors the house was tastefully if somewhat austerely furnished. There were one or two nice antiques, probably family heirlooms, and at the back big heavily curtained windows looked out over a spacious garden, much of which, Mrs Rutherford told her proudly, had been turned over to vegetables and chickens. Altogether it seemed to Helen to be a nice family house and the only problem with it was that it was extraordinarily cold.

The dining-room was coldest of all. In fact as she mouthed a slightly self-conscious 'amen' to Mr Rutherford's grace, it was as much as Helen could do to stop her teeth chattering. She wished she had Louise's place on the other side of the wide table with her back to the grate where three pieces of coal and two small logs were at least making some effort to produce flames. Louise had once told her that her father was the kind of man who never felt the cold, and certainly looking at him now, sitting stiffly at the head of the table while his wife brought in the food, Helen could well believe it.

She had only met Greville Rutherford once before, but even then she had been struck by his strict, uncompromising manner. He could hardly have been more different from her own liberal, easy-going father, who would have roared with laughter at the thought of saying grace at his own dinner table. Or anywhere else come to that.

Now as she listened to her host holding forth on the iniquities of the self-appointed Free French leader, General de Gaulle, Helen wondered suddenly how old he was. Mid forties, she would guess. Not much more than that, despite the hint of silver in the hair above his ears. He still looked pretty fit – she had some idea that Louise had told her he had been quite a sportsman in his youth. No, it was the disapproving frown and the clipped vowels that made him seem older. That and his extraordinarily outdated views.

But then Greville Rutherford was very much of the old school, the sort of man who thought that girls who lived in flats of their own and wore trousers were fast. As far as he was concerned a woman's place was in the home at her husband's side. Over a small sherry before dinner Helen had gathered that he was appalled by his wife's idea of opening a café, and the fact that Louise had defied his strictures and taken a job in an armaments factory was clearly a major bone of contention between them.

Certainly there was no love lost between father and daughter. Even as Greville Rutherford expounded his absurdly Francophobic views to Jack Delmaine, Louise leaned forward and pointedly reminded him that he shouldn't be too rude about the French because Helen was French herself.

Almost feeling sorry for him as he blustered to an abrupt halt in his diatribe, Helen smiled. 'Only a quarter, in fact,' she said mildly. 'Despite the name, it was actually my grandmother who was French.'

'But you've spent a lot of time there,' Louise prompted, clearly determined to discomfort her father as much as possible. 'You feel quite French, don't you?'

'I spent a lot of my childhood in the South of France,' Helen said. 'My mother died when I was quite young so I used to be sent to stay with my grandmother for holidays.'

Looking up she saw the sympathetic faces round the table and realised she might have given the wrong impression. Far from being a traumatic banishment for a young child, those carefree holidays had actually been some of the most pleasurable times of her life. Long sunny days, beautiful sandy beaches, jovial al fresco meals, and later in her teens, exciting trysts with glamorous French boys under the stars.

Thinking about it now it seemed incredible that all that was gone. And even more incredible that those same people who had taken the blonde little English girl into their hearts were now living under the fiercely anti-British Vichy regime, and thanks to the German propaganda would probably cash in an English airman or undercover agent to their German masters without a thought.

'I feel sorry for the French,' Louise said suddenly. 'I'm sure they are not all cowards like Daddy says.'

'Do be quiet, Louise,' her father snapped. 'Nobody wants to hear your opinion.'

'I had a holiday in France once.' Jack Delmaine broke the uneasy silence. 'Climbing in the Massif Central. We had a marvellous time.' He laughed self-deprecatingly. 'There was certainly no shortage of courage among the climbing instructors there.'

As Louise glanced triumphantly at her father, Helen eyed Jack Delmaine with new respect, impressed by his understated courage. As far as she was concerned anyone who did rock-climbing was brave; she herself was terrible with heights. Once as a child she had disgraced herself by being sick at the top of the Eiffel Tower, and on a school trip to Dover she had taken one glance over the white cliffs and fainted clean away. It was also pretty brave of Jack, of course, to stand up for Louise against her father, but then Sub-Lieutenant Jack Delmaine was a thoroughly nice chap. Handsome and at ease in his smart blue uniform, with Louise hanging on his every word, it wasn't hard to imagine him manning the bridge of some sleek Royal Navy frigate. Nor was it hard to imagine why Louise was so besotted with him.

Helen glanced at her friend wryly. Pretty and vivacious, Louise had always been besotted with someone. At one time she had been madly in love with Helen's old boss, Ward Frazer. After that there'd been some mysterious

Polish count. None of them had worked out, and Helen wondered if she would bring it off this time. She hoped so. Louise might be flighty and selfish but she was good at heart and she deserved a lucky break.

'And how do you spend your time, Lady Helen?' Greville Rutherford leaned forward suddenly. 'I'm sure you're doing your little bit for the war effort, aren't you?'

Amused by his condescension, Helen nodded. 'Oh yes,' she said. 'I work for the Inter-Services Research Bureau.'

It was true. It just happened that the Inter-Services Research Bureau was the innocuous-sounding cover name for the highly secret Special Operations Executive.

Not surprisingly Greville Rutherford had never heard of it. For a second he looked blank. 'Secretarial, is it?'

'That's right,' Helen agreed. 'They don't trust us girls to do much more than that.'

He laughed delightedly. 'I should think not.' Then he frowned at Louise. 'That's what you ought to be doing, Louise, something gentle and ladylike, not grubbing about in some factory getting grease under your nails.' Looking back at Helen, he smiled, clearly pleased to be able to use her as an example to his errant daughter.

Helen returned his smile sweetly and wondered vaguely what he would say if she told him the truth, that her 'gentle and ladylike' work actually involved providing background intelligence briefings to secret agents going into occupied France to sabotage and kill, that she rather relished the dirty undercover world of secrets and danger, that it had in fact crossed her mind to volunteer for undercover work in France herself ...

Suddenly Helen's idle musings stopped in an abrupt jerk, causing her to choke on her last mouthful of food. What had she just ... ? Quickly she replayed her thoughts.

It had crossed her mind to volunteer ...

Had it? Had it really? Her smile faded rapidly. And when had this mind-crossing taken place, she wondered. Because she had certainly not been aware of it.

Suddenly she realised she felt rather sick and hoped she wasn't going to disgrace herself. She didn't much like jugged hare at the best of times, but the last thing she wanted to do was vomit it all over the Rutherfords' dinner table.

After a moment she felt better and breathed again. Tentatively she allowed herself to examine the idea.

Well, why not? She spoke the language. She knew the terrain. She suddenly felt a sense of exhilaration. Goodness, that would show them, wouldn't it? All those condescending men. And it would prove something too. It would prove that she was more than a pretty face from a privileged background.

Becoming aware that everyone was watching her oddly, she smiled apologetically. 'I'm awfully sorry. I think someone must just have stepped on my grave.'

'You're cold,' Greville Rutherford said, standing up to kick the meagre fire. 'I'd better get some more coal in.'

'No, no, I'm fine really—' Helen began, then catching Louise's warning glance she bit back the rest as Jack leaped to his feet and grabbed the coal scuttle.

'Let me, sir.'

Greville Rutherford blinked. 'But you don't know where ...'

Louise threw down her napkin. 'I'll show him,' she said, and before anyone could speak they had both left the room.

'Well, really ...' Greville Rutherford turned incredulously to his wife, but Helen beat him to it. She had understood Louise's silent message. She knew her duty. Shoving her private mental turmoil to the back of her mind she leaned forward with her most interested smile. 'So where is your new café venture going to be, Mrs Rutherford? Near here somewhere?'

Outside in the hall, Louise glanced at Jack cautiously. He was so polite, so well mannered, that it was hard to know if he was finding the evening as much of an ordeal as she was. As he stood swinging the coal scuttle gently in his left hand with a small smile on his lips she couldn't tell whether he was pleasantly surprised or completely put off by her home and her parents. Let alone by her. She longed to know what he felt about her. Longed to know if he was as serious about her as she increasingly was about him. More than anything she wanted him to kiss her. To kiss her properly, deeply and passionately. Not just the polite little peck on the cheek he had given her in greeting earlier.

Of course he didn't know she was considerably more experienced than she looked. He wasn't to know that not so very long ago she had had a passionate affair with a somewhat athletic Polish count. She shivered. Not many people did know that, come to think of it, and she was going to have to make very sure Jack never found out about it. Or its unfortunate consequences. In any case she didn't feel experienced just now. She suddenly felt very young and very shy.

'I'm sorry about Daddy,' she said. 'I'm afraid he is rather overbearing, but I did warn you.'

Jack smiled. 'Your parents are charming and your friend Helen is delightful.'

Louise frowned. She didn't want him thinking Helen was too delightful. That wasn't the point at all. Then behind her through the door she heard Helen asking her mother about the merits of government-restricted five-shilling meals and decided to be generous.

'Yes,' she said. 'Helen's brilliant, isn't she? Do you think she was really cold or do you think she was just giving us an excuse?'

'An excuse for what?'

Louise stared at him. Surely he couldn't be so dense. Or was it just that he didn't feel the same way she did? Either way her heart sank slightly. Suddenly she wished she had worn something a bit more daring. After all, Helen's blue silk shift dress was considerably more sexy than the rather conservative cashmere twinset she had finally opted for in case Jack preferred his women demure. 'Well,' she said awkwardly, looking anywhere but at him, 'An excuse for us to be alone for a minute …'

When he didn't answer at once her heart sank another notch, but then eventually she had to look up and was disconcerted to find him watching her closely. As she met his eyes he smiled slowly and she saw at once that he'd known what she was after all along.

As the colour flooded her face, he laughed softly. 'I want more than a minute alone with you, Louise,' he said. 'I was thinking more in terms of the rest of my life.'

Louise's eyes widened. For a second, as the import of his words hit her, she thought she was going to faint. 'Oh Jack …' She wanted to say more, but before she could find air in her lungs he was putting up his hand.

'Don't say anything,' he said. 'Don't say yes or no. It's early days. We need to get to know each other first.'

'But how can we if you're stuck up in beastly Liverpool all the time?' Louise said. She didn't want to get to know him. She wanted to sign up for her future there and then.

He shook his head and smiled. 'We'll find time. There's no rush.' Then he raised the coal bucket. 'Now you'd better tell me where to find the coal, or your father will wonder what we've been up to.'

Helen had asked her taxi to come back for her at a quarter past ten. Nobody kept very late hours these days. The dreadful nightly bombing earlier in the year had knocked London's social life on the head, and even though the Germans' planes were nowadays far more busy bombing the guts out of the poor beleaguered Russians, the habit seemed to have stuck.

Helen felt far too strung up to go meekly home to bed, though. More than anything she wanted to think seriously about volunteering as an agent. Now she had had the idea she couldn't let it go.

If only there was someone she could talk to, but the very nature of the work precluded any possibility of that: the whole SOE operation was so secret that most government ministers didn't even know about it.

Then as the taxi driver turned out of the Rutherfords' driveway into Lavender Road, she suddenly realised there was someone she could talk to about it. Hugging her coat round her against the chilling cold she leaned forward and tapped urgently on his glass. 'I'm sorry, but I need to call at the pub on the corner there. The Flag and Garter. Please wait for me. I won't be long.'

Katy Frazer was pulling a pint when Helen came into the pub. She looked up as the door swung shut. As the colour left the other girl's already pale face, Helen winced, but Katy's reaction was not hard to understand. In the past Helen's arrival in the pub had so often spelt bad news.

It was Helen who had whisked Ward Frazer away from his and Katy's honeymoon for one last mission into France. Then when he hadn't returned it was Helen who'd had to tell Katy that the plane had crashed and that Ward was either dead or in the hands of the enemy. The only saving grace in her relationship with Katy had been that wonderful evening just over a month ago, the day Katy had reopened the pub after her father's death, when Helen had raced down to Clapham with the news from the International Red Cross that Ward was safe in a prisoner-of-war camp in Germany.

'It's all right,' she said quickly now. 'This is just a social visit. I was dining at the Rutherfords' and I desperately need a drink. Old man Rutherford is not very generous in that department.'

'He's not very generous in any department,' Katy said, and Helen remembered that as owner of the brewery, Greville Rutherford was in effect Katy's boss. He was obviously a hard taskmaster. Katy looked very tired. Her pregnancy was showing now and the effort of running the pub more or less single handed was obviously taking its toll.

Already Katy was pulling herself together, however, smiling a belated welcome, and waving a hand at the bottle-filled dresser behind her. 'Helen, it's lovely to see you. What will you have?'

Helen pulled off her gloves. 'Could you spare a tot of whisky? I can't stay long because I've got a taxi waiting.'

Katy reached for the bottle at once and poured a generous measure. As she slid it across the counter her eyes lit up suddenly. 'Did Louise tell you? I've had a letter at last.'

'From Ward?' Helen asked. 'And?'

Katy made a face. 'Well, it was written two months ago so it is a bit out of date, and it's heavily censored, but he sounds quite jolly. Well, as jolly as can be expected. He was obviously quite badly wounded. I think he must have been in hospital for a while, but he says he's on the mend.' She hesitated and bit her lip, then she looked up and there were tears in her eyes. 'He's alive, that's the main thing. And safe.'

'Yes,' Helen said. 'Thank God.'

Katy turned away then to serve another customer and Helen sipped her whisky and thought about Ward Frazer. Ward Frazer who could have had virtually any woman he wanted, but who, to everyone's astonishment, had chosen the shy little nurse Katy Parsons.

Looking at Katy now as she skilfully operated the optics, she realised that Ward had seen more in Katy than anyone else had. He must have seen more than the mousy, self-effacing asthmatic girl he had married. He must have seen the inner strength that had enabled her to survive the loss of her father, and the gritty courage that had enabled her to reopen the pub against the odds. Ward was a good judge of people. She wished he was here now.

As Katy turned back to her with an apologetic smile Helen downed the last of her drink.

'Katy,' she said abruptly. 'There's something I want to ask you. Is there somewhere private?'

'Of course,' Katy said. 'We can go into the saloon bar. There's nobody in there at the moment.' She sounded quite calm but as soon as they were in the other room she turned to face Helen. 'Is it something about Ward? Something I don't know?'

Helen shook her head quickly. 'No.' Then she stopped and went on more slowly, 'Well, not exactly.' She glanced over her shoulder to make sure they weren't being overheard, then turned back to Katy and made a slight face. 'There's nobody else I can talk to about this. I shouldn't even talk to you.' She lowered her voice. 'What would you say if I told you I am thinking of volunteering for overseas work?'

'Overseas work?' For a moment Katy stared at her blankly. Then her face paled. 'You mean … like Ward … Surely they don't take girls?' She stopped. 'No,' she said. 'Don't, Helen. Don't do it—' She saw Helen's expression and tailed off abruptly. 'But why? You've got so much. You've got a good job. A lovely lifestyle. Surely you don't want to … to throw all that away.'

'I don't want to throw it away,' Helen said, 'but I want to prove I'm more than that. I want to prove I've got guts. Courage.' She waved her arm round the room. 'Like you have with all this.'

'Goodness,' Katy said. 'It's hardly courageous to run a pub.' She shook her head. 'Please, Helen, don't do it,' she said. 'It's too dangerous.' She stopped again and Helen saw there were tears in her eyes. 'You and I both know that Ward is one of the lucky ones.'

Helen walked over to the window. 'But we're so short of good agents, and I've got the languages. With the right training I think I could do a good job.' She hesitated then turned back to face Katy again. 'Tell me, Katy. Honestly. What do you think Ward would say?'

For a second as Katy's eyes narrowed, Helen thought she was going to say Ward would be dead against it, but Katy was too straight, and she knew Ward too well.

After a moment's indecision she sighed heavily. 'Ward would say you have to do what you think is right,' she said.

The taxi driver was not pleased to have waited so long outside. He grumbled all the way back to Victoria about the inconvenience caused to taxi drivers by people wanting to trail about South London all night, and then from Victoria all the way round the Palace and up Park Lane he complained about the inadequacies of the Russians.

'That Stalin is moving his government out of Moscow, you know. Not much courage, them Ruskies, I don't reckon. Our leaders didn't leave London in the blitz, did they? Not even the King and Queen, not even them young princesses …'

He was finally only silenced in Curzon Street by an overly generous tip. 'Well, thank you, miss! And, of course, if you ever need a ride south of the river again …'

Smiling grimly, Helen ran up the marble steps and pulled the bell.

To her surprise, it was her father who opened the door, holding a cigar.

'Helen, my dear.' His handsome face lit up as always when he saw her but she could tell immediately that there was something on his mind. Sure enough, as soon as he had kissed her he stood back pensively. 'I'm glad I caught you,' he said. 'I'm afraid I've got some rather bad news.'

He drew on the cigar and blew out a small cloud of aromatic smoke. 'The house has been requisitioned,' he said. 'With all the hotels full to bursting, some damned Ministry lackey has decided they need somewhere for visiting dignitaries to stay.'

Helen stared at him blankly. It's starting, she thought.

It's like a sign. She looked up at her father. 'Will you contest it?'

He lifted his shoulders with a gesture of resignation. 'No. The place is too big for the two of us anyway.' He waved an arm benignly round the spacious marbled hall. 'Let them have it. I'll put the most valuable pieces into safe storage. The rest doesn't matter. Got to do our bit, after all.' He frowned. 'In any case, there's some talk about my going to Washington. I think old Winnie feels a bit of wining and dining over there might help pull the Yanks in a bit quicker. Until then I'll move into my club. The staff can stay here, of course, but what about you, my dear? Do you want to come to America with me? Or shall I get you a nice little flat somewhere?'

Helen smiled and shook her head. She wasn't fooled about the wining and dining any more than the Americans would be. Despite his easygoing manners, her father was a highly respected member of the British aristocracy, an active member of the House of Lords, and if he was being asked to go to America, there was going to be some very definite role for him to play.

As far as Helen was concerned, although the thought of a few months in America was tempting, she had other plans. As for where to live, she had had a flat of her own at the start of the war, but when the bombing had started it had seemed sensible to move back into her father's house with its deep bombproof cellars. In any case, to be honest she had missed the convenience of being waited on hand and foot. Employing staff might be a luxury these days, but they certainly made life more comfortable. However, she couldn't rely on her father for ever.

'It's all right,' she said now. 'I'll find somewhere here. Perhaps with a friend. Don't worry about me.'

He laughed as he flicked his ash on to the flaming logs in the grate. 'I never worry about you, poppet. You know that. You've always been far too sensible to worry about.'

Chapter Two

Katy Frazer was totting up her till takings from the night before when the district nurse called at the pub. Her heart sank. She was already running late. Her mother had been in one of her low moods this morning and by the time Katy had persuaded her to get up and have some breakfast and then go shopping, Aaref Hoch, the Jewish boy from up the road, was waiting downstairs to see what Katy needed for the pub in the way of cigarettes.

At first when Aaref Hoch had offered to provide her with saleable goods Katy had been concerned about their provenance, but after two months of running the Flag and Garter her qualms had been outweighed by more practical considerations. Without Aaref and his back-of-the-lorry supplies she simply wouldn't have been able to make ends meet.

Aaref was followed by the Rutherford & Berry delivery dray, and by the time the barrels and crates had been ponderously checked and lowered into the cellar by the elderly drayman Cyril, Katy was beginning to panic about being ready to open at lunchtime. Not opening meant no takings and that was one thing she certainly could not afford.

So, all in all, the last person she wanted to see was the district nurse, particularly as the pristine white-capped woman was looking around the empty bar with an expression of distaste. Having trained as a nurse herself for six months, Katy was used to sour-faced nursing sisters, and she didn't care one iota if this one found the stale smell of beer and old smoke distasteful. Katy didn't like it much herself but she had no choice. Running the pub was her only hope of providing a living for herself, her mother and her unborn child.

It was of course about the unborn child that the district nurse had called.

'You have missed two appointments at the clinic,' she said taking off her black leather gloves, 'so I thought I'd better call to see if everything was all right.'

Katy shook her head helplessly. 'I'm sorry,' she said, 'but I've been so busy here, I just haven't had time.'

Laying her gloves rather dubiously on the sticky counter, the district nurse withdrew a file from her briefcase. 'Now let me see. Your baby is due on the fifth of January. So all being well you will be taken down to our sector's maternity unit in Ashford on the first of December.'

Startled by Katy's gulp of astonishment she stopped and managed a faint smile. 'Don't look so concerned, Mrs Frazer. All my ladies love it down there. It gives them a chance to rest up thoroughly before the baby comes. And with so many of the London hospitals closed, we just haven't the antenatal facilities here any more.'

Staring at her in complete horror, it was a moment before Katy could find the words to speak. 'I can't possibly go out of London,' she said. She waved her hands around the bar. 'I run this place. It's my livelihood. I can't just abandon it.' Especially not at Christmas, she thought, the one time in the year when she might actually manage to make some money.

The district nurse was clearly taken aback by Katy's vehemence. 'I'm afraid there really isn't any choice,' she said. 'You can't work right up to the moment of confinement in any case. You should be resting already. Saving your strength.' She saw Katy's expression and frowned. 'Are you familiar with babies, Mrs Frazer? No.

Well, believe me, you'll need all the strength you can find when the baby is born.'

Katy did believe her. She had few illusions about how easy it would be to run a pub and nurse a small baby at the same time, but that was a bridge she would cross when she got to it. There were plenty of problems to overcome before then. Problems like how to attract sufficient customers night after night, how to get her mother to take her share of the work, how to persuade Mr Rutherford to extend the lease beyond the end of the year. For a second she felt the familiar stab of panic and shook her head. She didn't have time to worry about the baby. Not yet.

The district nurse was looking at her with some concern now. 'Surely you have staff, Mrs Frazer, who could man the ship while you're away, so to speak?'

Katy shrugged. 'I hold the licence jointly with my mother, but she finds working behind the bar very stressful and my evening barman isn't up to holding the fort on his own.' She wondered what the district nurse would say if she told her that Bob Carter, her barman, was a soldier who should have been back at his unit weeks ago after a prolonged sick leave for a non-existent bad back. She didn't like employing someone who was pretty much a deserter, but beggars couldn't be choosers and Bob Carter had proved to be an enormous help.

The district nurse consulted her notes. 'And your husband is in a prisoner-of-war camp. So there's not much chance of help from that quarter.'

'No,' Katy said, 'there's not.' Sliding her hand in her apron pocket she touched the single sheet of flimsy blue paper headed Oflag 1XA. Other than the small diamond ring he had bought her on their abruptly curtailed honeymoon, that closely written letter was currently her most precious possession. The only thing that was keeping her going at all in fact was the knowledge that Ward was alive.

For a second the district nurse studied her closely, then

she gathered up her gloves and attempted to unstick the file from the counter. She nodded, and there was genuine sympathy in her eyes. 'I can see it would be awkward for you to leave London, Mrs Frazer. I will see what I can do.' She hesitated. 'But I must urge you most seriously to consider your position carefully, both for your own sake and for the sake of your child. Healthy relaxed babies are born to healthy relaxed mothers, Mrs Frazer, and it is clear to me that you have far too much resting on your shoulders. At the very least you should be putting your feet up for a couple of hours each afternoon.'

Katy nodded obediently but inside she felt a bubble of slightly hysterical laughter. Where on earth was she going to find a couple of spare hours? Even as she opened the door for the district nurse and thanked her for taking the trouble to come round, her eyes were on the clock. Less than an hour to opening time and all the cleaning still to do, the new beer to spike, the fires to light, the glasses to wash from last night.

She sighed and glanced down the quiet street in the hopes of seeing her mother coming back from the shops, but there was no sign of her. The only people out and about in Lavender Road were Pam Nelson and her recently adopted child, seven-year-old George.

Katy waved and then groaned inwardly as Pam approached. She was fond of Pam but George was proving a difficult child and on the last occasion Pam had brought him into the pub he had broken three of her precious pint glasses and sprayed a soda syphon up the leg of one of her most valued regulars.

Now, though, she felt guilty for her dismay. Poor Pam Nelson looked at the end of her tether. Until George's adoption Pam had been used to a calm nine-to-five job in the Ministry of Information, and looking after an increasingly rebellious seven-year-old twenty-four hours a day had come as a shock.

'Where are you off to?' Katy asked, ruffling George's

golden head as he turned his deceptively angelic face up to smile at her.

Pam tapped the ration books in her basket. 'We're going shopping,' she said.

George had other ideas. 'I don't want to go shopping,' he said and emphasised his reluctance by grasping Katy's leg.

Meeting Pam's desperate eyes over the child's head, Katy felt herself begin to weaken. It was so unfair. Pam Nelson had longed for a child for so long, and when their friend and neighbour Sheila Whitehead had been killed in a bombing raid, Pam and Alan had struggled for months to be allowed to adopt her son George.

George himself, hating his uncle and aunt, had pleaded for Pam and Alan to have him, and then almost as soon as it was agreed, he started playing them up. Even now there were tears in Pam's eyes as she tried to prise him off Katy's leg.

Katy felt her heart twist. 'He can stay with me if he wants,' she said.

Pam looked relieved. 'Shopping would certainly be easier without him in this mood,' she said. 'He gets so bored in the queues. But do you mind?'

Katy shook her head then glared severely at little George who was now dancing round her clapping his hands with glee. 'But you're going to have to work because I'm very busy.'

He stopped clapping and looked rather taken aback. 'All right.'

She took a breath. 'I'm going to give you a cloth and you can wipe all the tables for me, making them nice and clean, and if you break anything I'll be very cross.'

Helen de Burrel spent the first hour in the office every day reading the papers. Part of her job was to scour the newspapers and Reuters reports for any news of interest to the organisation. Today the big headline news was that it was snowing hard in Russia. Sitting back in her chair, Helen couldn't help thinking how extraordinary it was that it mattered so much what the weather was like in Russia. But the Russian winter had finished off Napoleon's army in October 1812 and now of course everyone was hoping the same thing would happen to Hitler's in October 1941.

Also in the papers was a report that fifty French hostages had been shot in retaliation for the killing of a German officer in Nantes, and the Vichy government was blaming British secret agents for the murder. Helen didn't know if that was true or not but she rather doubted it. However, if the Germans were going to react to terrorist acts by randomly killing innocent local people, it was going to make the lives of agents in the field far more difficult.

She turned the page hastily. In the cold light of day the thought of volunteering as an agent didn't seem quite so appealing. Katy Frazer's reaction last night had brought home to her the realities of what she proposed. On the other hand fluent French speakers were needed badly.

'Well, good morning.'

Looking up, Helen saw Angus McNaughton lounging in her doorway smoking a cigarette. 'Is that the news you're reading? Or the court circular?' He smiled as she flushed slightly, and waved his cigarette at the newspapers on her desk. 'Any society engagements I should know about?'

Irritated by his attitude, Helen stood up suddenly. 'Angus, would you mind shutting the door?'

'Of course.' He clicked the door shut behind him and turned to face her.

She met his expectant gaze squarely. 'Angus, do you think I'd have any chance of being accepted for agent training?'

His face froze. 'Good God, girl, are you serious?'

'Perfectly.'

A scattering of ash fell off the end of his cigarette as he stared at her in silence. When he spoke his voice was low and serious, all his blasé dismissiveness had vanished. 'You know what this means? I don't need to tell you the dangers involved.'

Helen swallowed. 'No, you don't.'

He was frowning now. 'Have you thought what it's like being quite alone in enemy territory? Not knowing for certain who you can trust? Who might hand you in to the Gestapo?'

Helen nodded. 'Yes, I have thought about it.'

'And you still want to be considered.' It was a statement not a question. She realised to her surprise that she had passed the first hurdle, that of being taken seriously.

Walking over to the window he tapped his ash into the pot of a small ferociously spiked cactus that stood on the sill. 'You'd have to pass a psychological assessment interview, of course.' He looked at her thoughtfully. 'But you've got the languages, that's a start.'

Helen nodded again. She didn't trust herself to speak in any language just at that second. She had a nasty feeling her voice would come out as some kind of strangled squeak, or worse, not at all. It was partly to do with the way he was looking at her as though he was seeing her for the first time. Suddenly she realised that he probably was. For the first time he was seeing her as something other than a blonde, linguistically able, well-to-do young socialite. And his slow, assessing gaze unnerved her.

'What does your father think about it?'

Helen held his gaze steadily. She knew the question was a trick. To test her discretion. 'I don't know,' she said. 'I haven't asked him.'

'I see.' There was another pause, then Angus stubbed out his cigarette. 'The training programme is very tough,' he said suddenly. He turned to face her again. 'Physically and mentally. It has to be. This is not something anyone should undertake lightly. However, if you are certain, I won't stand in your way. We need agents, and who knows . . .' He stopped then shrugged slightly. 'There may be a delay. As you know, we are undergoing a change of leadership, but I'll certainly pass word up the line.'

'Thank you.'

He nodded. 'I hardly need say that you should not mention this conversation to anyone.' He looked at her again for a second, then he opened the door and went out of the room.

For a long moment after he had gone Helen stood where she was, staring at the door. Then she took a piece of her father's embossed notepaper out of her drawer, picked up her Parker fountain pen and wrote a note to Mrs Rutherford thanking her for dinner last night.

Celia Rutherford unlocked the door of the premises she had rented on the corner of Lavender Road and Lavender Hill and ushered Joyce Carter inside.

'What do you think?' she asked eagerly. 'It's coming on, isn't it?'

Joyce looked around. 'It's nice,' she said. 'Really nice.' She hadn't seen it since the ceiling had been painted. Propped against the wall, waiting to be hung over the fireplace was a magnificent picture of the King which Joyce had noticed at a WVS jumble sale and Mrs Rutherford had bought for ten bob. They had wanted Winston Churchill too but they hadn't been able to find one of him. There were eight tables. Chairs were in short supply these days but Celia had found half a dozen benches from a bombed-out school in the East End and Joyce's builder son Pete had cut them down to the right length. The linoleum-topped counter was six feet long. Joyce tried to imagine it set up with a tea urn, cups and saucers and plates of buns and cakes.

'I think we should open from half past seven until half past four,' Celia said. 'That means we'll be able to do breakfast, elevenses and lunch and tea and then we can use the rest of the afternoon for preparing the food for the next day.' She stopped and glanced anxiously at Joyce.

'Do you think you could get in by half past seven, Mrs Carter?'

Joyce felt a trickle of excitement. It was all suddenly becoming real. Her lifelong dream of running a little caff, or café as Mrs Rutherford called it. She nodded eagerly. 'Now Mick's at sea it's only Pete and Bob at home. Pete's gone by half seven and Bob lies in half the morning anyway.'

'What about your daughter? Isn't she coming home soon?'

'Jen?' Joyce frowned. 'Is she?' It was the first she had heard of it. This time last year Jen had gone off on a nationwide ENSA tour. It had been Jen's first real job as an actress, and to be honest Joyce had been glad to see the back of her. She certainly didn't want her back. The thought of her eldest daughter's tantrums, her prima donna ways, her fancy clothes and scornful attitude made her cringe. Joyce wanted things to stay just as they were now. Her and the two boys. Bob and Pete. Her two younger children were in Devon evacuated to a farm there at the beginning of the war. She'd been to see them once and had realised they were better off where they were. They were being well fed, well schooled and they were happy. She didn't miss them so much any more. And she certainly hadn't missed Jen.

Celia Rutherford was looking surprised. 'I heard she had got a part in one of the London reviews,' she said. 'Louise mentioned it. She'd heard from Katy Frazer.'

'Well, nobody has told me,' Joyce said sourly. Mind you, that was typical of Jen. She had always treated her family like dirt. Joyce squared her shoulders. 'I'm not staying at home to get Jen her breakfast, that's for sure. I've got my own life to lead now.'

Celia Rutherford laughed. 'That's the spirit, Mrs Carter.' She glanced round the room and Joyce could see that her eyes were sparkling. She felt a sudden fondness for her. She looked as excited as Joyce felt. Excited and a bit nervous. It was their first venture after all.

Joyce was glad it was Mrs Rutherford she was going in with, even though she knew they made an unlikely partnership: Joyce with her dropped consonants, bare headed in her old print-patterned dress and threadbare cardigan; Mrs Rutherford, with her nasal BBC voice, in her tweed coat and skirt and navy felt hat and her leather handbag on her arm.

It was as they walked slowly back up Lavender Road after locking up that Mrs Rutherford tentatively broached the subject Joyce had been trying to avoid thinking about all day.

'How did you get on with Mr Lorenz?' she asked, putting the keys in her handbag. 'Did he take you somewhere nice?'

Joyce groaned. 'It was a disaster,' she said. 'We went to this fancy place in Chelsea. All French and napkins and that. And my pilchards were full of bones and I couldn't think of anything to say.' She shook her head. Even now in the cold October air, she felt all hot and bothered about it. He'd made such an effort. 'Poor old Lorenz,' she said. 'I don't suppose he'll ever talk to me again.'

Celia Rutherford looked at her sympathetically. 'But I thought you liked him.'

Joyce hesitated. 'To be honest, I don't mind him but I get all flustered. I don't want him to think I'm keen, like.' She stopped and blushed. 'You know, hanky panky and that. I don't want anything like that.'

'Goodness no!' Mrs Rutherford looked appalled. Appalled and astonished. She moved her handbag from one arm to the other to cover her confusion. She glanced up and down the street nervously then lowered her voice. 'I'm sure he wouldn't be expecting anything like that, Mrs Carter. Not at our age.'

Joyce frowned. She wasn't all that sure that age had much to do with it. She didn't know about Lorenz, but

Stanley had certainly wanted his oats pretty regular and he was over forty. Mind you, she thought, it didn't sound as if Mr and Mrs Rutherford did much in the way of hanky panky any more.

They parted outside the Flag and Garter and it was only as Joyce crossed the road that she noticed the military vehicle parked outside her house. Two military policemen got out as she opened her front gate. 'Mrs Carter?'

'Yes,' she said warily.

'We're here about your son Robert Carter.'

'Bob? What about him?' But she knew well enough. Bob had been malingering ever since he'd been sent home from the army with a bad back. They'd been for him once before but he'd given them the slip.

'Do you know where he is?'

Joyce shook her head.

The policemen looked at each other. 'Do you know when he'll next come home?'

Joyce hesitated. She had mixed feelings about Bob. She didn't want him to get in trouble, but that Hitler needed stopping, and when every other young man in the country was doing their bit it went against the grain that Bob was lazing about at home.

The taller of the policemen looked severe. 'Mrs Carter, I have to warn you that sheltering a deserter is a serious crime.'

Joyce felt her heart kick. 'He's not a deserter,' she said. 'He's got a bad back.'

The other policeman gave a dry chuckle. 'Not so bad he can't knock off some floozy in the West End. Oh yes, we know all about that, Mrs Carter. What we don't know is what time he comes home.'

Joyce flinched. She didn't want any trouble. Not now that things were going so well. Bob would have to take the rough with the smooth like everyone else.

'Mrs Carter, I warn you …'

'He helps out in the pub opposite,' she said, nodding

over the roof of their car towards the Flag and Garter. 'Evenings. He normally clocks on around six.'

As soon as she got home from work Louise slumped in the drawing-room. It was a long walk up the hill from Gregg Bros., and since she'd broken her pelvis in the Balham bombing raid her legs ached terribly after a long day. She had hardly slept a wink for two nights since the dinner party. She had found it difficult to concentrate at work too and she needed to concentrate to keep up her output. She liked her job and she didn't want to get sacked for failing to meet her quota.

It was Jack, of course, who was on her mind. Jack Delmaine. She closed her eyes. All being well it would soon be Jack and Louise Delmaine. It sounded good. She just prayed nothing would go wrong.

On the way home she had called on Katy at the pub, just to remind her to keep her mouth shut about Stefan Pininski. She definitely didn't want Jack finding out about that fiasco. Not that Katy would say anything of course, there was nobody more discreet than Katy Frazer, but it was best to be sure.

Louise smiled to herself. She wondered when Jack would ask her to go to bed with him. This time she would refuse until the wedding ring was on her finger. She had learned her lesson. That was clearly the way to do it. She was certain Katy hadn't slept with Ward Frazer before they were married. Nice girls didn't. And lovely Jack Delmaine thought she was a nice girl.

Hearing her mother coming in, she called out that there was a letter for her on the sideboard.

'Oh, how nice,' Celia said, scanning the note. 'It's from Helen. Such a pleasant girl. So well mannered.' She stopped for a moment then frowned. 'Oh dear. She says she had a shock when she got home from here to find that her father's house is being requisitioned.'

Louise looked up. She thought how good Helen had

been the other night. How she had smoothed over the awkward moments. 'Perhaps we should offer her a room here?' she suggested. Suddenly the thought of having Helen actually living in the house was rather appealing. It would be nice to have a friend. Someone to gossip to about Jack. Someone to take the pressure off her as the only child still at home. 'With Douglas at school and Bertie at Sandhurst there's plenty of room.'

Celia looked surprised. 'Well, I suppose we could,' she said doubtfully. 'Of course, I don't know what your father would think of it.'

'Of what?' a voice barked in the hall. Greville Rutherford strode into the room. 'What would I think about what?'

Celia handed him Helen's letter. 'Louise suggested we offer her a room here.'

Expecting an abrupt refusal Louise was surprised when he shrugged slightly and dropped the letter on the occasional table. 'I don't see why not,' he said. 'She seemed a very pleasant sort of girl.'

It was five to six when Aaref came in with the cigarettes. Katy was polishing the glasses.

'I thought I saw Louise in here earlier,' he said casually as Katy opened the till and counted out the cash she owed him.

She glanced at him sympathetically. Aaref had had a crush on Louise ever since she taught him and his brothers English at the beginning of the war when they were newly arrived refugees from Austria. When Jack Delmaine appeared on the scene, Aaref had turned his attention to Molly Coogan, an old nursing friend of Katy's, but deep down Katy was sure that his devotion to Louise was unchanged and it worried her that Molly Coogan might be being led up the garden path.

'Yes, she was,' she said.

'How was she?'

Katy looked at him. 'Happy. Very happy.' It was an understatement. Louise had been sparkling with excitement, and Katy had had to stop crating up the empties to hear all about the dinner, about how the Rutherford parents seemed to have approved of Jack, and best of all how Jack had virtually proposed.

'She's going to marry him, isn't she?' Aaref asked flatly.

Katy nodded. 'Yes, I think she is.'

There was a long pause then Aaref looked up. 'You look troubled, Katy. Is it Louise?'

Katy sighed. 'No,' she said slowly. 'It's her father. The Rutherford & Berry agent was in here earlier checking up again. I'm pretty sure old man Rutherford is going to refuse to extend my lease.'

Aaref was looking pale. 'So,' he said. 'I've lost Louise and you've lost the pub.' Abruptly he shook his head and shrugged. 'Today we are unlucky. Tomorrow perhaps we will be lucky again.'

Katy felt chilled by the dark intensity of his gaze. 'Aaref.' She gripped his arm. 'You're not going to try and spoil it for her, are you?'

For a second he hesitated, then he looked away. 'All I want is for Louise to be happy,' he said stiffly. 'If I am sure this Jack Delmaine is making her happy I will be satisfied.' He shook his head. 'But you, Katy, are different. You need this business.'

'If only I had more customers,' Katy said, walking to the window and staring bleakly down the empty street. 'If I was buying masses of beer off the brewery he'd be more keen to keep us going, but it's been so quiet.'

Aaref spoke behind her. 'It takes time to build up a business.'

Katy sighed. 'Time is the one thing I haven't got.' As she said it she saw Bob strolling across the road. She glanced round at the clock. It was five past six, less than half an hour to opening time, but Bob was never in a hurry. Not like Katy who spent all her time flying around trying to get things done. But then apart from his chorus girl in the West End, Bob didn't have a care in the world. So long as he had a couple of pints and got his wages he was happy. And Katy knew she couldn't do without him.

She was about to turn away from the window when suddenly two uniformed men jumped out of a car and grabbed Bob's arms.

Katy's eyes widened in horror. 'Aaref, quick, look! What's happening?'

'Bob's being arrested, that's what's happening,' Aaref said, joining her at the window. He glanced at Katy's white face and sighed. 'You knew it was going to happen sooner or later. It was only a matter of time.'

Katy closed her eyes. She knew he was right, but the fact that Bob had been running on borrowed time didn't make her feel any better. She sat down heavily at one of the small bar tables. Poor old Bob, she thought. And poor me. Saturday was her best night. She had hired a pianist. She had ordered extra beer and now she wasn't going to have enough hands to serve everybody.

She felt the baby kick and suddenly she felt the fight go out of her. Bob had been her salvation. She knew she couldn't manage the pub on her own. Not seven months pregnant. Suddenly she felt very tired. She looked up at Aaref pitifully. 'What am I going to do?'

Aaref looked at her steadily. He was never one to give up. Three years ago, at the age of sixteen, having seen his parents killed and his home burned, he had led his two younger brothers out of Nazi Austria. After that nothing seemed too bad. 'You'll be all right,' he said bracingly. 'I'll help you out for a day or two until we can find you a replacement.'

Chapter Three

Lady Helen de Burrel moved into the Rutherfords' house on Saturday, 8 November. It was a wrench leaving her father and the staff but it had to be done. If she was accepted for agent training she would have to detach herself from her past anyway, and the fact that this first move had been accomplished so easily made it seem that fate was playing a part in her destiny, making everything fall into place.

To her surprise, when her taxi arrived at Cedars House it was Greville Rutherford who greeted her at the door.

'We were expecting you a little earlier. I'm afraid my wife's had to pop out,' he said as he carried her things up the stairs. Pushing open a door to a bedroom on the second floor at the back of the house, he stood back to let her in first. 'This is the room my wife has prepared for you. I hope you like it.'

Helen looked around. Apart from being extremely cold it was a very pleasant room. It had a single bed with a pink candlewick bedspread, a large antique wardrobe, flowery curtains, white distempered walls and a view out over Clapham Common.

'It's lovely.' Helen turned to smile at her host. 'Thank you so much.'

Greville Rutherford's eyes flickered slightly as he met her gaze, then he turned quickly for the door. 'Well, I'll leave you to unpack,' he said gruffly. 'The bathroom is at the bottom of the stairs on the left. We take tea at five thirty and dine at eight. If you need me I shall be in my study.'

When Helen descended on the dot of five thirty, however, there was no sign of any tea. Nor, sadly, of any fire in the drawing-room grate. Wondering if it would be rude to get her coat she wandered about looking for some sign of life.

She was in the kitchen toying with putting the kettle on herself when she heard a step behind her and nearly jumped out of her skin.

Greville Rutherford was at the door. He looked irritated and at once Helen began to apologise. 'I'm terribly sorry, but you mentioned five thirty …'

It seemed it wasn't Helen he was angry with but his wife. 'No, it's Celia's fault,' he said. 'We don't have any staff any more, you see, so she does the meals now. I can't think where she is. It really is very rude of her.'

'No, please, it really doesn't matter,' Helen said hastily. She eyed the kettle hopefully. 'Look, why don't I make some tea anyway? Then it will be ready for when she gets home.'

He looked appalled at the idea. 'But you don't know where anything is.'

Helen smiled. 'Do you?'

'Well, no, but …'

She never knew what the but was because at that moment Mrs Rutherford came hurrying in. She was clearly startled to find her husband in the kitchen, but she greeted Helen warmly. 'Oh dear, I'm so sorry I wasn't here when you arrived but there was so much to do at the café.' She smiled. 'We open next week, you see.' She glanced at the kitchen clock. 'Goodness, I must feed the hens before it gets dark.'

Before she had taken a step towards the kitchen door her husband intervened. 'Good lord, Celia,' he snapped. 'Surely seeing to our guest is more important than dealing with the hens?'

Embarrassed, Helen cut in quickly. 'Honestly,' she said. 'Please don't worry about me. I am quite able to look after myself.'

Celia looked relieved but Greville frowned. 'We couldn't dream of letting you look after yourself,' he said with stiff courtesy. 'You are our guest and we will treat you as such.'

The following day was Remembrance Sunday and Katy got up at six o'clock in order to have time to take her mother to church.

'Now don't forget, Mummy,' she said as they walked up Lavender Road. It was an icy cold day and their breath puffed in small clouds as they spoke. 'If we see Mr Rutherford we must make a point of saying how much we hope he will give us another year's lease.'

Mary Parsons looked anxious. 'But what about the baby, Katy?' You'll never be able to run the pub and look after the baby.'

Katy groaned inwardly. They had covered this ground so many times. Sometimes she felt as though she was banging her head against a brick wall. 'We'll have to manage,' she said patiently. 'It's our only chance. Without the pub we've got no income and nowhere to live.' She hesitated for a second and then went on cautiously, 'Perhaps by then you will be able to take on a little bit more?'

Mary Parsons quailed visibly. 'Oh Katy, I know I'm not much help to you, but I do as much as I can. I do the shopping.'

'I know you do,' Katy said, 'and it is a help. I just wondered if you might be able to do a little bit of dusting or polishing sometimes as well.' When her father had been alive her mother had done virtually all the pub's cleaning. She had even served behind the bar on busy nights. But now it was as much as she could do to rinse a few glasses, and even then she spent most of the time worrying about them being all the wrong sizes. She had always been a worrier, but since the pub was bombed she had been a bag of nerves. It wasn't surprising – she'd lost her husband that night, most of her personal possessions, and her home – but life had to go on.

Katy urgently needed someone to replace Bob, someone strong and reliable. It was one of the things she was going to pray for this morning. For the last six months all her prayers had gone to Ward, but now he was safe in a prisoner-of-war camp she hoped he didn't need them any more. As it was Remembrance Sunday she knew she ought really to be praying for those lost in conflict but she didn't think God would mind a couple of more personal requests. As well as a replacement for Bob, she needed some more customers. She needed an extension to her lease. And when the moment came she needed a quick and painless birth and a good quiet baby prepared to sleep all the time.

As they approached the sturdy redbrick church, Katy sighed. To be honest she didn't have much faith in God's goodwill any more, but it was worth a try.

It had come as somewhat of a shock to Helen to realise that she was expected to attend morning service with the Rutherfords.

'Daddy's reading the lesson,' Louise had whispered to her at breakfast, rolling her eyes expressively.

'I'm sure your father is a regular churchgoer, isn't he?' Celia Rutherford asked as she passed the toast.

Helen hesitated. 'Well, he ...'

Perhaps luckily she didn't have time to answer before Greville Rutherford appeared abruptly from behind his newspaper. 'Goodness, Celia, what an extraordinary question. How Earl Howe chooses to worship is entirely his own business.' He glanced at Helen. 'But I'm sure he would agree that people in our position need to set an example. Particularly in these difficult times.'

The times might be difficult for us, Helen thought, but it always seemed to her that God had it rather easy. Any mistakes in the world were attributed to man's folly while He took the credit for all the good things. However, wisely, she didn't say so.

'Of course,' she said instead. 'I'd like to go.'

Greville Rutherford nodded. 'Good,' he said and glanced pointedly at Louise. 'I'm glad that some young people take their faith seriously.'

Now, as she sat in the front pew between Louise and Mrs Rutherford, Helen realised the last time she had been in this church was for Katy and Ward Frazer's wedding. Then, she had sat at the back craning forward like everyone else to see the romantic embrace they had exchanged when Katy arrived at the front on her father's arm.

Sitting close to that spot now, Helen wondered what it must feel like to be as deeply in love as Katy and Ward had clearly been that day. She wondered if she would ever feel that strength of emotion. She doubted it. She certainly hadn't so far, and anyway, she wasn't sure that she would really want to. Falling in love meant giving up your independence, and she wanted to be her own person not someone else's.

She wondered how strongly Louise really felt for Jack. She certainly talked about him enough but Louise was so keen to get a husband that Helen sometimes got the impression that anyone in trousers would do. And then there were the Rutherford parents. There was no doubt that Greville ruled the roost there. Celia was making a valiant stab at independence by setting up the café but basically she was well under his thumb.

When Greville Rutherford got up to read the lesson, Helen watched him with interest. He did it well, his firm, clipped, unemotional voice reaching clearly to the back of the church. Helen smiled to herself. She was amused by him, by the way his stiff courtesy towards her contrasted so absurdly with his dictatorial attitude towards his wife and children.

Having been brought up by her easygoing but undemonstrative father she had little experience of marital arrangements. She knew that over the years her father had indulged in a number of discreet affairs, but none of the ladies had succeeded in persuading him to marry for a second time. She wondered whether the American women would fare any better. They would certainly try. Anthony de Burrel was still a very attractive man. His lazy manners and debonair good looks would go down well with the Americans. They went down well with everyone. In fact Helen was sure that one of the reasons she didn't have a boyfriend was because she could never find anyone who could match up to her father either in looks or in character. The young men of her acquaintance all seemed so insipid in comparison.

As Greville Rutherford stepped off the podium and retook his seat he glanced along the row and for a second caught her eye. Helen smiled politely and was surprised to see that he looked pleased. She would have thought Greville Rutherford was sufficiently confident in himself to be able to read the lesson without seeking her approbation.

Before she could amuse herself with any further speculation there was a rumble of movement as everyone got down on their knees, and Helen realised that as she was here she might as well use the time usefully and ask God to intervene on her behalf with the SOE bureaucracy in the hopes of getting a speedy and positive decision about her application.

Five rows behind her Pam was praying for patience. Patience to deal with little George's tantrums and moods and patience to cope with her husband Alan's inability to discipline him.

'He'll be all right,' Alan would say in his mild, tolerant way. 'He'll grow out of it.' But George wasn't all right and he showed no sign of growing out of it. If anything he was getting worse. He broke things deliberately. He dragged on her arm in the street. He wouldn't eat his food, he refused to go to bed at the appointed hour, and he screamed if he didn't get his own way.

Where Alan was happy to give in, letting him stay up as long as he wanted, pandering to his whims, Pam was close to despair. She just didn't know what they were doing wrong. George had always been such a sweet child. Now it was almost as though he hated her, and yet she loved him so much.

It was hard to be angry with the child, though. He had suffered so much. In three separate tragedies he had lost his brother, his father and his mother. He had suffered several months of hell with his uncle and aunt before they had sent him back to Pam and Alan, unable to cope.

Aware of a faint scuffling noise Pam opened her eyes. Crouched under the pew beside her, George was already fidgeting. Pam nudged him. George looked up. Perched on a thick tapestry kneeler, scrubbed and neatly dressed, his halo of blond hair gleaming, he looked as though butter wouldn't melt in his mouth. Pam prayed that the service wouldn't last too long. If only there was a Sunday school, or preferably a proper school, Monday to Friday, but so many children had been evacuated during the bombing that all the schools had closed. Although some had reopened in Streatham, so far there was nowhere locally he could go.

In the end after a short wrangle she let him stay on the floor under the pew for the sermon. At least he was quiet down there. She glanced at Alan and shrugged helplessly. He smiled and reached over the gap where George should have been to touch her arm. 'Leave him,' he whispered. 'He's not doing any harm.'

Pam sighed and looked away. She loved Alan dearly, but he was extraordinarily obtuse sometimes. He seemed impervious to her problems.

As the vicar launched into a solemn treatise on duty and self-sacrifice, suddenly Pam felt guilty. After all, George was being as quiet as a mouse down there on the floor. Poor little mite. It wasn't his fault that she didn't know how to deal with him. She would buy him a nice Christmas present, she decided. Something really special. A train set if she could find one, or a big teddy. She would ask Katy Frazer to look after him for a few hours one afternoon so she could go shopping. After all, it was only six weeks to Christmas. She would go early before the shops sold out.

A shuffling of feet and an outburst of coughing indicated that the vicar had reached the end of his sermon, but it was only as they stood for the final blessing that Pam realised why George had been so quiet throughout the service. Glancing down, she saw in utter horror what had been keeping him occupied under the pew. Where once there had been a beautiful tapestry kneeler depicting the St Aldate's altar cross, stitched painstakingly as a labour of Christian devotion by some elderly member of the congregation, there was now a bare canvas cushion and a few bedraggled strands of coloured silk.

'Goodness, Katy is getting big,' Louise remarked as she and Helen walked back from church. Greville Rutherford had stayed behind to talk to the vicar about parish business, and Mrs Rutherford had hurried on ahead of them muttering about needing to see Mrs Carter about something before lunch.

'I thought she looked tired,' Helen said.

'She always looks tired,' Louise said. 'And the baby's not even due till after Christmas. No wonder Daddy's worried about renewing her lease.'

So that's what it had been about, Helen thought. She had overheard Greville Rutherford brushing off some tentative question of Katy's in the churchyard. 'Not now,

Mrs Frazer,' he had said. 'Not on a Sunday. I don't talk business on Sunday.'

'Poor Katy,' she said now. 'It must be really hard for her without Ward.'

Louise didn't really want to talk about Katy. As usual what she wanted to talk about was Jack. 'I'm going to write to Jack this afternoon,' she said suddenly. 'Do you think I ought to tell him I love him, or will that put him off?'

Helen looked at her with interest. 'Do you love him?'

'Of course I do.'

'How do you know?'

Louise giggled. 'Because I want to go to bed with him of course.' She glanced at Helen curiously. 'Haven't you ever been in love with anyone?'

'No, I don't think I have,' Helen said. 'I've liked men. I've fancied some of them but I've never been in love. I don't really know what love is. It can't just be sex, can it? Take your parents for example. Do you think they are in love?'

'Goodness,' Louise said. 'I shouldn't think so, at least not in that way. Not any more. Actually it's hard to imagine Daddy ever being in love in that way.' She rolled her eyes. 'And Mummy is more in love with this stupid café than with him. Thank God the damn thing is finally opening tomorrow. She never thinks about anything else these days.'

Celia Rutherford was not the only person who could think of nothing else. Joyce Carter barely slept a wink that Sunday night, she was so nervous about waking up in time to open the café on its first morning's business.

As it was, they were both in the newly equipped kitchen by six o'clock. By six thirty they had the kettles boiling, the bread cut ready for toasting, the porridge made and the sausages frying gently. There were also a dozen eggs standing by, some from Mrs Rutherford's own hens. They hadn't been able to get bacon but the butcher had promised it to them for the following week.

On the dot of half past seven they flipped the closed sign on the door to open for the first time.

To Joyce's dismay the first person through the door was Mr Lorenz. She had only seen him once since that dreadful dinner at the restaurant, when she had bumped into him on Northcote Road and thanked him hastily without looking at him before hurrying on her way. Now she felt guilty, and she felt guiltier when he came in the following morning for breakfast, and the next. 'You don't have to come in every day,' she said, as he stood at the counter on the fourth morning in a row.

He looked concerned. 'Do you mind me coming in?'

'Well, no,' she said as she poured his tea. 'Of course not.'

'It's convenient for me, you see,' he explained. 'If I eat breakfast here, it means there's one less meal for me to worry about.'

Joyce nodded. She didn't have time to talk in any case. Mr Lorenz wasn't the only person who found the café convenient, and what with taking the money, working out change, ordering, cooking, delivering what was ready to the tables, keeping up with the clearing, washing up and re-laying the tables, she was rushed off her feet.

Celia Rutherford didn't know what had hit her. She had never done a proper day's work in her life before and by the Friday of the first week she was already suggesting hiring more staff.

'I think we need a waitress,' she said helplessly as she dashed into the kitchen with a tray of dirty dishes.

Joyce looked up from the sink. 'I reckon as we should see how we go. We don't want to overstretch ourselves. We'd best see what money is coming in first.'

'If we ever get time to count it.'

Joyce grinned at her. 'We get a day off on Sunday, remember. At least *you* do. I am going to spend it cooking up stuff for next week.' She glanced up at the store cupboard with their new catering rations neatly stacked on the shelves. 'Some scones and rock buns and that. I reckon they'd sell all right and they keep nice too.'

Celia shook her head. 'You're a wonder, Mrs Carter. You're in here at the crack of dawn and you're still going strong at four thirty. And now you're thinking of working on Sunday too. Where do you get the energy?'

Joyce wiped a sudsy hand over her brow. 'I've got nothing better to do,' she said. 'Anyway, I like being in here. I like to see people enjoying food I've cooked. Best of all I like to see them paying for it.'

'Oi, Louise,' Doris Smith shouted over the racket of the factory. 'You want to get a move on, love, or you'll get yourself sacked.'

Louise jumped guiltily. Doris was right. Larry Gregg was on the prowl round the factory floor and it would be dangerous to be caught slacking. Throwing a grateful smile at Doris, she quickly picked up her parting tool again and prayed she could make up the shortfall by the end of the day.

Louise had been at Gregg Bros. seven months and, odd though it seemed, she liked her job and didn't want to lose it. Before the war, when she was a pretty eighteen-year-old straight out of finishing school, it would have been the last job on earth she would have wanted. She had been a different person in those days, though, with stars in her eyes and high hopes for romance and happiness.

Then the war had come, and with it Stefan Pininski and Ward Frazer, and those stars had long gone, blacked out by a double heartbreak, a miscarriage and a broken pelvis. It had been in a desperate attempt to leave all that pain behind her that she had decided to take a job – and the only one she could get was this one.

It had been a shock, but if nothing else the unremitting noise of the factory had been enough to jolt her out of her self-pity. At first she had hated the anonymity of the baggy overalls, the monotony and the all-pervasive grime, but now she no longer cared. Somehow it didn't matter any more because she was good at the job, and that had given her back her self-respect. Frankly, who cared about the state of her nails if on a good day she could turn out a hundred and forty bolts? She was nearly as quick as her mentor, big Doris, who regularly did a hundred and fifty.

Today, however, she was finding it hard. She couldn't concentrate at all. Jack had written to say he had arranged to be in London over Christmas and that he wanted to spend as much time with her as possible.

Louise grimaced as her hand slipped. Sparks flew. If only the factory was closing over Christmas. As it was she would have to ask Larry Gregg for time off and he'd be reluctant to let her off because the factory was already behind on its government quotas.

'You up to target, ladies?' Larry Gregg's voice suddenly interrupted her thoughts.

Without faltering in her work, Doris nodded vigorously, making her multiple chins wobble alarmingly. ''Course we are,' she yelled back. 'Me and young Louise are the best workers you got, Mr Gregg. You know that.'

He grunted. 'I'm upping the minimum to a hundred and twenty. Anyone producing less than that is out.'

Louise felt a stab of panic. She knew she was unlikely to achieve a hundred and twenty today. Doris knew it too. 'Have a heart, Mr Gregg,' she said. 'We're not robots, you know.'

'More's the pity,' he said sourly. 'I'd be better off with robots. Robots don't need breaks. Robots don't need sleep. Robots don't keep asking about a blinking Christmas party.'

Doris chuckled. 'Are we having a Christmas party?' she asked.

Larry Gregg snorted irritably. 'It's the usual story. Everyone wants one but nobody wants to organise it.' He shook his head. 'I'd look kindly on anyone who took it on. It's good for morale, there's no denying, and I'd put a bit of cash in and all. But I'm damned if I'm doing it myself. They'd only complain about the venue like they did last year.'

'Well, it was a dump of a place,' Doris said, 'and the beer tasted like rat's piss.'

'I reckon it was rat's piss,' someone shouted across. 'There was definitely a bit of grey fur in my glass.'

As everyone laughed, Louise felt the sweat prickling her skin. Carefully she laid down her parting tool. 'I don't mind organising a party,' she said. 'I know a nice place.'

Larry Gregg's surprise was palpable. 'You?'

Louise shrugged. She knew with her classy accent and wealthy background she was an oddity at the factory. It was only because a couple of his tool workers had been killed in the bombing that Larry Gregg had taken her on in the first place. As much as possible she kept her head down and her mouth shut. Doris was the only person whom she had got friendly with. But now the moment had come to speak up. Organising the factory Christmas party would kill two birds with one stone. It would put her in Larry Gregg's good books and it would give Katy Frazer some much needed business.

'My friend runs a pub,' she said. 'The Flag and Garter up in Lavender Road. She'd put on a good do for us.'

There was a moment's hesitation and then Doris put her considerable weight behind the idea. 'It's a nice pub,' she said, turning round so her voice carried across the factory. 'I've been there a couple of times. No rats in the beer there.'

'Well, I …' Larry Gregg was looking extremely doubtful but before he could go on a burst of applause erupted round the factory floor. Whatever he had been going to say, he tactfully changed his mind and smiled bravely. 'Looks like you've been voted in,' he said helplessly.

Louise smiled sweetly back. 'Good. I'll come and see you later about that contribution you mentioned.'

As far as Helen was concerned the worst thing about living in Clapham was the journey into work each morning. She had known the Underground would be crowded, but she hadn't expected it to be quite so smelly. By the time she arrived in her office she felt grubby and irritable. Normally she tried to block out her surroundings by reading the newspaper but today the paper was full of the sinking of the HMS *Ark Royal* by a German torpedo off Gibraltar, and not only did she feel grubby, she felt sick.

She hated it when a ship went down. For some reason it affected her more than the loss of planes or a battle defeat. What turned her stomach was the thought of all those sailors trapped on board, struggling for the escape hatches or drowning slowly in the turbulent sea. As she unlocked the door of her office and took off her coat, she wondered how the men on board coped with that constant fear. Young men like Jack Delmaine. Or perhaps they didn't think about it until it happened.

She was sitting behind her desk reading the rest of the news when Angus McNaughton came into the room and closed the door behind him. Helen put down the newspaper. Suddenly she knew what he was going to say.

She was right. 'They want to see you this evening,' he said quietly. 'Six thirty. The usual room at the War Office.'

'Oh.' A shiver of anticipation ran down her spine.

Angus McNaughton spread his hands in a somewhat helpless gesture. 'Best of luck.'

'Thank you,' she said.

Chapter Four

Katy was delighted at the idea of throwing a Christmas party at the pub for the Gregg Bros. staff. Louise reckoned about fifty people would come. To everyone's amazement she had managed to persuade Mr Gregg into giving her twenty pounds towards it and she was going to arrange a collection in the factory as well. Doris reckoned most people would be prepared to put in a couple of bob. Katy was impressed. With twenty-five pounds behind the bar they'd be able to drink all night. She'd get Mrs Carter up at the café to do a nice spread of sandwiches and flans to go with the booze. All that was left was to choose the day. After some discussion they decided on Thursday 18 December. Thursdays were always quiet nights, the day before pay day, and being only a week before Christmas people would be in the right mood to enjoy themselves.

As Louise giggled about flirting outrageously with Larry Gregg to get the money out of him, Katy felt herself smiling for the first time in days. Things had definitely looked up since her visit to church the previous weekend. Not only had Louise brought her a lucrative bit of business but Aaref had produced his younger brother Jacob as a stand-in barman. Jacob was a thin, dark-eyed fourteen-year-old who rarely spoke and never smiled, but he was a conscientious worker and they had arranged that for five shillings a week he would come in for an hour before school each morning and again in the evening for as long as he was needed.

'What about his schoolwork?' Katy had asked. She knew Aaref had high academic hopes for his two brothers.

Aaref had shrugged. 'To take his place in the world Jacob must learn more than his studies. He must learn the skills of life.'

Katy wasn't sure what sort of life skills Jacob would learn swabbing floors and heaving barrels around in the Flag and Garter cellar, but she wasn't going to quibble. He was the answer to her prayer and she wasn't going to question God's judgement.

Looking at the clock now she realised with some horror that it was only five minutes to opening time.

'Goodness, Louise,' she said jumping up. 'I must get moving. I'm expecting a good crowd tonight for the news.' Having the wireless on for the news at nine each night had been Aaref's idea and it had worked well. People liked hearing the news. If it was good they celebrated; if it was bad they drowned their sorrows with beer. Tonight they would be waiting to hear how many of the *Ark Royal* crew had been rescued.

Katy smiled with a sudden burst of confidence. Maybe things weren't quite so bad after all. A few more good ideas and she would be home and dry. And Jen Carter was coming home in the New Year too. Jen might be a bit of a prima donna these days but she was good fun to have around.

Louise had just gone when Pam Nelson came to the door laden down with shopping. Dumping her bags on the floor she eyed Katy with a mixture of hope and trepidation. 'Has he been good?'

Katy stared at her blankly. Then suddenly she remembered. George! Where was George? She had had him all afternoon and he had in fact been very good, but since Louise arrived she had forgotten all about him. She was sure he hadn't gone out of the door. Perhaps he was with her mother upstairs.

She went to the foot of the stairs and called up

anxiously, but there was no response. Then a moment later he appeared up the cellar steps. Katy sighed in relief. Thank God he couldn't come to much harm down there.

She ruffled his hair and turned to Pam. 'Yes, he's been very good.'

Someone banged on the door then and she realised the first of the evening's customers were already queuing up outside.

She rolled her eyes and smiled at Pam. 'Here we go.'

Katy had been right about the *Ark Royal.* By quarter to nine the bar was full of men waiting for the news, and then suddenly as she pulled a pint she heard the faint wheezing noise that indicated the barrel was empty. Thankfully Jacob had just arrived for his evening stint.

'Quick, Jacob,' she called. 'The beer's running out. Go down and change the pump on to a fresh barrel. Make sure it's one I've already fined.'

Nodding silently he obediently disappeared down the cellar steps.

Katy smiled reassuringly at the line of men at the bar. 'It won't be a moment,' she said, pleased that she had taken the trouble yesterday to show Jacob how to change the pump over.

Even as she congratulated herself for her foresight, however, he reappeared.

'How do I know which barrel to use next?' he asked nervously.

'The fined ones have chalk crosses on them,' she said patiently. 'Like I showed you yesterday.' She groaned inwardly. She hoped he wasn't going to be a slow learner.

She waited for him to go back down but he stood biting his lip awkwardly. His long lashes flicked nervously over his dark eyes. 'They all have chalk crosses,' he said.

Katy stared at him. 'They can't have.'

Running down to the cellar herself a second later, she gasped in dismay. Every single barrel sported a bold cross.

Some had more than one. And the cellar wall was chalked with a picture of a diving aeroplane drawn in a childish hand.

George. Katy groaned. No wonder he had been so quiet. Then suddenly she caught sight of the finings tin lying empty in the corner and her dismay turned into panic.

Her customers were very fussy about their beer. The finings helped to clear the sediment in the beer, but if you used too much the beer started to taste of fish. In any case it took time to settle. If George had stirred finings into every barrel the beer would be undrinkable.

'Oh God,' she whispered. Suddenly she felt dizzy. Dizzy and sick. Putting one hand on her heavy stomach and the other on her forehead she leaned weakly against the damp wall as her whole financial security rocked before her eyes.

'Are you all right, Miss Katy?'

She realised Jacob was behind her watching anxiously.

She closed her eyes for a second, trying to drag back some of that earlier confidence, but it was hopeless. It had evaporated like a bad smell. She shook her head. There was nothing she could say, nothing to reassure him, because she knew she was very far from all right.

Slowly she straightened up and went back upstairs. Already there was grumbling about the delay. She was gathering her strength to say that the beer was off when the door opened and her old nursing friend Molly Coogan pushed her way into the bar.

Molly took one look at Katy's face and ran forward. 'What's the matter? Is it the baby?'

'No, it's the beer,' Katy said. She was close to tears. The cost of that ruined beer was unthinkable. 'That blasted child George has ruined the beer.'

Molly looked appalled. 'Are you sure? Every barrel?'

'I don't know. There's no way of telling, not just by looking at it. Only by the taste and I couldn't tell a draught from a stout—' Katy stopped as Jacob coughed awkwardly behind her.

Molly swung round. 'Who are you?'

'I'm Jacob, miss.'

'He's Aaref's brother,' Katy said.

'Oh.' Molly flushed. It was no secret that she was keen on Aaref. 'And what do you want?'

Jacob shuffled his feet. 'I was just going to say I don't think there was enough of the finings to ruin all the beer.'

Molly stared at him. 'Right,' she said. 'Then we'll have to get some of these men to taste it.' Snatching off her nurse's cap, she rolled up her sleeves and smiled grittily across the bar at the waiting customers. 'We're having a competition,' she announced. 'It's like a lucky draw. We're going to bring up half a dozen pints from the cellar and we want six volunteers to taste them. Whoever gets a good pint gets another free one on top. We'll go on until we find a good barrel.'

Helen was feeling uneasy.

The interview had started off well. Her unnamed interviewer was a bearded older man with steady eyes and a gentle smile. She had answered his questions about her childhood and schooling confidently. They had discussed her slightly unorthodox upbringing and she had talked about her holidays in France, explaining her knowledge of the language, her familiarity with French customs, her immense liking of the French people.

That was when things began to go wrong.

Her interviewer had looked up with an enigmatic smile. 'Even collaborators?' he asked mildly.

Helen knew it was a trick question, but that didn't make it any easier to answer. She shook her head with a smile. 'It is hard for me to believe that the people I knew would be collaborators,' she said.

He held her eyes. 'It is hard for me to believe that some of them would not be,' he said. 'The only reason the Nazis haven't occupied the South of France is because of its pro-German attitude.' Helen knew he was right but she didn't like hearing it. As she looked away he leaned back in his chair. 'How would you feel if you were betrayed by someone you knew?'

It was then that she remembered he was a psychologist. He wasn't so much assessing her knowledge and enthusiasm as her emotional stability, her psychological fitness for the job. The thought unnerved her.

'I don't know,' she said. 'I would be angry, I suppose.'

'Angry enough to kill?'

She swallowed. 'I suppose I could if my life was at risk. I don't know.'

He raised his eyebrows. 'Your life? Not someone else's? A colleague perhaps? A friend? A family member?'

Helen flushed. She knew he was trying to undermine her confidence and she didn't want to fall into a trap, but the idea of having to kill someone to protect a friend seemed so remote she could hardly imagine it. On the other hand she didn't want him to think she was squeamish. 'Of course,' she said. 'We are at war. Anyone opposing us with violence must expect to die.' She flushed again, hoping she hadn't gone overboard. She didn't want to sound like some blood-crazed assassin.

He fingered his beard, watching her closely. 'You are a pretty girl, Lady Helen. To what extent would you be prepared to use your feminine charms?'

Helen frowned. 'I don't know what you mean.'

'Don't you?' He hesitated for a moment, made a note on his pad, then looked up. 'Are you a virgin?'

Helen went hot and cold. 'I don't think you have any right to ask me that.'

'I have every right,' he said. 'You don't have to answer, of course, but I'm sure you realise how useful it can be to get close to the enemy.' He gave his faint enigmatic smile. 'Even the strongest men are like putty in the arms of a beautiful woman. Of course, you don't always have to go the whole way to get what you want. In some cases wanting is everything.'

'I don't know,' Helen said honestly. 'I don't know if I could do that.' She could feel the interview slipping away from her and with it her chance of proving herself. She hadn't realised proving herself might involve sleeping with some fat German officer. She looked up and saw that her interviewer was watching her thoughtfully.

'So you are prepared to give your life but not your body,' he said.

Put like that her scruples seemed ridiculous. 'I suppose it would depend on how important it was.'

'And perhaps how handsome the man involved?'

He was goading her. Tempting her into another trap. She felt a flash of irritation but squashed it, knowing that to show it would be fatal. She smiled bravely. 'I don't know,' she said. 'I doubt I'd feel much physical attraction for the enemy whatever he looked like.'

He didn't smile back. 'There's rather a lot of things you don't know,' he said. 'Would you say you are an indecisive person.'

'No,' Helen said. 'Not particularly. But you are asking me about situations of which I have no experience. I hope I would react well. I think I would. But until I tried it I wouldn't know. It would be wrong of me to pretend I know the answers.'

He looked at her for a long tense moment. 'I hope for your sake you never need to learn the answers,' he said, then he closed his notebook abruptly and stood up. 'Thank you, Lady Helen. I have enjoyed our discussion.'

'Is that it?' She glanced at her watch and was amazed to see that two and a half hours had passed. No wonder she felt so drained.

He inclined his head. 'That's it. I will send my report to Major Buckmaster.'

Pam didn't find out about the havoc George had caused at

the pub until the following morning when she called in at the café and Joyce Carter mentioned it to her. Her son Pete had been in the pub the night before and had come home full of the news of Molly Coogan's beer-tasting competition, how bets had been taken and quite a bit of money had changed hands. It turned out that four barrels had been ruined in all. It was the best evening he'd ever had in the pub, he said, but poor Katy Frazer had looked near to tears.

Joyce could well believe it. One good evening would never make up for four ruined barrels. She had felt so sorry for Katy that she had popped in on the way to the café and offered to do a bit of washing up for her on Sunday morning. Not that washing a few glasses would help much but it was the thought that counted.

'I don't reckon Katy would tell you herself,' she said now to Pam, 'but I thought you ought to know.'

Pam was horrified. Leaving her tea on the counter she grabbed George's arm and whisked him straight out into the street.

George was unrepentant. 'I was only trying to help,' he said huffily. 'I know she puts that stuff in the beer barrels, I've seen her do it before.' Then, wriggling against the pressure of Pam's fingers, he suddenly started to cry. 'You're always so cross with me, Aunty Pam. I know you don't like me any more. I wish my mummy was still alive.'

As she stood there watching his little shoulders shaking as the tears rolled down his cheeks, Pam felt the usual wash of helpless despair. She didn't know what to do.

She wanted to hug him. She hated it when he cried, but what he had done was extremely naughty. Certainly it was more serious than destroying the St Aldate's kneeler, and that was bad enough. The vicar had not been at all pleased. In fact he had been distinctly frosty about it. Now she would have to apologise to Katy Frazer as well. Katy

Frazer who had quite enough to worry about without four barrels of spoiled beer.

For a moment Pam thought of biting the bullet and going straight to the pub, but then she decided to wait for Alan to come home from the brewery. It was only fair that he should share in the responsibility. He could hardly brush George's misdemeanour under the carpet this time. This time it was serious and he would have to take some action.

She took George's hand and began to walk back up Lavender Road. 'We're going home,' she said, steeling her heart as he looked up at her pitifully. 'We'll wait there until Uncle Alan comes home and we'll see what he says about it.'

When Alan did come back at twelve thirty she discovered that the situation was even worse than she thought.

'Where's George?' Alan asked abruptly as he took off his coat.

Pam nodded down the passage. 'He's playing in the sitting-room,' she said. 'Alan, have you heard what he did to Katy Frazer?'

He nodded. 'Everyone is talking about it at the brewery. Saying she can't look after her beer properly.'

'But it wasn't her fault,' Pam said. 'It was George …'

Alan shook his head wearily. 'It doesn't make any difference. Old Rutherford's going to pull the plug on her anyway. He's been looking for an excuse not to renew her lease and now he has it.'

Pam stared at him in utter horror. 'Can't you talk to Mr Rutherford, tell him it was George? Anything?'

'It won't help. He would only say it was her fault for not supervising the child properly. What might happen when her own baby is born …'

Pam closed her eyes. If only she hadn't gone shopping. If only she had disciplined George properly. If only … She opened her eyes and looked at Alan. 'Oh God, what can we do to help her?'

'There's not much we can do,' he said, 'except offer to pay for the ruined beer.'

Of course Katy wouldn't hear of it. 'It wasn't your fault,' she said to Pam. 'I should have kept a better eye on him.'

'He's seven years old,' Pam said. 'We shouldn't have to watch him twenty-four hours a day.' She sighed. 'Alan is telling him off now, but it won't do any good. It just makes him worse. It's almost as though he's trying to test us to see how much wickedness we can take.'

'Perhaps he *is* testing you,' Katy said. 'Perhaps he's scared you'll send him away and he wants to see how far he can go before you do.'

Pam blinked. 'Does that make sense?'

Katy tried to smile but failed and looked away. 'Nothing makes sense any more.'

Pam felt a jolt of pain. 'You've heard the rumour, haven't you?' she asked hesitantly. 'About Greville Rutherford.'

Katy nodded.

'He's a bastard,' Pam said hotly. 'An utter bastard.'

Katy smiled thinly. 'He's also the boss unfortunately.'

By the weekend Katy had received formal notification that her lease would not be renewed at the end of the year.

Helen was shocked to hear the news when she called in on Saturday afternoon. Katy looked devastated. Her hand was shaking slightly as she poured the tea.

'I can't believe he would be so cruel,' Helen said. She really was surprised. She knew Greville Rutherford was tough and dictatorial but she hadn't realised he would be quite so heartless.

'He's a businessman,' Katy said. 'He's in it for the money. And the truth is that I simply don't bring it in.'

'I wish there was something I could do,' Helen said.

Katy mustered a faint smile. 'No chance of slipping some arsenic into his sherry?'

Helen laughed, but she knew it wasn't a laughing matter. In a few weeks' time Katy would have a tiny baby on her hands as well as a frail mother. With nowhere to live and no means of support she would be in dire straits indeed. It made her own worries about getting accepted for agent training seem trivial in the extreme.

As she walked home Helen felt a terrible sense of frustration. She felt guilty enough about Katy Frazer already, for sending Ward on that final fatal mission. Not that it was her decision of course, but she would never forget the look on Katy's face when she and the head of SOE French section at the time had arrived at their honeymoon cottage to take him away.

And now she had to stand by and watch her go out of business.

Letting herself into the house she was daunted to find Greville Rutherford alone in the drawing-room. He stood up as she came in.

'Helen. Let me help you with your coat.'

'Thank you,' she said stiffly, wishing she had gone straight to her room. The last thing she felt like doing was making polite conversation to Greville Rutherford.

Unfortunately as she shrugged off her coat, her cardigan came undone. Underneath she was wearing a thin white shirt through which her lacy French bra was clearly visible. Turning away quickly to repair the damage she felt the heat creep into her cheeks and thought suddenly of her prudish reaction last week when her interviewer had asked if she was a virgin. She was as it happened. Even though she had had the opportunity to lose her virginity several times, something had always held her back. Her upbringing of course, but also a sense of self-worth, a reluctance to let anyone get the better of her.

Even now as she looked round and caught the look in

Greville Rutherford's eyes she felt a shudder of revulsion. Oh no, she thought, please not that. Anything but that.

Chapter Five

'A terrible thing has happened,' Helen said to Katy the following weekend. 'I think Greville Rutherford has taken a bit of a shine to me.'

Katy's eyes widened. 'What do you mean? What sort of a shine?'

'The sort where he keeps looking at me,' Helen said, 'and when he catches me alone he's all smarmy and offers me drinks and things.'

'Oh, how ghastly!'

'He's even offered me a lift to the Tube station a couple of mornings.'

'Did you accept?'

Helen shook her head. 'I told him I liked the walk and the fresh air. I don't think I could bring myself to get in the car with him, he's beginning to give me the creeps.'

'What did he say?'

'He just smiled and said he admired my independent spirit.'

'I wish he admired my independent spirit,' Katy said sourly.

'That's the thing,' Helen said. 'He doesn't really admire any such thing. On the contrary, he keeps going on about how hopeless women are and how they lose their nerve in the face of danger.'

'What do you say to that?'

Helen shrugged. 'On that occasion I said that women had given a pretty good account of themselves in the blitz, but most of the time I just laugh and say nothing. Short of being rude, what can I say? I am his guest after all.'

'What a shame you can't tell him what you are going to do,' Katy said.

'I know,' she said. 'I wish I could. But I can't. Anyway, there's no guarantee I'll be accepted for training.' Two weeks had now passed since her interview and she had heard nothing.

'These things take time,' Angus McNaughton said when she asked him about the delay. 'There are a lot of considerations to be taken into account.'

'They'll take you,' Katy said now. 'They're bound to. You'd be brilliant.' She smiled. 'I just wish you could use your charms on Greville Rutherford on my behalf. Couldn't you hint that he might get a few favours if he renewed my lease, something like that?'

'Katy!' Helen said. 'I couldn't. I'd be sick if he touched me.'

'You don't have to touch him, couldn't you just talk to him? Explain my position?'

Realising Katy was serious, Helen swallowed. 'I suppose I could try,' she said, 'although I doubt it would do any good.' She stopped and looked at Katy closely. 'You really need this lease, don't you?'

'Yes,' Katy said simply.

By the end of November the Russian winter was beginning to take its toll on the Germans, making Hitler even more determined to take Moscow. In North Africa the Desert Rats were gnawing at the Nazi supply lines in a fluid ongoing battle. In London the autumn weather was deteriorating rapidly and people were gloomily predicting a renewed bombing campaign for the winter.

And then on Sunday 7 December the Japanese entered the fray with an unexpected attack on the American fleet moored in Hawaii at Pearl Harbor.

The news didn't break in England until the following morning, but then it spread like wildfire. The Flag and Garter was packed out that night and everyone was talking about the attack. The mood was optimistic. Surely this at last would bring the Americans into the war.

Joyce Carter was at the sink. She had already put in a full day at the café, but when she had called at the pub on the way home to discuss the food for the Gregg Bros. party, poor Katy Frazer looked so peaky that she had offered to come back later to lend a hand.

Katy had been grateful. She glanced round the smoky noisy bar. 'Jacob and I can cope when it's quiet, but when it's busy an extra pair of hands makes all the difference.'

'Couldn't your mother help a bit more?' Joyce asked.

Katy leaned on the counter. 'She does some cleaning for me, but she finds the evenings too much for her. She needs a lot of rest.'

Joyce sniffed. She'd never had much time for Katy's mother. Rest? The stupid woman needed a kick up the backside more likely, but she didn't say so. 'It's you as ought to rest,' she said instead. 'What with the baby coming and that.'

'That's what the health visitor keeps telling me,' Katy said.

'She's right,' Joyce said. She nodded at Katy's stomach. 'That's not just an inconvenient lump, you know. There's a human being in there, waiting to come out. Your child. Your responsibility.'

Katy paled suddenly and Joyce wondered if she had gone too far. It wasn't her place to say anything after all, but someone had to. That wet blanket of a mother obviously hadn't.

There were tears now in Katy's eyes. 'You're right,' she stammered. 'I've been trying not to think about it. The birth and that. Let alone afterwards.' She put her hands on the counter and shook her head. 'I suppose I've been hoping nothing will happen until I've sorted out this lease problem.'

Joyce shrugged. 'It will happen,' she said, 'and when it does you certainly won't be worrying about any lease.'

She was about to turn away when Katy leaned over and touched her arm. 'You've had children, Mrs Carter. Do you remember what it was like?'

Joyce thought back. Bob and Pete hadn't been too bad, but Jen … God. She remembered bloody Jen's arrival all right. That pain you thought you'd die of. So bad you wished you would. She'd hated Jen as a baby. For causing her so much pain.

Looking at Katy Frazer now she wondered if she would have the strength for it. She hoped she did, not just for her own sake but for the sake of that lovely husband of hers too. Ward Frazer. He was a catch and a half. It was a bloody shame he wasn't here now to give the girl some support.

She could feel Katy's eyes on her. 'It's bloody awful,' she said. 'There's no point in saying otherwise. But you'll cope. I've always thought you was tougher than you look.'

Moving away, Joyce noticed Mr Lorenz sitting on his own in the corner. She felt uncomfortable about Lorenz. He had been so good to her in the past, lending her stuff from his stock at the pawnbroker's and covering up when Mick took a potshot at him with a pistol stolen from the Home Guard. He had even found the premises for the café. But now she knew he thought she had given him the brush-off.

He wasn't looking at her. He was nursing his glass, apparently deep in thought. He was always on his own. She had never seen him with a friend. He came to the café every morning now, but she was always too busy to pass the time of day with him there. He had a cup of tea and two slices of toast and then he paid and went. She knew there was a kind of estrangement between them, and she didn't know what to do about it.

Suddenly she wanted to make amends, if she could. She just wasn't sure how to. She'd think about it, she decided. When she had more time. She had enough on her plate just now what with keeping up supplies at the café and helping a bit at the pub. And she'd have to start thinking about the Gregg Bros. party soon and all. She was going to do Katy proud on that. She'd do sandwiches of course, but some nice flans would go down well, she reckoned. And mince pies too if she could lay hands on some dried fruit and suet.

Louise was getting increasingly nervous about the Gregg Bros. party. What if it was a disaster? What if nobody enjoyed themselves? Then she would be blamed. Somehow her colleagues had already found out that her father owned the brewery which owned the pub. There had already been some jibes about keeping it in the family, putting a bit of business her father's way. Little did they know that the last person in the world she would try and help was her father. She couldn't say so of course. No more than she could let on that it was Katy Frazer she was trying to help. She just hoped Katy appreciated it.

It was more than anyone else had done for her, that was for sure. Oh, a few people helped in the bar from time to time – Aaref Hoch and Molly Coogan and that awful old Mrs Carter – but nobody else had gone out on a limb to bring her more custom.

Jack appreciated it of course. His letters were full of admiration. But then Jack didn't know the full details. He didn't know that Katy's lease was coming to an end. Louise didn't want him to think too badly of her father. Not just when he might be beginning to think of him as his future father-in-law.

With a sudden pang Louise wondered if Katy had written to Ward about the lease problem. Poor Katy, it must be ghastly trying to keep up a correspondence with Ward when the letters took so long. Jack's letters only took two days, but only now in December was Katy receiving replies to letters she had sent Ward in October.

Louise frowned. If only Ward was here and not in a blasted prisoner-of-war camp the whole situation would be different. She was sure her father wouldn't think twice about letting Katy continue at the pub if Ward was around.

Suddenly she sat up. She had an idea.

At supper that night she tried it out on her father. She waited for her mother to serve out the toad-in-the-hole, then she glanced at her father at the head of the table. 'Now that the Americans are in the war it will probably be over quite quickly, won't it, Daddy?'

He looked surprised. 'Good lord, yes,' he said. 'I doubt that fool Hitler will stand up against the combined strength of the Allies for long.'

'And then all the prisoners-of-war will be liberated?'

Her father frowned warily. 'Providing Hitler abides by the terms of the Geneva Convention.'

'So Ward Frazer might be home quite soon?' Louise said eagerly. 'And then he could help Katy with the pub. So perhaps you could reconsider and let her have the lease after all?' Catching Helen's eye she winked hopefully, but her father was not impressed by the argument.

'No, I will not reconsider,' he said. 'I have nothing against Katy Frazer personally. I am sure she has done her best over the last few months, but it is blatantly quite absurd to expect a young inexperienced woman to run a licensed establishment, let alone when she will shortly have a baby to look after.'

Louise flinched. 'But ...'

Greville Rutherford glared at her. 'I don't want to hear any buts or anything else.' He stood up and folded his napkin. 'For your information I already have another tenant in mind and he will be looking round the Flag and Garter later in the week with a view to taking over as soon as possible in the New Year. Now if you will excuse me I have work to do in my study.'

Helen was cold. Turning on to her side she tucked the covers closer around her and pulled her knees up to her chest, but it was no good. She had been cold ever since supper. Cold and cross. She had been steeling herself to talk to Greville Rutherford about Katy all day and then blasted Louise had blown it by jumping the gun over dinner.

Sitting up, she decided to go and get herself a hot drink. The thought of a steaming cup of Horlicks was very appealing. On the other hand the journey down the stairs and through the cold dark house was distinctly unappealing. It was made more unappealing by the fact that her torch battery had run out and her dressing-gown was in the wash.

'Damn it,' she muttered.

Chiding herself for being pathetic, she got out of bed, pulled off the bedspread, wrapped it round her shoulders like a cloak, and opened the door. If she wanted a Horlicks then she would damn well go and get one.

There was a moon but the blackout curtains made the house very dark. Dark and silent. She was already wearing bedsocks, so her feet made little noise, but tiptoeing along the landing and down the stairs, she couldn't help wondering why it was that floorboards which made no sound by day always squeaked so alarmingly by night.

Hugging the blanket round her she padded carefully down the stairs, across the hall, through the pantry and along the back corridor into kitchen.

Thankfully there the blackout was sufficiently in place to switch on the light and she had no difficulty lighting the gas. Aware that the new milk ration was only two pints per person per week she conscientiously diluted it with water before stirring in the Horlicks.

Even through the bedsocks, the stone floor felt cold and

she stepped from foot to foot hugging the blanket round her while she waited for the liquid to boil. Then she poured it carefully into a large cup, washed up the saucepan, turned off the gas and the light and began the journey back to bed.

After the light in the kitchen, the house seemed even darker than it had on the way through and Helen advanced cautiously, holding the cup and saucer with both hands to prevent the drink spilling.

She had just reached the pantry door and was fumbling for the handle when to her astonishment it jerked open from the other side.

Jumping back in alarm, Helen caught her foot in her blanket and went sprawling backwards on to the hard floor.

'Good lord, what's happened?' Through the pain and shock she heard Greville Rutherford's voice and then a torchbeam played over her. 'Helen?'

For a second as she lay there all she could feel was a cold throbbing in her left leg and a smarting sensation on her arm where the Horlicks had scalded her as it flew out of her hand. Then she saw where the torchbeam was pointing and suddenly all pain was forgotten as she realised that in her dramatic descent to the floor the blanket had fallen off her completely and her nightdress had ridden well up her thighs.

'Helen.' Greville Rutherford cleared his voice. 'I'm so sorry. I thought I heard something. Are you all right?'

'Yes, yes, I'm fine,' Helen muttered, staggering to her feet, although actually she did feel rather bruised, and as she brushed her nightgown down the pressure on her leg made her wince.

Greville Rutherford put the torch on the table. 'You're not all right. My dear girl, you're obviously in pain.' Suddenly he was standing very close to her. Close enough for her to feel the rough texture of his dressing-gown against the bare skin of her arm. Close enough to see the stripe of his pyjamas where the dressing-gown had come loose at the front.

'You're shaking,' he said. 'You're cold.' Abruptly he reached down and picked up the blanket. Draping it round her shoulders he touched the skin at her neck. She jerked away but he gripped her arm.

'Mr Rutherford, please, I ...'

'Greville,' he muttered. 'Call me Greville ...' Suddenly his hands were pulling her against him, and she could feel the hard wall of his chest crushing her breasts. He was breathing hard, and his hands were roaming over her back, clamping her to him as he leaned down and tried to kiss her on the mouth.

'No,' she said desperately. 'No! ...' Then, even as she began to struggle, they heard a voice. His wife's voice. Greville Rutherford froze.

'Greville? Are you there?' Celia called. 'It wasn't an intruder, was it?'

Leaping back from Helen, he hurried into the hall. 'No, no, my dear. It's just young Helen making herself a drink. I'll be up in a moment.'

Helen felt a terrible hot blush staining her face. She had never been so embarrassed, so abused, in all her life. How dare he? How *dare* he? As he turned back to her she gathered the blanket close around her. 'I'd better get to bed,' she muttered.

He tried to stop her. 'Helen, I ...'

She bent down to pick up the miraculously unbroken cup and saucer and put them on the table. There was remarkably little mess. The blanket had absorbed most of the Horlicks.

She didn't look at him. She couldn't. 'Goodnight,' she said coldly.

The following morning at breakfast Helen could barely bring herself to meet anyone's eyes. All she wanted to do was pack her bags and walk out, but she couldn't, not without an explanation, and good manners precluded an explanation. She could hardly tell Celia that her husband had assaulted her. It just wasn't the kind of thing you said. So she ate her breakfast quickly, exchanged vague remarks about Jack with Louise, and when Greville Rutherford waylaid her in the hall just as she was leaving the house she was distinctly frosty.

He looked pretty uncomfortable himself. 'I need to talk to you, Helen. Can I give you a lift to the station?'

Helen shook her head. 'No, thank you,' she said.

Glancing over his shoulder, he lowered his voice. 'Look, I'm sorry about last night. It was your legs. You're a very attractive girl, Helen. You must realise that.'

'I am also your guest,' Helen said coldly.

'Yes, of course,' he said. 'It won't happen again. And of course I trust your discretion ...'

Helen suddenly saw her chance. Probably her only chance. She met his eyes steadily. 'I'll make a bargain with you,' she said. 'You give Katy Frazer another year's lease, and I won't tell anyone what happened last night.'

For a moment the silence was deafening. Then he exhaled sharply, his breath cloudy in the cold early morning air. 'Nobody would believe you,' he said. 'It would be your word against mine.'

'Try me,' Helen said, but she could tell from the set of his face that she was wasting her time. She lifted her shoulders. 'It's your choice.'

As she limped down the steps she half hoped he might call her back, but he didn't.

'You're the prettiest girl I've ever clapped eyes on,' Larry Gregg whispered in Louise's ear as he waltzed her round the confined space in the Flag and Garter lounge bar to cheers of enthusiasm from the rest of his staff.

Louise laughed delightedly. The party was going well. The pianist was lively, Katy and Molly Coogan were rushed off their feet behind the bar and Mrs Carter had produced some surprisingly tasty sandwiches and flans.

Larry Gregg had stuffed a mince pie in his mouth just as they started to dance, but it was his hands that were causing Louise more problem. The one that was holding her hand was all right but the other one was edging lower and lower down her back.

'You like me and all?' He went on.

'Oh yes,' Louise whispered back. 'I like you very much, but before you try anything on I'd better warn you that my boyfriend is the jealous type. The last person who touched me up ended up in hospital.'

As his hand jerked up a few decorous inches, Louise giggled to herself. Actually she didn't know if Jack was the jealous type or not. She really didn't know him very well at all, but that would be rectified next week when he came back to London for Christmas. She felt a shiver of anticipation. She was certain that this time he would propose. What could be more romantic than a Christmas engagement?

'Is that your boyfriend over there by the bar?' Larry Gregg asked rather nervously. 'He looks pretty fierce.'

Looking up sharply Louise followed his gaze and saw Aaref Hoch watching her moodily. 'Goodness no,' she said lightly. 'Aaref's just a friend.' Actually she wondered about that. Aaref had acted so cold with her since she had started dating Jack. She knew it was because he was jealous of Jack, and although she pretended not to care, secretly she was rather flattered. It was nice to be so admired. Even if it was only by Aaref Hoch.

She giggled. 'Oh no, my boyfriend is much bigger and tougher than that.'

Three houses along on the other side of the road Pam Nelson was listening to the news recap. America was in the war now, thanks to Pearl Harbor, but that hadn't stopped two British ships getting sunk off Malaya where the

Japanese had already started threatening the British bases. In the Middle East the Allies were struggling to hold their new positions. The only good news was that in Russia a sudden reverse had killed thirty thousand Germans and put seven thousand Nazi tanks out of action.

As far as Pam was concerned the best news in the world was that the Lavender Road school was to reopen. Since the blitz the WVS had been using the local school as their headquarters, but now they were to confine their activities to just two classrooms, leaving the rest of the building ready for children.

For Pam the relief was immense. She was certain that school would make all the difference to George. He would find some friends. And teachers were far more experienced than her at dealing with recalcitrant children.

George had been subdued since the episode in the pub. Perhaps Alan's telling-off had had some effect after all. Dear Alan. She smiled suddenly as she heard him come through the front door.

Alan was in his Home Guard uniform. He listened quietly as Pam eagerly told him the news about the school. 'You're smiling at me,' he said, touching her cheek gently. 'That makes a change.'

Looking into his kind face, Pam suddenly felt guilty. It had been hard for her but it had been hard for Alan too. George's arrival had put a lot of pressure on their relationship. Pam's frustration that Alan wouldn't or couldn't discipline him had spilled over into a frustration with Alan himself. That, and a feeling of overwhelming stress and a fear that George would hear them, had completely put her off making love.

'Oh Alan, I'm sorry,' she said now. 'I really am. I can't tell you how different I feel tonight ...' She stopped as Alan drew her into his arms and kissed her gently on the lips.

When she kissed him back he seemed surprised, but when her arms crept round under his khaki jacket and burrowed under his shirt he started smiling. 'Ah, that sort of different,' he murmured. 'Now let me see.' He lifted her hair and kissed her gently on the neck. 'Do you feel different there?' He chuckled as a shiver ran through her. 'And what about here?' He eased her blouse away from her collarbone and kissed her there.

'Oh Alan,' she breathed as he slowly began to unbutton her blouse. 'I'd forgotten what this could be like.'

'Had you?' He shrugged off his jacket and took off his beret, then he smiled and pulled her into a chair on his knee. 'Well, I'm more than happy to jog your memory, my sweet.'

It was several minutes later, just as Pam was about to suggest they moved upstairs, when he suddenly stopped kissing her.

'You'll never guess what happened today,' he said. 'At the brewery.'

'What?'

'Old Rutherford changed his mind about the Flag and Garter.'

Pam jerked back to stare at him. 'What? You mean Katy can keep it?'

He saw her amazement and opened his hands. 'I know. It was the most peculiar thing. He's been like a bear with a sore paw for weeks and then today out of the blue he asked his clerk to draw up papers to renew the lease.'

'Does she know?'

'Not yet, but she will in the morning.'

Pam gaped at him. 'Alan, you must go and tell her at once!'

He looked aghast. 'What, now?' But Pam was already climbing off his lap.

'Of course you must.' She pulled him to his feet and began tucking in his shirt. 'God, don't you know the agony she has suffered over this? At least we can save her one night's worry.'

She stopped as Alan groaned despairingly. 'My darling,'

he said. 'You are the most frustrating woman I have ever known.'

However, he went. She had known he would. He was too kind not to. It was only over the road, after all. Glancing down at her unbuttoned blouse, she smiled to herself. She hoped he wouldn't be long.

Joyce was sweating. She had never known it so crowded in the Flag and Garter. What with the Gregg Bros. party and the regulars in as well, there wasn't enough room to swing a pint let alone a cat. Even now she was struggling getting back to the sink with some empties.

As someone pushed past in front of her she stepped back abruptly and felt her bottom make contact with someone's hip. 'Bumpsadaisy,' she said brightly, turning round, and was daunted to find herself nose to nose with Mr Lorenz.

He looked as embarrassed as she felt, but he recovered quickly. 'Good evening, Mrs Carter,' he said courteously inclining his head.

Joyce almost laughed. Lorenz was the only person in the world who would retain his impeccable manners even in a heaving scrum of well-over-the-top drinkers. As the person behind her lurched past again Joyce had to struggle not to bump him again. Already her bosom was pressed hard into his arm but there was little she could do about it. Better her bosom than the glasses she was holding. At least her bosom wouldn't break, whereas glasses were hard to come by these days.

She realised Lorenz was looking flushed and wondered if it was her bosom or the beer to blame. He was asking her something now, something about the party in the lounge bar, but over the din she couldn't really hear what he was saying. The only word she did hear was Christmas, and suddenly, to her astonishment, she heard herself inviting him to Christmas lunch.

Unfortunately he was still speaking and missed what she

had said. Clearly somewhat startled by her interruption, he cupped his hand to his ear. 'I'm so sorry, …'

Joyce could feel the sweat trickling down her face. 'I said did you want to have Christmas dinner at mine?' she bellowed. 'There'll only be me and Pete there so there's plenty of room.'

For a moment as he blinked nervously she thought he hadn't heard again and her heart sank. It hadn't been a particularly gracious invitation the first time round, but then she saw he was nodding.

'I would like to very much,' he said. 'It would be a great pleasure. An honour.'

He was about to say more, when over his shoulder Joyce saw Alan Nelson push his way into the bar looking distinctly dishevelled. She saw him glance round and then head determinedly towards Katy who was collecting up glasses off the tables by the fire. She saw Katy look up in surprise as Alan took her arm, and then Alan was shouting something in her ear.

For a second an expression of joy lit Katy's pale face, and then suddenly without any warning she doubled over with a sharp cry, and without another thought for Lorenz, once again Joyce started barging through the drinkers.

Katy couldn't believe the pain. She had had little twinges all day but she had thought nothing of it. It was three weeks until the baby was due after all. She had put it down to indigestion or anxiety about the party, but this was no indigestion. She knew it before Joyce and Molly Coogan came rushing over. She had never felt anything like that first painful stab and she didn't want to again. It seemed she had no choice, however, because a minute later it came again.

At first it came in waves. Waves of pain so intense that she couldn't help the tears coming to her eyes. She was aware of Molly Coogan and Joyce helping her towards the stairs. She was aware of people staring, of nervous offers of help, but she couldn't respond. She had no idea it would come on so quickly. Nor that the contractions would be so close on each other. She was barely up the stairs before the next came.

She heard Molly's urgent voice. 'Breathe, Katy, breathe. And try to relax.'

But she couldn't breathe or relax. She couldn't even think. She could only whimper and then scream and scream as the waves of pain turned into one long ongoing heartstopping agony.

She could hear them talking. She could hear her mother crying. She could hear the words doctor, danger and hospital, but she was beyond panic. Suddenly she knew beyond doubt that she was going to die and all she wanted was Ward Frazer. Her husband. She wanted just to see him once more before she died. She wanted to say goodbye.

The first Helen knew about Katy's collapse was when Louise woke her in the middle of the night. Helen had come home late from the office. One of the agents had failed to report in and they were waiting anxiously for a signal. When finally it came, it was obvious from the faulty password that he had fallen into German hands. She wondered how long he would be able to keep up the pretence that he was acting as a double agent before the Germans realised they were being duped. It was a dangerous game. All the way home she had felt chilled, but not as chilled as she felt now at Louise's description of Katy's pain.

'Thank God someone got a taxi,' Louise was saying. 'They rushed her off to the Wilhelmina hospital. You should have heard her screaming. It was terrible. And it took us ages to clear up the pub afterwards. I had no idea how much mess one night's drinking would make. No wonder she's tired if she has to do that every night.'

'Oh God,' Helen whispered, 'I hope she'll be all right.'

'I know,' Louise said. 'Especially now Daddy's given her the lease for another year.'

'He has?' Helen sat up abruptly. 'When? How do you know?'

'Alan Nelson knew,' Louise said. 'He'd only just told her when the contractions started.'

So it worked, Helen thought. My blackmail worked. Any satisfaction it gave her, however, was cancelled out by her total anxiety about Katy.

She touched Louise's hand. 'If you hear anything tomorrow, will you ring me at the office?' she said.

Louise nodded. 'Mr Gregg gave me the day off,' she said, 'so I'll go down to the hospital as soon as I get up. To see if there's any news.'

The following morning the underground trains were crowded, the windows steaming, the floors running with water. As she took a deep breath and climbed aboard, Helen suddenly found herself longing for summer, those long hot days, skimpy clothes, lazy drinks in the garden. As it was, she spent the journey shivering between a bony man in a sodden navy overcoat and a small woman in a wraparound rain hat and a spiky umbrella. I hate the winter, she thought. I hate it.

By the time she got to the office she was exhausted. There was no message from Louise. For once, the newspapers failed to interest her. All she could think about was Katy Frazer writhing in agony trying to give birth. Screaming.

When Angus McNaughton came into her office with a telephone pad saying he'd got news for her she stood up eagerly.

'From the hospital?'

'The hospital?' He looked puzzled. 'No, from Maurice Buckmaster. You have been accepted for agent training. The first stage is the arduous training course in Scotland.

You'll get joining instructions this afternoon. The course starts early in January.'

Part Two

Chapter Six

After a long, difficult labour lasting nearly sixteen hours Katy gave birth to a seven-pound baby boy.

It had been touch and go, everyone knew that; the baby had breached, punctured her bladder and only finally emerged into the world with the aid of forceps and the intervention of Sister Morris, Katy's old mentor from the Ethel Barnet ward where she had started her nursing training the previous year.

Katy had been almost unconscious and weak with pain and loss of blood when Sister Morris, alerted by Molly Coogan to the imminent disaster, had swept into the delivery room.

Sister Morris took in the desperate scene with one glance of her fierce blue eyes. She didn't need to hear the midwife muttering anxiously that contractions had stopped but it was too late for a caesarean. Ignoring the doctor and two helpless nurses she marched to the head of the bed where Katy lay in silent agony, her legs stretched high and wide in leather stirrups, her face bathed in sweat, white as the sheet that covered her upper body.

'What's the meaning of this?' she barked. 'What's all this nonsense I hear about you giving up? Do you want this baby or not?'

Galvanised by Sister Morris's voice, Katy managed to open her eyes, but it was almost too much effort to speak. 'I'm so tired,' she whispered eventually. 'I can't do any more.'

'Rubbish,' Sister Morris snapped. 'You're just being thoroughly selfish. Think of the baby. Think of your husband.' She snorted in satisfaction as Katy's eyes filled with tears. 'A reaction,' she said crisply, nodding at the doctor wielding the forceps. 'That's better.' She turned back to Katy and slapped her face quite hard. 'Now pull yourself together, young lady, take some deep breaths and *push.*'

It seemed a long time later that Katy opened her eyes. For a moment she thought she must be dead. She felt extraordinarily light, floating almost. The pain had gone. In fact her whole body seemed to have gone. The people had gone. Sister Morris had gone. The baby had gone.

Something grated in her mind. The baby? What had happened to the baby? She knew it couldn't possibly have survived that ordeal but she wanted to see it before they buried it. They hadn't wanted her to see her father when he had died but she had insisted and it had helped. He had seemed to be at peace. She hoped the baby would be at peace too. Desperately, she tried to sit up and at once a nurse appeared at the side of her bed.

'How are we feeling now?'

Katy saw the sympathy in the nurse's eyes and suddenly she felt very tearful. 'Would they let me see the baby?' she asked tentatively.

'Of course,' the nurse said placidly. 'I'll sit you up first and then I'll fetch him. Then I think we'll try a feed, shall we?'

'A feed?' Katy stared at her blankly as she was hauled up the bed.

The nurse nodded brightly. 'Best to get him started as soon as we can.'

Before Katy could speak she had left the room. A moment later she was back with a small bundle of trailing linen. Inside was a baby.

'That's it, hold the head,' the nurse said encouragingly

as she lowered it carefully into Katy's arms. Then she stood back and smiled. 'Isn't he gorgeous?'

Katy stared at it in bewilderment. 'It's alive,' she said. That was the only thing that could be said about it. It certainly wasn't gorgeous. It was, in fact, extraordinarily hideous. Its face was red and crumpled. It had sticking-out ears, shiny pink gums, a snub nose and no hair.

Katy looked up suddenly. 'Are you sure this one is mine?' she said. 'I thought mine was dead.'

'Dead?' The nurse looked astonished. 'Whatever made you think that?' She smiled at the baby fondly. 'No, he had a difficult birth but he's very much alive, I assure you. All seven pounds of him.'

When Katy didn't respond the nurse smiled gently. 'Does he look like your husband?'

Katy thought of Ward with his crisp dark hair, his steady grey eyes, his heartstopping smile. Then she looked down at the creature in her arms, the crinkled-red face, the dented head, the slitty eyes.

'No, not at all,' she said and burst into tears.

The nurses were kind but brisk. It was quite natural to feel low and distressed after such a long labour, they said. A lot of mums were tearful at first, but they soon pulled themselves together when they realised they'd got a new little mouth to feed.

Nevertheless they were clearly concerned about Katy, and although they allowed her mother to visit briefly the second afternoon, nobody else was allowed to see her until Christmas Eve.

By that time Katy was desperate for company. The nurses brought the baby in to her every four hours for feeding and changing and in between she lay in bed waiting for her internal wounds to heal and fretting about the pub.

To fill in time she wrote letters, to Jen, to Ward's aunts, the funny old Miss Taylors in Bristol, to Ward himself, telling him about the baby, his baby, even though she knew he wouldn't actually receive the news until February. The delay in their correspondence depressed her. She wanted him to know now. Today.

More than anything she wanted to talk to him, to hug him and hold him, to share her worries with him, but she knew she couldn't. It was bad enough for him to be locked up in a beastly camp, without him worrying about her. So she wrote a bright, careful letter, glossing over the problems of the birth and her financial worries, and not mentioning at all the fact that she was apparently entirely lacking in maternal feelings and still could not really believe the baby was hers.

What made it worse was that when she was finally allowed visitors everyone else seemed not only to be in festive spirit but also to find the baby genuinely beautiful when Katy still secretly thought it looked like some ugly little creature from outer space.

'Oh, I love him, I love him,' Molly Coogan giggled, delightedly dancing him round the room in her arms on Christmas Eve when she came off duty. 'Have you decided what to call him?'

'Malcolm,' Katy said.

Malcolm. Her father's name. It was Ward's suggestion, received only yesterday in a letter written back in October soon after he had first learned of her pregnancy.

Her mother had cried for half an hour when Katy had told her. 'Oh, he's a lovely man, your Ward,' she had sobbed. 'I just wish he was here to look after us.'

'Malcolm,' Molly said now. 'That's a nice name.' She giggled coyly. 'Nearly as nice as Aaref.'

'Goodness, what a pretty baby,' Louise exclaimed half an hour later. She was all flushed and excited after meeting Jack for tea. 'I hope I'll have one as pretty when I marry Jack.'

Katy's eyes widened. 'Has he proposed, then?'

'Well, no,' Louise admitted reluctantly. 'Not yet. I think he might be waiting for New Year's Eve.'

'Ooh, isn't he a little duck?' Joyce Carter gooed over baby Malcolm on Boxing Day afternoon. She glanced at Katy over the baby's head. 'Mr Lorenz sends his best wishes and all.'

'Mr Lorenz?' Katy blinked. 'How did he hear about it?'

Joyce flushed slightly. 'He came over for lunch yesterday,' she said.

'Oh, Mrs Carter.' Katy smiled her first smile since the baby was born. 'Do I sense romance in the air?'

'Romance?' Joyce looked appalled. 'Of course not, but I could hardly leave the poor man sitting alone, could I? Not on Christmas Day.' Avoiding Katy's knowing eyes she leaned over Malcolm again. 'At least your baby gave us something to talk about. I've never seen a more bonny baby.'

Katy nodded but deep down she felt almost jealous of baby Malcolm. Everyone seemed far more interested in him than in her. Hardly anyone enquired about her state of health; the fact that her bosoms ached twenty-four hours a day and she felt as though she was sitting on a pin cushion seemed to pass them by.

Helen de Burrel was the only person who seemed to remember she was a human being and not some kind of milk machine. In typical Helen style she brought with her a beautiful, soft-as-silk pram blanket for Malcolm and a huge bouquet of white winter roses for Katy. Katy stared at them in amazement. They must have cost the earth.

'I'm so sorry I haven't been before,' Helen said, sliding her chic fur-trimmed coat off her slender shoulders. 'I tried before Christmas and they wouldn't let me in.' Perching on the bed she glanced more closely at Katy. 'Tell me, how was the birth? I know there's some kind of conspiracy between mothers not to say, but was it truly awful?'

Katy blinked. 'How did you know?'

Helen lifted her shoulders. 'Pure logistics,' she said. She

nodded at the baby asleep in his hospital cradle. 'Squeezing something that size out of you-know-where must be the equivalent of blowing an orange out of your nose.'

For the first time in days Katy laughed out loud. 'Don't,' she gasped. 'Don't make me laugh.'

Helen smiled. 'Well, am I right?'

Katy shook her head. 'No,' she said, wincing as she moved slightly. 'Not an orange, more of a hedgehog, I would say. And it feels as if they've left another one inside.'

It was Helen's turn to laugh, but her eyes were sympathetic. 'How long is it going to be before you're up and about again? Back at work?'

Katy smiled bravely. 'I'm reopening the pub next weekend. Now Mr Rutherford has given me the blessed lease I'm damned if I'm going to let it lie idle any longer than necessary.' She hesitated. 'It was you who changed his mind, wasn't it?' She saw Helen's eyes flicker and nodded. 'I thought so. You've saved my life, you know. But how? How did you do it?'

Helen grimaced. 'He tried to kiss me one night and I threatened to tell poor old Celia if he didn't give you the lease.'

'Helen!' Katy's eyes widened. 'You blackmailed him!'

'It was in a good cause.'

Katy looked at Helen with new respect, 'You'll make a good spy.'

'Good,' she said lightly, 'because I start next week. Arduous training somewhere in the north of Scotland.'

Katy blanched. Surely Helen couldn't really be so cool about it. 'How do you feel? Really?'

Helen shrugged. 'I'm not scared of a few snow-covered mountains.'

In fact Helen was far too keen to get away from London and Greville Rutherford to worry about what awaited her at the other end. He had treated her with such stiff courtesy since his bungled attempt at a kiss that she was sure Mrs Rutherford or Louise would notice.

Luckily Helen had been away over Christmas, staying with some family friends in their beautiful Oxfordshire home. It had been a relaxed few days with blazing log fires and plenty to drink, and even the fall of Hong Kong to the Japanese on Christmas Day hadn't dampened the festive spirit too badly.

Back in London after the break, she found herself acting as chaperone to Louise and Jack. After Louise's unfortunate experience with the Polish count, Greville Rutherford was reluctant for her to spend any time alone with Jack, and although Helen thought he was a fine one to cast aspersions on his daughter's morals, she was happy to accept any invitations that kept her out of his way.

On New Year's Eve they went to the ballet with a friend of Jack's, and although the Sadlers Wells company were cramped in the New Theatre and the costumes rather tatty, and although they had to dance to a piano these days instead of an orchestra, Ashton and Fonteyn were quite brilliant and Helen would not have missed it for the world.

Jack's friend was pleasant but nothing special and Louise was disappointed that Helen didn't show more interest in him. 'Don't you like William, then? Jack and I thought you were getting on so well.'

'I like him very much,' Helen said, 'but he's not my type.'

'What is your type?' Louise asked.

'Oh, I don't know,' Helen said. 'William is a bit young for me. I think I'd want someone older, someone brave and strong, someone I can really respect . . .'

Louise was too put out that Jack hadn't proposed on New Year's Eve after all to give too much thought to Helen's requirements. 'I was so sure he would,' she grumbled now. 'He keeps saying he loves me, so why doesn't he get on with it and ask me properly?'

Helen smiled. 'I expect he wants to be sure. To know

that you are sure too. Marriage isn't something to jump into lightly.'

'I am sure,' Louise said crossly. 'I'd jump tomorrow if he asked me.'

Unfortunately Louise brought up the subject of William again at dinner in front of her parents. 'Poor William is head over heels in love with Helen but she says she's more interested in older men.'

Aware of Greville Rutherford's sudden glance in her direction, Helen groaned inwardly, hoping he hadn't got the wrong impression. 'Actually I'm not sure I want a husband at all,' she said. 'Not yet.' She certainly didn't want to be all a-dither like Louise waiting for some man to propose. Waiting for his whim. His decision. Waiting eagerly to become one of his possessions. I want my own life, she thought. I want to be something. I want people to respect me for myself, not just because I've found myself a man.

'Anyway,' she said, 'there's no point me looking for anyone just now because I've got to go away next week for a month on . . . an Inter-Services liaison tour.'

To Louise's dismay, Jack went back to Liverpool without proposing, even though she had taken the trouble to trail all the way up to Euston station to see him off in the hopes that he'd pop the question on the station platform as they made their tender farewells. Instead he just kissed her demurely on the cheek.

'Thank you for a wonderful, wonderful few days.'

'I can't wait to see you again,' Louse said bravely.

'You will wait, though, won't you?'

Louise pouted. 'I may do. So long as it's not too long.'

Jack looked at her anxiously. 'There's nobody else, is there? You're my girl, aren't you? You do love me, don't you?'

'Of course I do,' Louise said irritably. 'I've told you a million times.' Good lord, she thought, frustrated. What more could she do? If only she could go to bed with him she'd be able to show him how much she loved him, but she knew him well enough to know that it would be a mistake to offer anything on those lines. Jack was old fashioned in that way. The only time he had kissed her properly was at midnight on New Year's Eve. Being a gentleman, he called it. He wanted to wait. But for how long?

Jack shrugged apologetically. 'I wish I could get down to London more often, but the journey takes so long and I have so little leave.' He paused for a moment. 'Perhaps you could come up to Liverpool?'

For a second Louise thought things might be looking up, but then her face fell. 'Daddy wouldn't let me,' she said. 'Not unless ...' She stopped and flushed prettily.

'Unless what?'

She swallowed. 'Unless we were engaged or something. He might then.'

For a second he hesitated, then he shook his head decisively. 'I don't want to get engaged until I'm promoted. I'll have more to offer then. I'm due for it. I might get a second in command. I'm sick of this training role. I want a proper job. A job at sea.'

Looking at the sudden fire in his eyes, Louise sighed. Blasted men, she thought. Who cared about a promotion? If she was safe on a training ship in Liverpool harbour she'd rather stay there.

As the whistle blew, she felt something tug her heart. She liked Jack Delmaine, and she fancied him too. A lot. Even if his cool good manners and faint reserve drove her mad.

Even now, instead of giving her a proper goodbye kiss, he was just hugging her hard against him. 'Goodbye, sweetheart. Promise you'll be good.'

She smiled over his shoulder. 'I'm always good,' she said. And one day soon I'm going to get a proposal out of you, she thought, whatever it takes.

* * *

Joyce was rather startled when Mr Lorenz stopped her in the street and handed her a gasmask box.

Hardly anyone bothered with gasmasks any more, not since Hitler had laid off London and started bombing the Russians. Singapore was getting it now and all from the Japanese. Nobody liked Germans but the Japanese sounded even worse. She'd seen them on the newsreel. Sly-looking, little slitty-eyed men, them Japs. She reckoned Singapore didn't stand much chance.

Taking the box she was surprised to find it much heavier than she expected.

'It's sugar,' he murmured. 'You mentioned you were short the other day.'

Joyce blinked. Sugar? There must be a couple of pounds of it by the weight of the box. She hadn't seen that much sugar since the beginning of rationing. Nobody had. She didn't know what to say. They were amazing these Jews. It seemed they could lay hands on anything. It hadn't escaped her notice that that young Aaref fellow provided Katy Frazer with quite a bit of this and that and all.

'It's not for the café, Mrs Carter,' Mr Lorenz said shyly. 'It's for you. A little gift. I know you've got a sweet tooth.'

A little gift. Two pounds of sugar was more than a little gift, but Lorenz was rather good on gifts. He'd given her a handbag for Christmas. Said it had been handed in to him in hock. She didn't believe him of course. He was just saving her embarrassment as usual, because she hadn't got him a present. At least nothing other than the meal. Not that it hadn't been a good meal, because it had. And good fun and all. Even young Pete had been quite chatty for once. He and Lorenz had discussed racing. Lorenz had given him a tip for the Boxing Day race and Pete had won three bob.

She could do with three bob herself, she thought suddenly now. The café was all very well but there wasn't too much spare after the ordering and that. She didn't like to ask Mrs Rutherford for any more. The poor woman had put most of her savings into it as it was because that tight-arsed husband of hers wouldn't put his hand in his pocket to buy a bit of cutlery and crockery.

Lorenz was lifting his hat. 'Well, thank you again for the meal,' he said. 'I enjoyed it enormously.'

'You can come again Sunday if you want,' Joyce said. 'There's not much difference cooking for three than two after all.'

For a second Lorenz looked taken aback by the abrupt invitation, but then he smiled gravely. 'I would like to come again. Very much.'

She'd do a rabbit stew, she thought as she walked home, and she'd ask Mrs Rutherford to lend her a few apples for a pie. If she'd got a couple of pounds of sugar she might as well use it. Two pounds of sugar. She was smiling as she opened the front door.

There was a postcard on the mat. She picked it up and her smile faded abruptly as she read the flamboyant scrawl. 'Coming back Friday, 9 Jan. See you then. Jen.'

Joyce put a hand to her stomach. The thought of fancypants Jen sitting at the kitchen table with Lorenz for Sunday lunch made her feel quite queasy. Jen would spoil everything with her selfish ways and her mocking smile.

'I don't want Jen back here,' she said to Pete later over tea. She got on all right with Pete. He worked hard at his builders firm. He was a bit slow but he was a good lad. Steady. Not one to make a fuss like the rest of the family.

Pete blinked. 'But where will she go?' he asked. 'It's really hard to find anywhere just now. What with all the bombed houses and refugees and that, everyone's looking for rooms.'

Joyce looked at him. 'Of course,' she said slowly. There were lots of people renting rooms, like that nice Helen de Burrel Mrs Rutherford had staying. People like Mrs Rutherford called them paying guests. Everyone else called them lodgers.

Pete was frowning. 'Of course what?'

Joyce shook her head. 'Here,' she said briskly. 'As a special treat you can have a spoon of sugar in your tea tonight.'

The following day she carefully wrote out an advertisement on a piece of white card and stuck it up in the window of the café. 'Room to rent.'

By the next afternoon she had received three enquiries and had settled on a quiet studious-looking woman with a slight limp who turned out to be one of the new teachers at the soon-to-be-reopened Lavender Road primary school.

'You'll have to have your breakfast in the café,' Joyce said, 'but I'll do you an evening meal.'

Miss Philips nodded seriously. 'That seems very satisfactory.'

Yes, Joyce thought, for twelve bob a week it was very satisfactory indeed. And Jen could go and jump in the lake.

'Is this what Ward's aunts have sent?' Mary Parsons said, lifting up two tiny, intricately knitted cardigans from the pile of gifts on Katy's hospital bed. 'Oh Katy, aren't they lovely! And is this the gown Mrs Rutherford gave him?'

Katy nodded wearily. 'Yes …'

But her mother was well in her stride. 'Isn't it exquisite? I had no idea you could still get things like that these days. Oh, and are these the little gloves that Pam Nelson crocheted for him. Aren't they adorable? Oh dear …' She unfolded an enormous red and black tasselled shawl. 'What's this?'

'Mrs d'Arcy Billière sent it up with Aaref,' Katy said. Mrs d'Arcy Billière was known to be eccentric. She lived in the big house up on the common on the other side of Lavender Road from the Rutherfords. Before the war she had thrown wild parties and entertained glamorous foreigners, but she was good at heart. It was she who had taken Aaref and his brothers in when they arrived weak and penniless from Austria.

Katy touched the shawl. 'I think it's beautiful,' she said.

'Well, I suppose it's warm,' Mary Parsons said doubtfully. As Malcolm gurgled suddenly in the cradle alongside Katy's bed, she quickly put the gifts to one side. 'Oh dear, is he going to cry? I'd better go.'

'Mummy, when you come in tomorrow could you bring the order book with you?'

'The order book?' Mary Parsons looked anxious. 'I don't think ...'

It was odd, Katy thought, that her mother was more than happy to chat away about baby clothes, but as soon as Malcolm cried or she mentioned anything to do with the pub she got flustered.

'If I get the orders in tomorrow,' Katy said patiently, 'we'll be able to open on Friday evening. Can you put a sign up in the window so people know?' She was scared that in her absence all her customers would have absconded over to the Windmill on the common or to the rougher pubs down at Clapham Junction.

'But Katy, you only come out of hospital on Thursday.'

'So?' Katy smiled with a courage she did not altogether feel. 'I'll have a day to get organised.'

Thursday was the day Helen would be on her way to Scotland. She was so calm and confident about it. Sometimes Katy wondered if Helen really knew what she was letting herself in for. Ward had never said much about what he did, but Katy knew it was dangerous. The scars on his beautiful hard body had told her that, even if he himself had made light of them. Ward. She closed her eyes for a second, wishing she knew what he was doing, glad only that he was safe and she didn't need to worry about him any more.

She glanced in the crib at her red-faced baby. It was Malcolm she had to worry about now. Malcolm she had to provide for. She saw her mother's expression and put a hand on her arm.

'Mummy, it's all right,' she said. 'We'll manage.'

Surely looking after a child couldn't be that difficult?

Malcolm seemed a good quiet baby. And compared with arduous training in the Scottish Highlands in midwinter, reopening the pub would be a doddle.

Chapter Seven

It didn't take Helen long to realise the training course wasn't going to be quite what she had expected.

After a journey lasting nearly twenty-four hours with little sleep and less food she was hoping to be met by a comfortable staff car. Unfortunately she was met by a snub-nosed corporal with a canvas-sided lorry.

Ticking her name off a list the corporal jabbed his thumb towards the back of the truck. 'In there.'

There were several men already sitting on the narrow bench seats running along the side of the truck. They'd obviously arrived on the same train. Most of them were in uniform but one or two were in civilian dress. One looked familiar and she suddenly realised it was the man whose French she had tested all those weeks ago, the day she first went to dinner at the Rutherfords'. She hadn't liked him much then, but now as he leaned over to give her a hand in, she smiled at him gratefully.

'We meet again,' he said.

Before she could respond, the soldier had thrown her suitcases in after her and jerked the canvas down over the back, plunging them into semi-darkness. A moment later the truck roared into life and lurched forward, stopped abruptly and then started again, leaving one young man sprawling on the floor and the rest clutching their seats as all the luggage slithered to the back. After a bit of strained laughter and an offering-round of cigarettes nobody said much. It was too noisy and bumpy anyway. It took all their concentration to stay on the seats at all.

By the time they reached their destination about an hour later Helen ached all over. She was also freezing cold. Climbing out of the truck, ignoring the slush seeping into her shoes, she looked around with interest. They were in a rear courtyard of some largish house, a shooting lodge perhaps, but before she could get her bearings the corporal called her name and pointed towards a back stairs entrance.

'Up two flights, first on the right,' he said jerking his thumb upwards.

Helen nodded. 'What about my luggage?'

'What about it?'

'Will someone bring it up?'

For a second he hesitated then he shrugged. 'If you want it, you'll have to take it up yourself.'

So with the last remnant of strength she did, even though all she wanted to do was lie down and sleep for ever.

She had barely taken stock of the spartan room with its narrow iron-framed bed when someone banged on her door.

'Downstairs, five minutes. Map-reading exercise.'

She ran to the door. 'Excuse me,' she called down the passage after the man. 'I think there must be a mistake. I've only just arrived. I haven't even unpacked yet. I was told the course didn't start until tomorrow.'

He stopped and looked back, a thickset sergeant with small, beady eyes, a bristling ginger moustache and a strong Scottish accent. 'No, lassie, there's no mistake.'

'But, surely I …'

He walked slowly back to her and stood very close. Too close. When he spoke his voice was low and hard. 'Listen to me, Lady Helen de Burrel. I don't know why you've been picked for this work or what you've got to offer. All I know is that on this course it's each man for himself. It's a tough brutal world we're training you for. Nobody is going to do you any favours. Privilege counts for nothing with the Gestapo. Nor will it here. So you like it or you lump it. All right?'

Helen swallowed. Suddenly she felt ridiculously close to tears.

He held her eyes for a second longer then glanced at his watch. 'If you're not downstairs in five minutes you're off the course. Understand?'

As baby Malcolm started crying again, Katy closed her eyes and leaned weakly on the bar. Having been such a quiet baby in hospital, he had taken one glance at the Flag and Garter and screamed virtually nonstop ever since.

Katy was at the end of her tether. She had tried to feed him but he didn't seem hungry. She had tried to change him, but he was clean. She had tried to leave him to sleep, but he didn't want to do that either. She could hear him now, upstairs, bawling his head off, a grating roar of a cry which she simply couldn't ignore.

Pushing herself upright she rubbed her arm across her face and turned towards the stairs and wished her mother would just for once use some initiative. 'Mummy, can you pick him up?' she called up. He usually stopped crying if he was jiggled around a bit.

Her mother's anxious face appeared at the top of the stairs. 'Why's he crying?' she asked for perhaps the hundredth time that day. 'What's the matter with him?'

'I don't know why he's crying,' Katy screamed back at her, finally losing all semblance of control. 'All I'm asking you to do is pick him up. Can't you ever do something I say without questioning it?'

As soon as the words were out of her mouth she regretted them, but it was too late. Her mother had already disappeared and Katy could hear her sobbing quietly as she finally picked up the baby.

Putting her hand to her face Katy bit back her own

tears. It was her own fault. Everyone had said it was too soon to reopen the pub, that she needed some peace and quiet to get into a routine with the baby. She knew they were right but she simply hadn't got time for the luxury of peace and quiet. The pub had only been closed a couple of weeks and already there were bills piling up that she simply could not afford to pay. If she didn't start pulling in takings pretty damn soon she would go under, new lease or not.

At least the baby was quiet now. In a minute she would try and feed him again even though her nipples felt like red-hot pokers. She would make peace with her mother then. But she had a million things to do before opening at six. She took a deep breath and began to lift the chairs off the tables. After two chairs she stopped and closed her eyes as her arms fell weakly to her sides. A million things to do and absolutely no strength to do them with.

'Miss Katy?'

Blinking hard she swung round to find Jacob standing awkwardly by the door. Lost in her despair she hadn't heard him come in.

He cleared his throat. His voice was diffident, his eyes hopeful. 'Aaref said perhaps you will be needing me again?'

'Oh Jacob.' Katy stared at him through tears of relief. 'He's right. I need you more than ever.'

Jennifer Carter got out of the taxi and stretched languidly before paying off the driver.

So, she thought, glancing up and down the shabby little street, home again. It didn't look too bad. The gap where the Miss Taylors' house had once been had been tidied up since she was last here. Some quite large bushes had filled in the bomb site. Jen sighed. Yes, after fifteen months on the road she had been looking forward to coming back. Back in her own room with her own things around her and no nagging landlady checking to see how full she filled the bath.

Glancing across at the Flag and Garter she saw a sign stuck on the window announcing that they were opening again tonight. 'Please do pop in,' it said. Good old Katy, Jen thought. It would take more than a baby to stop her opening her precious pub.

She smiled to herself. Well, she would pop in later to celebrate her homecoming. She had a present for the baby too. A little train set. She knew it was a bit old for him but he'd quickly grow into it. She hadn't wanted to buy any baby things. Jen loathed babies. Having three younger brothers and a sister had been enough to put anyone off. The boys weren't too bad but once Angie was born her mother hadn't bothered much with Jen any more. She hadn't bothered much with her since either. She'd never supported her acting, never came to see her in the school play. In fact she'd been against Jen's chosen career from the first, saying she'd never make a go of it. Well, now Jen was going to have a solo slot in a West End revue and her mother was going to have to eat her words.

It was a satisfying thought. Smoothing her hair under the jaunty little tam-o'-shanter she had bought in Edinburgh, Jen picked up her suitcase and walked up the front path.

To her surprise the door was locked. She stared at it, wondering for a ridiculous moment if she had come to the wrong house. Eventually in response to her banging it opened tentatively to reveal a drab-looking young woman in a kind of shapeless grey dress that Jen would not have got into if it had been the last garment on earth. They eyed each other with equal astonishment.

'Who on earth are you?' Jen asked.

'My name is Eleanor Philips,' the woman said stiffly. 'I have lodgings here.'

'Lodgings?' Jen stared at her. 'What do you mean lodgings?'

Eleanor Philips blinked. 'I rent the room at the back.'

'That's my room.'

'Your room?' Eleanor Philips looked dismayed. 'But ...'

Jen was losing her patience. She was tired and she wanted this sorted out. 'Look, Miss Philips, where's my mother?'

'Your mother?' Eleanor Philips's eyes nearly popped out of her head. 'Mrs Carter is your mother?' She swallowed nervously. 'Well, she'll still be at the café, I expect.' She saw Jen's blank expression. 'Down the road on the left on the corner.'

Jen didn't bother to reply. She just turned on her heel and walked away.

As soon as she heard the door of the café rattle, Joyce knew it would be Jen. She had been listening out all day for the arrival of her daughter, dreading she would turn up and make a scene when the café was full of people. Thankfully it was closed now. Joyce had been just clearing up the kitchen and making a few flans ready for tomorrow. Flans were one of their bestselling items. You could make them up with this new powdered egg stuff that came from America. With a few boiled potatoes and a bit of veg, a slice of flan made a nice lunchtime meal for a couple of bob.

Rinsing her hands as the door rattled again, Joyce took off her apron and steeled herself for confrontation.

Before she had even opened the door she could see through the glass that Jen was in a furious temper.

'What's going on? Who's that woman in my room?'

'Miss Philips,' Joyce said calmly. 'She's a teacher.'

'I don't care what she bloody is,' Jen snapped. 'What's she doing in my room?'

'She's renting it.'

Jen glared at her. 'So where am I going to sleep? I'm not sharing with a fusty old teacher.'

'I didn't expect you to. In any case she's rented the whole room.'

'Well, I'm certainly not going in with Pete, whatever you—'

'Then you'll have to find somewhere else.'

Jen stopped mid sentence. 'Somewhere else?' She stared at her mother in amazement. 'What do you mean?'

'What I mean is I haven't got room for you, Jen. It's as simple as that.'

A sudden understanding crept into Jen's eyes. 'You got this teacher in on purpose, didn't you?'

Joyce didn't answer and Jen's voice rose. 'That's my home too, you know. You can't just hand it over to other people.'

'That's where you're wrong,' Joyce said. 'You lost your rights to that house when you moved out. And you're right. I don't want you back.'

Jen's eyes narrowed. 'You've changed,' she said. 'It's since Dad's been put away, isn't it? All that freedom. No more punches. No more bruises. It's gone to your head.'

Joyce bit back her fury. 'Maybe. I've come to my senses if that's what you mean. I've got my own life to lead now.'

Jen laughed. 'What life? Renting out rooms to mousy little spinsters and slaving your guts out in a piddly little café? What sort of a life is that?'

If Joyce had thought for a second she was being unfair, 'piddly little café' strengthened her resolve. It strengthened it so much that she wished she could punch Jen right in her pretty face. How dare she mock the café? Managing a place like this had been Joyce's dream ever since she was a child, and she was damned if she was going to listen to Jen running it down.

'It's better than anything I've ever had before,' she said grittily. 'It's certainly better than having you throwing your weight about. I've had enough of tempers and tantrums to last me a lifetime what with you and your dad.'

'Don't lump me together with Dad.'

'Why not?' Joyce said coldly. 'You're his daughter.'

For a second Jen looked taken aback, but in typical Jen fashion she rallied quickly. 'I'm your daughter too,' she snapped back. 'More's the pity. It's not my fault. I didn't choose my parents, did I? I certainly wouldn't have chosen a bitch of a mother who would lock me out of my own home.' Striking a dramatic pose she folded her arms across her chest and raised her neatly plucked eyebrows sarcastically. 'Tell me, Mummy dear, where do you expect me to go? Some hotel or what?'

Joyce looked at her. 'Quite honestly, Jen, I don't care. I simply don't care. You can go to hell for all I care,' and she shut the door.

A surprising number had come back to the pub for the reopening night. Katy was touched by their loyalty.

However, the unexpected amount of customers brought its own pressures. Jacob wasn't really up to serving yet. He was too young, too nervous and tentative with the pump and he spilt more beer than he got into the glass. Her mother kept calling to her to come and feed the baby. She had wanted to feed him at five thirty but he hadn't seemed hungry. Now of course he was crying again. As she measured out a gin and lime in the saloon bar Katy felt the tension building. If only her mother would help, but she refused to come downstairs if there were customers in the place. She said she couldn't face it. It was too upsetting, reminding her of her husband. Katy wished Aaref would come in, or Molly, but Aaref was busy on some deal up in North London and Molly was on duty. In any case Katy knew she couldn't always rely on her friends.

Suddenly she couldn't bear the baby crying any longer. The very sound of it seemed to tug on her breast in the most horrible way.

'Jacob,' she called. 'You're going to have to man the bar while I feed the baby. You know the prices. If there's a problem, shout.' She glanced round the bar. Everyone's glasses seemed full. Unless more people came in he should be all right for a few minutes at least.

As she turned to the stairs, the pub door swung open. When she saw it was Jen pushing through the blackout curtain, Katy's heart sank. Much as she had looked forward to seeing her old friend again, why did Jen have to choose this moment to arrive? Behind her she could hear her mother desperately urging her to come upstairs. 'I can't hold him for ever, Katy. My arms are getting tired.'

Jen was inside now, and forcing a welcoming smile, Katy went round the counter to hug her. 'Jen, you're back. How lovely to see you.'

Jen's smile was even more forced than her own, however, and leading her to the bar, Katy lowered her voice anxiously. 'Jen, are you all right?'

'No, I'm not bloody all right,' Jen hissed. 'My bloody bitch of a mother has let my room.'

Katy stared at her. 'Let it?'

'To some sour-faced old teacher.'

'Goodness. I had no idea.' Katy didn't know what to say. She was shocked. She knew there was little love lost between Jen and Mrs Carter, but it seemed a bit hard on Jen to come home and find she'd got nowhere to sleep. 'What will you do?'

'I was hoping you might put me up here.'

'Jen.' Katy stared at her in dismay. 'I can't. I really can't. I've got Malcolm now and Mum and there just isn't any room ...'

'Please, Katy.' Jen's eyes were pleading. 'Just for a couple of nights. I'm really stuck.'

Katy looked at her friend and, to her astonishment, realised Jen was close to tears. Jen never cried. She felt a stab of sympathy for her, although still she hesitated. She loved Jen dearly but she wasn't the easiest person in the world to deal with. In fact the thought of Jen, Malcolm, her and her mother all sharing two small bedrooms made Katy feel quite faint.

Before she could speak four large men entered the pub. Out of the corner of her eye, Katy could see Jacob quailing as they approached the bar purposefully.

'Four pints of Rutherfords.' Meeting Jacob's anxious gaze she nodded encouragingly and then turned back to Jen.

'Jen, …' She stopped. Jen might be outspoken and spiky but she was her friend. Probably her best friend. They'd been through rough times together before. She couldn't turn her away. She just couldn't. If necessary Jen would have to sleep in the cellar where they'd slept during the air raids last year.

'Katy!' Jen was looking at her in disbelief. 'You're not going to refuse me, are you?'

Katy smiled manfully. 'Of course not, but …' Even as her mouth formed the words she heard her mother calling her again, a heart-wrenching wail from Malcolm and a splintering crash as Jacob dropped a glass. A pint glass. One of the last decent ones she had.

Closing her eyes for a second Katy wondered how Helen was getting on. Suddenly a prolonged holiday in the Scottish Highlands seemed extremely appealing.

Helen was crouching behind a boulder. It was the only place she could find sufficiently out of the wind to look at her map. Even here the paper writhed and flapped as she tried to trace the line she had come. It was skirting round the enclosure of bulls that had thrown her off course. She had heard of Highland cattle but nobody had told her they had such enormous horns. The Gestapo were one thing but she was damned if she was going to get herself gored to death.

Desperately she forced her tired brain to concentrate. She was freezing cold and wet through, having slipped earlier and fallen into a peat bog, but according to her calculations she must now be near the check-in point. If she didn't get there soon she would die of cold, pain or exhaustion. The ghastly khaki denim overalls and thick leather boots she had been given for the exercise were not only the most unfeminine things she had ever worn but they were also extremely uncomfortable. Nor were they as warm as she had hoped.

During the briefing earlier in the cold stone hallway of the lodge they had learned that this part of the Western Highlands was where Bonnie Prince Charlie hid for five months while fleeing back to France after the 1745 rebellion. He had had a thirty-thousand-pound price on his head, the kilted Gordon Highlander instructor told them proudly, but not one of the locals had handed him in. Now, as Helen stood up stiffly and surveyed the bleak moorland terrain, she thought it was hardly surprising. It probably took poor old Bonnie Prince Charlie five months to find anyone at all, let alone someone who might have heard the news.

Bleak was certainly the word. She had never seen anything like it. The bare, grey, moonlike hills stretched in all directions, broken only by occasional snow-covered crags and interspersed with long, frozen lochs. There was no doubt it had a certain wild beauty, but it gave Helen the creeps, and it was beginning to get dark. Stamping down a vision of being lost out here for ever, Helen hunched her shoulders and headed determinedly down hill.

Surely over there somewhere, beyond the small reed-fringed loch … ?

Yes, there was a road. A thin line of grey. And on the road a dark shape parked in the shadow of some boulders. The truck. Thank God.

Crunching through some snow at the edge of the frozen loch, she consoled herself with the thought that by road it was only a couple of miles back to the house. Ten minutes at the most in the truck, and then surely something to eat, a hot bath, and blessed sleep.

Sleep. The thought of it spurred her on up the final stretch of heather and she was panting by the time she reached the truck. Oddly, there didn't seem to be anyone else there, only the corporal who had collected them from the station, smoking in the cab.

With her last strength Helen reached up and banged on the window. 'Am I the first?'

Winding the glass down lazily, he flicked his cigarette on to the verge where it sizzled and died in a patch of snow. 'No, you're the last, and you'll be the last back and all.' He started the engine. 'I only stayed on to see if you was still alive.'

'But … ?' She jumped back as the truck suddenly jerked into motion. The corporal leaned out of the window and laughed down at her. 'But . . . you'd better get walking, darling, or you'll miss your tea.'

Pam was nervous as she walked down the road to collect George from his first day at school.

It had been a difficult morning. He hadn't wanted to go. He had cried as they left home. All down the street he had dragged on her arm and she had virtually had to peel him off her leg to hand him over to his form teacher at the entrance marked 'boys'.

'I hope he'll be all right,' Pam said nervously. 'As I explained to the headmistress, he's had a difficult year.'

The teacher nodded briskly. 'I'm sure he'll be quite all right.'

Pam was not so sure. 'I'm only just down the road,' she said. 'If there's any problem.'

But nobody had come to fetch her and all day she had fiddled about nervously, thinking of George's last remark as the teacher marched him away to meet his classmates.

'You will be there when I come home, won't you?'

Pam had stared at his sad little tearstained face in

surprise. 'Of course I will. Anyway I'll be coming to fetch you at half past three.'

Now it was half past three, and as she joined the cluster of other mothers at the gate she realised she wasn't the only one who was nervous.

'I hope my little girl's managed all right. She's not been the same since her dad went.'

'My Peter's going to be ever so behind. What with being evacuated and that he's never been to school before.'

Before Pam could join in, a bell rang somewhere inside the school building. A moment later a door opened and the children streamed out.

George was one of the first out of the boys' door. He was barely out in the open before he was searching anxiously for Pam at the gate.

She waved and he waved back at once, slightly self-consciously. Concerned she might embarrass him among his new friends she restrained herself from hugging him but he seemed happy to take her hand as they walked back up the road.

'How did you get on?' she asked him. 'Did you like it?'

For a moment he seemed to think about it then he nodded. 'It was all right,' he said, 'but I don't really want to go again.'

'Oh.' Pam swallowed nervously. 'Why's that, darling? Didn't you make any friends?'

He shook his head. 'I don't want any friends,' he said. 'I just like being at home with you.'

Jen opened her eyes and groaned. It was still dark. The middle of the night. As usual it was the baby that had woken her. She was a good sleeper generally, even sharing the double bed with Katy wasn't a problem, but those ghastly, grating screams were enough to wake the dead. Even as she lay there pretending to be asleep she felt Katy getting out and heard her pad into the sitting-room where baby Malcolm slept. Slept? That was a joke. Baby

Malcolm didn't seem to know the meaning of the word sleep. Jen groaned again half in guilt and half in irritation. That baby was a damn nuisance. Worse than a nuisance. He was an absolute menace. She didn't know how Katy stood it. She was up and down all night like a bloody yo-yo. If it was her she would lock the blasted thing in the cellar and put a pillow over her head. Or its head preferably. But something told her that Katy might not agree to that solution.

Jen heard the creak of the cot as Katy lifted the baby out. The crying stopped at once. Closing her eyes again, Jen sighed in relief. Then she heard another noise, a hushed, sobbing kind of noise. Not one of Malcolm's normal noises. Katy, then? Jen frowned and tensed to listen, but before she could be sure, she heard Katy going downstairs.

For a moment Jen lay there, then she sat up. She didn't like the thought of Katy down there alone in the dark, deserted bar. There was nothing more depressing, Jen thought, than an empty bar. It was even worse than an empty theatre. At least theatres didn't stink of old beer.

For a second she wondered hopefully if her conscience would let her go back to sleep, and then with a deep sigh she threw back the covers and got out of bed and padded across to turn on the light.

As she pulled on her slinky satin dressing-gown she shivered and glanced at her watch. Four thirty. She grimaced. This was worse than the blitz. At least with the blitz you could normally hunker down in some air-raid shelter and sleep through it. At least in the blitz you were all in it together. Everyone was affected. Everyone was tired. But she could hardly waltz into rehearsals tomorrow expecting leniency just because some blasted baby had been keeping her awake.

It was dark in the bar. Katy hadn't bothered to turn on the lights but it was light enough for Jen to see the tears rolling down her cheeks as she wove her way slowly between the beer-stained tables with the baby in her arms.

She jumped as she heard Jen's step on the stairs and quickly brushed a hand over her face. 'I'm sorry,' she whispered. 'I didn't mean to wake you.'

Jen peered at her. 'This is ridiculous,' she said. 'What on earth are you doing? You can't spend the night walking about down here crying.'

Katy shook her head wearily. 'I know, but walking him is the only way I can keep him quiet. The minute I put him down he starts crying again.' She looked at Jen with tired, anxious eyes. 'If only he'd feed properly I think he might sleep, but he won't. He has a little bit then he stops. He's been like that ever since I brought him home.'

Jen frowned. 'What did that health visitor woman say this morning?'

Katy lifted her shoulders helplessly. 'She says I must try and get him into a routine, but he doesn't seem to like routines.'

Jen smiled. 'I'm not much of a one for routines myself.' But she could see Katy was near breaking point with worry and tiredness. Glancing at the baby, Jen groaned inwardly. She knew what she was going to have to do and she didn't want to do it one bit. She didn't like babies and she certainly didn't like baby Malcolm with his beastly little red face and bawling voice. It was incredible how a quiet, polite girl like Katy could have produced this ghastly little creature. Let alone Ward Frazer with his sleek good looks and perfect manners.

'Look,' Jen said suddenly. 'Give him to me. If walking around is the only way to stop him crying that's what I'll do, and you can get some sleep.'

Katy stared at her in amazement. 'But you don't like babies.'

Jen grimaced. Considering that she hadn't even touched baby Malcolm previously she could hardly pretend a sudden baby fetish now, but she felt she owed it to Katy.

'Okay, I don't like babies much, it's true, but I like you.'

'What about your rehearsals?'

Jen shrugged. 'I'll survive, but you won't if this goes on much longer.' As she took the baby she glanced at Katy. 'We're going to have to do something about this, you know.'

Katy nodded. 'But what?'

With some dismay Jen realised Katy was looking at her hopefully, obviously expecting an answer, maybe even a solution. 'God, I don't know,' she said abruptly, then grimaced as new tears filled Katy's eyes. Hitching the baby up into a more comfortable position Jen forced a reassuring smile on to her lips. 'Look, I'll think of something while I'm walking, Okay? Now for God's sake go to bed. And chuck me down a blanket on your way or I'll bloody freeze to death.'

When the wake-up klaxon went off at six in the morning, Helen had difficulty opening her eyes. That was nothing new. Even after a week of early mornings she still hadn't got used to rising in the dark. But this morning she really felt as though she hadn't slept a wink, and then she remembered that she hadn't.

She had barely got into bed last night before they were banging on her door insisting that she got up and subjected herself to an interrogation session.

God knows how long it had lasted. She didn't care any more, because in the end she had given them her secret. The map reference she had been told on no account to reveal.

It had taken them a long time to get it out of her. For ever, it had seemed, as she stood swaying with exhaustion in the corner of that bare, cold cellar room, repeating doggedly over and over again that she didn't know the crucial co-ordinates. That she simply couldn't remember them.

And then other questions. Cruel, taunting questions

about her father, her upbringing and her background that she knew she had to refuse to answer.

Eventually they had worn her down. It was the tiredness that had done it, and the glaring lights. She had been so disoriented when they suddenly turned off the lights and told her it was over and she could go, that she had felt almost dizzy with the relief of it. And that was when they had tricked her, by asking if she really had forgotten the map reference.

She had been angry then. Angry that they would never give her the benefit of the doubt, so she had told them, spat out the co-ordinates right into their mocking, sceptical faces.

They had laughed. Laughed and laughed.

And she had cried, but only in the privacy of her own room. She wouldn't give them that satisfaction.

Now she had to get up, go downstairs to the great panelled dining-room where breakfast was served and face them all again. In the knowledge of her failure.

She knew what was happening of course. She and the other candidates were being tested for toughness. To see how little sleep they could manage on. How much abuse they could take. The training officers were trying to make them crack. Trying to get rid of the slackers before they started the secret stuff. The stuff that really mattered.

Two men had left the course already. Helen had been tempted to go with them. Others had been surprised she hadn't.

'I thought you'd had enough,' Paul, the French speaker, had remarked one morning, catching her up as they tramped back to the lodge after a gruelling pre-breakfast session on the assault course.

Helen looked at him as he smiled quizzically and drew on his cigarette. Paul was tough and competent. Irritatingly competent, Helen thought. Despite the hint of cockney in his accent and his slightly flashy clothes, he was pretty much the star of the course. He was always at the front, always the first to volunteer, always there to support the stragglers. Basically he was too good to be true. He was also extremely nice looking. It annoyed Helen that his sleek good looks always seemed to survive the worst and dirtiest of exercises whereas she always ended up looking all flushed and sticky.

'What made you think that?' she asked stiffly.

He shrugged. 'You looked all in yesterday afternoon after the run.'

'I was tired,' she said. 'It's hard work.'

'You can't afford to be tired,' he said. 'That's when they get at you. That's when they try to break you.'

He was right. She was tired and they had broken her. She wished there was someone she could talk to, but there was no one. They had not been encouraged to make friends with other candidates. Paul was really the only one she had had any contact with and she knew even to admit her misery to him would be a mistake. He seemed a nice bloke, but if one hint of her uncertainty leaked out she would be off the course.

As she sat shivering on the edge of her bed, she realised she felt lonely, and she knew that was deliberate too. Being an agent in enemy territory was a lonely business.

Suddenly, perhaps for the first time, she felt able to imagine something of how Ward Frazer must have felt after the pick-up plane had crashed, as he lay alone and badly injured, facing death or certain capture, armed only with a pistol to hold the Germans off long enough for his Resistance friends to escape. She knew Katy had nightmares about that. It made Helen feel sick, because she knew grit and courage like that was what good agents were made of, and she was pretty sure now she hadn't got it.

'I'm not up to it,' she whispered. 'I'm simply not up to it.'

Outside her door she heard voices as two of the other candidates headed for a hearty breakfast. 'Apparently she lasted three hours,' one of them said. 'Amazing, isn't it? A fancy girl like that. Sergeant Porter is hopping mad. Said he just couldn't get her to crack. And now he and Major Maxwell are seriously short of sleep.'

'So they had to trick it out of her in the end?' the other one said.

The first voice laughed. 'He said it was either that or pull out her fingernails.'

Then they were gone. Helen could hear their boots clattering down the stone stairs.

So she hadn't done so badly after all. She was surprised at the enormous difference that sliver of knowledge made. Not that it made any difference to her body, she realised, as she stood up. It still left her dog tired. But her spirit had lifted. So Sergeant Porter and Major Maxwell were impressed, were they? They might have told her. Well, damn them, she thought. They weren't the only ones short of sleep. She squared her shoulders and smiled grimly. She would show them. All those condescending men. She would damn well show them what a fancy girl could do.

Chapter Eight

Jen's solution to Katy's problems was to get Pam Nelson to look after the baby for a few hours each day so Katy could either work in peace or, preferably, rest. The thought had come to her when she saw how eagerly Pam gooed over the baby when Jen was trundling his pram round the common one morning. As far as Jen was concerned anyone who gooed over baby Malcolm needed their head examined. Nevertheless, a baby-mad person was just what she was looking for, and indeed Pam seemed pleased to help. She admitted she was bored by day now that George was at school. They arranged that she would pick Malcolm up at nine after she had delivered George to school, and keep him until three, with one visit to the pub during the day for feeding.

'I can't afford to pay her,' Katy said anxiously when Jen put the plan to her.

'You don't have to pay her,' Jen said. 'She says she still owes you a fortune anyway for George spoiling your beer.'

Katy frowned. 'That wasn't her fault.'

'Well, she obviously feels guilty. She jumped at the chance of helping out.'

'But it's not right.'

'God.' Jen rolled her eyes impatiently. 'Well, let the poor woman do her penance for a week, then I'll pay her.'

Katy stared at her. 'You?'

Jen nodded. 'I'll give her what I should be giving you. Unless you'd rather I moved out.'

'No, please stay,' Katy said quickly. Oddly Jen's presence had been a help rather than a hindrance. The only drawback really was that Mrs Carter hadn't been in to help with the washing-up since Jen had been staying. On the other hand it was nice having a friend around the place, someone to talk to, someone to make you laugh. And best of all Jen took her turn with Malcolm at night.

She summoned a persuasive smile. 'Malcolm would be sad if you went.'

Jen groaned comically. 'Oh well. That's it, then. I'd better stay. I daren't upset baby Malcolm.'

The only person not happy with the new arrangement was George. He didn't like Pam looking after Malcolm. 'It's not fair. I thought you were meant to be looking after me now.'

Pam smiled fondly. 'I am. Nothing changes that. But Katy's little baby needs someone to look after it, and it's only while you're at school.'

George wasn't convinced. 'Can I see it?'

Pam nodded. 'Of course.'

So they went down to the pub where for once baby Malcolm was gurgling quietly to himself while Jen practised some music on the piano.

She stopped as Pam and George came into the bar. 'Katy's down in the cellar,' she said.

'Oh, don't disturb her,' Pam said. She certainly wasn't going to let George loose in the cellar again. 'We've only come to see the baby. Oooh.' Picking Malcolm up gently she crouched down with him so George could see him. 'There. Isn't he sweet?' She smiled at Jen. 'Do you think George could hold him?'

'I don't see why not,' Jen said. 'So long as he doesn't drop him.'

George backed away hastily. 'I don't want to hold it. I don't like it.'

Pam frowned. 'Don't be like that.' She stroked Malcolm's cheek. 'Look. He's a lovely little baby.'

George shook his head crossly. 'It's not, it's all red and horrid. And it smells.'

As Pam stood up in dismay, Jen laughed delightedly. 'I know how he feels. I just haven't liked to say so.'

Louise wasn't sure about the baby either. It was quite sweet, but since it had arrived Katy was all distracted and never seemed to have time to talk. And now she had that awful tarty-looking Jen Carter hanging around the whole time it was doubly difficult. Which was annoying because Louise wanted to consult Katy about Jack.

She finally caught up with her early one morning on her way to work. Katy was stacking crates outside the door of the pub, her breath coming out in clouds in the cold January air.

'That looks like hard work,' Louise remarked.

Katy straightened up. 'It would be easier if I wasn't so top heavy at the moment,' she said. 'With these enormous bosoms, once I've bent over I feel as though I'll never get up again. You should see my new bra. It's like two barrage balloons. If I lay on my back I reckon I could defend the whole of South London.'

Louise giggled, pleased to see Katy smiling for once. 'You do look rather, er … voluptuous,' she said. 'Lucky old Malcolm. He must be guzzling it up.'

As soon as the words were out of her mouth she knew she had said the wrong thing. Katy's sparkle faded. 'If only he would,' she said. 'Then he might put on a bit of weight and I might feel less like I'm about to explode.'

Louise didn't know what to say. Katy suddenly looked close to tears. She decided to change the subject. 'Have you heard from Helen at all?'

Katy shook her head. 'No, not a bleep.'

Louise frowned. 'She told us she was going on some

Inter-Services liaison meeting,' she said, 'but I don't believe it, do you?'

As she expected, Katy looked distinctly evasive. 'Why do you say that?'

Louise shrugged. 'Well, she works for the same organisation that Ward worked for, doesn't she? And we all know what Ward was up to when he went away.'

Katy blinked and Louise shrugged. 'Don't worry, I won't spill the beans,' she said crossly. 'I just think she might have told me, that's all.'

'She's not allowed to tell anyone,' Katy said. 'I only know because of Ward. And anyway, she's only training at the moment, she's not actually abroad or anything.'

Louise nodded reluctantly. 'Well, I wish she'd hurry up and come back,' she said. 'It's ghastly in the house without her. Mummy just goes on about her chickens or the blasted café and Daddy snaps my head off every time I open my mouth.' Suddenly she remembered why she had called by and glanced at Katy. 'By the way, Jack's coming back at the beginning of February for a weekend. Do you think I could make him propose if I said someone else was interested in me?'

Katy looked shocked. 'I think that's a bit mean.'

'Mean?' Louise frowned. 'He's kept me hanging on all this time. That's mean.'

'You've only known him a few months.'

'You only knew Ward a few months,' Louise said. She was glad to see Katy flush. Louise had never really forgiven her for pinching the gorgeous Ward Frazer from under her nose.

'Well,' Katy said quickly, 'that was different. I wasn't really in a hurry, but Ward—'

Louise realised she didn't altogether want to know what Katy was going to say. It was bad enough to have lost Ward without having it rubbed in how much in love he had been with Katy.

'Well, I am in a hurry,' she interrupted. 'So if Jack

doesn't pull his finger out and propose to me I will go off with someone else.'

Katy stared at her. 'Who?'

Louise tossed her head. 'I expect I could find someone. Jack Delmaine isn't the only man interested in me, you know.'

Katy was having a cup of tea with Molly Coogan when Aaref appeared with a camera to take a photo of Malcolm for Katy to send to Ward.

'You must be in it too,' Molly said to Katy as they walked over to Pam Nelson's to retrieve Malcolm. Glancing over her shoulder to where Aaref was fiddling around trying to get the camera to stand up on its own, Molly lowered her voice. 'Katy, will you do me a favour?'

Katy looked at the little nurse in surprise and saw she was blushing. 'Of course, if I can. What is it?'

Molly hesitated. 'I know I'm not very pretty or anything, but I'd really like to have a photo of me and Aaref.' She glanced at Katy pleadingly. 'Together, you know. Will you ask him for me? And then maybe you could take it?'

'I'll try,' Katy said, dreading on Molly's behalf that Aaref would refuse to pose with her, but Aaref seemed quite amenable. In fact he even put his arm round Molly as they stood shivering self-consciously in the ice-cold January breeze outside the pub.

'Smile!' Pam called, holding the baby while Katy disappeared under the black sheet at the back to make sure they were in the frame.

'I hope they come out,' Katy said.

'Oh, I'm sure they'll be lovely,' Molly said, hugging herself excitedly. 'I can't wait to see them.'

Aaref brought the photos round a week later. Katy admired the one of him and Molly.

'It's come out really well,' she said. 'You both look lovely.'

Aaref just shrugged. 'It's a good camera.'

The one of Malcolm and her was nice too. Katy was about to conceal it among some biscuits she was packing up for Ward's Red Cross parcel, when Jen grabbed it out of her hand.

'You can't send him that.'

Katy looked up startled. 'Why not? Malcolm looks sweet in it.'

'Malcolm may look sweet but you look awful,' Jen said.

Katy took the photo out of Jen's hand. 'What's the matter with it? That's what I look like. We can't all be glamour queens.'

Jen shook her head. 'Ward won't recognise you. When you were with him you were so bright, sparkling.' She grimaced at the photo. 'In this you look flat. Worn down.'

'Maybe I should cut myself out of it,' Katy said.

Jen laughed. 'Oh, that would be very reassuring for him.' She saw Katy's dismay and handed back the photo with a sigh. 'Oh, go on, send it, then. He'll be so delighted to get it he probably won't notice your expression.'

So Katy put it in. To be honest she couldn't really see anything wrong with it. Okay, so she looked a bit drab and down at heel but she couldn't help that. That was Adolf Hitler's fault. Anyway the photo was better than nothing, and she had nothing else very exciting to send him this week. She liked to send Ward little treats. It must be so awful for him there. The letters she was receiving from him now had been written well before Christmas, and although he guessed she would have had the baby by the time they arrived, she could sense his frustration of not knowing. Not knowing whether everything was all right or whether something might have gone wrong.

And then bizarrely by the next post a picture came of Ward. One of the camp guards had taken it apparently in exchange for some coffee Katy had sent over. 'It was a shame to give up the coffee,' he wrote, 'but I don't want you to forget what I look like.' She was touched. That was typical Ward, pretending he had done something for himself when she knew he had really done it for her. She could tell he was worried about her even though she tried so hard in her letters to hide the bad things from him.

'God, I'd forgotten how gorgeous he was,' Jen remarked when she saw the picture.

Katy smiled. 'I hadn't.'

Jen stared at her. 'That's the difference,' she said, watching Katy's face closely. 'You don't smile like that any more.'

Katy looked away suddenly as her eyes filled with tears.

'Katy, what is it? Ward?'

'No,' Katy said. 'It's Malcolm.' She hadn't meant to say anything but she couldn't keep her worries to herself any longer. 'He's not putting on weight. He's not eating properly. I know he's not. He doesn't suck properly any more. And he cries so much. I think there's something wrong with him.'

Jen was frowning. 'I don't know anything about babies, but if you are that worried you'd better get him checked out. If only for your own peace of mind. Ask the doctor. Promise?'

Katy nodded. 'Okay, I will.' She hesitated for a moment. 'Jen, I'm going to get him christened,' she said, and swallowed. 'Just in case. And I want you to be godmother.'

'Why me? I don't even believe in God.'

'You're my friend,' Katy said. 'I want you to do it.'

She would like to have asked Helen too, but Helen wasn't there, and she knew that Helen might not be there in the future much either. She shivered. I hope she's okay, she thought. I do hope she's okay.

Helen was okay. In fact since the night of her interrogation things had changed dramatically. Before that she had definitely been struggling to stay on the course at all. Now she was vying for top position. Vying with tough, competent Paul who had previously seemed quite unassailable at the top of the tree.

It was odd, Helen thought as she watched Sergeant Porter demonstrating a debilitating stranglehold on one of the candidates, what a difference confidence made. Grit and determination were all very well but it was confidence that made the difference. And it didn't take much. That one tiny, overheard sign that people were secretly impressed with her had been enough. It had been enough to make her realise that if she really put her mind to it she could win through.

Not only win through, but possibly even win, because although the course was physically and mentally tough, it wasn't academically difficult. It was just a matter of learning the short cuts, the tricks of the trade, keeping your wits about you and finding the best and easiest solutions to the problems they set. Each candidate's performance was being graded now and even on the physical side Helen was getting good scores.

She was fitter, of course, now than she had been at the start, and that helped. She was fitter, in fact, than she had ever been in her life. All those brutal assault courses and cross-country runs had developed muscles and strengthened tendons and sinews that she had never known existed, and now that she had finally begun to get over the pain and the exhaustion, she was aware of an extraordinary sense of physical well-being.

She knew the others felt it too. Now that this first phase of the training programme was drawing to a close, the loneliness and isolation they had all felt at the beginning had turned into a sense of camaraderie. They were the survivors after all. Plenty of others had fallen by the wayside: some voluntarily, glad to get away; others had been sent home after breaking bones or tearing ligaments or displaying evidence of weakness or lack of commitment.

Even the survivors had had their ups and downs. Helen's most recent down had been in the shooting range. To be fair it hadn't been just any old shooting range but a special shooting range with moving targets fitted in some old stables to simulate an urban environment.

It had been ridiculous, Helen thought crossly now, how terrified a person could be of a set of cardboard cut-out figures. The fact that they had jumped out in front of her, skidded across behind doors, and swung without warning from the ceiling on ropes was immaterial. They were cardboard cut-outs and quite unable to do her any harm despite the absurdly off beat sound effects that accompanied their dramatic appearances.

Nevertheless, as she entered the building she had been aware of the adrenalin pumping so hard in her body that she could barely breathe. So determined had she been to prove she wasn't scared of guns, that she had failed to discriminate between the targets, shooting instantly at everything that jumped out in front of her, regardless of its identity.

When she finally emerged into the open air of the stable yard she found everyone grinning and wished she had not been so trigger happy.

Even the weapons instructor was smirking as he totted up her hits. 'Three Wehrmacht officers, one Gestapo, two French Resistance, one greengrocer, one old lady and a baby in a pram,' he said dryly as she checked and cleared her revolver into the sand pit with a still shaking hand. 'Nine hits with nine bullets. Good aiming, lassie, but a wee bit random, we might say.'

Furious with herself for losing points, Helen smiled grimly and walked away from the group. She was perched moodily on the mounting block when Paul wandered up to her.

'I wouldn't want to be at the wrong end of your pistol,' he murmured, taking out a cigarette.

As he smiled at her through the flame of the match, to

her surprise Helen felt herself flush slightly. It had never occurred to her that Paul might fancy her, and although she respected his ability and appreciated his good looks, she certainly didn't fancy him. He just wasn't her type. He came from a completely different background to her, she could tell that from his accent. You couldn't hear it when he spoke French, but in English those slightly shortened vowels gave it away. Not quite cockney, but definitely East End. Certainly a million miles from the refined grace of her own upbringing in Mayfair. And yet there was something about him that intrigued her. A certain remoteness, an imperviousness that kept him slightly aloof from the rest of the group. Oddly, as he stood there, watching her enigmatically, she had the urge to confide in him.

'I was scared,' she admitted. 'That's why I shot everything.' It was true. That sense of real fear had disconcerted her. She had suddenly realised how very badly she didn't want to get shot herself. None of the tests they had done up till then had been for real. The simulated shooting range was the closest they had come to real life.

'It's been a game up till now,' she said. 'Suddenly for the first time it seemed real and I panicked.'

'That's what the training is for,' he said. 'To prepare us for real life. And death.'

Helen shivered. 'Don't,' she said.

He shrugged. 'It's true. In this game you can't afford to make mistakes.' He narrowed his eyes slightly as he drew on his cigarette. 'Over in France it's each man for himself. That's why it's important to be good. Very good. Only the very best will survive.'

Helen watched him extinguish his cigarette. 'And who's going to be the best on this course?' she asked. 'You or me?'

He grinned then. 'Me,' he said. 'You're just a girlie.

Girlies don't win. Not in tough games like this. Certainly not posh ones.'

They were called over for a debriefing then, but Helen was aware that something had changed between her and Paul. He had issued a direct challenge, thrown down the gauntlet, and it seemed to have caused a new frisson of competitiveness between them.

Two days later Helen put her foot down a rabbit hole on a map-reading exercise and only managed to limp in fourth. Once again Paul edged ahead on the points. But then she beat him in a memory test of street names from a fictional French town. And again in a weapons assembly competition.

'That's the advantage of being a girlie,' she said. 'Nimble fingers.'

When the scores were read out the evening before the final exercise, they were neck and neck.

'I reckon you're still working too hard,' Molly remarked to Katy as they laid white doilies on the bar tables. 'You're not getting enough rest. Maybe that's what's wrong with Malcolm.'

Katy groaned. That's what everyone said. That's what the health visitor had said, but what difference would rest make if Malcolm wouldn't suck properly? And when did they think she had time to rest anyway? Even now she was frantically trying to get ready for the party that would follow the christening. She had had no idea so many people would want to come. Even Ward's aunts, the Miss Taylors, and their dachshund, had come up from Bristol for the occasion.

'It was a long journey, but we had to see little Malcolm, Katy,' they said, and then fell into raptures about how like Ward he was. Katy had smiled nervously. She loved the Miss Taylors dearly, but they were sharp old birds and she was terrified they would pick up on her anxiety about Malcolm's health. The last thing she wanted was them writing to Ward and worrying him unnecessarily. But luckily they were smiling happily as they trundled off down the road to the Rutherfords' where it had been arranged for them to stay for the weekend.

'Katy,' Molly said suddenly. 'Do you think it would matter to Aaref that I'm not Jewish? You know, if it ever got really serious.'

'Oh Molly!' Katy said. 'Do you think it might?'

'Well, he did give me a necklace for Christmas,' Molly said, 'and he's taken me out quite a few times, to the cinema and that. He kissed me yesterday. You know, a proper kiss.' She stopped, blushing furiously. 'Do you think I'm wrong to be excited?'

'Well, no,' Katy said cautiously. She looked at Molly's eager little face. The last thing in the world she wanted was for Molly to get hurt, and she didn't know why but she had a nasty feeling that was exactly what was going to happen. 'But do try not to get too keen. Not until you're sure.'

Molly sighed. 'I can't help it. I've been mad about him ever since I set eyes on him.'

Sliding the last doily into place, Katy smiled and glanced at the clock. Any minute now Joyce Carter would be turning up with the sandwiches. It would be the first time Joyce had set foot in the pub since Jen had come home. Jen had taken herself off deliberately to be out of the way although they were bound to come face to face later at the christening.

Joyce had been apologetic when Katy went to the café to ask about the sandwiches. 'I didn't mean you to get lumbered with Jen,' she said gruffly. 'I bet that's the last thing you needed.'

Katy smiled. 'Well, I must admit I was a bit daunted at the time, but actually she's been very helpful.'

'Helpful?' Joyce had been incredulous. 'Jen?' She snorted. 'I'll believe that when I see it. If she ever lifts a hand to help me I'll drop down dead with shock.'

Katy had hoped to try and smooth things over between Joyce and Jen but it was clearly a lost cause. In any case Jen would have nothing to do with any attempt at reconciliation.

'You must be joking,' she had said when Katy suggested it tentatively. 'And don't think I don't know why she wanted me out of the house. So she could set her cap at that old bugger Lorenz, that's why. Pete says he's round there at lunch every blasted Sunday. God knows what Dad would say if he found out. I know Dad's a bastard but he is her husband even if he is in the nick.'

'Lorenz has been very good to her,' Katy said mildly.

'I don't care what he's done to her. It's embarrassing. Worse than that it's disgusting. A woman of her age should know better. And he's a Jew.'

Now as Katy glanced out of the window and caught sight of Joyce Carter and Mr Lorenz carrying trays down the street she was glad Jen had kept clear. Glancing the other way to make sure Jen was well out of the way, she saw something that stopped her short. Aaref and Louise standing together on the corner, chatting. Even as she looked, Louise laughed and touched Aaref's arm lightly. Katy was aware of a dreadful sinking feeling in her stomach. She was also aware of Molly coming towards her across the bar.

Oh no, she groaned inwardly. Please God, no. Not today. Not any day.

'Molly,' she said, turning quickly away from the window. 'Here comes Mrs Carter with the sandwiches. Could you clear some space in the kitchen?'

The final course exercise was designed to be a test of all the 'tradecraft' the trainee agents had learned so far. The 'scheme', as they called it, was a mini version of the big exercise that Helen knew completed the entire training programme, when fully trained operatives were put out of a van in a strange town with no money or papers and had to fend for themselves, make contact with so-called 'friends', find a 'safe' house, complete various tasks without being followed or captured, and wireless relevant information back to base.

For the Scottish 'scheme' they were to be dropped off one by one in a nearby town and had to make their way to a certain map reference as quickly as they could, having first collected specific information and completed some prearranged tasks.

They weren't armed of course. As Major Maxwell said at the briefing with a wry glance at Helen, they didn't want the local population decimated unnecessarily. But there was a good chance, he added, that the trainee 'agents' would be captured by directing staff acting as 'enemy', in which case they would be locked up, interrogated, and very likely miss the evening train to London.

Helen was determined not to be captured. On the other hand she was also determined to be first at the rendezvous.

It seemed strange being back in civilian clothes. She had been wearing baggy fatigues or khaki overalls for so long that her own clothes seemed remarkably insubstantial.

The real world felt strange too. The town they had been dropped off in seemed small and claustrophobic after the great wide expanses of moorland she had become accustomed to over the last month or so.

The first few tasks were relatively easy: finding out the Christian name of the local baker, getting the licence-plate number of the Inverness bus, the times of the local church services. Memorising the street names without drawing attention to herself was more difficult, and she was standing on the steps of the library, checking she wasn't being followed, when she sensed a movement behind her and jumped. Paul was at her elbow.

He grinned, clearly amused to have startled her. 'How are you getting on?'

Helen glanced round warily. They had been told at the briefing not to make contact with each other. She had studiously ignored the other candidates she had seen around the town. 'All right,' she said. 'I've got most of the answers.'

'And I've got a vehicle. What d'you say we pool resources? We'd get through quicker that way.'

'Paul, we can't.' Helen felt a stab of disappointment. If Paul had a vehicle, there was no way she could beat him to the rendezvous. Tempting as the offer was, though, joining forces was tantamount to cheating.

He shrugged. 'Suit yourself. I just thought you might want to catch the earlier train.'

'It's not fair on the others.'

'They'd never know.'

'No, Paul, I couldn't do it. It's not right.' She frowned. 'Anyway, I want to prove I can beat you fair and square.'

'Not much chance of that,' he said. 'I'm invincible, darling. You should know that by now. Still, it's your loss. That early train isn't as crowded as the later one.' He winked. 'Who knows, we might have even got a sleeper, had a bit of fun together.'

Helen stared at him incredulously. 'Paul, I ...' She cleared her throat. 'I wouldn't dream ...'

'Why not?' he said. 'We're both young, healthy and fit. Oh, I know you think I'm beneath you, but that wouldn't stop us having a good time. Nobody need know.'

Helen tried to gather her thoughts. She had never been propositioned so crassly in all her life. If Paul had made such a suggestion at the beginning of the course she would have found no difficulty at all in giving him an icy-cold setdown, but now after they had shared so much it was harder to know how to react. Despite their social differences they were in effect comrades in arms, and as such she owed it to him to let him down gently.

'Paul, look, I know we've been quite friendly on the course, but that doesn't mean that I want to take it further. In any case, I don't do that sort of thing. I'm not that sort of girl ...'

For a second she thought she saw a flicker of hurt or anger in his eyes, then he shrugged negligently and she realised she must have been mistaken. 'As I said,' he said. 'It's your loss.'

He left her then, melting away inconspicuously as a group of chattering women came out of the library behind them.

Momentarily stunned, Helen stared after him, then spotting one of the instructors strolling down the other side of the road, dressed as a farmer, she quickly stepped inside the library.

Twenty minutes later, equipped with answers to all the questions they had been set, she emerged from a little-known back door of the library, followed a small side road to the outskirts of town and then headed west. She knew they would be watching the main northern routes out of town in the direction of the rendezvous, and this way she should avoid any checkpoints.

She had only been walking about five minutes and was already wishing she was in army boots rather than her own slim-heeled shoes, when a butcher's van drew up alongside her. Paul leaned over to open the window. 'Still sure you don't want a lift?'

'Yes, quite sure,' she said crossly. 'How did you get hold of that van anyway?'

He tapped the side of his nose. 'Tricks of the trade.' He revved the engine. 'See you next weekend, darling, on the parachute course.'

As he drew away with a squeal of tyres Helen couldn't help hoping he had a puncture.

He didn't, and by the time she reached the checkpoint a weary and footsore hour and a half later, Paul was long gone.

Chapter Nine

Katy wasn't enjoying the christening at all.

It had started off well enough at the church. The vicar had spared them a long sermon, and to her relief Malcolm had slept peacefully on her lap. Even at the font he had lain quietly in Jen's arms, in fact it was probably the longest period of quietness he had had since he came home. He wore the same christening gown she had worn, a dreadful grey old thing, but everyone thought it was wonderful of her mother to have kept it, so her mother was pleased. And Malcolm didn't cry. Even when they got back to the pub he didn't cry, and Katy had been able to greet everyone properly.

The Miss Taylors had come, armed with some lovely presents for Malcolm and touchingly a beautiful cardigan they had knitted for her. She was touched too by the christening cake that Mrs Rutherford had dropped off earlier. Amazingly it had icing. Mrs Rutherford smilingly said that Joyce had come into a bit of sugar.

It was only as the party got underway that Katy realised that things weren't going quite as well as they seemed.

She was first alerted to the underlying tensions when Mr Lorenz presented her with a beautiful silver mug. 'I thought it was appropriate for a pub baby,' he murmured as Katy enthused in delight. Realising Jen was at her side, she held out the mug. 'Look, Jen, isn't this wonderful?' But

Jen barely bothered to look at it and Katy could have kicked her for her rudeness as Mr Lorenz flushed and backed away, mumbling something about a drink.

'Jen.' Katy turned on her crossly. 'That was cruel. He's a sweet man, and it is a generous gift.'

Jen sniffed. 'He's a pawnbroker, Katy,' she said. 'He didn't buy it, did he? It's only something some poor bugger put in hock and couldn't afford to buy back.'

As Katy looked again at the mug in her hand, across the room she caught Joyce's sharp gaze. Smiling hastily, she held up the mug. 'It's lovely,' she mouthed. It was. She didn't care where it had come from. Nor did she care that Jen flounced off towards the other bar where George was playing on the floor with the train set she had bought for Malcolm. Katy sighed. It was the thought that counted. And it was too exhausting trying to keep everyone happy.

Even now she could tell that Jen was angry to see her mother chatting to the Miss Taylors. Jen thought Ward's aunts were *her* friends. Their friend Mrs Frost, Jen's old singing teacher, was here too. They were all staying at the Rutherfords'.

Katy had asked Mrs Frost if she would play the piano later on. She hoped Jen might sing. Everyone loved it when Jen sang, but judging from Jen's expression it was unlikely she would sing today. Katy sighed and was heading for the kitchen when her mother touched her arm.

'Katy,' she murmured, 'the Miss Taylors have kindly asked if I'd like to go back with them to the country for a little holiday and I wondered what you thought?'

Katy blinked. 'Well,' she began hesitantly, 'it's very kind of them, but ...'

'It's just that I do so need a break, dear. I'm very tired and I find it all so worrying what with the pub and the baby and that, and I do so miss your father.'

Katy stared at her in amazement. What about me? she wanted to shout at her. I'm tired too. Don't you think I find it worrying? Don't you think I need a break? Don't you think I miss Dad too? And Ward? But she didn't say it. She couldn't. Her mother looked so eager. Perhaps it would do her good to get away. Perhaps she would come back refreshed and renewed and full of vigour.

'Of course you must go,' Katy said. 'I'm sure Jen and I can manage for a week or so.'

At least Malcolm was still quiet, she thought as she turned away, in fact he looked quite sunny for once, jiggling in Pam Nelson's arms, although she knew it wouldn't last for long. She'd better get the food going before he started crying.

In the kitchen she found Molly Coogan in tears.

'Molly, what's the matter?' But she knew. Louise and Aaref had been chatting together in the saloon bar ever since they'd got back from the church. Louise was looking good today. She had bought a new skirt, and the shorter utility hemline showed her shapely calves to their full advantage as she sat provocatively cross legged on one of the bar stools.

'I thought she had her own boyfriend,' Molly muttered. 'Why can't she keep her hands off mine?' Molly had never liked Louise. She thought she was spoilt and rich, and now it seemed her prejudice was justified.

'I'm sure it doesn't mean anything,' Katy said helplessly, wondering why her friends would choose today of all days to let her down so badly. 'They're only chatting.'

'I can't go out there,' Molly said. 'Not with her draped all over him like that. Everyone knows he's my bloke. It's demeaning.'

'Of course you must go out there,' Katy replied. 'Show them you don't care.'

Behind her, with a sinking heart, she heard Malcolm start crying. As she hurried over to take him from Pam, to her relief Katy heard Mrs Frost strike up the first notes of a lively quickstep. Then she saw Louise jump to her feet pulling Aaref up with her.

'Come on, lazy bones,' Louise giggled. 'Let's have the first dance!' Smiling through her lashes at him she added softly, 'Although it will have to be a slow one, because of my hip.'

To Katy's horror, at exactly the same moment that Aaref took Louise in his arms, Molly emerged red-eyed from the kitchen. A second later George threw the train set into the fire. As sparks flew all over the floor, Molly fled unseen back into the kitchen and baby Malcolm started howling again. Looking round for some help, Katy saw Pam Nelson shouting at Alan to do something about George, and Joyce Carter, red-faced and angry, snapping something at Jen on the other side of the room. Meanwhile Aaref and Louise were swaying together, apparently oblivious, by the piano.

Katy closed her eyes in despair. 'This is as bad as it gets,' she muttered to herself. 'At least it can't get worse.'

And then the door opened and Jack Delmaine walked in.

Helen arrived back from Scotland that afternoon, tired to the point of exhaustion. The train had been slow and cold and she had spent most of the journey huddled in the corner of a carriage while the other candidates drank and smoked themselves into oblivion around her.

It was mid afternoon by the time the train eventually lumbered into King's Cross with a final snort of steam and a juddering of brakes. Shouldering their packs her companions got blearily to their feet.

'Oh well,' someone said. 'Back to the real world.'

They dispersed quickly once they were through the ticket barrier, and oddly, Helen felt sorry to see them go. Having lived alongside them for the last month she had got used to the group atmosphere, the feeling of all being in it together. She had grown fond of them and she knew they liked her. They respected her for what she had achieved, not for who she was. It was odd being alone again.

It was also disorienting to be back in London. The buildings seemed bigger and dirtier than ever and the streets more crowded. It was even more disconcerting to step out of the taxi at Cedars House to find nobody there except a small, rather motheaten dachshund. She smiled as it followed her laboriously upstairs. Recognising it vaguely, she had a feeling that it might belong to Ward's aunts and realised they were probably up visiting Katy's baby.

For a second she wondered about walking along to the pub, until she saw her bed. It was only five o'clock in the afternoon, but who cared? It was a bed. A warm snug bed with a proper mattress, clean white sheets and thick blankets. And along the passage was a bath. She prayed the water would be hot. Under Greville Rutherford's regime there was hardly ever enough hot water, but this time she was lucky.

Half an hour later she wrote a note and pinned it to the outside of the bedroom door. 'Home again, having early night,' and slid into the bed.

She was instantly asleep. Far too deeply asleep to feel the dachshund hop up and burrow down next to her under the bedclothes.

Katy was furious with Louise and Aaref. It was bad enough that they had made Molly so unhappy, but to waltz off to the pictures together at the end of the party, leaving poor Jack completely in the lurch, really was the end. Katy had had quite enough on her hands with a smouldering carpet, Molly sobbing in the kitchen and the acrimony between Jen and Joyce, without having to console Jack for an hour. Give him his due, like a true Englishman, he took it bravely, although it wasn't hard to see that underneath the stiff upper lip he was extremely upset.

They didn't talk about it of course. Instead they talked about the war: the recent loss of Benghazi in the desert, the humiliating surrender of Singapore announced on the news that very morning, the worrying naval setbacks, the terrible carnage wreaked on the merchant ship convoys by the German submarines. There was no doubt it was a bleak phase. The only light on the horizon was the arrival of the first American troops, but even that was a cause for controversy. They had disembarked in Northern Ireland and now the Irish government were saying that they had violated Eire neutrality.

'Bloody Irish,' Jack muttered. 'Do you know they are letting German subs refuel in their harbours?' He smiled grimly. 'Well, they won't be refuelling there much longer once I get my hands on them.'

Jack couldn't wait to get to sea, and Katy admired his courage. The last thing in the world she would want to do was go to sea and face the hidden threat of those beastly U-boats, but Jack said the detection systems were improving all the time and he was confident that sooner or later the tide would turn in the Allies' favour. He was expecting to hear of his promotion, he said, and with it his posting to a North Atlantic convoy escort frigate.

He had seemed eager then, and for a second his patriotic enthusiasm had lifted Katy's spirits, but then he had remembered Louise and the excitement faded rapidly from his eyes.

'I'm sorry,' he said abruptly. 'I've stayed too long.' As he stood up and shrugged on his greatcoat he sighed sadly. 'Perhaps it would be for the best,' he said, 'if I was away at sea.'

Katy felt her heart twist. She touched his arm. 'Don't give up hope,' she said. 'Louise has had a bad time one way and another. I think she's just a bit unsure about things at the moment. I know she's very fond of you ...'

He brightened slightly. 'Do you think I should call and see her?'

Katy shook her head. 'No. I think you should go straight back to Liverpool. It might teach her a lesson.'

After he had gone she swung angrily round to Jen. 'Why am I trying to help this relationship,' she asked, 'when I feel like flattening Louise?' Come to think of it, she felt like flattening Jen too for making a scene with Joyce, but as Jen had managed to stop Malcolm crying for the last hour she couldn't be too angry with her.

Jen shrugged. 'God knows,' she said. 'If you ask me, Louise is an out-and-out bitch and that bloke would be much better off without her.' Hitching Malcolm up on to her shoulder she glanced round the empty bar and rolled her eyes. 'Well, that was fun,' she said sarcastically. 'What a bloody fiasco. Anyway, now that it's finally over could you possibly take this blasted baby and feed it before my arms drop off?'

'I've never known anything like it,' Celia said to Joyce in the café on Monday morning. 'She was asleep when I got in yesterday afternoon and she was still asleep when I left this morning. Goodness, they must have worked her to death on that Inter-Services conference.'

'Not literally, I hope,' Joyce said as she checked the bread toasting under the grill. 'You're sure she was only asleep?'

Celia looked appalled. 'Don't say such things, Mrs Carter. No, she was definitely asleep, and can you believe it, she had that dreadful animal of the Miss Taylors in there with her? Right in the bed? The Miss Taylors were so relieved when I found it there. They were in a terrible twitter, thinking someone had stolen it. Greville was most annoyed about it when I told him. Said it was unhygienic. Made a dreadful fuss about it.' She frowned. 'I'm rather worried about Greville. He has been very irritable recently. I suppose it's the war. These setbacks are enough to make anyone irritated.'

Joyce sniffed. As far as she was concerned Greville

Rutherford was always irritable. It was general knowledge that he was a bastard. Not that she could say so to Mrs Rutherford of course. They were pretty friendly these days but not that friendly. Not friendly enough to criticise her husband. Anyway old Rutherford probably was no worse than most. He was certainly no worse than Stanley. She shuddered and reached for the margarine to spread the toast.

'Men,' she said. 'They're a menace.'

Celia smiled. 'Not all men surely. I'm sure you don't think that about Mr Lorenz?'

To her dismay Joyce felt herself colouring. 'Lorenz?' she said. 'He doesn't count. Just because I give him the odd meal. Poor old bugger. I feel sorry for him, that's all.'

Helen slept for seventeen hours. When she finally woke at midday on Monday, she was alone in the house. There was no sign of the Miss Taylors although the dachshund's presence showed that they were still in residence. Having bathed and dressed she telephoned the office and was told to take the day off.

'I expect you need it,' Angus McNaughton said. 'Oh, and well done. I gather you made a good impression.'

If it was odd being back in London it was even odder being at a loose end. For the last month she had been on the go every second of the day, and often night. Now as she mooched about the house she felt distracted and fidgety. And yet despite her restlessness she felt distant and remote from day-to-day things. It was a strange feeling. She wondered if the other candidates were feeling it too.

Even when the Miss Taylors and Mrs Frost came in, having been to the matinée of Jen Carter's new show, she felt as though she was talking to them through a dense fog.

'It was marvellous,' they twittered eagerly. 'And Jen really was very good. Very professional. Her singing voice has come on enormously. You must go one evening. Oh look, Winston wants to sit on your knee.'

When Helen escaped down to the pub, the banter in the bar all seemed distant there too, far removed from her recent experiences. Most of the talk was war talk of course. The bar was busy, people shocked into drink by the shattering fall of Singapore.

She sat on a bar stool nursing a small whisky, and in between pulling pints Katy told her about the awful christening party, Louise's mistreatment of poor Jack, Molly's distress and Pam Nelson's horror when little George threw the train set into the fire. None of it really sank in, though. Helen still felt remote from it all as though she was listening from afar.

It was only Katy's evident anxiety about the baby's health that finally pierced her strange cocoon.

'I had to take him in to the hospital for tests,' Katy said. 'The health visitor arranged it. She's obviously worried now too. They couldn't find anything wrong with him except that he's underweight.'

Tests. Helen was appalled. However you looked at it tests sounded ominous. She didn't know what to say. 'Katy, …' There was only one way she could help. 'Katy, if he ever needs treatment or anything, you must have it. The best. I'll pay. No.' She held up her hand. 'It's the least I can do.'

Katy was clearly touched. 'Well, if it comes to it, I'll ask you,' she said reluctantly, 'but I'd only accept it as a loan. If … when Ward gets back, we'd repay you. I promise.'

'Well, we'll see,' Helen said. 'And how is Ward? Are the letters still getting through?'

Katy nodded. 'Once a week more or less,' she said. 'Thank God.' She looked round the bar and then back at Helen. 'You know, I don't think I could cope with all this if I didn't know he was alive.'

'You would,' Helen said, and she knew it was true. For all that she looked so frail, Katy was tough. Katy had survived the loss of her father, the capture of her husband, being bombed, reopening the pub against all the odds, a difficult birth and now a sickly baby. Compared to that lot a few tough weeks in Scotland seemed like child's play.

'How about you?' Katy said. 'How was your "conference"?'

'Oh, it was all right,' Helen said. 'Hard work, but interesting.'

'What's the next step?'

Glancing round to make sure they weren't overheard, Helen took a deep breath. 'Parachuting. Then explosives.'

Katy shuddered. 'How do you stay so calm?'

Helen shrugged. 'I don't think about it. That's one thing I've learned. You just do it. You don't think about it. You can't afford to.' She realised Katy was looking at her closely. 'What? What is it?'

'You look different,' Katy said. 'Kind of fit and self-contained.'

'Do I?' Helen said. 'I don't mean to, but you're right. I do feel a bit odd. I suppose that's what they're trying to achieve. They want to detach us from reality, from our ordinary lives.'

'So you were pipped at the post,' Angus McNaughton said. 'How galling for you. Although I do also gather that Paul was a particularly good candidate throughout.'

Detecting the faint sense of satisfaction in his tone Helen bridled slightly. After all, she had been a good candidate too, and actually what was galling was Angus's attitude that it was somehow inevitable that Paul, a man, would have won. Helen shrugged. 'He was good,' she said. 'He was very good. Although I still can't quite work out how he got hold of that van on the final exercise. I can only assume he bribed the butcher.'

'So?' Angus raised his eyebrows. 'What's wrong with that?'

'Only that we were told not to take any money with us.'

'Oh dear,' Angus said. 'This sounds like sour grapes.'

'No,' Helen said calmly. 'I just don't see why Paul should get all the praise by breaking the rules.'

Angus laughed. 'Your integrity does you credit, Helen. Integrity is important of course, but there's another important quality our agents need, and that's initiative. I expect Paul would say that in bypassing the rules he was using his initiative.'

'I expect he would,' Helen said, but actually she didn't really care. She had shown she could do it and do it well, and that was all that mattered. In any case, the attitude of the other members of staff outweighed Angus McNaughton's pennypinching praise. Nobody had been told where she had been or what she was doing, but somehow everyone knew and it boosted her confidence to see the new sense of respect in their eyes.

Things weren't quite so good at home, however. Louise was cross with her for not telling her about her agent training, but then Louise had been in a black mood ever since Jack had disappeared back to Liverpool without bothering to say goodbye.

'You might have told me,' she had said. 'Don't you trust me?'

'Of course I do,' Helen said, 'but it's a secret. Nobody's meant to know. Not even my father knows.'

'Well, I won't tell anyone,' Louise said.

'Not even Aaref Hoch?'

Louise glared at her. 'Aaref and I are just friends. I don't know why Jack made such a stupid fuss about it.'

'Perhaps he was hurt,' Helen suggested mildly.

'I'm the one who's hurt,' Louise said crossly, flouncing off. 'And don't you start nagging me about it, I've had enough of that from Katy.'

One way and another Helen was glad to be going away again, but Greville Rutherford wasn't pleased about it. When she found him painting a five-inch plimsoll line on the bath in accordance with new government guidelines, she was taken aback by the vehemence of his reaction.

'This is ridiculous,' he said straightening up, unaware that he had a smear of paint on his cheek. 'My dear girl, you've only just come back from the last one. Surely there is someone else who could go in your place, one of the other secretaries?'

Helen tried to imagine one of the secretaries standing in for her on the SOE parachute course. She shook her head. 'Not really.'

He rubbed his cheek now, making the paint smear worse. He glanced at the door and lowered his voice. 'For heaven's sake. What do you think it's like for me when you keep going away?'

Helen was startled, and for a moment she didn't know what to say. Trying to make light of it she smiled. 'We are at war,' she said mildly. 'We all have to make sacrifices.'

To her horror he reached out suddenly and took her hand. 'Oh my dear girl,' he said. 'Is it a sacrifice for you too? Do tell me it is.'

Desperately Helen tried to pull her hand away. 'No, Mr Rutherford, please. I ...' She stopped. I ... what? What was she going to say? Mrs Rutherford was downstairs in the hall arranging flowers and the last thing Helen wanted was for her to hear her husband making a fool of himself, but she had to say something. Already he was pulling her towards him.

'What are you doing?' she hissed. 'No, stop it, you mustn't ...'

'Oh, come on, Helen,' he said gruffly. 'Just a little kiss and a cuddle. You know you want it as much as I do.'

'I certainly don't.'

'Yes you do. You only said the other day that you wanted an older man.' He laughed. 'And you shouldn't prance about in those ridiculous figure-hugging trousers if you expect me to hold back.'

Helen stared at him incredulously. 'Is that it? Just

because I wear slacks you think I'm fair game.' She jerked her hand away. 'That's ludicrous. I'm an independent modern woman and I can wear whatever I like.'

Suddenly he was angry. 'Oh yes,' he hissed, 'you think you're so modern and independent with your little job and living away from home, but you're not prepared to take the consequences, are you? Well, you can't have it both ways. Either you're independent or you're not. And if you're not, then you should get yourself a husband to look after you.'

Helen shook her head. 'I don't need a husband to look after me. I can look after myself. We women are capable human beings, you know, we're just as good as men.'

To her amazement he started laughing. 'You are priceless, my dear. You show me a woman as capable as a man and I promise to eat my hat!'

Helen gritted her teeth. It was so, so tempting to tell him what she was doing, where she was going, but she knew it would be unforgivable. Instead she met his sceptical eyes squarely. 'Okay, it's a deal,' she said grittily. 'One day I will show you a woman as capable as a man. And you will eat your bloody hat.'

Jen was worried about Katy. So worried in fact that she forced herself to go and see Sister Morris.

She didn't want to go to see Sister Morris. She didn't particularly like Sister Morris, and she knew she disapproved of her. On previous encounters, she had made no secret of the fact that she thought Jen was a bumptious little madam. Nevertheless Sister Morris was the only person who Katy took notice of and that was why Jen had ventured into the hospital.

She had intended to ask Molly Coogan to do it, but stupid Molly Coogan was so distraught about Aaref Hoch dropping her flat in favour of Louise that she never came near the pub now for fear of bumping into one or other of them. Pathetic behaviour, Jen thought. If she was Molly

Coogan she would tell that shifty little bastard Aaref Hoch to bugger off once and for all.

Jen had a pretty dim view of men. Having a violent vindictive father didn't help of course, and her brothers weren't much to write home about – poor old Pete couldn't even add up. And she'd spent the last year fending off stage-door johnnies who reckoned if they gave you a bunch of flowers they could get your knickers off. Sean Byrne was the only man she had ever really liked and he had run off to Ireland never to be seen again, except in a photograph in the paper standing on the steps of an Irish jail with a pretty girl in his arms. No. They were all the same. You simply couldn't trust them. Even blasted Ward Frazer, the one man you might have been able to trust, had got himself caught and locked up in some German prisoner-of-war camp just when Katy needed him most.

Poor Katy. There was no doubt she had had a rough time of it, and now just to cap it all this blasted baby was ailing. Even Jen could see he was getting weak. He was definitely too small for his age.

'He's had checks but they can't find anything wrong with him,' Jen said to Sister Morris when she at last managed to pierce a fierce guard of rustling ward nurses to gain admittance to the inner sanctum of Sister Morris's office. Small was certainly not an adjective you would ever apply to Sister Morris, she thought, as she looked across the desk at Katy's former mentor. Sister Morris's mighty bust alone must weigh at least six times little Malcolm's puny weight.

'Katy's worried to death,' Jen went on quickly, dragging her eyes back up to Sister's stern face. 'She's convinced he's going to die. She's so busy all the time, and her mother's gone away now so she's got even more to do.'

'And what do you want me to do about it?' Sister Morris said. 'She's no longer within my jurisdiction. I don't want to step on the health visitor's toes.'

Goodness, Jen thought, if you stepped on the health

visitor's toes the poor woman would be lame for life. 'I thought just a casual visit,' she said hopefully. 'Katy would be so pleased to see you. She was very disappointed you couldn't make the christening.' She smiled ingratiatingly. 'We all were.'

Sister Morris was not impressed. 'That's quite enough of your mealy mouth, Miss Carter. My opinion of you has risen recently and it would be a shame to spoil it by deliberate insincerity.'

Jen felt colour staining her cheeks. Somehow in a few short words Sister Morris had made her feel about three and a half. Covering her confusion in a light laugh she stood up abruptly. 'In that case, I won't outstay my welcome,' she said, 'but I hope my visit hasn't been in vain?' At the door she stopped and smiled sweetly. 'If you are ever in the West End I'd be more than happy to get you tickets to my show.'

Sister Morris snorted. 'If you think I want to waste my time watching girls like you prancing about on the stage you've got another think coming.'

Jen shrugged. 'Well, never mind. It's probably a bit racy for you anyway.'

The parachute course was held at Ringway airport near Manchester the weekend of 21 February. Having successfully put the prospect of jumping out of a plane out of her mind for the last week Helen now spent most of the journey reminding herself that she was no longer scared of heights. As a child she had been terrified, but that was a long time ago, and anyway, she had guts nowadays. She had proved that in Scotland, where, to her secret amazement, she had even managed a bit of basic rock climbing.

The thought of Scotland reminded her of Paul and, forgetting her fears, she spent the last few miles of the journey wondering what it was going to be like seeing him again.

But when she bumped into Paul in the hallway of the beautiful old manor house they were staying in a few miles from the airport, he seemed strangely subdued. He barely gave her a second glance at dinner the first night, and even at the airfield the following day, apart from asking her if she had had a good week off, he mainly kept himself to himself.

At first, as they learned how to pack a parachute and practised rolling on landing having jumped off a couple of hay bales, Helen thought it was because he was piqued by her refusal of his advances last weekend, but on the Sunday morning, as the time of their first real jump approached, it had become increasingly clear that Paul was scared.

Helen was amazed. The brilliant Paul was scared. So scared he had lost most of his colour and was visibly shaking. She could hardly take her eyes off him as he climbed into the plane and sat with the other two candidates hunched on the opposite side of the fuselage, bulky in the British army paratroopers' camouflaged smocks, helmets and X-type parachutes. It was surprisingly dark inside the plane and she couldn't see his expression but she guessed from the way he held his stomach as the engines roared and the rattly old Dakota began to judder as it lumbered along the runway that he was feeling pretty bad.

It was only as the plane lifted off that she realised the unpleasantly combined odour of petrol, sweat and leather in the fuselage was making her feel rather queasy too.

Before she could account for the prickling sensation on her skin, the plane banked steeply and the sergeant instructor leaned over to slide the jump door open. Light flooded in at once, and as the world underneath them veered away violently to the left, Helen's stomach lurched. In the distance Manchester swung across the horizon, a blur of brick and slate shrouded in rain. As she tightened her grip on her seat, Helen glanced quickly at Paul. He looked dreadful and she felt a sudden stab of sympathetic fear.

Then she realised it wasn't just sympathetic. It was real genuine, heart-hammering, clammy-palmed fear, and it was all her own. Suddenly she was six years old again, standing in utter terror at the top of the Eiffel Tower as the buildings and streets and parks swum sickeningly far below her in a blur of tears. Oh my God, she thought as the panic tightened in her throat. Oh my God.

The plane was climbing steeply now. The RAF sergeant instructor was already lining them up, clipping them to the anchor line, giving them the jump order. Gerry. Doug. Helen. Paul.

Helen swallowed hard. In a moment the green light would come on and she would be expected to throw herself out of the door. Into the air with only a few ropes and a flimsy piece of silk to support her.

The instructor touched her arm. 'One minute.'

In a terrible flash of clarity she realised that she had been so busy telling herself how marvellous and tough she was that she had forgotten to be frightened, but now all that belated fear was gushing through her veins as though there was no tomorrow. Come to think of it, if her chute failed to open there would be no tomorrow. She felt sick. Faint. She felt the weight of the parachute pack, the helmet on her head, and something liquid moved in her bowel. In horror she gripped her buttocks together.

The plane was turning back over the airfield now. Far below she could see the hangars, the aircraft standing in neat rows on the wet black tarmac. She could see people, their faces turned up into the rain, waiting to see the jump. She saw the ambulance waiting. She saw herself splattered on the ground, torn silk billowing around her.

'Thirty seconds.'

The red light began to flash.

I can't do it, she thought. I simply can't do it. Turning

back to look at Paul she saw the hesitation in his eyes and she knew he wasn't going to do it either.

Thank God. She was filled with relief. She wasn't alone. She and Paul would get to France some other way.

'Go!' Swinging back, she saw the green light was on. The instructor was slapping Gerry on the back, and then Gerry had gone and Doug had gone and the sergeant was pulling her forward.

'Go!'

'No!'

For a second everything seemed to be moving in slow motion. She felt the instructor's hand on her back. Trying to shove her out. To overcome her reluctance. But she knew without doubt she was going to die and her panic gave her strength. Screaming and screaming, she found herself swivelling round, but even as the wind hit her like a charging bull, she clung on.

And then through a haze of terror she heard swearing, shouting, and she was being hauled unceremoniously in. A moment later the instructor was unclipping her line and sliding Paul's forward.

'No!' she screamed as she was flung back and crashed in a painful crumpled heap on the uneven floor of the fuselage. 'He's not going.'

But he was. Without hesitation.

As soon as he was out of the door the instructor rounded on her. 'You stupid little bitch. You could have been killed.'

Helen stared at him. Of course she could have been killed. That was why she hadn't jumped. Already she could feel the relief surging over her like a warm wave. She was safe. Safe. *Safe.*

'Get up,' he yelled at her. He shouted something down the intercom to the pilot and the plane banked steeply.

'We're giving you one more chance,' he said, reaching for her static line.

For a second she couldn't make out what he was saying,

then as the panic hit her again, she shook her head, heavy under the helmet. 'No,' she said, backing away from him frantically. 'No! I don't want another chance.'

He looked at her grimly. 'If you don't go now, you never will.'

'I never will.'

'You know what that means?'

Suddenly despite all her resolutions she was crying. She knew what it meant all right. A successful jump was a prerequisite for staying on the course, but even though she knew it, she couldn't do it. She simply couldn't. Whatever shred of courage she might once have had had gone. The realisation hit her like a bullet in the heart. She was a coward and deep down she always had been.

Chapter Ten

To Katy's astonishment on 22 February, in the middle of the busiest Sunday lunchtime for ages, Sister Morris swept into the pub in full nursing regalia, white starched fan cap, cloak, belt and all.

'What's all this nonsense about the baby?' she shouted, marching past the astonished regulars and pinning Katy with an iron gaze behind the bar.

For a second Katy felt she was back in the Wilhelmina hospital as a petrified probationer nurse. All the terror and feeling of inadequacy came back to her with a jolt. 'I'm sorry, Sister,' she stammered humbly. 'I … It's just that he's not putting on weight.'

Sister Morris glared at her. 'I don't suppose you are feeding him properly. Although I don't see why not, your breasts look full enough to me.'

As a chuckle of appreciative laughter coursed through the bar, Katy remembered where she was. Glancing around helplessly she caught sight of Jacob standing goggle-eyed at the top of the cellar steps. Sliding swiftly out from behind the counter she asked him to take over and ushered Sister upstairs where Malcolm was grizzling in his cot.

It was no easier upstairs. Sister Morris was in high dudgeon. It seemed she had questioned Molly Coogan almost to pain of death about Katy's lifestyle and hadn't liked what she heard. Nor did she like the look of Malcolm.

'What a miserable little specimen,' she said plucking him out of the cot. Stripping off her gloves, she undressed him and glared at Katy. 'This child is seriously undernourished. You have quite clearly been skimping on your feeds. From now on you will feed him three hourly. If necessary we will get you a pump so you can express your milk. What's more you will rest for two hours morning and afternoon. And I mean rest. I don't want to hear any nonsense about not having time to rest. If you want this baby to live you will make time. Now, are you eating properly?'

Katy stared at her aghast. 'You mean he really might die?' she whispered. She had thought the words often enough but she had never really thought they might be true. Not really.

Sister Morris shrugged. 'If he does it will only be your fault,' she said brutally. 'You are letting yourself down with this absurd preoccupation about the pub. And you are letting your husband down too. I know you have to earn a living, but he's trusting to you to look after this baby. This is his baby. Not only that, it's a person in its own right. A human being. I am deeply shocked that a former nurse of mine would treat human life in such a cavalier fashion.'

Katy couldn't speak. She couldn't think. It was as if suddenly some barrier had been taken down and all she could see was Malcolm. Ward's baby. Her baby. Her little baby. In danger of his life. She couldn't bear it. She couldn't bear the thought of losing him. As she lifted him up her eyes filled with tears. 'Oh, I'm sorry, little baby,' she whispered, turning away in shame from Sister Morris. 'I'm so sorry.'

Sister ignored her. Without further ado, having delivered her opinion, Sister Morris was now pulling on her gloves and heading for the stairs. At the top she paused and glanced back briefly at Katy. 'I'm giving Nurse Coogan leave of absence for a few days to start you off.'

Katy gulped back her amazement. 'Thank you, Sister,' she said meekly. 'She'll be an enormous help.'

Sister Morris sniffed. 'Good. Because she's no use to me at the moment snivelling around the place all the time.'

'Where's George?' Alan asked, appearing suddenly in the kitchen as Pam made some pastry.

Pam looked up from her rolling pin and sighed. 'He's upstairs in his room. I told him off for breaking a cup and he went off in a sulk.' She felt the tears prickle her eyes. 'I hate telling him off all the time, Alan, but he keeps breaking—'

But Alan wasn't listening. 'He's not,' he said.

Pam blinked. 'What?'

'He's not upstairs. And he's not in the front room.'

Pam felt a shiver of anxiety run up her spine. 'He must be hiding.'

They searched every cupboard in the house, under every bed. Alan even got a chair and climbed up to look in the attic, but to no avail. No George. Nor was he in the garden, not even in the air-raid shelter where he sometimes played. Frantically Alan flung open the front door, but there was no sign of him in the street. A couple of passersby said they hadn't seen him.

'Oh Alan,' Pam cried, as suddenly the frustration and despair welled up in her. 'I can't bear it. What are we going to do?'

It was a bigger question than it sounded, and Alan knew it, but it was the immediate problem that he addressed. 'We're going to stay calm,' he said. 'He can't have gone far. There's nowhere for him to go. I'll go and ask round a bit.' He hesitated. 'If I have no joy I'll go on down to the police station.'

'Oh God.' Pam closed her eyes. She loved George so much. All she wanted was for him to be safe. As Alan picked up his coat, she grabbed his arm. 'What will I do?'

'Stay here in case he comes back.'

* * *

Helen arrived back in Clapham at five o'clock. Within an hour of her abortive parachute jump she had been put on a train back to London. She had seen nobody. In a way she was thankful for the hasty departure. The thought of facing Paul and the others in the knowledge of her disgrace was too horrible to contemplate, but her dismissal from the course had been so abrupt she still couldn't quite believe what had happened.

Now, in retrospect, the parachute jump seemed so easy. So quick. The others had landed within minutes. Perfectly safely. So why hadn't she just jumped and got it over with?

That question had been churning over and over in her mind like sour milk all the way home, but she knew the answer. There was no point in pretending she didn't. The time for pretence was over. Everything was over. She simply hadn't got what it took. It wasn't just that she hadn't jumped, although that was bad enough. No, the reason they had shunted her off that course so fast wasn't just because she was lacking in the guts department but because she had committed the cardinal SOE sin. She had lost control and panicked in the face of danger, and they didn't want her contaminating the other candidates.

'This it, love?' The taxi driver glanced over his shoulder as he turned off the common. 'Nice-looking place.'

Helen nodded numbly. Oh God, she thought. We're here. As she paid off the cabby she remembered her arrival back from the last course and prayed that once again everyone would be out.

This time of course Mr Rutherford was in the hall to meet her.

'Helen.' He came forward quickly, holding out his hands. 'My dear girl, what's the matter? Are you ill? I thought you said you'd be away a week.'

She tried. She tried very hard, but the craving for reassurance was too great, and when he drew her into his arms she didn't resist. For a moment she clung to him, desperate for some human contact, desperate for warmth, security, and then she felt his arms stiffen and the telltale movement in his groin and pulled away quickly.

'Helen, I …' His voice was ridiculously formal. She turned away, embarrassed for him for getting aroused. Angry with herself for being so weak. Desperately she tried to pull herself together.

'Where is everyone?' she asked over her shoulder.

'Out.'

He was trying to turn her round, but she couldn't bear to face him.

'Come to me, Helen,' he whispered. 'Come to me again.'

'No,' she said, taking a deep breath and turning round. 'I'm sorry, Mr Rutherford, I'm really sorry, but I can't allow you to feel like this. It's not right.'

His brows drew together. 'Don't say that.' Grasping her arms he pulled her hard up against him. 'Don't you know what you do to me? You torture me, blowing hot and cold like this.'

'I'm not blowing hot and cold. I'm not doing anything.' The pressure on her arms was hurting now. She tried to ease away but he wouldn't let her. His face was close to hers. She could smell alcohol on his breath.

'Oh yes you are. Why else would I feel like this?' He grabbed her hand and thrust it on his groin. 'I'm aroused for you, Helen. I want you. I need you.'

For a second Helen was shocked into immobility. Then she began to struggle. But he was strong and he was enjoying it. Already he had ripped open her jacket and was trying to grope through her shirt for her breast.

She hadn't attended the unarmed combat sessions in Scotland for nothing, however. Coldly, calculatingly, even as the buttons flew off her shirt, she worked out his vulnerable spots. Only the fear that she would hurt him irreparably held her back.

But then he kissed her, his lips hot and wet and his tongue probing, and without thinking further, she kicked him hard in the shin. At the same time she jerked her arms up and then hard down and out, twisting out of his grip as he cried out in shock.

As he hopped about in agony she grabbed her suitcase and opened the front door.

'Helen, wait.' His voice was strangled. 'Where are you going?'

'Out,' she said and slammed the door.

Actually it was a good question. As she half walked, half ran up the drive she thought of going to Katy, Katy had her own problems, and she didn't need Helen's too, but Helen didn't know anyone else well enough to ask. Not in Lavender Road. Even after living here for three months.

Stopping on Clapham Common Northside, she closed her eyes for a second. She didn't belong in Lavender Road, any more than she belonged in the SOE. Her father was in America, he couldn't help her. All the hotels were full of Americans. Biting back tears, she looked around helplessly then glanced across the road at the wide expanse of Clapham Common. She needed to be alone. She needed time to think, and where better than on the grey lonely common.

Louise was beginning to think she had made a big mistake. She couldn't believe that Jack would disappear like that without a word. She had been so certain he would plead with her to come back to him, pester her in increasing desperation, and, if things went to plan, eventually propose.

But things hadn't gone to plan. She hadn't heard one word from him for a week. No letters or phone calls, no message, nothing. And the only person pestering her was Aaref Hoch. Aaref was all right for the odd trip to the pictures and a bit of flattering attention but he wasn't the sort of man she wanted to marry. The sort you could take to smart parties and show off to your friends. Admittedly Aaref was quite attractive in that dark foreign sort of way, but there was a big difference between an officer of Her Majesty's Royal Navy and a Jewish evacuee from the back streets of Clapham.

Nor was she in love with Aaref.

That was the crunch. She simply didn't feel that same shiver of excitement when she was with Aaref as she did with Jack. That sense of nervousness, the constant craving for his good opinion. Aaref's admiration was pleasant enough, but nothing compared with the heartstopping effect of just one of Jack's cool smiles. And now she had gone and ruined it. Spoiled her chances. She would probably never see one of those smiles again.

What was worse, she had lost the support of her friends. Helen had been really off with her last week and Katy was furious with her for upsetting that stupid ugly Molly Coogan. That beastly Jen Carter had laughed when she overheard her telling Katy how much she missed Jack. 'Well, it's your bloody fault, isn't it?' she had said, and it had annoyed Louise that a cheap, tarty piece like Jen Carter should look down her nose at her for behaving badly.

Even Doris down at Gregg Bros. this morning wasn't entirely sympathetic. 'If you've found a good man, I reckon as you should of hung on to him,' she said. 'They're few and far between, after all, and you can't afford to kick them in the teeth.'

'I didn't kick him in the teeth,' Louise said crossly. She hated these Sunday shifts. She had only volunteered for this one to avoid accompanying her mother to her grandparents', and now Doris was being annoying she was beginning to wish she hadn't bothered. 'I was just trying to make him jealous by spending a bit of time with someone else, that's all.'

Doris paused in her work for a moment to wipe the back of her hand over her sweaty brow. 'Comes to the same, doesn't it? You've hurt his pride. That's a strong thing for men, pride.' She shrugged her copious shoulders.

'Mind you, that Jewboy's a nice looker and all. Maybe you'd be better off with him.' She chuckled heartily. 'Lucky to have a choice, I say. It's more than what I've got.'

Louise glared at her. 'That's the whole point. I haven't got a choice any more. Jack seems to have disappeared off the face of the earth.' She paused for a second as a cold shiver ran up her spine. She hoped to God Jack hadn't disappeared off the face of the earth. Hadn't gone on some stupid manoeuvre and been blown up by a U-boat or something.

'Well, you'd best write to him, then,' Doris said. 'Tell him you're sorry and you miss him and love him and can't live without him and all the rest of that old gobbledygook they like to hear.'

Louise looked at her doubtfully. 'Isn't that a bit demeaning?'

Doris snorted impatiently. 'Good God, who cares? The poor bastard will probably be torpedoed before long anyway. Might as well get your hands on him while you can.'

'Why are you crying?'

Helen had been sitting on the cold bench for a long time when a small voice behind her asked the question.

Swinging round, she found herself looking at a child. A young boy. A vaguely familiar boy.

'Are you sad?'

'Yes,' she said shortly. She wasn't very good with children at the best of times, and the last thing she needed right now was some kind of juvenile interrogation.

'Very sad?'

'Well, yes. I suppose so,' she said. She cleared her throat and looked hopefully round the adjacent area for some adult to call him away, but there was nobody about any more. It was obviously later than she thought. In fact it was getting quite dark. Even the gun emplacements over by the road seemed deserted. It was also cold. Very cold.

'Why have you got a suitcase?'

Helen groaned inwardly. 'I was staying with some friends,' she said, 'but someone was horrid to me so I don't want to stay there any more.'

'So you've run away?'

Helen smiled faintly. 'Sort of.'

'I've run away too.'

It was spoken as a kind of challenge. Startled, Helen looked at him more closely. She recognised him now. He was Mrs Nelson's adopted child. The one who had ruined Katy's beer.

He hesitated for a second and then he nodded proudly. 'They've been looking for me but they haven't found me.' His tone implied he was more pleased that he had evaded capture than that they had been looking for him, but the wistful expression on his pinched little face made Helen think it might actually be the other way round. For a moment she felt a stab of sympathy for him. If nothing else it was awfully cold. She could feel the vibrations of the boy's shivers as he leaned over the back of the bench.

Realising that she was going to have to do something about him, she sighed. Much as she wanted to, she could hardly just shrug him off. It was clearly a choice between grabbing him and frogmarching him home, or trying to find out what was wrong and hopefully persuading him to go home off his own bat. She glanced at him assessingly and decided the former was out of the question. He looked like a slippery little blighter and the chances of manoeuvring both him and her suitcase across the common singlehandedly were slim.

'What will your mother say about you running away?' he asked suddenly.

Helen shook her head. 'My mother's dead,' she said.

'So is mine,' George said. 'She was killed by a bomb,

and my daddy was killed by the Germans. And my brother was killed by a car.'

Helen swallowed. 'But you've got new parents now, haven't you?'

'Aunty Pam looks after me now, but ...' He stopped.

Suddenly he had lost his perkiness. He began kicking the tufts of grass at the base of the seat.

'But what?' Helen asked gently.

He was silent a long time.

'She looks after a baby too.' This announcement was followed by another long pause and more kicking.

'Don't you like the baby?'

'No,' he said, 'but Aunty Pam does.' He glared at Helen suddenly. 'I think she likes it better than me. Even though it smells.'

For a second, despite his evident distress, Helen was hard pushed not to smile. Quickly she looked away and blew her nose. 'I don't like babies very much either,' she said.

'Don't you?'

'No. To be honest I'm not sure that anyone does much. After all, they've got nothing to say for themselves, have they? All they do is lie there. Some of them aren't even very pretty. And they smell sometimes, like you say. But it's a funny thing, you know, that everyone *pretends* to like them. It's like a sort of game that everyone plays.'

George was staring at her, whether in disbelief or suspicion it was hard to tell. At least he had stopped kicking though, which was a relief. He frowned as he worked out the implications of what she had said and then a faint flicker of hope appeared in his blue eyes. 'So you think Aunty Pam is pretending to like the baby?'

'Well,' Helen said slowly, 'some people like them more than others, of course, but I simply can't believe that anyone would like a miserable little baby more than a ...' She paused, wondering what description would please him most. 'A tough, sensible boy like you.'

He liked tough, but he wasn't sure about sensible. 'Most people say I'm naughty. Like running away. And I break things.'

She shrugged. 'We're all naughty sometimes. Look at me. I've run away too. But I reckon you're sensible enough to know that Aunty Pam will be really worried about you by now, and that maybe the time has come to go home.'

He looked doubtful and she thought the time might have come for the grab and drag technique. No one was going to steal her suitcase now. Another few minutes and it would be too dark to see it anyway.

Once again George surprised her. 'Okay,' he said grudgingly, 'but only because I'm cold.' He gave the grass one final kick. 'And only if you'll come with me.'

'Me? But why?'

He slanted her an appealing look through his lashes. 'Aunty Pam won't be so cross if you come too.'

Aunty Pam was far too relieved to be cross, and too astonished. When she opened the door and found Lady Helen de Burrel on the step her mouth fell open, but then she noticed George lurking behind her and the relief washed over her like a warm wave.

'George! Thank God.' It was only as she picked him up and hugged him that she remembered her anxiety. 'Where have you been? You naughty boy.' Then she met Helen's eyes over his head and stopped abruptly.

There was something wrong here. She didn't know Helen well but she had seen her around often enough to know that dishevelled clothes and a tearstained face were a long way from her normal immaculate, confident appearance.

Lowering George to the ground, she smiled at Helen tentatively. 'Will you come in?'

Helen shook her head hastily. 'No thanks, I . . .' She took a step back and nearly tripped over her suitcase.

A suitcase? Pam stared at it in blank amazement, but before she could speak, George was clutching at her hand.

'She must come in. She's run away too. Someone was horrid to her, but she can stay here with us, can't she?'

'No, no. Honestly. I'm fine.' Helen was clearly appalled. Already she was backing away down the path.

'Please,' Pam said quickly, 'please stay at least till I've found someone to tell Alan the worry's over. Then I'll put the kettle on. It's the least I can do to thank you for bringing George back.'

'He wanted to come back,' Helen said. 'He just …'

Pam glanced at George. 'Why don't you run upstairs and get a jumper? You're freezing.'

George looked mutinous. 'Only if she stays,' he said.

Pam looked at Helen and smiled gently. 'I think you're outnumbered.' Nevertheless she felt self-conscious leading Helen into the kitchen. Helen was such a lady with her classy accent and manners and that, and Pam was suddenly very much aware of the shabby little kitchen, the clothes horse covered in Alan's vests, the row of dirty cups on the wooden draining board, witness to her anxious afternoon. I should have put her in the front room, she thought, as she rattled the cups under the tap. And then another thought occurred to her.

'It wasn't George that upset you, was it?' she asked.

Helen looked up at once. 'No, no. George was sweet.' She made a visible effort to pull herself together and managed to muster a reassuring smile. 'He's jealous of Katy's baby, that's all,' she said. 'I think you looking after it has made him feel insecure. He's worried you love Malcolm more than him.'

Pam blinked. It was so obvious. So glaringly obvious she couldn't think why it hadn't occurred to her. Or to Alan. She felt a sudden rush of gratitude towards Helen, but before she could express it properly, Helen was on her feet again.

'Look, I'd better go …'

Suddenly noticing the torn buttons at the front of her jacket, Pam's eyes widened as a possible rather shocking explanation for Helen's disarray occurred to her.

'Look, I don't want to pry, but if what George said was right, perhaps you, um … don't want to go back to Cedars House?' She saw Helen tense and rushed on quickly. 'Seriously. We can give you a bed for the night if it would help. We've got a spare room. It's not very large but …'

To her dismay Helen's shoulders began shaking. 'Oh God,' she mumbled. 'I'm so sorry. You're so kind. I've made such a mess of things. I don't know what to do.'

'Don't do anything now,' Pam said gently. 'You look too tired to decide anything anyway. Stay here and sleep. Sometimes things seem clearer in the morning.'

'She's very sad,' George said helpfully from the door. 'That's why I brought her home.'

Pam nodded. 'I know,' she said gravely. 'It was a sensible thing to do.'

Arriving home after her Sunday shift, Louise nearly jumped out of her skin when her father leaped out of his office like a madman and grabbed her arm.

'Oh,' he said. 'It's you.'

'Of course it's me,' she said, staring at him aghast. 'Who did you think it was?'

'I …' He stopped and ran a hand through his oddly dishevelled hair. 'I thought it might be your mother.'

Louise began to wonder if he was drunk. Not that he usually drank. He was generally pretty mean with alcohol. Mean with everything come to that. But there was a distinct smell of whisky in the air, and he was definitely behaving oddly. 'Mummy's at Granny's,' she said. 'She said she'd leave a cold supper out ready for us.'

He thumped his head with a parody of forgetfulness. 'Oh yes, of course,' he said. He half turned away and then swung back abruptly. 'What about Lady Helen? Have you seen her at all?'

Louise stared at him. He was either drunk or mad. 'Of course I haven't seen her,' she said crossly. 'She's away at another conference.' Or her so-called conferences, she added silently to herself. 'Why? Did you want her?'

He didn't answer at once and she looked at him more closely. There was definitely a mad glazed look in his eyes. When he saw her staring he shook his head violently. 'No, of course not,' he said.

'Well,' Louise said uneasily, 'I'm going to have a bath now, so I'll have my supper later.'

Abruptly her father turned back to his study. 'Well, don't use too much water.'

Louise groaned silently. He obviously wasn't so drunk he would forget about his stupid new plimsoll line.

She was halfway up the stairs when the telephone rang. She turned back at once, but to her astonishment her father was out of the study and across the hall like a dose of salts.

'Yes,' he barked. 'Yes. Who … oh.' He lowered the receiver and glanced at Louise. 'It's for you. Trunk.'

It was Jack.

Louise couldn't believe it. Only ten minutes ago she had dropped into the pillar box in Lavender Road a letter written in her tea break on paper scrounged from Mr Gregg's office and virtually dictated by the long-suffering Doris.

'Louise? Is that you? Look, I had to ring. I need to talk to you …'

'Oh Jack,' Louise breathed. Just the sound of his husky voice sent shivers up her spine. 'I've just written to you,' she said.

'Oh?' His voice sounded stiff now. 'To say it's all off?'

Louise shook her head violently even though he couldn't see. 'No,' she said. 'On the contrary. To say I'm sorry for the other weekend. I was only trying to make you jealous. I know it didn't work, but I …'

'It did work.' At least she thought that's what he said.

The line was crackling unnervingly and she felt a stab of panic. Surely they weren't going to be cut off. Then his voice came again and he sounded as frantic as she felt. 'Louise, are you there?'

'Yes, I'm here.'

'It did work. I've never felt so terrible in all my life …' He stopped, and started again abruptly. 'Look, my promotion has come through and I wanted, I wondered …'

'Yes?' Louise was hopping about now in a dread anticipation, clutching the phone to her ear. Another crackle obliterated his next words and she screamed down the line. 'What? Jack? What did you say? Say it again!'

She heard the hiss of exhaled breath at the other end. 'I asked if you would consider marrying me. I know I should ask in person really, but …'

'Oh yes,' she said. 'Oh Jack. Yes please.'

There was a long silence at the other end and again she thought they had been cut off, then she heard a soft laugh. 'Thank God for that. I've been summoning up the courage to ask you all week.'

She couldn't speak. All week she had worried unnecessarily. She heard the operator cut in to say his time was up.

'I'll come down as soon as I can,' he shouted. 'You'll wait for me this time, won't you?'

'Of course I will.' She would wait for ever for him now he had asked her to marry him. Marry. Marriage. A wedding. A husband. Louise could hardly breathe as she lowered the telephone back on to its cradle.

Her father was still hovering in the hall. She stared at him. Inside her she could feel a great welling excitement, a great bubble of happiness and overwhelming relief. She wanted to laugh and cry. She wanted to dance and sing and fly and positively explode with happiness. But she couldn't dance or sing or fly. Or explode. She would have to tell someone instead. It was a shame that her father was the only available person but he would just have to do. It was far too great a piece of news to keep to herself.

'Jack's proposed,' she said. She looked at him expectantly but he didn't seem to take it in. 'Daddy.' She raised her voice. 'Jack's asked me to marry him.'

Her father looked at her blankly, then he frowned. 'If he had any manners he would have asked my permission first,' he said, and then he went into his study and shut the door.

Pam Nelson was intrigued. 'Old Rutherford must have had a go at her,' she whispered to Alan in bed that night. 'Her buttons were all torn, and there's nobody else there. Bertie is away at training camp and the other boy Douglas is at school.'

'It might not have been him,' Alan said mildly. 'It could have been some drunk up on the common—'

'No,' Pam interrupted him. 'That's the thing. It was at Cedars House. She doesn't want to go back—' She stopped abruptly as Helen's voice rose in an eerie wail from the adjacent room. 'Oh God. She's sleeptalking now.' At first it was hard to hear the words, but then quite clearly they heard Helen's shout. 'No! Don't make me. I can't do it. Oh God!' Then a scream, and then the voice again. 'Two shots. Oh no. I've killed him. I've killed them all.'

'Oh my God,' Pam whispered with a nervous giggle. 'Who do you think she's killed? The Rutherfords?'

'Well, she hasn't killed Louise,' Alan whispered back. 'I saw her going down to the pub earlier. Mind you, she was running.'

'Alan, don't!' Pam hit him playfully on the chest in the darkness. Of course Helen hadn't killed anyone. She was far too ladylike.

Calling at the pub the following morning to pick up baby Malcolm as usual, Pam was surprised to find Molly Coogan scrubbing the floors while Katy lay in bed with

Malcolm asleep in the crook of her arm. Jen meantime, dressed in a slinky satin dressing-gown, was wafting about in the kitchen making breakfast.

'It's a new regime.' Katy smiled at Pam's amazement. 'I'm under strict orders to rest, and it seems to work. Malcolm's been asleep for two hours since I fed him at seven. It's a miracle.'

Pam smiled. It was a miracle to see Katy relaxed and smiling. Suddenly she thought of Helen's distress last night, those dreadful nightmares. 'Alan said he saw Louise come in last night,' she said hesitantly. 'Was she all right?'

Katy laughed. 'She was more than all right. She was over the moon. Jack had just rung up and proposed.' She grimaced. 'Although I dread to think what Aaref will do when he finds out.' She looked at Pam and frowned. 'Why?'

'Well, it's just that ...' She stopped. 'Well, nothing really. I just wondered.' After all, she didn't want to spread gossip, and it suddenly occurred to her that just for the time being Helen might not want people to know where she was.

She was right. Helen didn't want to see anyone or talk to anyone. Helen just wished the world would stop so she could get off. She was grateful for Pam's discretion. Grateful for the tea and toast she brought up to the plain little bedroom, and even more grateful when Pam offered to go down to the telephone box to call Helen's 'office' to tell them Helen was sick and wouldn't be in for a couple of days.

She was even more grateful when Pam tentatively suggested that she stay on a few days until she was 'feeling better'. She liked it at the Nelsons'. She felt safe there in their cosy little house. It was tiny compared with what she was used to, but it was neatly kept. And it was warm. And nobody bothered her.

Mostly she read or slept but once or twice she offered to

cook a meal and one morning she even struggled with the ironing. Pam was fully occupied with Katy's baby by day, and in the evenings Alan liked to listen to the wireless with his feet up in front of the fire. Helen took a strange comfort from the solid normality of the national news, *The Brains Trust*, and the stereotyped humour of Tommy Handley's *ITMA* characters, even though the absurd pomposity of Colonel Chinstrap reminded her of Greville Rutherford. Oddly, each afternoon she even looked forward to George coming home from school. Helen had never really known a child well before and had never realised the sense of self-worth that having a small child cuddling up to you could bring.

However, she couldn't hide at the Nelsons' for ever. Sooner or later she knew she was going to have to rejoin the real world.

By Friday she had made the decision to resign from the SOE. She just couldn't go back there. Her credibility had been shot to pieces. She knew she would have to face telephoning Angus McNaughton later. First, though, she was going to the café to tell Mrs Rutherford that she had decided to join her father in America, and she would then pack up her things and move down to her friends' in Oxfordshire until she could get a passage.

On the way to the café she called at the Flag and Garter. She hadn't seen Katy since she came back from the parachute course. She hadn't seen anyone except the Nelsons. Katy would want to know what had happened, and now, after five days of rest and recuperation, Helen reckoned she was just about strong enough to tell her without crying.

Helen had heard from Pam that Katy's health and spirits were vastly improved by her own regime of rest, so she was surprised to find her white faced and shaking, leaning helplessly against the bar. Quickly she ran up to her. She saw the letter clutched in her hand, the envelope lying on the table with its distinctive Red Cross stamp, and her heart kicked.

'Katy! What's happened?'

For a second Katy stared at her blankly, then she handed her the flimsy paper. 'Tell me,' she whispered. 'Tell me I'm wrong.'

The letter was from Ward. Hastily Helen scanned the writing. At first she couldn't see anything wrong. He wrote of some football game the prisoners had played against their guards. He thanked her for her letters and said he loved the photograph Katy had sent, but he wished she had been smiling. He missed her smile.

Helen glanced up. It all seemed pretty normal stuff but Katy's face made her look down again and at once she saw her own name mentioned. Abruptly her eyes jumped to that spot.

'How is Helen?' he wrote casually. 'Give her my love and ask her to give my best wishes to the boys. Tell them I am hoping to see them again soon.'

At once Helen's blood ran cold. Suddenly she understood Katy's panic. Katy knew as well as she did who the boys were. The 'boys' were Jean-Luc and Pierre, two Resistance fighters Ward had worked with in France, organising sabotage and setting up escape routes for downed airmen. His message was clear. He was intending to escape and was going to try to make contact with the 'boys'.

'The boys will look after him, won't they?' Katy whispered. 'If he gets that far?'

Helen could feel Katy's fear sweeping across her like a draught. She didn't know what to say, where to look. Katy was looking to her for reassurance. Reassurance she simply couldn't give.

Helen felt her knees give way and she sat down heavily. Trying to escape was bad enough. Everyone knew that the chances of a successful escape were minimal, that the Germans shot escaping prisoners on sight.

But what neither Ward nor Katy knew was that the boys' Resistance network had been compromised weeks ago and anyone trying to make contact with them would be in serious danger.

Part Three

Chapter Eleven

Ward's letter changed everything. Much as she longed to run away to the country, Helen knew she owed it to Katy to try and find a way of warning him about the danger surrounding the boys, if he hadn't already escaped. Or tried to. That was another thing she would have to try and find out, which meant staying in London for the foreseeable future, and worst of all meant going back to the office.

Even now as she sat on the number 2 bus trundling up Park Lane she could feel the sinking feeling of dread in her stomach. She hadn't told Katy she had intended to resign, nor had she told Katy about the boys. She couldn't. Not when Katy had been looking at her with such hope and trust in her eyes. In any case, the fact that the boys were compromised was classified information.

She had told Katy that she had failed the parachute course though, and Katy, despite her anxiety, was sympathetic.

'Oh, you poor thing. How ghastly. Mind you, there's no way you'd ever get me to jump out of an aeroplane.'

Helen shook her head. After all, Katy was the person who had risked her life by crawling through a teetering mass of rubble when the Whiteheads' house was bombed last year to rescue little George. 'You would if it was life and death,' she said.

Katy thought about it. 'Well, maybe,' she conceded reluctantly, then she touched Helen's arm. 'But so would you. If it really was life and death.'

Helen didn't need to think about it. She had thought about it all week. Dreamed about it. Cried about it. 'No,' she said. 'I really don't think I would.'

Anyway it didn't matter any more. She was off the course and that was that. And now she was on the bus getting inexorably closer and closer to the moment when she would have to walk into the SOE offices full of men all quite happy to jump out of an aeroplane at the drop of a hat.

It wasn't quite as bad as she thought. It was Friday and for some reason the building was always quieter on a Friday. Most people's doors were closed in any case and Helen only saw two people she knew on her way to Angus McNaughton's office, and although they glanced at her in a knowing way, neither of them stopped to talk.

To her relief Angus was in his office alone. He stood up at once when she came into the room. 'Helen,' he said. 'How are you? I was sorry to hear you were ill.'

She could hardly bear to look at him for fear of seeing the expression in his eyes. She didn't know if it would be pitying, I-told-you-so or merely embarrassed. One thing was for sure – he certainly knew she hadn't been ill.

'Angus,' she said, 'I wasn't going to come back, but Ward Frazer is going to escape and he doesn't know that Jean-Luc and Pierre's network is compromised.' She explained about Katy's letter and added, 'Can we warn him somehow? I couldn't bear it if he managed to escape and then got picked up trying to contact the boys.'

Angus didn't reply at once. Instead he waved her to a chair and lit a cigarette. 'There's no way we can warn him,' he said. 'Not without endangering his escape attempt. Any urgent message we tried to send into his camp could easily have the effect of making the Germans more vigilant.'

'But would that matter?' Helen asked. 'Surely it's better for him to stay there safely.'

Angus looked shocked. 'Good God, girl. It's his duty to escape if he can.'

'His duty?' Helen gaped at him. 'What do you mean it's his duty? Is it his duty to walk into a trap?'

'It's his duty to try to get home. We need all the men we can get. And in any case, the more prisoners who try to escape, the more Germans there will be tied up guarding them.'

Angus spoke sharply and Helen looked down at her hands. He was right of course. It *was* Ward's duty to try to escape. She knew that really. But in her current emotional state safety seemed more important than duty. The thought of risking a bullet in the back during a mad dash across no-man's-land made her stomach clench painfully.

Angus blew out a cloud of smoke. 'Just as it's your duty to come back to work,' he said. 'I know you are upset about failing the jump, of course you are, but it's no disgrace, you know. Particularly not for a girl. Precious few men get through that course successfully, and there's no guarantee that even those who do won't fail when put to the real test.'

He was being kind. He wasn't surprised she had failed. She realised that he had never really expected her to pass. Somehow that knowledge made her feel even worse. If it hadn't been for Ward Frazer and the need to keep an ear to the ground she would have walked out then, never to return. As it was, she kept her seat and listened while Angus McNaughton outlined a new role for her.

'We need to set up a liaison with the Free French in London,' he said. 'General de Gaulle's lot. I have talked to Maurice Buckmaster and he agrees you are the perfect choice. The French are playing their cards pretty close to their chest, but we need to know what they are up to. And, being French, they'll do anything for a pretty face.'

Helen stared at him blankly, and then she understood. They didn't trust her any more. Not really. So she was being shunted out. Shunted into a job where once again it was her pretty face that was the crucial factor. Not her brain. Or her guts.

'What do you think?' Angus was watching her closely.

Helen nodded. 'All right,' she said. After all, it was only what she deserved.

'So what do you think?' Pam whispered to Alan in bed that night.

Alan shrugged slightly. 'You don't like having lodgers.'

'But Helen's different,' she said. 'She's so helpful. And nice. And George likes her.'

It was true. George had been like a different child all week, sunny and endearing, making it easy for Pam to hug him and Alan to tease him and generally show him how much they loved him.

Pam frowned, disappointed by Alan's reaction. She liked Helen, and the thought of some extra cash in the money box was appealing. Their standard of living had dropped alarmingly since she had given up work to look after George. With a bit extra coming in they might even be able to take George on a little holiday in the summer. To the seaside perhaps, if there was anywhere left where the beaches weren't mined. She sighed. 'So you don't want her, then?'

She jumped as Alan's hand slid over her stomach. 'It's you I want,' he murmured, nuzzling her ear.

Pam giggled. 'Alan, shh. She'll hear.'

'No she won't,' he said. 'She's far too busy dreaming about killing people.'

Pam pushed him back a little. 'You don't really think . . .?'

'No, of course I don't, but I wouldn't be surprised if there's more to her "office" than meets the eye. She was friendly with that Ward Frazer, after all, and we know what he did for a living.'

Pam frowned. 'Do we?'

'Well, we know he was in France when he was captured and I doubt he was there on a wine-tasting mission.'

Pam shivered. 'So you think Helen works for the secret service?'

'Or some equivalent. That might account for her dreams.'

Pam thought about it. It was possible, she supposed, although it was hard to imagine the ladylike Helen de Burrel being involved in the dirty world of spies and saboteurs, even in an administrative capacity. On the other hand, Helen had been rather reticent about what she actually did at her so-called 'office'.

'So does that mean you do want her to stay, or not?' she asked. 'I'll have to let her know tomorrow. Poor girl. She was embarrassed enough about asking to stay one extra night.'

'If you want her, that's good enough for me,' Alan said. 'Maybe we could use the extra cash on a holiday for George?'

Pam smiled and turned over so she could kiss him. 'That's what I was thinking.'

'Great minds,' Alan murmured. Then after a moment he added, 'And great bodies too.' He chuckled softly as he slid his hand up under her nightie to stroke her breasts. 'In your case, anyway.'

'Katy, you aren't concentrating,' Molly Coogan complained. 'I've asked you twice what I ought to do and you just stare into space. What's the matter?'

'Nothing,' Katy said quickly. 'Nothing's the matter. I think you ought to wait, that's all. Aaref is still upset about Louise's engagement. I think it's too soon to rush back in. He's treated you badly enough as it is.'

'You think I'm stupid, don't you? You think I'm wasting my time.'

Katy shook her head. 'I don't think you're stupid,

Molly. I think you are lovely. And I'm sure Aaref will realise it sooner or later.'

Molly was not reassured but she promised not to approach Aaref for at least another couple of days.

After she had gone Katy closed her eyes. She was finding it a strain pretending everything was going on normally. And yesterday evening, with every nerve on edge, she had spent an hour listening to Louise panicking about an imminent visit to Jack's parents' home in Surrey.

'What happens if they don't like me?' she had asked nervously.

'I'm sure they'll like you,' Katy replied. 'Just show them how much you love Jack and they're bound to like you.'

'It was so easy for you with Ward's parents being in Canada,' Louise had said crossly. 'You didn't have to go through all this.'

Katy had longed to tell her how very much less than easy things were now, but Helen had warned her to tell nobody about Ward's possible escape. As the ghastly 'Keep Mum' posters said, 'Careless Talk Costs Lives' and you never knew who might get to hear of it and who they might tell. If Ward was going to escape, the last thing they wanted was a German patrol waiting for him on the other side of the barbed wire.

However, she had told Jen. She had to. It was impossible to keep a secret from Jen. In any case, Jen had noticed her renewed anxiety. To her surprise Jen just laughed. 'I knew you shouldn't have sent that dreadful photograph,' she said. 'One look at your miserable face and he probably started digging there and then.'

That afternoon in her 'rest period' Katy wrote a letter to Ward saying pointedly how much better she was, how Malcolm was putting on weight at last (not entirely true but at least he wasn't losing it any more) and how much she was looking forward to seeing him again 'when the war was over'. Even as she wrote it she had a premonition that he wouldn't get it. If Ward had been considering an escape six weeks ago when his letter had been written, it would be surprising if he hadn't done anything about it by the time he got this one five or six weeks hence.

Finishing the letter, Katy sealed it and glanced at Malcolm fast asleep beside her. From the look of him she might still have another half an hour's peace and quiet. She sighed because she didn't like the task awaiting her, then carefully so as not to disturb him, she drew her account books on to her lap.

Downstairs the wireless was still on and Katy could hear some discussion about the new man Sir Arthur Harris who was taking over as head of RAF Bomber Command. He was reputed to be tough and intended to increase the intensity of raids over Germany. Katy shivered. She hoped he wouldn't intensify them over the area where Ward was trying to make his escape, and she hoped the Germans wouldn't retaliate. Just about the only good thing about the last couple of months was that there had been no bombing. Not here. Other places had suffered, of course, but nothing like the dreadful raids of last year.

For a second she allowed herself to remember one of those raids when Ward had caught her dodging the flak down at Clapham Junction on her way back from the hospital. Angrily he had dragged her back between the pillars of Barclays Bank and pinned her against the wall as a German plane strafed the empty road behind them. It had been the first time he had held her close. In fact it was the first time he had held her at all, and even now, well over a year later, she could remember exactly the extraordinary mixture of excitement and reassurance she experienced during that first embrace.

As the figures in her account book began to blur and swim on the page she took a deep breath and sniffed determinedly. There was no point being sad. There was no point dwelling on the past. She had to try to be brave, she had to try to look to the future, and more than anything she had to try to work out why the pub still wasn't making any money.

It was odd, Helen thought, how when you were feeling happy and well everything seemed so easy, but when you felt down even the smallest things became a problem. In the old days she would have been able to extricate herself from Cedars House with smiles all round and everyone thinking what a nice polite girl she was, but now, somehow, with her excuses about not wanting to outstay her welcome, she seemed to have managed to upset everyone.

Mrs Rutherford was clearly put out and apologised rather huffily, when Helen went to collect her things, for not looking after her as well as she should have because of her commitment to the café. Louise was simply cross and said that she thought it was mean of Helen to go just when she needed her most to help her with all the wedding preparations.

Greville was just angry. Not in public of course. In fact she didn't see him until a few days after she had moved her things to the Nelsons', but then he overtook her on Lavender Hill one morning as she walked down to Clapham Junction. As soon as she saw the car slow down she took evasive action, but she wasn't quick enough. He was out of the car and running after her before she had even turned the corner on to St John's Road.

'Helen.' He caught her up outside Arding & Hobbs and grabbed her arm.

Terrified they would be seen Helen shrank back against the sandbagged window.

Mistaking her concern for fear of physical assault he dropped her arm abruptly. 'I'm sorry,' he said stiffly. 'I need to talk to you. I know I behaved badly that day,' he said, 'but it won't happen again. Come back to Cedars House. It's not the same without you.'

Helen shook her head. 'I can't,' she said. 'I'm sorry but I just can't. It's not right. For me. Or for your family.'

He looked annoyed. 'It's up to me to decide what's right for my family. As for you, I've apologised, what more do you want?' It was obviously a rhetorical question because before she could answer he went on irritably, 'I don't understand you, Helen. You are a sensible girl. It's quite obvious you are better off with us than at the Nelsons'. I know Alan Nelson well. He works for me. They're nice enough people but you must understand they're not of our class. It's the same with Mrs Frazer. People like that don't really know how to go on.'

Suddenly Helen realised the problem. He was scared to death she would spill the beans to his employees. 'The Nelsons are kind, sincere, trustworthy people,' she said coldly, 'and Katy Frazer is a close friend. But don't worry. I haven't said a word about …' she hesitated '… about what happened.' Although of course Katy had guessed immediately.

'I should think not.' Greville Rutherford flushed slightly, then quickly changed the subject. 'That would be quite unnecessary and most unfair. You were as much to blame as me.'

Helen stared at him incredulously. 'I …'

'Oh yes, and not just that time. You have led me on from the first, with all that smiling and laughing and talk of independence. You can't play with men's affections like that, Helen, and expect to get away with it. Men's urges are stronger than women's and less easy to control. Next time you start flirting with a man you should think about that.' With that he turned on his heel and strode back to his car, leaving Helen standing numbly on the pavement.

She didn't want to think about it. She didn't want to think about anything. She just stood there wishing she was a million miles away.

* * *

25 February 1942

Dear Katy,
I'm sorry I haven't written before but it is so lovely down here, so peaceful, that I didn't want to spoil it by thinking of London. I feel so much better here. At the weekend I took the mud at Weston-super-Mare and it did wonders for my bad leg. I think it might be beneficial for me to stay on a little longer. The Miss Taylors have kindly said they don't mind having me. Now you've got Jen there you don't need me so much, anyway, do you?

Love from Mum.

27 February 1942

Dear Katy,
Just a little note to thank you for the lovely christening party. We thought Malcolm was a darling little baby, and good as gold. I expect you have heard by now that your mother wants to stay on with us a little while. We do feel it might be good for her health, but if you need her there you must let us know and we will encourage her to return. I hope you didn't mind us inviting her in the first place, but she did look so fraught and we thought it might give you and Jen a little break and a little more space too.

With all our love to you all,
Your old friends, Esme and Thelma.

P. S. We had a lovely long letter from Ward today. He sounded very positive and we were rather reassured because in his previous letter he seemed rather brought down. We do hope he's getting enough to eat.

'What do you think?' Katy asked Jen anxiously, showing her the letters. 'Do you think I ought to try and get her to come back?'

Jen shrugged. 'Poor old trout, let her stay there if she wants. Personally, I think we're getting on better without her.'

It was true, Katy realised suddenly, although it seemed a bit disloyal to say so, but things were a hundred per cent easier without her mother fussing about all the time. Especially if Jen carried on doing the shopping before she went to the theatre each day. 'Well, maybe you ought to move into her bedroom,' she said. 'I'm worried you're not getting enough sleep in with Malcolm and me.'

Jen grinned. 'I was hoping you would say that.'

Jack had borrowed a car from a friend to take Louise down to see his parents in Surrey.

'They say driving for pleasure is going to be banned soon,' he said as he settled Louise in the passenger seat, 'but as Johnny's given us half a tank of petrol we might as well make the most of it.'

Louise nodded, but she wasn't sure if going to see Jack's parents was really her idea of pleasure. It was more like a duty, and a particularly terrifying duty at that. So terrifying in fact that she barely spoke as they sped out of London on virtually empty roads.

They were through Streatham and well on their way to Purley, passing the bombed-out perfume factory by Croydon airport, when Jack noticed his fiancée's unaccustomed silence.

'Are you all right, sweetheart? I'm not going too fast for you, am I?'

Anything faster than a snail's pace would be too fast, Louise thought, but she shook her head. 'No, I suppose I'm just a bit nervous about meeting your parents, that's all.'

'Goodness, you don't need to be nervous,' Jack said. 'They'll love you, and I hope you'll like them too. I'm sure you will.' He smiled. 'You should do, because they're just like me.'

Louise smiled dutifully, but it occurred to her that she didn't really know what 'just like him' was. The truth was that she didn't really know him. In some ways he was so tough and brave. He hadn't flinched about asking her father formally for her hand in marriage, and he talked so confidently about the navy, the ships, the prospect of going to sea and experiencing some real action. He could hardly wait to drop his first depth charge on some unsuspecting U-boat.

In other ways, however, he seemed unusually sensitive. He was so well mannered, polite almost to the point of prudishness. Even now they were formally engaged he hadn't kissed her. Not properly. And yet she was sure from the way he looked at her sometimes that he fancied her like mad.

It was 1 March and as they left the straggling buildings of Croydon and turned south the sun came out suddenly, casting a bright silvery light on to the road. Most of the trees on the steeply wooded hillsides were bare against the pale blue sky but here and there pink and white blossom hung on the smaller trees like confetti.

Louise sighed and leaned back in her seat, half closing her eyes against the light. It was nice to be out of London even if there was an ordeal ahead. Turning her head slightly she looked at Jack. She had been disappointed that he wasn't in uniform when he had arrived at Cedars House earlier, but now she realised she liked his more casual appearance. Above the tweed jacket with leather elbows, checked shirt and old school tie, he looked relaxed and happy. Happier than she had ever seen him, in fact, and she knew with a flicker of excitement that it was being with her that made him smile like that. Even as she watched he turned his head slightly and caught her gaze.

'What are you looking at?' he asked.

She felt a blush trickle into her cheeks. 'You,' she replied.

'And?'

She smiled innocently. 'And what?'

He laughed softly. 'And do you mind if I kiss you?'

Louise blinked. That wasn't what she had expected him

to say at all. 'No,' she stammered, flushing wildly now. 'Of course not.' As he reached a hand behind her head and drew her towards him she had a moment's alarm that they would crash while his eyes were off the road, and then, just as his lips touched hers, she realised that they were in fact stationary already.

It was a gentle kiss, gentle and to be honest a bit tentative, but that didn't stop her heart accelerating wildly in her chest and she barely dared to breathe for danger of spoiling it.

'Oh Louise,' he murmured, drawing back. 'You're so lovely.'

So was he. She was shocked by how much she wanted him. Even now as he took her hand and held it gently to his cheek she longed for him to shove her back against the seat, longed to feel the power of his body, longed for him to rip her clothes off and make love to her as though there was no tomorrow.

But there was a tomorrow and there was a today. Already he was regretfully giving her back her hand and straightening his tie self-consciously. Trying to control her sudden craving passion, she took a slow breath and looked out of the window.

They seemed to be parked halfway down somebody's driveway. Ahead of them a lovely old ivy-covered house sprawled behind a wide sweep of gravel.

'Where are we?' she asked.

He smiled and started the car. 'We're here,' he said, letting in the clutch and running the car out of the trees and on to the gravel.

Louise gaped. 'This is your parents' house?' She had no idea it was going to be so grand. As she blinked in amazement, the enormous front door swung open and a smiling grey-haired lady ran down the steps accompanied by two equally smiling Labradors.

'Darlings, you've made it. How exciting.' She was hugging Jack before he was even out of the car, and then to her astonishment Louise found herself being hugged too. 'And you must be Louise. Oh, what a pretty girl, Jack. We're so glad you could come. We've been dying to meet you. Down, dogs! Ferdie, stop it! Oh dear, I am sorry, Louise, I'm afraid he does do that sometimes, but we are all so excited, aren't we, boys? Now do come in. Lunch is all ready but we thought we'd crack open a bottle of champers first. By way of celebration.'

And so it went on. After the stuffiness of her own parents, Louise could hardly believe it. Jack was laughing. One of the dogs was barking, the other was thrusting its nose up her skirt. Four other people had been invited to lunch and they were already well into the sherry in the beautiful drawing-room overlooking the sweeping lawns at the back of the house.

Somewhere along the line Mr Delmaine appeared and poured generous measures of champagne and everyone toasted the engagement with great gusto and Louise found herself smiling and laughing along with the best of them. Everyone was so nice and so friendly and so interested in her, and they obviously adored Jack. Even the dogs insisted on lying right on his feet all through lunch, and when he took Louise down to the lake afterwards they bounded at his heels and barked insistently for sticks to be thrown into the water so they could fetch them and swim them back triumphantly to him and shake all over him as they waited for the next turn.

Feeling immensely happy Louise sat on a carved wooden bench and watched him. I love him, she thought. I really love him. And I love his home and his family. This is what I want life to be like. She closed her eyes for a moment and let the future drift towards her, the wedding, a white dress, bridesmaids, the honeymoon, Jack's beautiful body, making love, a lovely house like this, not quite as big perhaps, but definitely ivy clad, children playing on the lawn, dogs, Jack earning lots of money, endless champagne …

She stopped abruptly as a shadow fell across her. Opening her eyes she saw Jack standing in front of her. Lovely, bright-eyed Jack, his golden hair tousled from the game with the dogs, a cautious smile on his lips.

'Louise, darling, I want to ask you something.' He put a hand into his trouser pocket and drew out a small box. 'Mummy has given me this. She thought it might make a nice engagement ring. I think it belonged to my grandmother, but if you'd rather have something new, you must say, and just keep this for parties and things.'

Louise took the box and opened it. Inside nestling on a piece of rather limp cotton wool was the most exquisite ring she had ever seen. A simple gold band supported an intricate antique setting of small rubies and diamonds.

'Oh Jack,' Louse whispered, and then to her dismay she burst into tears.

At once Jack was on his knees beside her. 'Louise, what is it? Don't you like it?'

Sniffing manfully she smiled blearily at him. 'I love it,' she said. 'I'm only crying because I'm so happy.'

'So am I,' he said, and taking her hand he slipped the ring on to her third finger. Then he looked up at her and his blue eyes were sparkling with tears too. 'I've never been so happy in all my life.'

Chapter Twelve

It was March and suddenly London was full of Americans. In the centre, around Leicester Square and Piccadilly Circus they were everywhere, in the shops, in the cafés, and more than anything they were on the streets, hanging around, smoking and laughing and watching the girls go by.

For Jen, getting to the theatre without verbal molestation was increasingly difficult, and getting home again was like some kind of crazy human assault course. The theatre management loved it. Ticket sales soared and an extra man was taken on to hold back the throng of stage door Yankees waiting for the showgirls to emerge.

As a soloist, albeit a minor one, Jen had her fair share of admirers but, following the example of the principals in the show, she tried to stay aloof, and although she was happy to autograph the proffered programmes, she refused to respond to the banter and invitations that rose to a crescendo as she left the theatre each evening.

Some of the chorus girls, on the other hand, thrived on the attention and giggled endlessly in the wings, to the irritation of the rest of the cast, about Hank and Walt and Dirk and other ridiculous names.

'Good God,' the leading lady remarked to Jen after one particularly distracting burst of backstage laughter. 'You'd think the little scrubbers had never seen men before.'

Pleased to be singled out, Jen nodded in agreement. But when the little scrubbers started sporting new nylons, which were impossible to find in the shops any more, and ostentatiously smoking Lucky Strike cigarettes in the dressing-rooms, she began to think she might be missing out.

'How far do you reckon I'd have to go to get a couple of lipsticks off them?' she asked Katy one night as they sat chatting over a cup of Horlicks.

Katy looked dubious. 'You'd better be careful,' she said. 'The papers are full of how violent they are. Some poor man bumped into one of them the other night in the blackout, and when he started to apologise the American flattened him.'

Jen laughed. 'That's what'll happen to Lorenz if Dad gets to hear about all those Sunday lunches he's having with Mum over the road.'

'Jen, don't, that would be awful.'

'Not as awful as having Lorenz as a stepfather.'

Katy was gaping now. 'You don't think they ... ?'

'Who knows?' Jen said. 'Frankly, who cares? I certainly don't. She can do what she bloody likes as far as I'm concerned. All I'm interested in at the moment is a couple of new pairs of nylons and a nice red lipstick.' She grinned suddenly. 'So don't be surprised if I'm a bit late home one of these days.'

By the middle of March, Helen had begun to think that Ward Frazer's escape plans must have been foiled. Despite her embarrassment about her own disappointing foray into the undercover world, she had forced herself to ask everyone she could think of in the organisation if they had heard anything at all about an escape attempt from Oflag 1XA. But although the intelligence grapevine was humming with rumours about an imminent commando assault on the Nazi submarine base at St Nazaire in France, there was no word about any missing prisoners-of-war.

Discovering about the highly confidential St Nazaire raid, however, caused Helen problems of its own. She was finding her new liaison role between the SOE and General de Gaulle's Free French headquarters difficult enough as it was.

The SOE had an ambivalent attitude towards the French. As representatives of a defeated nation they were considered to be untrustworthy. Popular opinion said they had let Britain down once before and might well do so again. It didn't help Helen's own morale problem to discover that one of the additional reasons for the SOE distrust was that earlier in the war a Free French agent had been flown to Morlaix for a mission in Brittany and at the last minute had refused to jump.

Their dashing uniforms, eye for the girls, and general disinclination to learn or speak English didn't help their popularity among British men, and the York Minster pub in Soho where they tended to congregate was generally considered to be an iniquitous den of vice.

On the other hand the Free French represented a potentially important fighting force and a crucial link to Occupied Europe and as such, within reason, they had to be kept sweet. It was Helen's job to tell them what was going on. Only the mundane things of course; all the really top secret stuff went on at a higher level. Nevertheless, under the guise of giving information she was expected to keep her ear to the ground on their side of the intelligence fence to ensure there weren't plans afoot of which the SOE knew nothing.

It had only taken her a couple of visits to de Gaulle's headquarters in Carlton Gardens to realise that her so-called liaison role was a bit of a farce. Her opposite number in the Bureau Centrale de Renseignements et d'Action, Jean-Claude Monet, a young French captain with intelligent eyes and an enormous beaky nose, knew it too.

'Come on, Hélène.' Jean-Claude smiled wearily as he drained his small cup of rich black French coffee. 'We both know there is to be a commando attack on St Nazaire. We both know your organisation is involved. We both know the Resistance will play a part. Now will you tell me when it is due or do I have to find out from other sources?'

Helen sighed. They both knew he could almost certainly find out from other sources. The proliferation of secret units all operating on more or less the same territory was a nightmare for security. There were so many leaks and releaks that sometimes Helen wondered why the powers that be didn't just put the information in *The Times* and be done with it.

'I don't have any information about any such raid,' she said now.

To her surprise Jean-Claude stood up. 'Then we are wasting our time.' He saw her dismay and raised his shoulders in a typically Gallic gesture. 'I am sorry, Hélène. I have enjoyed our meetings but there is no point in continuing if we are to always be treated as second-class citizens.'

Helen stared at him in disbelief. He couldn't just stop. Could he?

Clearly he could. Already he was opening the door for her politely, but before she could move there was a commotion in the passage outside. She couldn't see exactly what was happening but a burst of hilarity preceded some kind of struggle and then a box flew into the room, burst open on landing and scattered dozens of tiny brown packets across the floor.

'*Merde!*' someone shouted, and then suddenly the room was full of men. Some uniformed young Free French officers were already scrabbling on the floor, others stood by the door laughing. It was a moment before they realised that a lady was unexpectedly present and then the laughter ceased abruptly.

Helen was more taken aback by the sudden shocked silence than by the initial invasion. Aware that every pair of eyes was on her she covered her embarrassment by crouching down quickly and scooping up some of the packets nearest to her. Nobody else moved.

Standing up again she glanced around for someone to give them to, but now nobody was looking at her, they were all staring rigidly at the contents of her cupped hands.

For a moment she couldn't think what was wrong. Even Jean-Claude was avoiding her gaze. Casting around helplessly, it was only when she read the word '*Capotes*' scrawled on the fallen lid of the box on the floor that it dawned on her belatedly what the packets must contain. What the English called French letters.

To her dismay she felt colour flood her cheeks although actually it wasn't so much the contents of the packets that embarrassed her as the fact that it had taken her so long to work out what they were.

She felt she had been standing there for hours but it was in fact probably only a couple of seconds before one of the men took pity on her. Stepping forward from the doorway he cupped his own hands under hers. '*Donnez-les moi, mademoiselle*,' he murmured. Then, as she opened her hands and let the beastly things fall into his, he smiled. 'These should see me through the weekend.'

He spoke in French, probably assuming that as she was in the building she must either be French or at least speak it. Or perhaps he didn't speak English.

Unfortunately Helen found she couldn't speak at all. She wanted to thank him. She wanted to brush the incident off as a joke as he had done, but she couldn't do anything. One quick glance into his face had rendered her utterly tongue tied.

She couldn't look at him again. The best she could manage was a gruff '*Merci*,' as she edged away from him towards the door.

At once Jean-Claude leaped into action, hastening to her side to escort her from the room.

At the door she glanced back curiously at the man who

had come to her aid. He was already depositing the French letters he had taken from her on to the table but she couldn't help noticing that even as a couple of the young officers reached forward eagerly, he surreptitiously slid a couple of packets into his own pocket.

She frowned. That first glance had made her think he was handsome, but he wasn't. Not classically so at least. His features were too strong for traditional filmstar good looks, his nose a little too prominent, his chin too firm.

It was a distinctive face, though, a hard face, the high, almost aristocratic cheekbones softened only by the long eyelashes and a coolly sensuous mouth. The clothes he wore, a dark jacket and short grey flannels, didn't seem to suit, or indeed fit his strong, broad-shouldered frame. For a moment Helen was surprised by a faint sense of disappointment and wondered why she had been so affected by him before.

And then, as he glanced back at her, she knew at once.

It was his eyes. Behind those soft lashes his gaze was self-possessed and utterly direct. She had never seen such a strength of purpose reflected in someone's eyes before. What's more he was clearly quite unfazed that she had seen him pocket the contraceptives. He simply smiled faintly and nodded her a courteous '*Au revoir.*'

As she muttered an awkward response, she felt oddly humbled by those eyes. Instinctively she knew they belonged to a man who knew what he wanted and got it. Not just in terms of women but in terms of life. There was energy, passion, and even perhaps a hint of frustration there, as though there were barriers in place that even he couldn't overcome.

Chiding herself for being fanciful she turned away quickly and followed Jean-Claude down the passage.

'I'm sorry, Hélène,' Jean-Claude said at the front door. 'Very sorry.' He was clearly mortified by the incident. 'The young officers ...' He shrugged expressively, a mixture of distaste and apology.

'It doesn't matter,' Helen said.

'You will come tomorrow?' Jean-Claude said. 'I did not mean what I said about wasting time.'

Helen blinked. She had forgotten about their earlier impasse. Jean-Claude, however, was now clearly too embarrassed to refuse to see her again, so one good thing had come out of her awkwardness. At least she didn't have to go back to Angus McNaughton and say she had failed again.

'All right,' she said. 'I'll come tomorrow.'

That night, instead of scrubbing her face bare when the last show came down, Jen left some of the stage make-up on. Before leaving the dressing-room, she stared grimly at herself in the mirror. 'Think of the nylons,' she said and took a deep breath.

As usual the little posse of Americans had congregated at the stage door.

'Hey, darling, you were great. Can't we buy you a drink?'

Checking to make sure that none of the principals were in the vicinity, Jen squared her shoulders and smiled brightly. 'Okay.'

They were so used to her brushing off the offer that her unexpected acceptance caught them off guard. Suddenly, instead of potential rapists, Jen saw them for the young awkward lads they were. She laughed as she peered at them through the darkness. 'Are you boys old enough for a pub or am I going to have to bring you out some lemonades?'

'No, Mam, we're old enough,' one of them responded hastily, reaffirming her belief that Americans had no sense of humour.

Eager to move away from the stage door, she rubbed her hands pointedly. 'So where are we going, then?'

There was a pause. 'Do you know any nice places?' one of them asked her hopefully.

She shook her head. 'Not round here.'

Eventually they took her to a shabby pub off Long Acre. There then ensued a debate about which of them would buy Jen's drink, and yet another about what they would have themselves. While the barman drummed his fingers on the bar irritably waiting for a decision, Jen thanked her lucky stars that there was only about twenty minutes to closing time.

Once they were all equipped with their drinks, they exchanged names, made a few polite remarks about the King and Winston Churchill and then looked at Jen expectantly.

At first Jen was at a loss as to what to talk to them about, but then she hit on the ingenious trick of asking them each where they came from. Immediately they would then launch into a proud travelogue about the wonders of Denver, Colorado or Tampa, Florida or Salt Lake City, Utah.

Rather to her surprise, Jen found that the avid stage-door attendance was more to do with boredom than lust. When they were sent to England they thought they were going straight into action, Dirk explained, but now they found themselves stuck in drab old London with plenty of money and nowhere to spend it. The shops were virtually empty. The pubs were unfriendly and served warm beer. The clubs were mostly reserved for officers. The PX canteen served better food than they could get in restaurants. The cinemas were showing films they considered to be out of date and they had no taste for serious theatre.

Variety shows like the one Jen was in offered some relief from the boredom, but what they really wanted, Steve from Salt Lake City confessed, was to find a cosy English pub where they would feel real welcome. One which served cold American beer, Dirk added with a wide big-toothed grin, and preferably full of pretty girls eager to meet nice young Americans.

Jen laughed. 'I know just the place,' she said.

They looked amazed. 'You do?'

'Sure I do,' Jen said borrowing one of their favourite phrases. 'It's called the Flag and Garter and it's in my sunny home state of Clapham. Hey,' she put on a Texas drawl and grinned round at them, 'why don't you all come on down, Sunday? It's a bit of a hike but what the hell, you'll love it when you get there.'

Katy was appalled. 'But I haven't got any American beer.'

'Aaref will get that for you on the quiet,' Jen said airily. 'I bumped into him on the way home.'

'If old Rutherford gets to hear of this, I'll be dead,' Katy wailed. 'And what about these girls you promised them, where are they coming from?'

Jen grinned. 'I'll get some of the girls in the chorus to come, and I thought your Molly Coogan could provide the rest. There must be some off-duty nurses who'd like to meet some lovely Yankees on a Sunday night.'

'But are they lovely?' Katy asked dubiously. The last thing she wanted was a lot of rowdy American louts wrecking the place.

'Well, they're tall with white teeth,' Jen said. 'What more do you want?'

The next day Angus McNaughton gave Helen permission to tell Jean-Claude in strictest confidence that the St Nazaire raid would take place some time the following week.

Jean-Claude was pleased. 'Good. Perhaps we can now give you some information about St Nazaire. One of our men used to work in the docks there.'

Helen felt cheered. This was just the sort of co-operation the SOE were seeking. For the first time in months she felt she had been of some use, and then as she began to think about who in the organisation Jean-Claude's man should best talk to, she had a thought.

'It's not the man I met yesterday, is it?' she asked. 'The one who … er … helped me?'

Jean-Claude burst into laughter. '*Mon Dieu!* Hélène, you make me laugh. You think the man you met yesterday looks like a dock worker?'

Helen shrugged. 'Well, he looked quite strong and he was wearing rather strange clothes.'

Jean-Claude found this even more hilarious. 'Hélène. I assure you. This man is not a dock worker.'

'Well, who is he, then?'

Jean-Claude lowered his voice. 'This was André Cabillard,' he said. 'He only arrived two days ago.'

The name meant nothing to Helen. 'Arrived from where?'

'From Spain,' Jean-Claude said. 'Before that from France. He sailed a small boat from St Tropez to Barcelona, then came from Santander by merchant vessel.' As Helen's eyes widened, Jean-Claude shrugged. 'This is why he was wearing as you say strange clothes. He had no room in his boat for *haute couture*, only for some of his family's heirlooms to save them from the Germans.'

'So now he is joining the Free French?'

Jean-Claude shrugged and spread his hands. 'Perhaps. Tomorrow he will talk with *le Général*.'

Will he indeed, Helen thought as she walked the familiar route back to Baker Street. This André Cabillard was clearly no slouch. Nor apparently was he just another bit of cannon fodder. It was inconceivable that General de Gaulle interviewed every possible recruit personally, so what was so special about André Cabillard, she wondered sourly, that caused him to get special treatment? She didn't somehow imagine that the autocratic, imperious General de Gaulle would be much influenced by a sexy voice and a pair of shockingly direct midnight-blue eyes.

For the first time in ages Helen was smiling as she turned into Kendrick Place and entered the small doorway which was the back entrance to the SOE headquarters.

She was still smiling when one of the new young cipher clerks called her name. She stopped smiling abruptly when she heard what he had to say.

'You know you were asking about escapes?' he murmured. 'Well, something has come in from Bletchley Park. A break out from a train near Dresden this morning. It seems they were moving prisoners from one camp to another.'

'And?'

'It's not confirmed of course, but it sounds as though there was some shooting. At least two prisoners died. It's not clear how many got away, if any.'

Helen swallowed. 'When do you think we might know?'

He shrugged. 'If they put out descriptions to the Abwehr, we'll know some got away. Otherwise we wait for the Red Cross.'

'But they haven't put out descriptions yet?'

He shook his head. 'Not that Bletchley Park have heard, but then it takes time for Jerry to count up and ascertain who's missing. I doubt the other prisoners are very forthcoming in these cases.'

Helen closed her eyes for a second and he frowned. 'Are you all right?'

'Yes,' she said. 'I'm fine. Let me know if you hear more. And thanks. Thanks very much.' But she wasn't all right. She suddenly felt rather faint, and turning on her heel she went quickly into the washrooms. I can't tell Katy, she said to herself as she doused her face with cold water. I can't. Not yet. It's not fair.

'What is the matter with Aunty Helen?' George asked Pam as they sat together in the café having elevenses on Saturday morning. 'Why does she talk in her sleep?'

'I don't know,' Pam said. 'Sometimes when you are anxious about things they come into your dreams and then you can say things in your sleep without knowing.'

George was silent for a moment. 'Do I say things in my sleep?'

Pam smiled. 'I've never heard you.' She was lifting her toast to take a bite when she saw his thoughtful expression and put it down again. 'Why?' she asked. 'Are you anxious about something?'

'Not really,' he said.

Pam looked at him. 'You can tell me,' she said gently. 'Even if it's only a tiny thing.'

He kicked the leg of his chair a few times then looked up. 'It's about Katy's baby,' he said. 'Malcolm.'

Pam waited.

'Well, I know he's only a baby now but when he grows up he will call you Aunty Pam, won't he?'

'I suppose so,' Pam agreed, puzzled.

George frowned. 'Well, I call you Aunty Pam.'

Pam nodded. 'I know you do ...'

'It's not fair,' he burst out suddenly. 'I don't see why baby Malcolm should call you the same.'

Pam stared at him. She didn't know what to say. She had thought she had proved to him over the last few weeks that he came first in her affections. Then as he raised his eyes pleadingly to hers she felt a jolt of excitement. 'Maybe you'd like to call me something else,' she said cautiously. 'Something more special?'

Another long pause ensued during which Joyce Carter approached to clear their cups. Catching her eye Pam shook her head and with a startled look Joyce withdrew.

'I know I'm not your real mother,' Pam said hesitantly to his bowed head, 'but I sort of am your mummy now . . .'

'"Mummy" is a bit babyish,' George said abruptly.

Pam hid her disappointment carefully, but before she could speak George had looked up again. 'What about Mum?' he said. 'Would you mind if I called you that? Some people at school call their parents Mum and Dad.'

Pam felt tears stinging the backs of her eyes. 'Of course

I wouldn't mind,' she said gravely. 'I'd like it. I'd like it very much.'

'Do you think Uncle Alan would mind if I called him Dad?'

'I think he'd be delighted.'

'And I'd be the only person allowed to call you that?'

Pam smiled. 'Well, yes, of course you would, darling.'

George nodded. 'Good,' he said. 'Then everyone will know you love me best.'

At first, Jen thought the inaugural Sunday evening American Night at the Flag and Garter on 22 March was going to be an unmitigated disaster. It wasn't that the preparations had not gone well, because they had. Everything had worked out just as Jen planned. Thanks to Aaref Hoch there were six crates of pale American beer, and there was a huge American flag draped over the entrance. American music played on the gramophone Katy had borrowed from Louise. There was even a small posse of sensibly clad off-duty nurses and a number of less sensibly clad chorus girls eyeing each other dubiously as they waited hopefully at the bar. The only thing they were lacking was Americans.

As she tried to jolly the girls up a bit, Jen was aware that Katy was avoiding her eye. She knew Katy had had to buy the beer outright and if it didn't get drunk she was going to suffer. Certainly none of the locals seemed interested in it. They were far more interested in half a pint of Rutherford & Berry bitter and a good gawp at the girls to go with it.

When Aaref Hoch came in the girls brightened, but as one of the chorus girls remarked loudly, 'One bloke isn't going to last long among us lot, is he?'

'He's not going to last any of you,' Molly Coogan hissed from behind the bar. 'He's my feller and he's not up for grabs.'

Jen was surprised. 'I thought that was all over,' she said

to Katy. 'I thought she was never going to speak to him again.'

Katy smiled wanly. 'He asked her to go with him to the pictures and she couldn't resist.' She bit her lip and for perhaps the hundredth time she glanced at the door. 'Jen, I don't like to say this, but … ?'

Jen groaned inwardly. 'They'll come,' she said. 'They promised.'

To everyone's abject relief, twenty anxious minutes later they did come. An enormous utility van with a great white USA painted on its black sides drew up outside with a screech of brakes. Two soldiers jumped down from the cab.

Oh God, Jen thought. Only two. She recognised one of them as Steve from Salt Lake City, or was it Kirk from Colorado, and ran for the door.

'Hey, did we have one hell of a time finding this place,' Steve or Kirk called jovially as he locked up the cab.

'Well, you're here now,' Jen called back. Thank God. At least two was better than none at all. She smiled gratefully at the other soldier. 'Come on in.'

'Sure,' he said. 'Just let me let the other boys out of the back.' To Jen's amazement he flipped down the back of the truck and about twenty tall, grinning soldiers leaped out into the street and converged on the doorway.

'Oh, my word. I've just died and gone to heaven,' one of the chorus girls said behind her.

Backing up hastily in the face of the onslaught, Jen laughed. 'Doreen, let me introduce Kirk from Colorado.'

The handsome young American shook his head sadly. 'You never get it right, Jen. You know something? I reckon deep down you don't care.' He grinned briefly at the simpering Doreen. 'Hi. I'm Dirk from Seattle, Washington State.' Then as his compatriots headed for the bar, he winked at Jen. 'I guess I'll save the girls for later, where's the beer?'

* * *

'Miss de Burrel?'

Helen looked round sharply as someone called her name softly up the passage. When she saw it was the young cipher clerk she turned round quickly and walked back to him. 'Any news?'

'Yes and no. Jerry has been tight with information on this one, but we've got names from the Red Cross of the four escapees who were recaptured.'

Helen took the proffered sheet of paper. Staring at it blankly, it took her a ridiculously long time to see that there was no 'Flight Lieutenant Ward Frazer' or anything like it on the list.

The cipher clerk produced a second piece of paper. 'I have some other descriptions here,' he said: 'One: short man, blond with scar on left cheek. Two: tall man, dark hair, grey eyes, slight limp. Three: Tall, older man, grey curly hair, blue eyes. All were armed and considered a danger to the Reich. Do any of those fit the bill?'

Helen swallowed. Tall man, dark hair, grey eyes, slight limp. Armed and dangerous. That sounded awfully like Ward Frazer. He had told Katy in his letters that although his injuries were mended he still had stiffness in one leg.

'Where did you get that list?' she asked abruptly. 'It's not the dead, is it?'

'Lord no.' The cipher clerk looked surprised. 'Bletchley Park intercepted it from an SS alert. It's the escapees.'

Helen hesitated. 'Number two sounds pretty close.'

He grinned cheerfully. 'Well, in that case it looks as though our man's on the run.'

Pam sat at the kitchen table and stared at the calendar. Alan was out on Home Guard duty. Helen was working a late shift at her so-called office. George was asleep in bed, the paw of his Christmas teddy as usual clutched in one hand.

And Pam was sitting at the kitchen table with a cup of

Bovril and a strange shaking sensation somewhere in the region of her stomach.

She must have got it wrong. She must have missed a week somewhere. She must have miscalculated. Suddenly she checked back to make sure 1942 wasn't a leap year, but it wasn't. In that case she must just be late.

But she knew perfectly well that she was never late. Never. For those four long years when she and Alan had been so desperate, her heart had sunk regularly as clockwork on the morning of the twenty-ninth day.

Since Alan had had the tests and been told he was not capable of fathering a child she had stopped checking. And, oddly, the relief from constantly frustrated hope had been almost greater than the disappointment of knowing they would never have children of their own.

And then Sheila had died in the bombing and they had inherited George.

George. George who over the last few weeks had turned from a whining, scratchy bag of nerves into a sunny endearing little child. George, who now called her Mum almost without thinking. Little, vulnerable George who hated babies.

At that moment the door opened and Alan came in, clumping up the passage in his heavy boots. Dropping his kitbag on the floor, he took one look at her and stepped forward quickly.

'Sweetheart? What is it? You look as though you've seen a ghost.'

Pam felt a lump in her throat and didn't know if it was dread or a terrible shocked excitement. She knew she shouldn't tell him. Not yet. It would be cruel to raise Alan's hopes, only to have them dashed. He had suffered enough one way and another. Much better to wait until she was sure. Then they could decide what to do.

Taking a valiant grip on herself, Pam pushed all her anxieties to the back of her mind and stood up. 'I'm fine,' she said. 'I'll make you a Bovril. You must be gasping after a night on patrol.'

Chapter Thirteen

Despite the loss of quite a number of commandos, the raid on St Nazaire was considered to be a success. On 27 March, defying heavy fire, the specially strengthened destroyer *Campbeltown* sailed up the Loire estuary to ram the dock gates at twenty knots. Five tons of explosives then put the important dry dock out of action and the Nazi U-boat base was left a raging inferno. The French Resistance played a part in the attack, but although information given by the Free French ex-St Nazaire dock worker helped enormously in the planning of the raid, Jean-Claude made it quite clear to Helen that the Free French in London were piqued that they had not been involved in the action.

It was as she once again walked back to Baker Street after a rather unsatisfactory meeting that Helen became aware of the unnerving sensation that someone was following her. Forgetting all the lessons learned in Scotland just a few weeks ago, she stopped abruptly and swung round to stare down the street behind her. The pavement was quite crowded with people, as usual nowadays the number of uniforms exceeding the number of people in civilian dress; just in this short stretch she could see three different-coloured berets – green for commandos, maroon for airborne and two dark blue of the exiled Polish forces. But there was no sign of anyone particularly interested in her. There was nobody staring suspiciously into any shop window. No one hiding behind the fruit and veg. stall on the corner.

Feeling stupid, Helen walked on, but the prickling sensation at the back of her neck remained, and knowing that she shouldn't lead any unwelcome tail to the SOE headquarters, instead of turning left in Portman Square as she normally did, she turned right and marched briskly along Wigmore Street.

By the time she reached the Wigmore Hall she was convinced she was over-reacting. She had done all the tricks of looking for reflections in shop windows, pausing to retie her shoe, glancing at her watch and quickening her step but none of her manoeuvres had apparently discomfited anyone behind her and she was forced to conclude that her prickling neck was merely a manifestation of her general loss of confidence. She had felt very unsure of herself ever since her abortive parachute jump, and the news of Ward Frazer's escape hadn't helped. She had been dreading telling Katy, although actually when the moment came Katy had taken it remarkably well.

Now as Helen turned round and headed back towards Baker Street, she berated herself for being so ridiculously jumpy. Who would want to follow her anyway? The only person interested in her these days was blasted Greville Rutherford. Even that rather sexy Frenchman André Cabillard had barely given her a second glance.

Giving one last check over her shoulder, she put her hand out to open the discreetly unmarked door and then nearly fainted in terror as someone grabbed her shoulders from behind and put his hands over her eyes.

'Long time no see,' a voice whispered in her ear.

Helen felt her whole body go rigid. As her assailant took his hands away and swung her round to face him, she stared in amazement. It was Paul. Paul whom she had last seen throwing himself from the plane while she clung to the fuselage, sobbing.

Amused by her shock, he glanced round with interest. 'So this is where the brains behind our esteemed organisation hang out, is it?' He grinned. 'Thanks for showing me the way.'

'I find it hard to believe that as the SOE star pupil you didn't already know the whereabouts of your own headquarters,' Helen retorted.

He laughed. 'And I find it hard to believe that someone who has attended one of the SOE special training schools couldn't make a better effort to throw off a tail.'

Helen laughed too. 'Oh, but what a tail,' she said, widening her eyes in a parody of admiration. She had heard only last week that Paul had completed the training programme with flying colours throughout.

'So am I allowed in?'

She shook her head. 'Not unless you have special permission from Major Buckmaster. Agents aren't really meant to know anything about HQ.'

'You would have known quite a bit, wouldn't you?'

'Well, yes, but I didn't make it, did I?'

He shrugged. 'That bloody parachuting. It nearly killed me too.'

But it didn't, Helen thought, did it? Paul had done the jump despite his fear. That was the difference between them.

'I was sorry to see you go off the course. I thought we would have made a good team in France, you and me.'

He sounded genuine and she wondered why the remark sent shivers up her spine. Was it the idea of being in France or the idea of being with Paul? I'm a snob, she thought. He's a good-looking, highly competent man. Most women would fall at his feet. It's only his background and accent that's holding me back. Looking at him now, however, she realised it wasn't just that. There was something else about him. Something intense and demanding. Almost devilish. As though, given a chance, he would take more than your body and your heart. He would take your soul too. She knew some women would find that exciting but Helen found it scary. She didn't want to lose her soul.

'Come for a drink with me?'

'Paul, I can't.'

'Tonight, then, or some time over the weekend?'

'No Paul, really, …' She tailed off. There really was no excuse, and he knew it too.

His eyes narrowed. 'You don't like me, do you?'

'Of course I do,' she said dropping her gaze. 'I admire you enormously, but …'

'Then the least you can do is kiss me goodbye.'

That jolted her. She looked up sharply. 'Goodbye?'

He lifted his shoulders. 'I'm going over. Early next week.'

Helen gulped, but before she could move he had taken her shoulders and drawn her up against him. The kiss was cool, hard and experienced and Helen found it extraordinarily unnerving. She didn't respond but she didn't struggle either. Passivity was the best she could manage, but she knew he could hear her heart hammering in her chest.

'You see now what you've been missing,' he whispered against her lips. Then he kissed her again, lightly, almost flippantly. 'Goodbye, sweet Helen, and thank you. At least now I'll have something to remember when I'm scared and lonely behind enemy lines.'

And then he was gone, quickly and inconspicuously, melting into the crowds on Baker Street, leaving her feeling shaken and uneasy on the SOE doorstep.

Forcing herself to concentrate Katy laboriously totted up the column of figures once more. Then she scribbled the total in the margin, compared it with her previous efforts and groaned aloud.

'I just don't understand it,' she complained to Jen who was gargling noisily with salt and hot water at the sink. 'I used to be quite good at maths at school, but I've added my outgoings up three times now and each time I get a different number.' She stared at the page moodily. 'And all of them are far more than they should be.'

Spitting out the liquid, Jen wiped her mouth on a towel. 'Don't ask me,' she said waspishly. 'I wouldn't know an outgoing from an ingoing. All I know is if I don't get rid of this sore throat pretty bloody sharpish I'll be out of a job.'

'Maybe you should take a couple of days off,' Katy said. 'Give your voice a rest. You have been singing three shows a night virtually nonstop for nearly three months.'

'That's my job,' Jen said. 'That's what I'm paid to do.' She shook her head. 'No, all I need is some hot honey and lemon. That's what I used to have as a kid. But where the hell do you get honey and lemon from nowadays? I haven't seen a lemon for months.'

Katy smiled. 'There is a war on, you know.'

Jen grimaced as she picked up her coat. 'Don't, Katy, please. Don't make me feel guilty. I know I've been moaning on about my throat when you are worried to death about Ward. And about Malcolm. And about your accounts. But this is my career. My livelihood. I just can't afford to keep getting sore throats. If I start missing shows I'll get sacked. It's as simple as that.'

'I didn't mean to make you feel guilty,' Katy said truthfully as Jen pulled on her gloves and headed for the door. 'How could I when you've helped me so much with Malcolm? And as for the accounts, what money there is in the till is only thanks to your Americans. And God knows, nobody can do anything about Ward.' She frowned. 'But I do think you are pushing yourself too hard. Everyone gets the odd cold. I'm sure the producer would understand if you asked for a few days off. You could even go away, have a few days down in Bristol with Mum and the Miss Taylors perhaps?'

Jen was never one to take advice but now at the door she hesitated and ran a hand over the painful glands in her neck. 'Maybe you're right,' she said. 'Even if they wouldn't give me sick leave, I suppose I could ask for a couple of days' holiday.' As she pulled open the door she grinned back at Katy suddenly. 'Thankfully my understudy sings like a dog on heat, so there's not much chance of her usurping my role while I'm away.'

After Jen had gone, Katy tried to refocus her attention on her accounts, but it was easier said than done. For a second she recalled the Miss Taylors' little cottage outside Bristol. The rolling green hills, the wide skies. She remembered the wooded hill behind the village, which she had climbed with Ward one afternoon. She remembered the way he had carried her over a patch of mud and then gone back to lift his aunts' little dog across too. More than anything she remembered that as she sat on the war memorial at the top staring in wonder at the magnificent view, Ward had told her he wanted to make love to her.

She closed her eyes reliving that shocking, wonderful moment. Then she opened them again and almost cried to find herself back in the dingy public room with yesterday's smoke still hanging on the air, the floor sticky underfoot and her account books and receipts spread out in front of her on one of the beer-stained tables.

They hadn't made love of course. Ward was far too much of a gentleman for that. In fact they hadn't made love until their honeymoon a couple of months later, but that moment up on the war memorial had been the turning point.

Suddenly with an almost overwhelming urgency she wanted to revisit that place on the hill, to re-create that moment of breathless excitement. The craving made her grimace almost in pain, but she knew it was impossible. She couldn't possibly get away. Even if she could find someone to stand in for her she couldn't afford to pay them. Now, after seven months of trying to make ends meet, she finally understood why her father had never had a holiday.

She felt like a hamster on a wheel, constantly struggling to get to the top but never achieving it. And there was

Malcolm to think about. He wasn't sufficiently off the danger list yet to traipse him all the way to Bristol. In any case, although it would be nice to see her mother and the Miss Taylors, it wouldn't be the same there without Ward.

Even if Ward did come back it would be impossible to re-create that moment of innocent, unfettered love. Too much had happened since then. Too much worry. Too much waiting. Too much pain.

Looking back at the accounts Katy found her eyes were blurring with tears. Angrily she blew her nose, and trying to blot out of her mind that next week was her first wedding anniversary she gritted her teeth and began totting up her columns again.

'Perhaps I could help you?'

Almost jumping out of her skin Katy swung round to find Jacob standing diffidently by the door watching her. She had no idea how long he had been there but he clearly thought her distress was caused by her inability to add up. As in part it was. But she could hardly ask a fourteen-year-old boy to look after her account books. Jacob did far too much for her already. A couple of nights previously, at nearly midnight as she locked up she had found him sitting on a barrel in the cellar frantically doing his homework for the following day.

He had explained then that he was working hard for exams that might give him a scholarship to Dulwich College or the Emanuel School in Wandsworth. Ultimately, he admitted shyly, he wanted to go to Oxford University to read law.

Katy had been startled by his ambition. Nobody who lived in Lavender Road would ever normally dream of going to Oxford University; even Louise's brothers would probably not aspire to those giddy heights. In any case Bertie Rutherford, after his brief, unpopular period of conscientious objection, was now training to be an officer, and the younger boy, Douglas, was all set to join up when he left school.

'Jacob, no,' Katy said firmly. 'I can't let you do any more. You'll never get your schoolwork done.'

Jacob looked disappointed. 'But you are so unhappy when you do the books, Miss Katy,' he said. 'It would not make me unhappy.'

Katy laughed. She couldn't help it. In his own shy way Jacob was as appealing as his older brother. 'Well,' she said hesitantly, 'maybe you could do the adding up for me. Just this once.' She smiled wryly. 'But you mustn't tell anyone how badly I'm doing.'

Jacob smiled too. 'Perhaps if I do the books you will not be doing so badly after all.'

The last thing in the world Helen wanted to do was to go out again with Louise and Jack and Jack's friend William, but Louise was insistent. 'Oh, go on, Helen. A night out will be good for you. You've been so down recently. I know Ward has escaped and everything, but it's not going to make any difference to him if you stay in or go out, is it?'

The problem was that almost for the first time in her life Louise was genuinely happy and she wanted everyone else to be too. Certainly she didn't want her joy spoilt by long faces and gloomy foreboding.

Jack had decided to push the boat out and book a table at Prunier's. Louise was thrilled, and when the evening came, Helen couldn't help enjoying the rare treat of smoked salmon, braised chicken, chocolate mousse and a desperately expensive bottle of 1937 French wine.

It was as Jack and William ordered cigars to go with their port that Louise leaned over and whispered to Helen that someone was looking at her. 'He's been watching you all evening on and off,' she said. 'At first I thought he knew Jack but it's definitely you he's looking at.'

Helen felt the old prickling sensation on her neck. It's Paul, she thought. It must be. She groaned and caught

Jack's quick glance. How on earth was she going to explain Paul to Jack and Louise?

'He's sitting in the window,' Louise whispered. 'With two other men and a couple of women. He's rather handsome.' She touched Helen's arm. 'Quick, you could look now, they're getting up to leave.'

Helen couldn't look but Louise was still staring across the room. 'Just ignore him, Louise,' she said sharply. 'If it's who I think it is I don't want to talk to him.' She had been unnerved by that last meeting. By that kiss

'Well, you're going to have to,' Louise giggled nervously, 'because he's coming over.'

As her table companions fell abruptly silent, Helen felt a warmth spread over her bare shoulders like a cloak. She could sense his approach. She could almost see him now out of the corner of her eye as he skirted a nearby table. She could feel his eyes on her, she could sense the faint smile playing round his lips. Rigidly she stared at the white starched tablecloth as she racked her brain for something sensible to say.

As soon as he stopped beside her she knew something was wrong. Her reaction was wrong. Her heart was thumping in the wrong way. Shocked, she looked up and knew at once why.

It wasn't Paul at all. It was the aristocratic Frenchman, André Cabillard, last seen slipping a couple of contraceptives into the pocket of his ill-fitting trousers.

Helen couldn't believe it. She stared at him blankly. There was nothing ill fitting about him tonight. On the contrary, he looked distinctly smooth and sophisticated in an extremely well-cut dinner jacket. She felt she should stand up but somehow she had become glued to her seat.

It took her a moment to realise that Jack was not similarly afflicted and had in fact risen rather threateningly to his feet. 'Now, look here ...'

Jerked out of her coma, Helen interrupted hastily,

leaning over to tug at Jack's sleeve. 'No, no, Jack. It's all right. This is someone else. This is someone I met …'

As she tailed off helplessly, the Frenchman smiled at her confusion. 'André Cabillard,' he said, holding out his hand to Jack. 'You don't need to knock me down. I promise I have only met your friend very briefly. And this is a very civilised restaurant.'

This time he spoke in almost perfect English, but it was the same voice she remembered from before. That slight drawl, the underlying hint of humour.

She was so busy watching him shake hands with Jack and William and Louise that she was completely unprepared when he turned to her. 'Lady Helen de Burrel,' he murmured. 'At least now we can be properly introduced.'

Helen blinked. His hand was dry and cool but his eyes were warm for the brief second they caught her gaze at least, and then he was glancing over to his friends who were waiting somewhat impatiently by the door.

Suddenly Helen knew he was going to go, and that would be that. Worse than everything, he now clearly thought she was romantically linked to Jack. Even as she muttered some meaningless platitude, she was desperately trying to think of some inconspicuous way of putting the record straight, but it was Louise who saved the day.

'What a shame you are leaving,' she said brightly. 'You could have joined us for a glass of port.'

He smiled then and glanced at the empty wine bottle which still stood on the table. 'I would have preferred a glass of the Bordeaux.' He grinned briefly at Jack. 'A good choice, I think?' He lifted his shoulders in polite regret. 'Unfortunately my friends are waiting. We are going on to a nightclub. Maybe you know it? It has a suitably French name, Le Petit Club.' He hesitated for a fraction of a second. 'Perhaps you would like to join us there?'

'Oh, do let's.' Louise looked round at the others eagerly.

William nodded good naturedly. Jack glanced doubtfully at Helen.

'Well, I …' she began.

André didn't give her time to finish. 'I will tell Madame Vaughan on the door to expect you. *A bientôt.*' And, raising a casual hand, he was gone.

He had barely turned his back before Louise was on to Helen. 'Goodness.' Her eyes were round with intrigue. 'You're a dark horse. You've kept him pretty quiet.'

'I hardly know him,' Helen said. 'Honestly, I only met him once and even then I …' She stopped, aware that she was sounding flustered. 'Look, we don't have to go to his club. I'm quite happy to go somewhere else.' She glanced at her watch. 'It's quite late. Maybe we ought to think about going home.'

But Louise wouldn't hear of it. 'I've been dying to go to Le Petit Club,' she said. She smiled winningly at Jack. 'Oh, go on, darling. Just to see what it's like. We needn't stay long.'

Jack clearly couldn't resist her smile. 'Only if you promise not to disappear into a dark corner with some sweet-talking Frenchman,' he said, mock severely. 'And only if Helen doesn't mind?'

Louise looked astonished. 'Of course Helen doesn't mind. With those incredibly sexy come-to-bed eyes waiting for her at the other end, Helen would be mad to mind.'

But I am mad, Helen thought as Jack resignedly called for the bill. I am mad enough to wish I had never set eyes on André Cabillard. I am mad enough to wish I hadn't witnessed that incident with the contraceptives at the Free French headquarters. And I am mad enough to hope he's not married.

Le Petit Club was in St James's. It was considerably larger than its name suggested and was presided over by a smart, beady-eyed woman, presumably the Madame Vaughan André had referred to. Directing a minion to take their coats, she led them round the crowded dance floor to the table occupied by André and his friends, the number of which seemed to have grown considerably since they left the restaurant. Already the table seemed far too small to accommodate them. However, as André rose and greeted them with apparent pleasure, more chairs miraculously appeared together with fresh glasses and several bottles of wine. With introductions effected with some difficulty over the music and hubbub of conversation and laughter, they quickly found themselves absorbed into the multinational group.

Somewhat to her dismay, Helen found herself squashed between a vivacious Dutch girl and a French-speaking Pole. Irritated with herself for minding that André had not seated her next to him, she glanced round the table. Two along, Louise was proudly showing off her engagement ring to two aristocratic-looking Frenchwomen while Jack smiled self-consciously beside her. William was struggling along in schoolboy French with a Belgian officer, and up at the other end of the table André was apparently being well entertained by the two prettiest girls there.

No wonder he didn't want me sitting next to him, Helen thought. However, as she attempted to translate into French a joke the Dutch girl was telling, for the benefit of the Pole, she inadvertently glanced back across the table and caught André looking at her. Faltering in her translation, to her horror she felt herself blush and was grateful for the club's low lighting.

Abruptly resuming her explanation of the joke she chided herself for reacting so violently. After all, she had seen plenty of handsome men before. It was just those wickedly direct midnight-blue eyes that made this one so sexy. Nothing more, nothing less. Like all Frenchmen he had an eye for the ladies and Helen knew she was looking pretty good tonight. Louise has insisted they dress up for the evening, and although Helen had groaned at the time, there was no doubt that the off-the-shoulder pre-war Chanel dress still suited her. It was simple but elegant and the string of pearls at her throat set it off perfectly.

Not that she cared what she looked like, she added to herself as André stood up to take one of the girls at the end of the table to dance. He wasn't that handsome anyway. He was too tough looking, his features too strong, his nose too big, his chin too square. It was only that air of confidence that made him seem attractive, that sense of leashed energy, and of course that ridiculously sexy smile.

But when he asked her to dance later, it wasn't his smile that affected her so much as the touch of his fingers on her skin. He had chosen a slow number, a lazy, mournful tune Helen didn't recognise. At first as she moved into his loose embrace she thought she had drunk too much of his delicious wine, but then with belated alarm she realised it was his proximity that made her feel so suddenly languid.

She was so busy fighting a sudden panicked desire to run off the dance floor and out into the street, that it was a moment before Helen realised that André was talking to her. It was more the vibration of his chest that alerted her than his raised voice, because the noise of the club was now such that it was almost impossible to hear anyone speak even if they shouted. Guiltily switching her gaze from the pearl buttons on his crisp white shirt to his face, Helen found to her surprise that he seemed amused by her inattention.

'*Alors*, I won't flatter you any more if you don't want me to.'

Helen stared at him. Had he really been flattering her? The twinkle at the back of his enigmatic eyes made her think that he was teasing, but she couldn't be sure, and as he held her gaze steadily she found she was overwhelmed with a desire to hear his compliments.

But it was too late. Already he was asking why Jack had been so hostile in the restaurant.

'I thought at first he must be your boyfriend,' he said, 'but now I see he has eyes only for Louise.'

She shook her head. 'No, he was just being protective. I thought at first you were somebody else.'

He raised his eyebrows. 'An unwanted admirer?'

'Sort of.'

He smiled. 'It must always be a problem for a pretty girl. And this William,' he said. 'Is he in love with you too?'

'No,' she said. 'William is a friend of Jack's. I've only met him a couple of times before.'

André shrugged. 'I don't think that would necessarily stop him being in love with you.' This time he spoke in French and quite softly, and although she wasn't sure she had caught the words correctly over the general din of music and shouted conversations, Helen felt a strange tightening of her throat. Quickly she looked down, back to her study of his shirt buttons. She didn't know what to say, so she said nothing, and as if aware of her confusion he didn't pursue it. He just drew her slightly closer to him as he moved her on efficiently round the dance floor.

They danced two dances in a row, then as the music subtly changed again, out of the corner of her eye Helen saw Jack glance at his watch and say something to Louise. Suddenly anxious that they were going to go and leave her behind she looked up at André.

'I'm going to have to go in a minute,' she said.

'You can't go yet. I want to talk to you.'

'You were talking to me just now.'

He waved a dismissive hand round the crowded room. 'We can't talk in here. Not properly. It's too noisy. Anyway just now I prefer to hold you in my arms.'

'Oh.' She felt herself blushing and laughed to cover it up. 'That's a good excuse!'

'It's not an excuse,' he said, nodding to Jack who was looking at them expectantly from the table. Courteously, with a hand at her back, he led her off the dance floor, but on the way back to the table he stopped and turned to face her. He suddenly looked quite serious. Almost businesslike. 'But I would like to meet you again, Lady Helen de Burrel.

There is something I want to ask you. What are you doing tomorrow?'

'Tomorrow?' He was nothing if not direct. Tomorrow was Sunday. 'Well,' she stammered. 'Nothing much. I'm not working or anything.'

'So can I come and see you? Perhaps in the evening is best.'

'But I live right down in Clapham,' she said.

'It's no problem.'

Suddenly she felt embarrassed at the thought of him turning up at the Nelsons' shabby little house. 'It's not my home,' she said. 'I'm in lodgings.'

He inclined his head. He was smiling, but under the long soft lashes, his eyes were cold. 'Aren't we all? We have Adolf Hitler to thank for that.' He produced a piece of paper and in silence she wrote down the address.

He barely had time to read it before Louise was on them. 'William's managed to get a taxi,' she said breathlessly. She giggled and glanced coyly at André. 'So *if* you're coming with us, Helen, you'd better hurry.'

'Of course I'm coming,' Helen said. 'I'll just get my bag.'

André escorted them to the door where he shook hands with Jack and William. Then politely in the French manner he kissed the two girls. 'It has been a pleasure,' he said. '*Au revoir. A demain.*'

Chapter Fourteen

Joyce was just about to dish up the Sunday lunch when she heard the front door open. Glancing up the passage, expecting to see Pete coming back from the pub, she did a double take when she saw a soldier pulling off his beret in the hallway.

'Bob?' She stared at her eldest son in amazement.

He grinned and ran a hand through his hair. 'That's me. It's all right, Mum, you needn't look so worried. I'm not AWOL this time. The regiment is off to war and they've given us twenty-four hours' embarkation leave, that's all.' He spread his hands. 'So here I am, and it smells like I got here just at the right moment.'

'But I thought you were still behind bars.'

He shook his head. 'They let me out a couple of weeks ago. I reckon they need all the cannon fodder they can get.'

He spoke lightheartedly but Joyce could tell he was nervous. Suddenly she felt nervous too. For all his faults, Bob had always been her favourite son. 'Where are you going?' she asked.

Unbuttoning his battledress jacket he shrugged. 'We don't know. Not officially. But from the kit they've issued us it's not hard to guess we're destined for the desert.'

'Oh.' Joyce frowned. She'd rather lost track of what was happening in the desert these days. For months the news had been full of a British push and then a British withdrawal and then another push, but for the last few weeks all anyone had heard was about poor little Malta being under siege and this new Arthur Harris fellow at RAF Bomber Command and his round-the-clock bombing of German factories and cities. Perhaps the fact there was no news from the desert was a good sign.

Before she could question him further Pete came in from the pub with a jug of beer. When he saw Bob he stopped so suddenly that some of the beer slid over the side of the jug.

'Well, well, if it's not pea-brained Pete.' Bob punched his younger brother on the shoulder. He glanced at the beer. 'How did you know I was coming?'

Pete grinned. 'I'd have got two if I'd known you was coming.'

Bob laughed. 'Things must be looking up if you can count as far as two.'

While they indulged in brotherly banter Joyce busied herself with the vegetables. In a minute she knew Bob would notice the table was laid for four and—

'So who's coming to lunch?' Bob interrupted her thoughts. 'Jen?'

'No, not Jen,' Joyce said coldly.

'Jen's on holiday,' Pete said. 'She's gone to them old ladies in Bristol. The Miss Taylors.'

'Has she indeed?' Joyce said. 'Nice for some. We'd all like a holiday but not all of us can afford it.' Even with Miss Philips's rent, Pete's contribution and her wages from the café, Joyce was finding things tight. It worried her that the café wasn't making more, but there never seemed to be enough money in the till to pay the bills.

'She'd got a sore throat,' Pete said. 'She thought a few days off might cure it.'

'A bit less razzmatazz with American soldiers might cure it,' Joyce said sourly.

Bob was frowning. 'So who is coming to lunch?'

'Well,' Joyce said, 'Miss Philips, the lodger, is coming.' She hesitated. 'And I've asked Mr Lorenz to pop over too.'

Bob's eyes widened incredulously. 'You've asked that old pawnbroker to lunch? You're joking.'

'She's not joking,' Pete said. 'He comes every Sunday.'

'And what does Dad say about that?' Bob asked.

'He doesn't know,' Joyce said sharply. She put down the saucepan she was holding. 'I'm not interested in what your dad thinks any more.'

'But he'll be out of prison in a year or so,' Bob said. 'What's going to happen then?'

Joyce shrugged and turned back to the sink. 'I don't know.'

Bob stared at her. 'No wonder Jen doesn't come any more,' he said. 'Well, I'm not going to sit down to lunch with a bloody Jew either.'

Joyce swung round angrily. 'That's not why Jen doesn't come. She's not invited, that's why she doesn't come.'

There was a moment's silence then Pete cleared his throat awkwardly. 'Lorenz is a nice bloke,' he said.

'I don't care if he's bloody Jesus Christ himself,' Bob said. 'I can't stand by and watch some other bloke eating in Dad's place. Specially not a Jew.' He took a step towards the door and then stopped. He turned round and stared defiantly at Joyce. 'It's either me or him.'

For a moment as she looked at his stubborn, angry face, suddenly so like his father, Joyce was tempted to say 'him', but then she thought of the desert. All that sand. All those guns. The lorries full of waving soldiers they showed you on the newsreels. And the ones they didn't show you with the big red cross on the side. This might be the last time she saw Bob. She couldn't turn him away.

Silently she dished up a portion of food on to a plate and handed it to Pete. 'Run this over to him,' she said. 'Tell him I'm sorry but he can't come today, and then call Miss Philips. She's upstairs, I heard her come in from church earlier.'

André Cabillard arrived at eight thirty and by that time

Helen had spent over an hour deciding that he definitely wasn't going to come. She knew a lot more about him today than she had known yesterday. It seemed that Louise, intrigued by their enigmatic host, had spent most of the time at Le Petit Club grilling the two Frenchwomen about him.

Helen now knew that he came from one of the best families in France and was in fact heir to several magnificent Provençal wine-producing estates. 'I think she said several,' Louise had giggled in the taxi on the way back to Clapham. 'She might have said seven, but nobody would be heir to seven magnificent estates, would they? Not even your lovely André. No wonder he mentioned the wine.'

'He's not mine,' Helen had replied. 'I hardly know him.'

But now as she glanced at him over the banister as he stood talking to Pam in the hall she realised she was looking forward to knowing him better.

Tonight he was wearing a rather nice wool tweed jacket over a dark roll-necked jersey. It was casual but stylish and Helen was pleased as she went downstairs that she had decided to wear her new nine coupons' worth of sleek navy slacks from Fortnum & Mason and her old but still elegant white Strassner pullover. She didn't want him thinking she was dressing up for him, not on a Sunday night in Clapham, but she didn't want him thinking she was a wartime scruff either.

Hearing her step on the stairs he looked up and smiled. 'Hélène.' He took her lightly by the upper arms, kissed her fleetingly on both cheeks. 'How are you today?'

Out of the corner of her eye Helen caught Pam's rather startled look. Pam Nelson clearly wasn't used to continental manners. Come to think of it she felt rather flustered herself. There was something about André Cabillard that unnerved her badly. The Nelsons' hallway suddenly seemed rather small for the three of them.

'So,' he said. 'Shall we go? I thought the pub opposite looked quite nice.'

Pam smiled. 'Oh, it's very nice,' she said. 'A friend of Helen's runs it.'

'How convenient,' he said. He turned to Helen. 'Then if you are agreeable we will go there?'

It was only as they crossed the road that Helen remembered it was American night at the Flag and Garter, but André didn't seem to mind. 'I like the Americans,' he said as she hesitated at the door. 'I like anyone who will help us get rid of this tyrant in Germany.'

The soldiers in the Flag and Garter showed more sign of getting rid of Katy's American beer than of Adolf Hitler. The pub was packed and throbbing with noise. By the fire three young soldiers had pretty girls sitting on their knees. Behind the bar Katy and Molly Coogan were battling against a mounting tide of orders.

Thankfully there was a small table free in the saloon bar. As André went up to get drinks, Katy slid over to Helen.

'Why's everyone looking at me?' Helen whispered.

Katy giggled. 'This is a pub, you know, not a Hollywood movie set. You can't waltz in here cool as a cucumber with a divine man in tow and not expect people to stare.'

'I don't feel all that cool,' Helen said.

Katy followed Helen's eyes to the bar where André was giving a wide-eyed Molly his order. 'I'm not surprised,' she said dryly. 'Molly doesn't look too cool either.'

'What do you think?' Helen whispered. 'Do you think he's all right?'

Before Katy could answer, André was coming back with the drinks. Putting them down on the small table he shook hands with Katy as Helen introduced them.

'It's a nice place you've got here,' he said. 'A very nice barmaid too.'

'She's a nurse really,' Katy said. 'She's only helping out.

I'll tell her later you thought she was nice. I don't want it going to her head.'

André laughed. 'I already told her,' he said.

'Goodness,' Katy giggled. 'She'll never nurse again.'

They're getting on, Helen thought. She likes him. Mind you, she could hardly fail to. André certainly knew how to please. Helen watched as he complimented Katy on the decor, laughed about the rowdy Americans next door and offered to buy her a drink which she refused.

'I'd love to join you,' Katy said innocently, 'but as you can see we're desperately busy.' She winked secretly at Helen as she turned away. 'Enjoy your evening.'

Somewhat to her surprise Helen found she did enjoy the evening. André was easy to talk to. They chatted about the restaurant last night, about the club. He asked about Louise, so she told him all about meeting Louise at finishing school and staying at the Rutherfords', making him laugh with her descriptions of the awful stiff meals she had endured there, although she drew the line at telling about Greville Rutherford's embarrassing attachment to her. They talked about the two years André had spent at Oxford University, which explained his excellent English, and they talked a lot about the South of France and discovered they had several favourite places in common. Whether by design or luck, they kept off any potentially contentious topics such as Helen's work or the Free French.

It was some time later that André glanced across at Katy joking with a couple of the Americans as she poured out some beers at the main bar. 'Your friend Katy runs this place on her own? But she wears a wedding ring. Is her husband serving?'

'Not now,' Helen said. 'He was captured in France by the Germans just about this time last year.' She stopped abruptly as she realised it was in fact almost a year to the day that Ward had failed to return from that last fateful mission. Poor Katy.

'In France? This time last year?' André was looking puzzled. 'He was a pilot?' It was an obvious assumption. There had been no Allied ground forces officially in France this time last year.

Helen hesitated. The fewer people who knew the truth about Ward the better. Nobody knew how many spies the Germans were running in England, but there was no doubt certain secrets got out. It was thought now in the SOE that the Germans must have had prior warning of the St Nazaire raid. Already certain fingers were pointing at the Free French, and yet looking at him now, Helen had an overwhelming urge to tell André the truth. There was something about him that made her trust him.

'Ward was in the RAF,' she said at last, 'but he wasn't actually flying at the time.'

André looked at her. 'You knew him well?'

Helen nodded. 'Yes. Very well. I worked with him.'

'So now he is a prisoner-of-war?'

'Well, yes and no,' she said. She saw his surprise and lowered her voice. 'You see, he's escaped. Or at least we're pretty certain he has.'

André didn't ask how they knew. Instead he raised his glass slightly and smiled. 'A man after my own heart.'

'Of course,' Helen said, glad to change the subject. 'Jean-Claude at the Free French told me how you escaped from France.'

He shrugged it off. 'That was nothing. Just a short trip in a sailing boat.' Taking a drink of his beer he eyed her thoughtfully over the glass. 'So you asked Jean-Claude about me, did you? Why was that? What did you want to know?'

'I wanted to know who you were, that's all,' she said. 'After all, you did rescue me from a rather embarrassing situation that day.'

'Is that the only reason?'

It was the first hint of a flirt and Helen found herself blushing. He was French. What more could she expect?

But as she raised her eyes and met his defiantly she felt something lurch inside her. For an odd second as something flickered at the back of his eyes she was sure he felt it too. Or almost sure. It was hard to tell if that faint reaction was lust or disappointment.

'Of course,' she said. 'What other reason could there be?'

He didn't answer. He merely inclined his head, then he drained his glass and stood up.

'Come on,' he said, holding out his hand to pull her up. 'There is something I want to ask you and it is too public in here.'

'Well, well, well,' Molly Coogan murmured to Katy as they watched them leave. 'What goldmine did she dig him up in?'

Katy smiled. 'You liked him, didn't you?'

'Ooh, that accent,' Molly purred. 'And those eyes! To be honest I was too flustered to make any rational decisions like that. You talked to him longer than I did. What did you think of him?'

Katy hesitated. 'I don't know,' she said. 'He was charming enough, and utterly gorgeous, but there was something else. I don't know what it was.' She shook her head. 'Maybe he was just too charming and too gorgeous.'

'That's what I used to think about your Ward,' Molly said. 'It was that look in his eyes. That strong, hard sort of look. I don't know what it was, but it used to give me the shivers.'

Katy stared at her for a moment then looked away. 'In Ward's case it was courage,' she said. 'Stupid, thoughtless, over-confident courage. I don't know where these men get it from but it makes them think they're tougher or stronger or more invincible or something. I don't know, special, anyway.'

Molly smiled forgivingly as she began to rinse some glasses. 'Well, your Ward was pretty special. Hey.' She nudged Katy's arm. 'What's the matter? You've gone all pale.'

Katy stared at the counter. 'Sometimes I hate him, you know,' she whispered. 'I really hate him for causing me all this anxiety.'

Molly put down the glass she was washing. 'You only hate him because you love him,' she said. 'If he walked in here now you'd go berserk with happiness.'

'I don't know,' Katy said. 'I really don't know. 'She shook her head and looked up at Molly. 'All I know is that if I was Helen I'd run a mile.'

Molly looked astonished. In silence she reached behind her and poured a small whisky. 'You're tired,' she said, handing it to Katy. 'Drink this and go to bed. I'll finish off here.'

It was chilly on the common. A recent April shower had left a sheen of dampness over the grass. In the thin moonlight it glinted and shone as they walked in a kind of ghostly phosphorescence.

The common was deserted. Even the searchlight and gun positions seemed empty. As they strolled towards the silent bandstand it occurred to Helen that she was mad to come up here alone with André. He could be anybody. There was no proof he was who he said he was or who Jean-Claude said he was, and yet she wanted to be here. She liked him. As a person, not just as an attractive man. And she was pretty sure he liked her too. It was a strange feeling. On the one hand some of her old confidence had crept back into her. On the other she felt almost breathless with nervous anticipation.

As he stopped suddenly by a bench at the edge of the path it was the nervousness which predominated. He indicated that she should sit down, and it certainly wasn't the slightly damp bench that caused a shiver to run through her as he sat beside her.

'I'm sorry,' he said. 'You are cold. I promise I won't keep you long.'

It seemed an odd thing to say in the circumstances and she suspected he was wondering how quickly he could kiss her, but then he spoke and she realised that he wasn't wondering any such thing.

'I am going to ask you something,' he said abruptly, still staring at his knees. 'You don't have to reply. I already know you are discreet, I think you are in a position to help me.'

For a second he paused, then he turned his head to meet her startled gaze. 'I want to go back to France.'

When she didn't reply he went on, his voice low and intense, 'Not just on my own but with equipment. Sabotage equipment. Weapons. Guns. Explosives. I'll need to know how to use them and how to get more.'

Helen stared at him blankly. He had certainly taken her breath away but not quite in the way she had hoped. She was aware of an icy chill washing over her. In desperation she tried to concentrate on what he was saying. 'But what about the Free French … ?' she began.

He shrugged. 'The Free French are forming up as traditional land forces. In any case, they are at the beck and call of the Americans now. That's fine. Eventually the Allies will invade mainland Europe. I suppose that's how we will win ultimately, but there is so much that can be done in France first. I want to be there. There are other people at home who will help me.'

'But your part of France is still free.'

'Technically, but we all know the Vichy government is hand in glove with the Germans.'

So this was why he wanted to see her. To talk to her. Not because he fancied her after all. He merely wanted her to like him so she would help him. All that cosy chat in the pub had just been to impress her. He needed her good opinion. He needed her to make a good report on him to the people that mattered.

Suddenly, as the reality of the situation hit her like a punch in the stomach, Helen was glad of the darkness. At least it meant he couldn't see the pain in her eyes. She looked away anyway as the cold hand of disappointment began to squeeze her heart. She knew she had to say something, but she was afraid if she spoke she might cry. 'I see,' was all she could manage, and that sounded stiff and cold even to her ears.

She sensed him frowning. He put a hand on her arm. 'I know you can't promise anything, but you don't mind me asking, do you?'

'No, of course not,' she said. She moved her arm and he took his hand away. Yes, she thought. I mind dreadfully. I'm shocked by how much I mind.

'Hélène, I don't know how to put it, but if there's anything I can do for you in return ...'

She blinked. What was he offering now? A bribe? Money? One of his salvaged heirlooms perhaps. Or something more physical? Perhaps he thought he could put her out of her misery with a bit of efficient French lovemaking? The horrible truth was that he probably could.

She stood up. 'I'd better get back. It must be quite late.'

'Of course.' He stood up too.

They walked back in silence. Outside the Nelsons' he handed her a piece of paper. There was a telephone number written on it. 'You can contact me here,' he said.

She was pleased that her fingers were steady as she took it.

'Thank you,' he said. He paused for a moment then went on. 'It has been a pleasant evening.' He lifted his shoulders slightly. 'I am only sorry I had to spoil it by talking business.'

Don't, she wanted to scream at him. Don't pretend. As he looked at her thoughtfully, with the last vestige of self-control she managed to return his smile. 'There was nothing to spoil,' she said. 'As far as I am concerned business is the only thing of importance at the moment.' She was pleased with that. It was a classy rebuff. She wished she could have seen his reaction but his eyes were shuttered as he leaned forward to brush her cheeks in a fleeting farewell kiss.

'Business before pleasure,' he murmured dryly. 'Already we are adopting German ways.' Then he dropped his hands and stepped back. '*Au revoir, Hélène. Dormez bien.*'

Pam and Alan were making love when they heard the front door open. Pausing, they listened automatically for footsteps.

'She's on her own,' Alan whispered.

Pam was shocked. 'Goodness,' she said. 'She wouldn't bring him in here. She's far too ladylike. Anyway, as far as I know it was the first time she had been out with him.'

Alan shrugged. 'Well, you'd better check she knows the facts of life if she goes out with him again. You know what those Frenchmen are like. We don't want her getting pregnant. The last thing we need right now is a baby in the house.'

As Pam suddenly went completely rigid under him, Alan levered himself up on his elbows. 'What's the matter, darling? Did I hurt you?'

Pam couldn't speak. She couldn't move. She knew she was going to have to tell him, but now the moment had come she simply couldn't find the words.

'Alan I …' she started and then stopped again. It took Alan a moment in the darkness to realise that Pam's shudders were distress rather than desire. When he did, he rolled off her and drew her into his arms gently.

'Pam, what is it? What's happened? What have I done wrong?'

'You haven't done anything wrong,' she mumbled into his chest. 'You've done something right.'

She knew he was frowning, completely puzzled. 'So why are you crying?'

She took a slow shuddering breath and pulled back from him slightly. 'I'm pregnant.'

'Pregnant.' Alan repeated the word as though he had never heard it before. Since Alan had been declared infertile, it was in fact a word that rarely passed between them. Pam felt his hesitation and then to her horror a slight withdrawal.

'Alan, what is it?' She grasped his wrist. 'I … I thought you might be pleased. Or are you worried about George too?'

She felt a jolt of emotion course through him. 'Pleased?' He sounded incredulous. Then he steadied himself. 'Whose is it, Pam? You can tell me, I'll try not to mind.'

Suddenly she understood his shock. 'Alan, darling, it's yours.' She giggled slightly hysterically. 'Unless it's a virgin birth. The second coming or something. I certainly haven't been to bed with anyone else. I just think that stupid doctor you saw must have been wrong. Either way I'm definitely a couple of months gone, which makes it due in early December.'

'I can't believe it,' Alan whispered. 'Oh Pam.' His voice was choked. 'No wonder you cried. I didn't mean what I said about a baby in the house.'

Pam grimaced. 'You did,' she said. 'And I've been worrying to death about it too. George will go mad. He's so determined to be the only one, and he hates babies at the best of times.'

'I don't think we should tell him,' Alan said. 'Not yet. It's quite a while until December, after all.'

'We'd better not tell anyone else either, then,' Pam whispered. 'In case it slips out. The secret, I mean, not the baby, although I'm afraid there's still a chance that might happen too.'

Alan shuddered. 'Don't even think about it,' he said. He shook his head. 'Okay, it's our secret. Even though I want to shout it from the rooftops.' He was silent a moment then he kissed her. 'Is it ridiculous to say I feel proud?'

Pam smiled in the darkness. 'It's not ridiculous. It's sweet,' she said. 'Is it ridiculous to say I feel scared?'

He hugged her close. 'Don't be scared, darling. I'll look after you.' He kissed her again tentatively. 'The only thing is, I have to confess this news has rather taken the wind out of my sails.'

Pam kissed him back. 'What a shame,' she said. 'I was quite enjoying it.' Slowly she slid her hand under the covers. 'Perhaps I can do something to help?'

In the silence that followed, to their dismay they heard muffled sobs coming from Helen's room.

Pam hesitated. 'Should I go to her?'

Alan shook his head violently. 'No. Certainly not. You're my wife and the mother of my child-to-be. Your duty lies in this bed and if you stop what you are doing for one second I'll divorce you.'

Chapter Fifteen

After a tortured night Helen had finally woken up feeling angry. Angry with herself for getting upset over a man, and angry with André Cabillard for being more interested in his country than in her. And yet grudgingly she had to admit she admired his courage and his patriotism. In a way, that almost made it worse. She admired him for the very things that prevented him from seeing her as anything other than a means to an end.

She hated the idea of being used, but even worse she hated the idea of pining for a man who was not interested in her. Eventually, as she ate a hasty breakfast, avoiding Pam Nelson's eyes, she decided she would do what he had asked and that would be the last she would think about him.

When she explained the Frenchman's interest in the SOE to Angus McNaughton later that morning, however, Angus seemed reluctant to follow it up.

'We don't normally take volunteers,' he said, standing up and walking round his desk to push the door to. 'We have to be careful,' he went on, perching on his desk and lighting a cigarette. 'We don't want the organisation infiltrated by enemies. That's always a danger with volunteers.'

Helen was shocked. 'André is not an enemy. He's desperate to fight for us. The Allies. For his country.'

Angus blew out smoke. 'Those wealthy French,' he said,

making a slight face. 'It's in their interest to collaborate with the Germans. Look at Monte Carlo.'

Helen frowned. It was well known that over the winter, glamorous, sophisticated Monte Carlo had become a favourite watering hole for high-ranking German and Italian officers.

'André Cabillard is not like that,' Helen said. 'He's got integrity.'

'Hmm, integrity,' Angus said. He let the word hang between them for a moment while he tapped out ash, then he looked up and frowned. 'How long have you known this man, Helen?'

'I've met him three times,' she said.

'I see. And in that short time you have ascertained that he has all the physical attributes we look for in our agents, as well as courage, dedication … and integrity?' Angus leaned back in his chair. 'Are you sure it's not his Gallic charm that has influenced your judgement?'

Helen felt a bubble of anger form somewhere in the region of her stomach. 'Of course I'm sure,' she said. 'Anyway, I'd hardly be likely to recommend someone I was interested in for this kind of work, would I?'

Angus held her gaze for a second then he shrugged slightly. 'Not if you have any sense,' he said dryly. He glanced at the notes he had jotted down and drew thoughtfully on his cigarette. Then abruptly he made his decision. 'All right. I'll pass his details up the line.' He stubbed out his cigarette. 'I'll let you know if they want to see him.'

'Thank you,' Helen said.

'By the way,' Angus added as she turned for the door, 'your friend Paul has arrived safely.' He looked at her with faint amusement as she stopped in mid stride. 'I thought you'd like to know. We got a signal in from him this morning. He had a good landing and has already set himself up with accommodation and a cover job in Marseilles.'

Helen's primary reaction was relief. Relief that Paul was in safely. Her second reaction was that it could have been her too looking for accommodation and a cover job in Marseilles, indeed should have been her too, and she felt her knees tremble just at the thought. She never could have done it, she realised. Never.

Realising that Angus was still watching her, she nodded. 'Good for him,' she said.

Jen came back from the Miss Taylors' renewed and refreshed with her sore throat apparently recovered.

Katy was pleased to see her back. She had missed her. The pub had seemed quiet without her. Baby Malcolm had missed her too. He had been fretful and unwilling to feed while she was away and Katy had begun to worry all over again whether he would ever catch up all that time he had lost in the early days. He was still underweight but his fingers were definitely stronger and once or twice he had even shown signs of wanting to sit up on his own.

Jen had brought back a knitted animal the Miss Taylors had made for him from a pattern they had found in a magazine. She laughed as Katy unwrapped it. 'It's meant to be a donkey,' Jen said, 'but it looks to me more like a giraffe.'

'It has got rather a long neck,' Katy said doubtfully. 'And its head is a bit floppy.'

'They tried to stuff its neck a bit more,' Jen said, 'but then it looked as though it had eaten a tortoise.'

Whatever it was, Malcolm adored it. Once he had got it clutched in his skinny little fingers he adamantly refused to let it go.

Jen laughed. 'Well, there's no accounting for taste.' She watched Malcolm putting one of the animal's gangly legs to his mouth then turned back to Katy. 'Any news?'

Katy knew she meant news about Ward. 'No,' she said, 'but then we won't hear unless he makes contact with one of Helen's secret lot in France.'

'Or unless he turns up here,' Jen said. 'The Miss Taylors are convinced that's what will happen. Mind you,' she added dryly, 'I'm not sure that they quite appreciate the problems of being on the run in Nazi-controlled Europe.' She saw Katy's expression and shrugged. 'But I'm sure you'll be glad to know that they are so certain he'll get back that they are going to start knitting another jersey for him.'

Katy had to smile at that. The Miss Taylors had succeeded in sending a jersey out to Oflag 1XA for Ward, but although he had thanked them profusely he had confessed in a separate letter to Katy that it would have fitted a man three times his size.

Katy was about to reply when she heard footsteps on the stairs. It was Jacob.

'I'm sorry to disturb you,' he muttered looking at Jen awkwardly. 'I was wanting to ask you about the accounts, but if you're busy ...'

Jen stood up. 'Perhaps I'll make a cup of tea,' she said. It amused her that Jacob was so much in awe of her.

'What is it, Jacob?' Katy asked. 'Have you found a mistake in my adding up?'

'A few,' he said, 'but it's not that. It's just that I was thinking it might be better to have two sets of accounts. Obviously you want to seem to make enough to keep the brewery happy, but then there are the extra things you get from my brother. Like the American beer ...'

'Oh,' Katy said. 'I see.' She swallowed. It wasn't in her nature to be dishonest, but then if Greville Rutherford found out about the American beer she'd probably be closed down anyway.

'Well, perhaps that's the best thing to do,' she said. It occurred to her that putting her entire livelihood in the hands of a fourteen-year-old schoolboy might not be the wisest course, but on the other hand he was certain to be better at it than her, and he seemed to like doing it.

'Thanks, Jacob,' she said as he edged towards the door. 'I appreciate it.'

'Good old Jacob,' Jen said coming in with the tea. 'These Jews are all the same, aren't they? Give them a sniff of money and you can't hold them back.'

'Jen, shh.' Katy glared at her. She hated Jen's anti-Semitic attitude. 'Anyway, if it wasn't for your Americans there wouldn't be any money,' she said. 'Talking of which Dirk left a package here for you on Sunday.' She reached over to the dresser and handed it to Jen. 'He was devastated you weren't here to receive it.'

Jen smiled as she opened it. 'I thought it was Hank who liked me. Oh yes!' Her smile widened as she produced three pairs of sheer American nylons and two red lipsticks. 'This is more like it. No bloody bare legs for patriotism for me.' She held them up. 'What do you think?'

'I think I feel sorry for Dirk,' Katy said. 'He's mad about you, you know.'

But Jen was far more interested in her new lipstick. Already she was at the mirror trying it out. 'Mmm, mmm,' she mumbled. 'He's only a kid. I don't want to go out with a kid.' She smacked her lips and surveyed the effect. Then she adjusted her gaze, blinked and swung round abruptly. 'Katy!' she said. 'Look at Malcolm! You didn't tell me he could sit up on his own!'

On 16 April the small island of Malta in the Mediterranean was given the George Cross for surviving over two thousand German air raids.

Stuck in an endless round of work, sleep and the dreary journey in between, Helen almost found herself wishing there would be a few air raids on London. At least it would break the monotony.

It was an odd time in London. In other parts of the world the war was proceeding, mostly badly, admittedly, but proceeding. Even in other parts of England they were suffering a few raids, on the unprotected cathedral towns mostly, but in London nothing was happening. Except that the weather was getting better. The cherry trees in Lavender Road were covered in blossom now and last year's daffodils were coming out among the leeks and cabbages in people's new vegetable patches. Even the bomb sites were beginning to look quite pretty as self-seeded Rosebay willow herb and butterfly-covered buddleia filled the unsightly gaps.

Usually the coming of spring lifted Helen's spirits but this year she felt flat and defeated.

Then, at the beginning of May, Angus McNaughton suddenly informed her that Maurice Buckmaster wanted André Cabillard brought in for an interview.

Jerked out of her lethargy, it took Helen some time to steel herself sufficiently to telephone him. When she dialled the number he had given her, a husky-voiced woman answered. André wasn't there. Reluctantly Helen left her number.

When he rang back a couple of hours later Helen's heart was thumping before she even lifted the receiver.

'Hélène? *Comment ça va?*' He sounded ridiculously relaxed and yet he must know that after all this time she was calling with important news.

'I'm fine,' she said. 'Look, I don't know if you are still interested in the matter we discussed, but if you are, there is someone who would like to meet you.'

'Good,' he said. 'Yes, I am very interested.'

Helen took a steadying breath. He was the one who should be nervous, not her. 'Then you should go to the War Office at three p.m. on Monday and ask for room forty-five. It's only a preliminary interview. You do understand that, don't you?'

'Yes, I understand.'

He seemed slightly hesitant and she frowned. 'That is what you wanted, isn't it?'

'Yes,' he said. 'Of course. And I'm very grateful to you for arranging this. *Vraiment.* Thank you.' He paused and for a second she thought he might be going to ask to see her again, but then he just thanked her once more and rang off.

So that's it, she thought dully. The end. I have done my bit. Served my purpose. Now it's up to him.

But it wasn't the end. On the Tuesday morning Angus told her that the initial interview had gone well, that the Frenchman had been recommended for further assessment. Two weeks later, just as the news arrived that the hated SS Obergruppenführer Reinhard Heydrich had died from his injuries in Prague after his car was attacked by SOE-trained Czech paratroopers, Helen heard that André had been accepted for training.

That same afternoon a bunch of flowers was delivered to the Nelsons' house with a polite note from André thanking her for her help and asking if she would consider accompanying him to a reception at the Russian embassy at the weekend.

'Goodness!' Louise looked up from her mother's desk where she was laboriously addressing the wedding invitations. 'You've got Mrs Carter on the list, Mummy. Surely we don't have to ask her.'

Greville Rutherford glanced up from his newspaper. 'Mrs Carter? Oh, I don't think so, Celia. Quite unnecessary.'

'Of course we must ask her,' Celia said. 'She's my business partner.'

'Business partner!' Greville Rutherford snorted. 'I'd hardly call your little venture a business, my dear. Knocking up a few sandwiches doesn't have much impact on the British economy, does it? Or the war effort, come to that.'

'People have to eat,' Celia said grittily. 'Just as they have to drink.'

'Exactly,' Louise chipped in irritably. 'Running a brewery doesn't help the war effort much either, does it?'

Her father's negative attitude got on her nerves. It was her wedding after all and she wanted it to be fun. All she was doing was trying to get the invitations written.

But her father was glaring at her for her untimely intervention. 'Running a brewery makes money, young lady. That's the difference. My brewery is paying for your wedding. I haven't noticed any contribution from your mother's café.' He turned his glare on Celia. 'Or is your precious Mrs Carter pocketing the profits?'

'Of course she's not,' Celia snapped.

As her father reddened alarmingly Louise blinked. She had never heard her mother raise her voice to him like that before. 'Well, I'll do one for Mrs Carter anyway,' she muttered as Celia stood up and walked to the door. A second later she looked up again. 'You've got Mr Lorenz down here as well,' she said incredulously. 'Surely he doesn't have to come.'

Her mother stopped at the door. 'Yes, he does have to come,' she said shortly.

'But I'm going to run out of invitations,' Louise wailed.

'Oh, for goodness' sake.' Celia closed her eyes. 'Put him on the same one as Mrs Carter, then. I don't suppose she'll mind.'

As her mother left the room, closing the door behind her with a distinct click, Louise glanced nervously at her father. He still looked ominously red in the face. Deciding it might be wiser not to remark on her mother's abrupt departure, she busied herself back in her task.

'At least there's no problem with Helen,' she murmured to herself, sucking her pen thoughtfully. 'Although I wonder if I should put "Helen and partner". Or if André should have a separate—'

'What?' Her father's abrupt question made her jump so badly she nearly rammed the pen down her throat.

Coughing as her eyes watered, Louise shook her head. 'Nothing,' she said. 'I was just wondering if Helen de Burrel's boyfriend needed a separate invitation.'

'I didn't know Helen had a boyfriend,' he said. 'Who is it? That William fellow?'

'Goodness no,' Louise giggled. 'He's called André Cabillard. He's some kind of French aristocrat, and he's terribly glamorous.'

'I see.' Her father turned away to kick the fire. 'And how long has this been going on?'

Louise probed the bruised roof of her mouth with her tongue. 'Well, I first met him just over a month ago,' she said. 'She's been rather cagey about it since then, but I do know he's taking her to some frightfully grand reception at the Russian embassy tomorrow night. Why?' Busy shovelling coal on to the fire, he didn't reply. 'Why?' she repeated. 'Why did you want to know?'

'What? Oh, no reason,' he said, but his eyes were angry as he glanced at the pile of invitations on the table. 'I just don't want too many hangers-on at this wedding, that's all. The damn thing is going to cost quite enough as it is.' He glared at Louise. 'I'm going to my study now. You can tell your mother that I want to see the accounts for that café by the end of the week. I'm sick and tired of these women pretending they know how to run a business.'

At the door he hesitated and turned round. His eyes were cold. 'You can tell your friend Katy Frazer that I'll be sending someone to collect hers too, and if they are not up to scratch I'll close her down.'

With that he strode out of the room leaving Louise with her mouth open. It was only a minute later, when she felt an unusual warmth on her back and swung round in alarm, that she realised that she hadn't seen such a blazing fire in the house for years.

The Russian embassy was in Kensington Palace Gardens. Compared with the surrounding houses with their broken fences, damaged brickwork, peeling paint and long grass, it looked extremely spruce. As her taxi drew up, Helen wondered if it had been dolled up for the occasion or whether Ivan Maisky, the Russian ambassador, kept it permanently in good shape as a defiant gesture of comparison with his beleaguered homeland.

To her relief, André was already there waiting for her.

'Good evening, Helen. How are you?' For a moment as he helped her out of the taxi he seemed stiff and slightly remote. 'You look very beautiful tonight.'

'Thank you,' she said. He didn't look bad himself in his formal evening dress, but she didn't say so. She just nodded, not quite meeting his eyes.

As he led her towards the front door which was flanked by two Cossack guards Helen felt awkward at André's silence. 'I've never been here before,' she said brightly. 'It was nice of you to ask me.'

'It was nice of you to come,' he said.

Something in his tone made her glance at him quickly, but his eyes were guarded. Helen looked away. It's all going wrong, she said to herself, and it's my fault.

Suddenly, she had a ridiculous, overwhelming urge to cry. She had never in her life met anyone with the power to upset her so easily. I'm not up to this, she thought. I was stupid to think I could see him without feeling hurt. If only I could go home now and never see him again.

But then he touched her arm. 'I'm sorry,' he said quietly. 'I didn't mean to be rude. I certainly didn't mean to upset you.'

He sounded sincere. There was even the faintest catch in his voice. Looking up at him Helen suddenly found she didn't want to go home after all. On the contrary, she wanted to throw herself against his broad chest and make him fold his arms tightly round her. Luckily she managed to restrain herself. 'You weren't rude,' she said. 'I was just stupid. I really am pleased you asked me.'

He smiled then. 'And I really am pleased you are here.'

Suddenly it was all right again. Helen could hardly believe it. It was as though a cloud had drifted across the sun, momentarily casting a shadow, and now it had gone, and everything seemed bright again.

Before she could think about it in too much detail there was a slight stir as the Duke and Duchess of Kent arrived in a chauffeur-driven Rolls-Royce.

'Well, I can't vouch for the party,' André murmured as they stood back to let the royals in first, 'but we seem to be in good company.'

'I can see why they are here,' Helen muttered back, 'but why are we here? What's your connection with the Russians?'

'My father once entertained Ivan Maisky to a meal. I was there.'

'Once?' Helen stared at him. 'You must have made a big impression.'

He smiled. 'Russians have long memories,' he said as they gave up their coats to a liveried footman, 'and my father has mildly Communist leanings.'

Something in his voice made Helen turn to look at him. 'You disapprove?'

André shrugged. 'It is easy to have left-wing leanings when you own some of the wealthiest estates in the South of France, but it will not be so easy for him to give them up to the Fascists.'

Helen felt a shiver course down her spine. 'That's really why you want to go back, isn't it?' she said abruptly. 'To make sure you don't lose your estates.'

For a second as she looked at him accusingly she thought she saw anger in his eyes. It was gone so quickly she was left wondering if she had imagined it. When he spoke his voice was low and steady. 'I want to go back to make sure I don't lose my country,' he said.

It was a good reply. A clever reply. But his hesitation had worried her. She realised she didn't want him to have purely selfish motives, nor did she want him to lie to her. 'Don't worry,' she said crossly as he led her into the beautiful chandeliered reception room. 'You don't have to impress me now. I've done my bit. What happens now is up to you. I can't affect your future any more.'

To her surprise he laughed then. A short private laugh. 'No? I also would like to think that is the case, but I am a little afraid you may be wrong.'

Something in the wry smile that accompanied the words made Helen's heart start thumping again, but before she could ask what he meant he had stopped a passing waiter and was encouraging her to try a blini. 'It is like a little pancake,' he said as she eyed it dubiously. 'On top is sour cream and Black Sea caviar, which probably makes it the most expensive snack in the world.'

Helen couldn't help smiling at that. Biting into it carefully her eyes widened in delight. 'And the most delicious,' she said, licking her lips.

'Ah.' André nodded to the waiter. 'The lady has taste. You should wash it down with vodka,' he went on, looking round for some. 'Yes, over here,' he said, leading her off to a table covered in rather oddly shaped bottles. 'Just the thing.'

By the time Helen had downed a couple of throat-burning pepper vodkas and several more blinis she was definitely enjoying herself. Somehow she found herself talking to a distinguished newspaper columnist who was extremely good company, while only yards away she was amused to see two portly Conservative MPs attempting to make hearty conversation with the inscrutable Chinese ambassador, Wellington Koo, and the American ambassador, John Winant, who looked as though he had had one vodka too many.

André was the perfect escort. He was charming and attentive, but equally he let her hold her own in conversation with other people. She appreciated that. So often men wanted to answer her questions for her, to put their opinions instead of listening to hers. Either that or they disappeared and left her stuck with some dreadful bore, but André was never far away. Even if he was talking to someone else, from time to time he would glance over or offer her a snack as an excuse to check up on her.

It was as she watched him joking with the newspaper columnist that it came to Helen with a jolt that she really liked him. It was obvious that other people liked him too. He was also inordinately attractive. All evening she had found her eyes drawn to him, not even really for his looks but for that indefinable quality she had noticed that very first time they met at the Free French headquarters, a kind of suppressed energy, a certain self-possession that seemed to lift him above other men.

She wasn't the only one affected by his charisma. Even now the Duchess of Kent was glancing at him somewhat covetously and Helen was surprised by the irritation she felt in intercepting that look. I'm jealous, she thought. I can't believe it. I'm jealous about a man I hardly know.

Looking back at him her heart jumped violently to find his eyes on her. For a second as he held her gaze everything seemed to stop. It was like a film caught in the projector. A moment frozen in time. Flickering at the edges. Even the sound in the room was momentarily blurred.

Oh God, Helen thought with rising panic. Oh no. Please no. Please don't let this be happening. Please let me just be at home, safely with the Nelsons listening to *ITMA* or *The Brains Trust*.

As though he could read her mind André raised his eyebrows slightly. She knew he was asking if she had had enough, if she wanted to go, and it occurred to her that for someone she hardly knew, they communicated very effectively without speech. She nodded imperceptibly and a moment later he was at her side effortlessly extricating her from the mêlée.

Within minutes he had retrieved her coat and asked one of the Cossacks to signal a taxi. Hoping desperately that it was the vodka that was making her feel so light-headed Helen allowed herself to be led outside.

'Where to?' the taxi driver asked over his shoulder as André opened the door for her.

André glanced at her in the semi darkness. 'To Clapham?'

'Yes please,' Helen said.

The taxi driver grunted irritably but seemed mollified when André told him he would be coming straight back again.

'So,' André murmured, getting in behind her and settling back in the corner. 'No chance of tempting you back to my bed, then.' He spoke in French, presumably for the benefit of the driver, but nevertheless, the words hit Helen with an almost physical jolt. Somehow in the space of that instant she managed to feel both hot and cold. His remark was so unexpected. So brazen. So casual. So utterly sexy.

She didn't even know if he was serious. It was too dark in the back of the cab to see his expression clearly. In any case, he wasn't looking at her. He seemed far more interested in gazing out over the dark expanse of Kensington Gardens. There were no railings any more, Helen noticed. They must finally have been taken up for the war effort.

'I can't,' she said. 'I couldn't possibly.' She realised that this was the same response she had given Paul, although this time she didn't really mean it. This time she could. Very easily. But she would probably hate herself afterwards. And him.

He looked round, apparently unperturbed. 'I know you couldn't,' he said. He leaned forward to slide the driver's glass partition shut. 'I'm not asking you to. I just thought you ought to know how I felt.'

He didn't seem to be expecting a reply, but she felt she had to respond, she had to get the tension out of her somehow. The only problem was that she didn't know what to say. They were round Marble Arch and heading south down Park Lane before she remembered the French letters he had picked up that day, and some of the heat in her evaporated.

'You probably say that to all the girls,' she said.

'I know you think that,' André said, 'and I can't deny I like girls, but this is different. Completely different.' He stopped for a moment and shook his head. 'I'm sorry, Hélène. *Je m'excuse.* I didn't mean this to happen. I have been fighting it hard since I first met you. And then I saw you in the restaurant that evening and I knew I was lost.'

She didn't know whether to believe him or not. He sounded so matter of fact. So cool. She frowned. 'I thought you just wanted an introduction to the organisation.'

He nodded. 'I did. I tried to make that all I wanted. Ever since our last meeting I have tried. But all the time I have been wondering how I could arrange to see you again.'

'And now you have.'

He inclined his head in the darkness. 'And now I have and now of course it's even worse.'

'Worse? Why?'

He moved his position slightly. 'Because now I don't just want to make love to you, I want more than that.'

'Is that bad?' she whispered.

'Yes,' he said. 'Very bad. What I ought to do is kiss you goodbye tonight and never see you again.'

Helen flinched. 'Why?'

'Because tomorrow I go to Scotland.' He hesitated. 'I'm not sure how long the training programme lasts, but after that ...' He stopped. They both knew what happened after that.

'You're going tomorrow?' She had no idea he would be called forward so soon.

'You see,' he shrugged, 'it is very bad.'

He was right. She knew he was right. She also knew he was trying to give her a chance. A chance to withdraw. She respected him for that. In any case, it was utter madness to do anything else.

'There are gaps in the training,' she murmured. 'Not for the first month. But after that. A few days here and there between courses.'

It was an admission. An admission of far more than her knowledge of the SOE training programme. She knew it. He knew it. Probably for all she knew the taxi driver knew it. She hoped he couldn't hear. Either way she waited tensely for André to take advantage of it, but he just raised his eyebrows.

'So perhaps a few months? If we are lucky. I wonder if it will be enough.'

'Enough for what?'

He smiled. 'Enough to make you fall in love with me.'

If he smiles at me like that again it won't take five minutes, Helen thought. In fact it was almost certainly already too late.

Even as she had the thought he slid his arm round her shoulders, drawing her closer to him. Then with his spare hand he turned her face to his. 'I'm sorry,' he murmured. 'I know it's not the thing to kiss in the back of a taxi, but suddenly I can't help it.'

Helen didn't care where they were. All evening she had wanted to get close to him, and now she was in his arms and it was the most wonderful feeling in the world. His kiss was brief. His lips were cool, measured, appreciative. Even when a spark of passion flared between them he didn't lose control. He just turned his head away slightly and held her close. She could feel their hearts thumping in tandem. She could feel the tension in him and she wanted to lose herself in him. In his arms. She felt drugged, languid and excited at the same time, and yet a small voice of caution urged her to be careful. It would be so easy to make a fool of herself, but it felt so nice. So right.

He kissed her again then drew back a fraction and frowned. 'I hope you don't really think I am just another amorous Frenchman.'

Helen smiled. 'Aren't you?'

He laughed then. 'Well, yes I am. Of course. But it's not just amorousness I feel right now.' He touched her cheek with cool fingers. 'It's something more—'

He was interrupted by the taxi driver sliding back the partition. 'Oi,' he shouted over his shoulder. 'Which of you love birds knows the way, then? All these South London streets look the blinking same to me.'

The untimely interruption was bad enough but the look on André's face caused Helen to get an equally untimely attack of the giggles, and then André started to smile too and suddenly they were both rocking with laughter.

Completely taken aback at their hysteria the taxi driver turned round and glared at them. 'I don't know what's so funny.'

Somehow that made it even worse, but controlling herself with difficulty Helen leaned forward and directed him briskly to Lavender Road.

She was still smiling when André got out with her and instructed the driver to take a turn round the block while he said goodnight to her.

As the driver moved off reluctantly with a crash of gears, André put his hands on her shoulders. 'A month suddenly seems a long time,' he said.

'It is a long time,' Helen said.

He frowned. 'Shall I let the taxi go? I can always walk home.'

She looked at him appalled. 'No. You must go home now. Get some sleep. You need all the sleep you can get. And try to sleep on the train too, because they won't give you a moment's rest once you get there.'

'You seem to know a lot about it.'

Quickly she looked away. She knew more than he realised. Much more. It was on the tip of her tongue to tell him, but then she stopped. She couldn't possibly tell him, because to do so would mean telling him about her failure, and she didn't want to admit to that. Not when he apparently thought she was so wonderful.

It occurred to her that she could give him advice, tips. She could tell him about the surprise night exercises. About the interrogation training. How to make it easier for himself. She could but she didn't. She didn't tell him anything. Suddenly, very desperately, she wanted him to fail.

'André?'

'What? What is it?'

But already she could hear the taxi approaching.

'Oh God,' he groaned. For a second he closed his eyes. Then he cupped her face gently in his hands and kissed her softly on the lips. 'I hate this. I hate goodbyes. But next time will be different. Next time there will be time. I promise.'

'Come on, mate,' the taxi driver bellowed. 'Wrap it up. I can't hang round here all night. There's a war on, you know.'

André kissed her once more. 'If you see news tomorrow of a murdered taxi driver,' he murmured against her lips, 'please don't tell anyone it was me.'

Chapter Sixteen

Opening her front door to an urgent banging, Joyce was astonished to find Celia Rutherford on the step. She was even more astonished by the other woman's dishevelled appearance.

'What? What's happened?' At the very least she thought Celia was going to say she had been assaulted in the street by some drunken American soldiers. Joyce had seen them outside earlier, standing around waiting for the pub to open, and she'd seen Jen too, from behind the curtain, running up to them, laughing and flirting; she even kissed a couple of them. Joyce had seen her lifting her skirt to show off her nylons, and even from across the road she had heard the raucous laughter and whistles that had greeted the sight of her daughter's shapely knees.

'My husband wants to see our accounts,' Celia was saying now. 'The café accounts. But we haven't really got accounts, have we? And I don't know what to say to him.'

Joyce felt a stab of anger. What did their café have to do with bloody Greville Rutherford? It was theirs, hers and Celia's. He hadn't even set foot in it yet, as far as she knew. She looked at Celia's anxious face and knew that if the café wasn't making enough money, Greville Rutherford would put his foot down and insist they closed it. All he cared about was profit. He didn't care that his wife was enjoying it; he didn't care that people liked to pop in for a chat and a sandwich; nor that without it Joyce would be out of work and virtually destitute. It didn't pay much but it paid her enough to keep going, to keep the house and a bit of food on the table.

'What are we going to do?' Celia asked. 'I don't know anything about ledgers and things. I didn't think we needed them. It all seemed to be going so well.'

'I suppose we could ask Mr Lorenz,' Joyce said doubtfully.

Celia sighed in relief. 'Of course. Why didn't I think of that? He runs a business, after all, and he'd do anything for you.'

Joyce felt a faint flush creeping up her cheeks. Glad of the falling dusk she sniffed. 'Well, I've given him enough lunches. He owes me the odd favour.'

Helen glanced at Katy over the rim of her glass and made a slight face. 'I think I've fallen in love.'

Slightly to her surprise Katy didn't break into the immediate smile she expected. Instead she swilled the lemonade in her own glass and almost frowned. 'It's early days,' she said. 'Maybe you shouldn't rush into thinking you're in love.'

Helen was taken aback. 'Don't you approve?' she asked. 'I thought you liked him.'

'I did like him,' Katy said. 'I suppose I just think he is a dangerous man to fall in love with, that's all. You've had a rough time recently and you don't need any more trauma. And the more fond you get of him the worse it will be when he goes.' She paused a moment, looking into her glass. 'At least when Ward went into France that last time, he thought he was coming back. You know more about these things than I do, but as André is French presumably he'll be expected to stay in France. At least until the end of the war. And the way things are going that could be years.'

It was true, but it was so unlike Katy to put a dampener on anything that Helen was still surprised, and jolted. It was crazy to fall for someone in André's position, and yet when she thought of that last taxi ride – his restrained kisses, their shared laughter, his unexpected sincerity – she knew it was already too late.

She had never intended to fall in love. She had had no idea what it would be like. She had always secretly laughed at girls who declared themselves in love, believing that all they really wanted was a nice home and husband and imminent children. She didn't want any of those things. All she wanted was André.

'You can't really know him very well yet,' Katy said suddenly. 'Are you sure you aren't in love with the idea of him? A glamorous, dashing Frenchman. And what about him? Are you sure you can trust him not to hurt you? Not to take what he wants and then wave goodbye without another thought?'

Helen swallowed. She wasn't sure. How could anyone be sure of such a thing? How could she really be sure she hadn't fallen for some soft-soap Gallic charm from an experienced ladykiller?

'You're right,' she said. 'I don't want to get hurt. I'll try not to think about him too much while he's away. Perhaps the feeling will wear off.'

But not thinking about him was hard, particularly when reports began filtering through from Scotland that André was performing well on the arduous training course.

'You're not the only one he's impressed,' Angus McNaughton remarked dryly. 'The instructors up there are raving about him.'

Something in his voice made Helen frown. 'But you're not?'

Angus shrugged. 'It's not my job to question the opinion of our training officers. I just wonder about his motivation, that's all. He got one lot of treasures out, maybe he wants to go back for some more.' He saw Helen's shocked expression. 'But he's only at the beginning of the programme, after all. If I'm right and there is a problem it will all come out in the wash sooner or later.'

'Of course there's no problem,' Helen said. 'André

simply wants to do the best for his country like the rest of us. You're just cynical.'

Angus laughed suddenly. 'Maybe that's it. Or it could be that I simply don't trust the French.'

For Louise, June 1942 was the happiest month of her life so far. For once she was the centre of attention wherever she went. She was the bride-to-be. At work everyone looked at her with new respect. Not only had she organised the best Christmas party in years but she was the girl who was going to marry a naval lieutenant. An officer. Doris had already started up a collection for a wedding present. As a precaution against anything too common Louise had hinted that she wanted some white cotton linen. What she really wanted was lace-edged pillowcases, feminine and pretty, but linen was hard to come by these days and she knew she would have to be grateful for anything she got.

At home there were fittings for the wedding dress, which was being remade from her mother's dress. She would have preferred a brand new one, but there was simply no material in the shops any more. Even her neat little going-away suit was being made out of an old ream of Harris tweed that had been ordered for her brother Bertie ages ago and never made up. Bertie didn't need it now because he was shortly to depart for Egypt as a newly commissioned officer in the Royal Artillery.

To her surprise, Louise felt quite proud of Bertie when he called in briefly at the end of June. He looked good in his uniform, and his manner was crisp, cool and unemotional. Altogether a far cry from the effete, drawling conscientious objector he had claimed to be when he first left school. Even her father had seemed grudgingly impressed with his errant son, and to everyone's astonishment had actually shaken him by the hand as he left. Louise had kissed him, and her mother had cried as the three of them had stood on the step and watched him stride away down the drive without a backward glance.

It was a shame Bertie wouldn't be at the wedding, of course, but it seemed he was needed in Libya where blasted Tobruk had fallen to the Germans yet again.

Louise could hardly imagine that her brother was going to make much difference to Rommel's apparently unstoppable advance but she supposed he had to do his duty. In any case, there would be plenty of other people coming to the wedding. The seventy invitations would be going out soon, a small marquee had been ordered, food was being supplied by Fortnum's, and the old fellow who had the flower stall in Northcote Road market had been charged with finding as many white roses as he could for the big day. Despite her father's constant niggling about the cost of everything, 1 August was definitely going to be a big day.

It even sounded good, Louise thought. Saturday, 1 August. My wedding day. And Jack's of course, she added belatedly. Lovely, romantic, generous Jack, who as a special treat, at vast expense, had booked them into the Compleat Angler hotel at Marlow for their two-week honeymoon.

In fact, apart from the continually miserable war news, her father's ill humour was the only cloud in Louise's sky. It wasn't just Louise he got at, her mother was suffering too. It had all started that day when he had asked to see the café accounts. He had clearly expected either a faltering admission of their having no accounts at all, or at best badly managed ones. When her mother had later presented a sparkling, perfectly balanced ledger and an extremely respectable balance sheet, he had been almost too annoyed to look at it. It didn't help that the Flag and Garter books were apparently equally up to the mark and certainly did not justify him closing Katy down.

Katy had laughed when Louise had asked her about it late one evening when she popped into the pub just after closing time. 'Oh well,' Katy had said lightly, glancing casually at young Jacob behind the bar. 'I'm glad your father was pleased with them.'

Before Louise could question her further, an eerie wailing siren started up in the street outside. It was so long since they had heard that noise it took them a moment to realise what it was. Then they looked at each other as memories came rushing back. For Katy, the loss of her father, the devastation of the pub. For Louise, the terrifying blackness of Balham Tube station, the gushing water, the agonising crack as falling debris hit her pelvis.

'Oh God,' Louise whispered. 'I can't bear it. It's only a month to the big day. If that bloody Hitler starts that beastly bombing again and spoils it for me I'll die.' She glanced at Katy for sympathy.

But Katy wasn't there, she was already halfway up the stairs, running to fetch Malcolm. 'Lock the door, Louise, and bolt it,' she shouted down. 'And stamp out the fire.'

'Thank God my mother's not here,' she added a minute later as she and Louise hurried down the cellar steps with Malcolm and a couple of blankets. 'She'd be having fifty fits by now.'

The raid wasn't serious, but it reminded everyone what life might have been like for the last year if Russia hadn't taken the brunt of Hitler's offensive. Nevertheless, it and the intermittent incendiary raids that followed it had the effect of putting London back on full alert: sand buckets were refilled, stirrup pumps were brought out of dark corners and volunteer fire-watchers once again took turns in patrolling the streets at night for incendiaries.

A lot of people were worried that the incendiary raids might be a precursor to more heavy blitz-type bombing, but for Helen, July brought an infinitely more nerve-racking prospect: that of André's imminent return.

She had tried very hard not to think about him. Tried very hard not to mind that he hadn't written to her to tell her when he would be back, but he hadn't. She knew of course. It wasn't difficult to find out when the course was due to finish or to work out which train he would be on. What was more difficult was convincing herself that she mustn't contact him. She must wait for him to contact her, and if he didn't then so be it. After all, it was likely that the month in Scotland would have convinced him of the futility of any kind of relationship.

In any case, as Katy had said, it was madness to hope to find happiness with a man like André. However much he professed to like her she would always be second best to his patriotism.

Now, as she sat in her office and tried to read an ominous report that the Vichy leader, Laval, had agreed to let Gestapo forces into unoccupied France to hunt for enemy radio transmitters, despite the seriousness of the subject, she found she simply could not concentrate on it. How could she when she knew that in less than an hour the *Highlander* would be steaming into King's Cross?

Glancing at the clock she assessed the situation. Angus McNaughton was at a meeting at the War Office. Maurice Buckmaster was away visiting one of the SOE 'finishing schools' in Sussex. Nobody would notice if she slipped out. If she walked up Baker Street to Marylebone Road she could take a bus straight along to King's Cross, see the train come in, watch André get off and be back within the hour.

Watch was the operative word. She wasn't going to let André see her. She didn't even want to talk to him. She just wanted to see him. Just for a moment. Just to test the effect it had on her.

Abruptly she stood up and reached for her jacket. At the door she hesitated again.

'This is completely ridiculous,' she said, taking out a small mirror and touching up her lipstick. 'And pathetic. Probably the most pathetic thing I have ever done in my entire life.' For a second she glanced back at her desk, then she opened the door and walked briskly down the passage.

King's Cross was crowded, hot, and unbelievably noisy. Shrill whistles, shouted orders and a babble of voices almost drowned out even the hissing steam and thumping and clanking of the trains as they manoeuvred in and out. The hot July sun beating down on the glass in the roof was turning the station into a sweltering greenhouse, but as she pushed through the scrum of bodies and luggage towards the ticket barrier and felt the sweat prickling under her arms, Helen knew it wasn't entirely the heat of the station that had raised her body temperature.

She was just in time. The *Highlander* was coming in. She could feel the ground vibrating, hear the screech of braking iron, the shuddering pants from the massive engine as it edged forward the last few yards of its journey.

Taking up a discreet position in good view of the platform, but half concealed behind a pile of crated luggage, Helen was aware of her heart thumping in nervous anticipation.

With a final coughing wheeze the great train ground to a halt. Suddenly the air was full of smoke and steam and people were thrusting forward waving and shouting as the doors clunked open and hundreds of weary, travelworn passengers spilled out on to the platform and joined the long queue at the ticket barrier.

Scouring the crowds, Helen felt like some ridiculous teenager waiting at the stage door of a theatre for a glimpse of her screen idol.

And then she saw him. Almost at the barrier. Tall and striking as ever with ruffled hair and a dark shadow on his chin. Suddenly, desperately, she didn't want him to see her. Something about his hard unshaven jaw, the easy strength in the shoulders as he swung his suitcase from one hand to the other and reached into his pocket for his ticket made her cringe away behind the crated luggage, but it was too late.

Already his head was turning as though drawn by a noise, although she hadn't spoken. Indeed the hubbub of the station was such that he couldn't possibly have heard even if she had. And yet he was looking her way. For a second a faint puzzled frown narrowed his eyes and then, even as she tensed to flee, he saw her.

As their eyes met Helen felt an almost physical jolt. She had forgotten the power of those eyes. The unbelievable heartstopping quality of his smile.

The ticket collector was asking for his ticket. Reluctantly jerking his eyes away he handed it over, then he was through the barrier and pushing through the crowds towards her.

Helen didn't move. She couldn't move. As everyone milled about her she stood rigid and stiff like some strange modern statue.

A moment later he was right there in front of her. 'Hélène?' He put his suitcase down, and resting his hands on her shoulders, kissed her on each cheek. He was wearing a high-necked grey sweater under a loose-fitting navy blazer, and although he was clearly hot and travel weary and smelt of cigarette smoke he still somehow contrived to look glamorous and debonair.

'*Merde*,' he said. 'What a journey. I had to stand all the way.'

'All the way?' Helen was appalled. 'After what you've been through for the last month? God. You must be exhausted.'

He raised his eyebrows quizzically. 'You should know.'

It took her a moment to realise what he meant, then as the truth dawned she drew back. 'You know? You've heard about my . . .?' She looked away. 'Oh no, how awful.' It had not occurred to her that he would find out about her abortive attempt at agent training. They were so security conscious up there. So tight lipped. Oh no, she thought, mortified. What will he think?

But he seemed more puzzled than disgusted. 'Why awful? I heard you were gutsy and tough.' He smiled faintly. 'Ladylike in adversity, was how someone described you. Did you know the instructors had a bet about how quickly you would cry? And you never did.'

Helen shook her head. 'I did,' she said. 'In private.' She actually felt suddenly close to it again now. Perilously close. But she had to know the worst. 'So you didn't hear what happened afterwards?'

'The parachute jump, you mean? Yes, I did hear.'

She couldn't look at him. Couldn't bear to see his expression. 'I was scared and I panicked,' she said. 'I … Oh God,' she sniffed. 'And now I'm crying. I'm sorry to be so pathetic!' She stopped abruptly as he muttered some expletive under his breath.

'Helen, for God's sake,' he said. 'No one who survives what you survived in Scotland is pathetic. You are a legend up there. So what if you didn't jump that day?'

She stared at him in astonishment for a second then struggled a handkerchief out of her bag and blew her nose. 'I failed the course,' she said flatly. 'I made a fool of myself.'

He shook his head. 'No,' he said. 'Nobody thinks you are a fool.' His eyes were serious. His voice was low. 'Sometimes it takes more courage to say no than to say yes.'

'But …'

He took her arm and shook her gently. 'Helen, listen to me. You weren't yourself that day. You were under enormous pressure, and you were tired. Look around you. Everyone is tired. That's what two years of war does to people. You'd been through the blitz. You'd suffered privations. Danger. Loss. And that was before that month of hell in Scotland.' He looked at her closely. 'You're still tired.' He touched her cheek gently with a cool finger. 'It shows in your eyes.'

That small touch sent a shiver running up her spine. She looked away quickly, scared what else he might see in her eyes. It was nice of him to be so forgiving but he was wrong. It wasn't tiredness that day. It was fear, pure and simple.

He was silent a moment then suddenly he spoke again, briskly now. 'You need a holiday,' he said. 'A complete break. Listen. I've got until the weekend free. Why don't you take a few days off and we'll play?'

'André, I can't. I must work …'

'Phh,' he said dismissively. 'You can't work for ever. When did you last have a holiday? Look.' He pointed upwards to the grimy glass roof through which sunlight was streaming in distinct rays like an old religious painting. 'For once London has good weather. We must not waste it. You need to feel the sun on your skin. You need to relax. To have fun. To forget completely about your work.' He smiled. 'When did you last relax in the sun with a handsome Frenchman at your side?'

Helen sighed. It sounded so good. So appealing. But dangerous. Katy's words of warning rang in her head: 'You simply can't afford to get hurt.'

'Well?'

'You're right, I do need a break,' she said hesitantly. 'But I've been thinking while you've been away. I think it would be a mistake for us to get too … um, too involved.'

He didn't answer at once and her heart sank. She had blown it now. Ruined everything. He was a man after all, and what men wanted was sex. And yet she tried to convince herself perhaps it was for the best. Raising her eyes cautiously she caught a thoughtful expression in his face, but then he shrugged.

'Okay. No problem. So we are just friends.' He spread his hands and smiled easily. 'Now, what do you say to spending a few days together?'

Helen felt a bubble of happiness form in her chest. She swallowed hard to resist the appeal of that smile. 'All right.'

André went home to change and shave. Helen went back to Angus McNaughton to ask for a few days off, which to her surprise he gave her without question.

It was a wonderful few days. Four long sunny days torn from the grim reality of war.

They sat in deckchairs in Hyde Park. They did the *Times* crossword. They picnicked on bread torn from the loaf and slices of American Spam and washed it down with wine straight from the bottle. André seemed to have an unlimited supply of wine. Sometimes they spoke in English, sometimes in French.

Most of all they laughed. In both languages André had the power to make her laugh. As André had promised, Helen found herself forgetting the war, the privations, and the fact that on Friday he would be leaving for the parachute course followed immediately by three weeks' specialist explosive training in Sussex.

One night they went to see Jen Carter's revue and André insisted on waiting at the stage door with a horde of Americans so he could tell Jen he thought she was the best thing in it. The following day they took the train to Oxford and punted on the Isis and ate sandwiches bought from the Cadena as they drifted past green meadows and shady overhanging trees.

Although André often touched her, getting in and out of the punt or ushering her through a doorway or across the street or to attract her attention to a swimming water rat or a small solemn family of passing ducks, he never made her feel awkward by trying to make love to her. In one way Helen appreciated his sensitivity but in another she was piqued that he apparently found it so easy to resist her.

It was on the last day, when she glanced at him casually

over the rim of her glass and saw the sparkle in his eyes as they picnicked on Hampstead Heath, the lazy sprawl of his long limbs as he poured the last of the wine, that she realised how much she owed to him.

'André, thank you,' she said suddenly.

He looked up, squinting slightly against the sun. 'What for?'

'For rescuing me,' she said. 'I'm sure the last thing you expected or wanted when you got back from Scotland was to find me snivelling at King's Cross. And now you've given up all your precious free time to make me better.'

He shook his head. 'I know,' he said. 'What a saint I am to sacrifice things like going to the bank and sending my clothes to the laundry, in order to spend time with the most wonderful girl I have ever met in my entire life.'

Helen laughed. 'André, don't,' she said. 'Don't tease.'

He was silent for a second. 'I am not teasing, Hélène. It is no hardship at all for me to be with you. In fact the thought of being without you again for the next few weeks is very bad.'

'Is it?' Helen searched his eyes. Sometimes it was so hard to know if he was telling the truth. 'Really?'

He didn't smile back. For a second she thought he might even be angry for putting him on the spot. Then slowly, deliberately, he began to clear the remnants of the picnic from the space between them: the bottle, the corkscrew, long-stemmed wineglasses begged off Katy for the occasion. When he had finished he reached over and drew her into his arms.

She could feel the strength in his limbs, smell the warm, clean masculine scent of him, the thick, healthy texture of his hair under her hand.

For a minute they lay there, entwined in silence, so still that Helen could hear the faint twittering of swallows high above them and a blackbird scratching under a nearby tree.

After a while, André rolled her on to her back, raised his head and kissed her.

For a fleeting heartbeat Helen felt nervous, but it was only a brief kiss and now his hand was on her face, stroking the hair back off her forehead, tracing her features. She opened her eyes and saw the warmth in his deep blue eyes.

'Hélène,' he whispered. Lowering his head, he kissed her again, a soft exploratory movement of lips and tongue, and suddenly she found herself responding.

It felt so right. So perfect. So simply wonderful.

But even as something turned over in her stomach, André was drawing back.

'You see, Hélène,' he murmured, 'we have so much. We like each other. We desire each other. Maybe we even love each other. We have everything.'

Helen looked up at him, his dark head framed by a cloudless blue sky, and she felt her eyes prickle with tears. 'Everything except time,' she said.

He touched her cheek. 'We have time,' he said. 'Not now, I know, but after the next course. And the next one.' He swung up into a sitting position and flexed his shoulders. 'In any case, I doubt they'll be sending me over before Christmas.'

Helen felt a stab of relief. Christmas. Five months away. Five months! She sat up abruptly and looked at him curiously. 'But you were so impatient before.'

'I know,' he said, 'but to do the job properly there is a lot to learn. So, *ma belle Hélène*, do not look sad. We have plenty of time.'

Joyce Carter didn't get much in the post these days. What with Pete now on his way to Egypt and Mick trundling back and forth to America on the Atlantic convoys, and the two kids in Devon so thoroughly absorbed into country life, she sometimes went several weeks without any mail.

So it was a surprise when she came in from the café to find two envelopes on the mat.

One was hard like card, the envelope white and crisp and the address written in a rounded hand. The other was in the usual wartime poor quality envelope, the writing a jerky mix of capitals and ordinary letters, and its very presence in her hand caused a curl of fear to circle Joyce's heart. Stanley.

She didn't want to hear from Stanley. She had done a good job in forgetting about Stanley. She didn't want to hear about life in jail. She didn't want to hear his gripes and moans about the food and the lack of drink. She certainly didn't want to hear that he missed her.

Hesitating only a moment she picked up the smart white envelope and slit the seal with her thumbnail and drew out the card.

> Mr and Mrs Greville Rutherford request the pleasure of your company on Saturday, 1 August 1942 for the marriage of their daughter Louise Elizabeth to First Lieutenant Jack Walter Delmaine at St Aldate's Church, Clapham Common, and afterwards at Cedars House.

Joyce stared at the crisp white card. She had never seen anything so smart in all her life. What's more, she had been with Celia Rutherford all day and she had never said. Never even hinted that Joyce would be invited to the wedding. Let alone Lorenz. Because there it was written on the top in the same rounded hand as the envelope: 'Mrs Carter and Mr Lorenz'.

Joyce couldn't help smiling at that. It was almost as though they were a couple. She knew old Lorenz would be pleased and all. She was pleased he'd been asked, because she never would have dared go on her own, not with all those toffs and fancy people the Rutherfords knew. What if she spilt her drink or got tipsy or something and said the wrong thing? And what would she wear? Then she shook her head. Lorenz would find her something to wear. He always had outfits in hock, he'd be bound to turn up some nice summer frock for her. Perhaps even a hat. She stood up. She'd pop over and see him now, show him the invitation and ask him to look out for something.

It was only as she turned for the door that she noticed Stanley's letter still lying on the table. Picking it up she tore it open quickly.

> Dear Joyce,
> I've heard word that you are making a fool of yourself over that Jew. He's been seen coming to the house more than once. I won't have it. I won't have you seeing him. You're my wife for better or worse. And if you don't stop it you'll pay. I'm not having you make a laughing stock out of me. You best not forget I've got friends in the area. Friends who keep me informed. Friends who will see me right.
>
> I'll be out of here soon and I'm damned if I'll have people saying that you were messing around while my back was turned. So you watch your step.
>
> Your loving husband,
> Stanley.

Almost as if the sun had shone deliberately on their happiness, as soon as André had gone the weather broke, bringing rain to London for most of July. But oddly Helen didn't care. The cold damp weather fitted her mood. Missing André the second time was much worse than the first. She knew now what she was missing. The image of him had been fleshed out. There was also the scary thought that next time he was back in London she might even go to bed with him.

The thought thrilled her. If fact she could hardly think about it without a shiver of anticipation running up her spine. It was madness, she knew, but the world was mad at the moment. Mad and sad. Only a few days ago a whole Arctic convoy had been lost off Greenland because of a simple Admiralty mistake, and in Yugoslavia seven hundred innocent civilians were taken from their homes and shot by the Germans in reprisal for the assassination of the Gestapo chief in Zagreb.

And tomorrow, Helen thought, among it all, Louise was going to be walking up the aisle, achieving her dream and marrying a handsome, eligible man, a man who quite obviously adored her to bits, a man who would shortly be joining those beleaguered Atlantic convoys, a man whose life expectancy, by any standard, was poor.

Not that Helen would dream of saying so of course. As chief bridesmaid she would throw herself into the spirit of the wedding with the best of them.

Even Katy was excited about the wedding. Katy, who lived with the knowledge that somewhere in Nazi Europe her husband was still on the run, still in danger. That was of course if he were not already lying dead somewhere unrecognised or unreported.

Helen was just trying to force her mind away from this unpleasant thought when Angus McNaughton came into her office.

One look at his face told her that whatever he had to say was not good news. Suddenly, with a horrible sense of certainty, she knew it was going to be something about André. An accident. A negligent discharge, a mistimed bomb. Or if not André, Ward, news of his recapture. A shooting. His death.

She could barely wait for the two seconds it took Angus to close the door and turn back to face her. 'The Autogiro network in France has been infiltrated by the Gestapo,' he said. 'Fifteen of our agents have already been rounded up. God knows how many French.'

Helen was shocked. Partly by the appalling news, but mostly by her dreadful sense of relief that it was nothing to do with André, or Ward.

'Oh no,' she muttered. 'How awful.'

'Awful?' Angus glared at her through his exhaled smoke. 'It's a bloody fiasco. A calamity. It means that apart from Paul and one or two others we've got virtually no reliable agents in the field at all.'

'So what's going to happen?'

'What's going to happen is that if we're not careful we'll lose the confidence we've built up over there, so we're sending in as many as we can next week. To pick up the pieces.'

Helen blinked at him. 'But who? There are hardly any French speakers ready, are there? Not fully trained.' She knew the SOE chiefs were worried about the lack of French-speaking candidates successfully passing out of training. The fact that she wasn't the only one to fail had been some small comfort to her, but of course it meant that now, when qualified agents were needed, there was none to be had.

'We're going to take the best out of training,' Angus was saying. 'It's the only thing to do. It's not an ideal solution, but they'll just have to do their best.'

Helen nodded. It wasn't an ideal solution. Sending semi-trained operatives into the field was clearly a dangerous course, both for the SOE and for the agents themselves. Looking up she realised Angus was watching her.

'I thought you'd like to know,' he said.

And suddenly, belatedly, she realised why he was telling her all this. It wasn't for her general edification. It wasn't just casual conversation. It was because of her link with one of those 'best' candidates.

'André,' she whispered. 'They're sending André?'

Angus lifted his shoulders slightly. 'I told you before, they rated him highly.'

Helen stared at him. 'They can't,' she said. 'He's barely begun his training. It's far too dangerous. How can he hope to survive?'

'He didn't have to agree,' Angus said. 'He was given every chance to say no, but apparently he jumped at it. We're hoping to get him over there early next week. They're briefing him now down at Brockenhurst. I just hope to God they know what they're doing.'

Helen sat down again. She couldn't speak. She couldn't think.

Angus looked at her. 'I'm sorry, Helen,' he said awkwardly. 'If I'd known you felt this way about him I would have broken the news more gently.'

Gently or brutally, it really didn't matter. What mattered was that André was going. Leaving her. Without a second thought. Just as Katy had predicted.

Part Four

Chapter Seventeen

Pam was polishing the kitchen windows when she felt the baby kick. At once she stopped and put a hand on her stomach. Her pregnancy was progressing well. She had suffered no sickness or cravings, which was lucky, Alan said, because unless she developed a craving for tinned meat or lettuce, which were virtually the only things in the shops right now, she was going to be disappointed.

Catching sight of her reflection in the newly polished window, Pam couldn't help but notice her rosy cheeks and shining hair. There was no doubt she was blooming. Her only problem was that the lump was beginning to show. It wouldn't be long now before people noticed. Last year's summer skirts were far too tight in the waist, and only by dint of sewing in a strip of precious elastic discovered in Arding & Hobbs was she able to continue wearing them at all.

Suddenly she heard a noise behind her and swung round to find George staring at her. 'What's the matter, Mum? Have you got a tummy ache?'

Pam quickly took her hands off her stomach. She knew she had to tell him. The last thing in the world she wanted was for him to find out from someone else. She had been putting it off day by day, but now the moment had come when she knew she was going to have to bite the bullet.

'No, I haven't got a tummy ache,' she said, 'but I have got something to tell you.'

'Is it a bad thing?' he asked nervously as she sat him down at the table.

'No. It's a nice thing. Or I hope you will think so, anyway.' Gathering her courage she sat down on the other side of the table. 'George,' she said. 'You're the first person we've told, but I'm going to have a baby.' She patted her stomach. 'It's on its way already. A baby that will be born in December. Just in time for Christmas. A little brother or sister for you.'

She smiled at him expectantly but he didn't respond. For a moment he looked as though he didn't believe her and she wondered nervously if she was going to have to explain the facts of life. And then very slowly, painfully slowly, the expression on his face turned from disbelief to dismay. It didn't stop there: fleetingly she saw anger, terror, pain and then abruptly, to her utter horror, his face crumpled, but before she could move to touch him, to comfort him, he was up and running.

'George. Darling. Stop! Where are you going?'

But it was too late. He was gone. At high speed. Sprinting down the passage, flinging the front door open and slamming it behind him before Pam had even got to her feet.

Helen was in her old bedroom at the Rutherfords' putting on her bridesmaid's dress. Louise had wanted frills and flounces but Helen had persuaded her towards a simpler style, something she could use again, a slimline summer shift of pale lemon. Louise had miraculously found the material in Debenham & Freebody and they'd all clubbed together on clothing coupons to get enough for Helen and the two little bridesmaids, cousins of Jack.

She was just about to roll on the brand new stockings that Jen Carter had procured for her from some American serviceman, when the door opened. Expecting Louise, she was dismayed to find Greville Rutherford entering the room.

'Hello Helen,' he said. He rubbed his hands together with a slight laugh and glanced around the room. 'Funny you being in here again. Just like old times, isn't it?'

'Not really,' she said. 'Things have changed quite a bit since then.'

He looked at her for a moment then gave a short caustic laugh. 'Oh, the new boyfriend, you mean? Yes, Louise has told me all about him. Some French aristocrat, I believe. What a shame he can't be with us today.'

Ignoring his sarcasm, Helen nodded. 'Yes, isn't it?' she said stiffly. It was actually looking increasingly likely that she would never see or hear from André again. She had waited in the office until eight o'clock last night hoping he would ring, but he hadn't. Not a word. And no letter this morning. Nothing but silence. Painful, heartbreaking silence.

'What's the matter, Helen?' Greville took a step towards her. 'I didn't mean to upset you.'

For once he sounded genuine and Helen had to grit her teeth to stop sudden tears springing into her eyes. Abruptly she turned away from his outstretched hand. 'Nothing's the matter,' she said, staring fixedly out of the window. 'Absolutely nothing.' She was determined not to throw a dampener on Louise's happy day. In any case, Greville Rutherford was the last person she would tell.

Behind her she heard his patronising voice. 'I suppose he's giving you the runaround, is he?' he said. 'I can't say I'm surprised. Take my word. You can never trust a Frog ...'

But Helen was no longer listening. Gripping the windowsill she leaned her forehead against the glass. Below her there was a clattering of china as two men in striped aprons unloaded the Fortnum & Mason van which was parked in the drive. Beyond, at the end of the drive the wide expanse of Clapham Common stretched away. And then she caught a glimpse of a running child.

'I told you before, what you need is an older man ...'

Narrowing her eyes against the bright sunlight, Helen tensed, then turned and ran across the room. 'Excuse me.' She brushed past Greville and swung the door open. 'I've just got to go out for a moment.'

She was already halfway along the passage when she heard his bellow behind her. 'Helen! For God's sake. What are you doing? Helen! I was talking to you ...'

As she raced barefoot down the stairs, Louise appeared on the half landing looking anxious in a long lacy dressing-gown. Her hair had been dressed in falling ringlets and her face was smooth and carefully powdered. Her eyes widened as Helen pelted past. 'Helen! Where are you going?'

Helen didn't even pause. 'Back in a minute,' she shouted over her shoulder as she sped down the final flight into the hall, dodging the caterers as she flew out of the front door.

'I need you to help me with the dress,' Louise wailed. 'Now!'

But Helen had gone. Looking up, Louise saw her father leaning over the banister rail. 'Where's she gone?' she shouted. 'What have you done to her?'

To her surprise he flushed and drew back. 'I haven't done anything to her. Don't be absurd.'

'George! Wait!'

The yellow dress was tight. Pausing for a second at the end of the drive to hitch it up, Helen padded cautiously across the road then sprinted barefoot across the cool grass after the small figure.

She caught him up at the bandstand.

'Leave me alone,' he cried as she grabbed his arm and swung him round to face her. 'I'm all right.'

'Then why are you crying?'

'I'm not.'

Helen touched his face and showed him her damp fingertip. 'Well, what's this, then?'

He was silent for a moment, head hanging like a broken doll. 'Mum's having a baby.'

'Mum?' Helen gaped at his downturned head. 'Pam?' She looked back across the common towards Lavender Road. Was it possible? Helen had been so distracted recently that Pam could have developed wings and learned to fly for all she would have noticed. But now she came to think of it Pam had put on a bit of weight, and there had been a vague sense of mystery in the small house.

'Goodness,' she said. 'When's it due? When did she say it was coming?'

George pulled away from her and scuffed his foot in the dust. 'For Christmas,' he said. 'She says it's so I can have brothers and sisters but I don't *want* any brothers or sisters.' He looked up suddenly as a thought occurred to him. 'She said it's already on its way, but if I told her I didn't want one, perhaps she could send it back?'

He looked so hopeful Helen barely had the heart to disabuse him. 'No, I don't think she'll be able to send it back,' she said gravely. 'It's in her tummy, you see, and it will be growing quite big already.'

George looked appalled and Helen glanced round quickly. 'Here, why don't we sit on this bench for a moment?' she said, sitting down herself. Eventually after a long pause he heaved himself up next to her and sat with his feet dangling over the edge.

'You know,' she began casually, 'when I was young and I had a wish, like on a birthday cake or a Christmas pudding, I always longed for a younger sister.'

'Did you? Why?'

'I thought it would be fun. Grown-ups are all right, but can never be friends. Not properly. Not like brothers and sisters. Think how nice it will be for you to have someone to talk to, someone to share secrets with, someone to be naughty with.' She smiled. 'And think how nice it will be for the baby to have a grown-up brother who can tell it things, help it along, teach it to walk and talk.'

George looked away. 'Aunty Pam won't want me if she's got a baby, will she? It will be like that horrid Malcolm baby all over again but worse. I'll just be in the way.'

'Oh, I don't think so,' Helen said. 'I think she'll want you more than ever. To help with things. Babies are hard work.' He didn't look convinced, and Helen frowned. 'George. Listen to me,' she said suddenly. 'Loving someone doesn't mean that you stop loving someone else less. I love André but that doesn't mean I love my father any less. Or you.'

He stared at her. 'Do you really love me?'

'Of course I do.'

'And you still will when the baby comes?'

Helen was touched. 'Of course I will.' She smiled. 'Anyway, I told you once before I don't like babies very much.'

George was silent for a minute, swinging his legs. Helen noticed his knees were grubby and bleeding where he must have fallen in his precipitous flight.

She was just about to say more reassuring things about the baby when he looked up suddenly. 'André's going away, isn't he? I heard you tell Aunty … Mum last night.'

Helen nodded. 'Yes, he is.'

'Will you be sad?'

'Yes.' It was her turn to look away.

After a moment she felt a small slightly muddy hand creep into hers. Turning back she gave him a watery smile.

'You were sad before and we made you better, didn't we? Mum and Dad and me.'

'Yes.'

George frowned. 'Perhaps we can do it again.'

Jen was tired. She wished now, as she walked back from Clapham Common Tube, that she hadn't gone to the party, but when the leading lady singled her out and asked her to an impromptu gathering after the last show she could hardly refuse, and then of course it got far too late to get home.

Actually she had enjoyed the party. The leading lady's Hampstead house was wildly bohemian, and her friends were funny and irreverent. The producer of the show was there too, and as he talked to Jen she suddenly realised he thought she was good. Really quite good. Perhaps even good enough to get somewhere. And then, as she talked and laughed and drank the rather odd-tasting punch, she had felt the uncomfortable roughness in her voice come on and her heart sank.

She couldn't say anything of course. The last thing they wanted to hear was that she had a problem with her voice. In any case the cigarette smoke and music covered any telltale huskiness. As she bedded down eventually on a sofa, she had prayed to every God she knew that by morning it would have worn off.

It hadn't, of course, and after a bleary-eyed cup of tea with her hostess's husband, Jen made a hasty exit.

Last time she had had the throat problem one of the Americans had given her some throat lozenges. By numbing her throat slightly they had just about enabled her to get through three shows each night.

Now as she walked briskly along Clapham Common Northside she felt renewed anxiety. A singer without a voice was not a good prospect. She tried humming a few notes and grimaced as the sound faltered. It seemed so cruel that this should happen just when doors were beginning to open to her.

Shaking her head crossly, she decided to try not to worry yet. She would gargle, change, try to catch up on an hour or two's sleep, then head back to the theatre and hope that Dirk or one of his mates would be there later to ask about the lozenges.

As she passed St Aldate's, she saw a few people standing around expectantly in fancy clothes and prewar hats, and remembered it was Louise Rutherford's wedding day and that she had promised to look after Malcolm while Katy went to the wedding.

Further along the road at the Rutherfords' house, someone had tied a white ribbon on the gatepost. On the other side of the road she saw Helen de Burrel with the Nelson child walking hand in hand across the common towards her. Helen waved, but Jen pretended not to see her. She had a nasty feeling that if she had to talk to anyone she might cry. Jen never cried.

Quickening her step she turned the corner and walked slap bang into her mother and Mr Lorenz hurrying the other way.

Jen almost didn't recognise her mother. She had never seen her so done up. Wearing a spotted navy and white summer dress with a matching navy boater, handbag and gloves, she looked almost attractive. She even had a touch of lipstick on. Lorenz too was looking extraordinarily dapper in a dark morning suit with a crisp white shirt and wing collar. Jerking back from his steadying hand, Jen gaped at them in astonishment. Only then did she realise that they were going to the wedding.

Suddenly she felt a stab of jealousy. How was it that she, a pretty up-and-coming star, was dragging back to the pub, feeling like death, while her drab old mother was waltzing off to a society wedding on the arm of a rather nice-looking man? Not that Jen had ever had much time for Louise Rutherford of course – frankly she considered her a spoilt little brat. Nevertheless it was galling that she hadn't been invited.

Taking a pace back she hid her pique in sarcasm. 'Goodness,' she said. 'Aren't we fancy today? I wonder what Dad would say if he could see you now.'

For a second her mother's eyes flickered nervously but then she straightened her shoulders in an unexpected gesture of defiance. 'Not as much as he'd say if he saw you rolling home at twelve in the morning after a night on the razzle,' Joyce said coldly. 'You'd best get out of sight before anyone sees you. You look a right mess. It's obvious what you've been up to and it's embarrassing.'

Jen could not believe her ears. Embarrassing? Her mother was embarrassed by her. Jen almost choked. When she tried to speak her voice was husky. Putting a hand to her throat she coughed and felt her eyes water. She wanted to scream at her mother that if anyone was embarrassed it was her. Nobody else's mother pranced around in public with a fancy man. Nobody else's mother refused to house their daughter. Nobody else's mother dressed herself up like mutton to go to a wedding far beyond her station.

Before Jen could say anything, Pam Nelson came flying up the street like something demented. 'Have you seen George anywhere?' she asked.

'Yes,' Jen said. 'I saw him a minute ago on the common with Helen de Burrel.'

'What's the matter with your voice?' Joyce asked as Pam gasped out something in relief and ran on.

'I've got a bit of a sore throat, that's all,' Jen said.

Joyce sniffed. 'Not surprising, if you ask me. It's your own fault for messing around with them Yanks. You've most likely picked up some nasty disease.'

It was unfair. Bitterly unfair. Once Jen would have fought back but today she simply hadn't the energy. All she wanted to do was go to bed. As she swallowed painfully she felt tears in her eyes. She saw Lorenz looking at her and turned her head away. She didn't want Lorenz's sympathy.

'Well, I didn't ask you,' she said coldly. 'And if that's your opinion of me you're welcome to it.'

Pam could have cried with relief when she turned the corner and saw George and Helen crossing the road hand in hand, but instead she waited until they reached the pavement and then crouched in front of him.

'Sweetheart, I didn't mean for you to be upset about the baby. I hoped you'd be pleased.'

George wouldn't look at her. 'I don't want to talk about it.'

'Oh darling. Don't be like that. I do understand how you feel, but the baby's not coming until December so there's plenty of time for us all to get used to the idea.'

'I don't want to talk about it.'

Over his averted head, Pam met Helen's eyes. 'All right,' she said, straightening up. 'We'll talk about Meccano instead.'

He did look at her then, a brief wary glance. 'Meccano?'

Pam shrugged. 'I saw in the paper that Arding and Hobbs got some Meccano in yesterday, and if we're quick we might be able to get some.'

'Can Helen come?'

'No,' Pam said. 'Helen's got to go to the wedding. Will you come with me?'

There was a moment's pause, then George detached his hand from Helen's and thrust it into his pocket. 'All right,' he said.

Pam nodded. It wasn't much, but it was something. A concession.

It was a wonderful wedding. Despite clothes rationing and government strictures on economy there was a profusion of pretty hats and dresses. The Northcote Road street trader had surpassed himself and the church was filled with the scent of roses. Reunited with her shoes Helen felt distinctly choked as she walked slowly down the aisle behind Louise and Greville to the accompaniment of crashing organ music. Ahead, Jack and William, his best man, stood stiff and straight. Behind her, the two little bridesmaids were solemn and pretty as dolls.

Louise herself looked prettier than Helen had ever seen. As she walked back up the aisle after the service with her veil lifted she was quite clearly radiant with joy, and Jack couldn't take his eyes off her. It wasn't surprising. Regardless of his love for his bride, it seemed so out of place somehow to see such innocent prettiness. The frills and flounces on her dress made such a change from the grim austerity of war, and the reception afterwards was like a throwback to a more luxurious age. There were economies of course: the cake icing was paper thin, barely enough to cover the Victoria sponge inside, and where once Fortnum's would have produced vol-au-vents, devils-on-horseback, and melt-in-the-mouth cheese biscuits, now the canapés were predominantly made of standard issue brown bread, and after a couple of sips of the rather tasteless wine it occurred to Helen that Greville Rutherford must have watered it down.

Nevertheless it was a good show and Helen tried very hard to enjoy it. Determinedly banishing all thoughts of André, and carefully avoiding Greville Rutherford, she dutifully spent time with William, exchanged remarks about the wonderful weather with various Rutherford relatives, shared a mild joke about the wine with Katy and the food with Mrs Carter and found herself touched by the old-fashioned courtesy of Mr Lorenz.

It was while she was talking to Jack's utterly charming parents that a commotion suddenly occurred at the entrance to the marquee. For a moment, Helen couldn't tell what was happening. All she could see was Greville Rutherford arguing rather heatedly with some latecomer.

'Oh dear, I do hope it's not some old boyfriend of Louise's,' Mrs Delmaine whispered.

'It looks more like some kind of tramp,' her husband replied, craning across to see.

And then the sea of heads parted and Helen saw who it was.

At the same moment, Louise suddenly screamed out, 'It's André! It's all right, Daddy. Let him in. It's Helen's boyfriend.'

For Helen everything seemed to stop. All she could see

was André, standing there, staring at her across the crowded room.

She could understand Greville Rutherford's dismay. André was certainly not dressed for the occasion. On the contrary, he looked like some kind of belligerent French peasant in shabby navy trousers and baggy shirt. All he needed to complete the image was a beret, a loaf of French bread and a string of onions, Helen thought, as he began to stride towards her through the sea of guests.

'André,' she gulped. Staring at him in amazement, it was a moment before she remembered her manners and introduced him to Jack's parents who were still standing next to her trying manfully to hide their astonishment.

'Hélène,' he murmured urgently. 'I must talk to you. I don't have very much time.'

Looking wildly around the crowded marquee, Helen couldn't see anywhere to go.

'Perhaps the garden?' Mrs Delmaine suggested gently. 'Look, you can squeeze through this flap.'

Out of the corner of her eye Helen could see Greville Rutherford bearing down on them ominously, closely followed by Louise and Jack, but André was already urging her out of the gap in the tent.

Hitching up her skirt she clambered through and a moment later they were out plunging through one of Mrs Rutherford's dig-for-victory vegetable patches and running for the safety of the garden shed. Beside it, out of sight of the marquee, André took her into his arms and held her against him for a moment.

Burying her face in his shoulder, Helen tried to steady her breathing. I must be brave, she thought. I must not cry. He has made the effort to come. I must not let him down by crying.

Slowly he pushed her away so he could see her face. 'You have heard what's happened, haven't you?' he said.

Helen nodded mutely.

'They have lost one of the main southern circuits,' he

went on. 'They want me to go and set up another. In unoccupied France. So we are ready in case the Germans take over, as they surely will.' He was holding her hands. Holding them hard as though he never wanted to let her go, and he was looking at her intently. 'You know why I've come, don't you?' he asked.

Helen could feel the sun beating down on her shoulders. She could smell the tangy creosote paint sweating on the shed door. She could feel her heart beating heavily in her chest as she looked up into his steady, midnight-blue eyes.

'You've come to say goodbye,' she whispered.

For a second he looked surprised then he shook his head. 'No,' he said. 'I've come to ask you to go with me.'

Chapter Eighteen

It was hushed in the Rutherfords' garden. The noise of the wedding was muted by the thick canvas walls of the marquee. Only the vague murmuring and scratching of Mrs Rutherford's chickens and a lone song thrush on the wall disturbed the lazy August silence. Despite the fact that Mrs Rutherford had turned much of her garden over to vegetables, the heavy scent of late summer flowers hung on the still air. Roses and honeysuckle and the soft emotive aroma of the jasmine climbing over the wall.

Helen and André were standing close to the shed. They seemed very still. Very quiet. Katy grimaced to herself as she approached them. She knew it was a bad moment to intrude. Of course it was. André wouldn't have come barging into the middle of Louise's reception unless he had something important to say.

'Um … Look, I'm really sorry to disturb you,' she said awkwardly, 'but Louise is refusing to leave without saying goodbye.'

The tension in the air was almost tangible. Katy couldn't help noticing that André's fingers were overtight on Helen's bare arm, nor that Helen was looking anywhere but at him. Katy felt the hairs on her own arms prickling. For an awful moment she thought nobody was going to speak. Or move. That the three of them would be stuck there in a strange emotional tableau for ever more.

Then Helen straightened her shoulders. 'I must go,' she said.

André inclined his head. 'Yes of course.' His hand fell slowly from Helen's arm, leaving four red weals, and Katy wished she was a million miles away.

As Helen walked away towards the house, Katy looked uncertainly at André. 'Will you come too?'

He shook his head. 'I'll stay here. I don't want to upset Louise's parents any more.' He smiled then, but Katy could see the effort it took and she looked away quickly. She knew that look, that sense of closed-down emotion. She had seen it in Ward's eyes too.

'He's going, isn't he?' she asked as she caught Helen up at the back door.

Helen nodded.

Katy touched her arm. 'You poor thing. I'm so sorry.'

Helen smoothed her dress. 'It's worse than that,' she said over her shoulder as she stepped into the house. 'He wants me to go with him.'

For a second Katy didn't take it in, then she put a hand over her heart. 'Oh my God,' she whispered, then she tripped on the step in her high heels and would have fallen sprawling headlong into the kitchen if Mrs Rutherford hadn't been there to catch her.

'Goodness,' Mrs Rutherford exclaimed, blanching as Katy's elbow embedded itself in her stomach. 'Are you all right, Katy?' Steadying Katy back on her feet, she frowned at Helen. 'There you are! We've been looking for you everywhere.'

'I'm sorry,' Helen said. 'I'm afraid something rather urgent cropped up.'

'I see,' Celia said doubtfully. She peered over their shoulders. 'And your, um … friend? Has he left?'

'No,' Helen said. 'He's waiting in the garden. I hope that's all right.'

Celia looked rather taken aback. 'Yes,' she said. 'Yes, of course, but …'

Helen smiled blandly. 'We'd better go and wave off the happy couple.'

Marvelling at Helen's coolness, Katy followed her through the house.

Louise was already at the car kissing everyone goodbye. She was clearly dying to get to the hotel. There were no last-minute maidenly nerves for her. It was Jack who looked nervous as he ushered his giggling, excited bride towards the waiting taxi for the short ride to Clapham Junction station.

No, Katy thought, catching Louise's smile as she leaned back provocatively against Jack for a moment, Louise wasn't going to be shy on her wedding night. But then Louise had done it before. Not that Jack knew that of course. Jack was presumably under the impression he was going to have to deflower his virgin bride. No wonder he looked so pale.

With a sudden pang Katy remembered her own wedding night in a little country cottage near Oxford. She had been so nervous she had nearly spoiled the whole thing, and it was only Ward's wonderful tender lovemaking that had saved the day. And the six idyllic days that had followed it, before he was called away for that last fated mission.

Now André was also being called away. Too soon. Even Katy knew that. He couldn't possibly have finished his training yet. As for Helen, she had barely even begun hers before she had come off that parachute course, and yet now she had the opportunity to go with him. To France.

Helen looked so cool, so composed as she kissed Jack and hugged Louise goodbye, and all the time André Cabillard was waiting in the garden. Waiting presumably for Helen's decision. Katy shivered. As much as she had loved Ward, it was not a choice she would have wanted to make. As she stood in the sun among the smiling wedding guests, Katy felt a cold hand close round her heart. Whatever happened, whichever course Helen chose, Katy knew that it was bound to end in tears.

Behind the polite smile, the laughter, the good wishes and farewell kisses, Helen was miles away. Back in Scotland, cold and tired, learning to handle the .32 Colt they thought would suit a girl's hand better. She heard again the constant shouted instruction. Speed. Attack. Two shots. Always two shots. Running crouched down alleys, flinging open doors, knowing that behind one of them would be a Nazi dummy.

'Come with me, Helen,' André had said, and it sounded so good. So brave. She and André working together for the freedom of France. She could feel the adrenalin pumping through her veins as if she was already on the way.

But then reality reasserted itself. The constant fear, the looking over your shoulder wondering who is behind you, waiting for the knock on your door. Waiting for the bullet in your back. Or worse, the horror of interrogation and torture.

Nobody knew exactly what depths the Germans would sink to, but nobody doubted Adolf Hitler's capacity for mindless cruelty. Already there were reports of Nazi death camps for so called 'enemies of the state'. Jews. Traitors. Spies. Mass extermination in conditions too horrible to think about. Like everyone else Helen could only hope it was propaganda, but deep down she feared it was true.

Then suddenly through her uneasy reverie she saw something coming straight at her out of the blue sky. At once she was back in Scotland again with a live hand grenade arching towards her and she leaped away in horror.

It was a second later, as Louise wailed her name in dismay and Katy and William bent quickly to retrieve the scattered flowers, that Helen realised Louise had deliberately thrown the bouquet to her. And she had dropped it.

It wasn't Jen Carter's day. She had only been back at the pub a few minutes before the door opened and she found herself staring across the bar straight into the grinning, wide-eared face of her younger brother Mick.

'Good God,' she said straightening up. 'What on earth are you doing here? I thought you were bobbing about on the high seas somewhere with a cargo of Spam.'

Mick shrugged. He was used to Jen's sarcasm. 'We're having a refit, so I thought I'd come home for a bit, but the house is all locked up. Mum's not away, is she? I hope not because I've brought her some maple syrup specially from America.'

Jen eyed him suspiciously. Since when had Mick cared two hoots about Joyce? Smarmy little bugger, she thought, just because he wants a bed for his leave. She made a mental note, nevertheless, to ask Dirk and the boys if they could get her some maple syrup.

'She's at Louise Rutherford's wedding,' she said shortly.

'Cor.' Mick looked impressed. 'She's gone up in the world.' He heaved his canvas bag back on to his shoulder. 'Give us the key, then, Jen, and I'll dump my stuff and have a wash.'

'I haven't got a key,' Jen said stiffly. 'I don't live there.'

'What? Has Mum thrown you out? What have you done?'

'I haven't done anything,' Jen said crossly. 'I wouldn't want to live there anyway. Not with that awful Lorenz hanging round there the whole time.'

Mick frowned. 'He's all right, Lorenz. I know he's a Jew and that, but if he's kind to old Mum, that's all that matters, ain't it?'

Jen laughed mockingly. 'What've you got? Religion or something? What about Dad? You used to be such a Daddy's boy. And if I remember rightly you once took a pot shot at Lorenz with some pistol you nicked from the Home Guard.'

Mick's freckled face coloured slightly. 'I didn't know better then, did I? But Lorenz didn't bubble me. And what's Dad ever done for Mum apart from beat her up?'

'He's her husband. For better for worse.'

'I reckon as she ought to get a divorce.'

Jen stared at him. 'A divorce? What do you know about divorce?'

Mick scratched his head. 'I know as when you're out in the dark ocean and you know that Jerry is there but you don't know if he's got his sights on you or the next ship, then you know that there's not any point in winning the war for people to be unhappy.' He shuffled his feet, suddenly self-conscious. 'It's like you get time to think at sea.'

Jen almost laughed. Was this really her cack-handed kid brother talking? With his freckly face and big ears he still looked like an oversized schoolboy. It was hard to imagine him sitting on some dark, heaving deck, thinking. It made her feel uneasy, and she was almost relieved when he reverted to type and grinned his old cocky grin.

'Pull us a pint, Jen.'

Jen shook her head. 'You're underage,' she said, but one of the locals bought one for him anyway. Already they were gathering round eager for news.

'What's it really like at sea? Eh, Micky? What about the navy, how much protection do the convoys really get? Have you seen a U-boat?'

Despite herself Jen found herself listening in. 'Saw one last but one trip,' Mick said nonchalantly. 'Lit up by the light of a burning coal freighter. We reckoned we was goners and all, but he left us alone.' He grinned. 'That's twice that's happened since I joined the *Topaz*. Some of the lads reckon I'm like a lucky charm.'

'I'd have thought you'd be more like an albatross,' Jen said sourly, but the allusion was lost on Mick.

'I've seen one of them and all. Great big bugger. I've seen all sorts. Dolphins, flying fish. Saw a whale last week. Bigger than a double decker, that was. Quite friendly though. It kind of smiled at us as it went past.'

My brother the raconteur, Jen thought grimly, turning away. There was no problem with Mick's voice.

Maybe I should give up altogether, she thought. Maybe I should join the Forces. Or maybe I should get married like Louise. Nobody cared if stupid Louise could reach top C or not. Louise was set up for life. All Louise had to do now was be suitably subservient to her husband and bear him a couple of babies. But I don't want to be like Louise, Jen thought, clearing her throat. I don't want to have to be subservient to some cocky young man. I want to sing. I want to act. I'm good at it. I want to do it.

Just then baby Malcolm started wailing upstairs and Molly Coogan appeared on the stairs. 'Jen, can you come and help?' she called. 'Malcolm's just been sick all over the playpen.'

'Hélène?' It was only half a question because as soon as he saw her walk out of the house and down across the lawn towards him André knew she had made the decision.

'Oh, André.' Her voice was full of despair. 'It wouldn't work.'

'Is it the jump?' he asked. 'You could do it if you were with me. If they drop us at four hundred feet, we'll be down in less than twenty seconds.'

Helen shuddered. Even now she could feel the chill of remembered fear. She was on that plane again, circling Ringway aerodrome, the grey blur of Manchester tilting away under the wing like a toy town.

'It's not just the jump,' she said and there were tears in her eyes as she looked away down the long garden. 'I want to be with you, but I know I would let you down and then you would despise me. Even more than you probably do now.'

He took her hand then and put it against his cheek. 'I would never despise you, Hélène,' he said. 'I told you once before it takes more courage sometimes to say no.' Gently he pulled her into his arms.

Closing her eyes Helen leaned into the warm strength of him, loving him more now than ever before. She couldn't believe his understanding. Nor could she believe the pain of his imminent departure. She could feel his regret, his disappointment, even as he rested his cheek on her hair.

'Oh, André,' she mumbled. 'I'm so sorry.'

His arms tightened for a moment, reassuring her where most men would have accused her of not loving them enough. 'Don't be sorry,' he murmured. 'I do understand. And it's not for ever. One day the war will be over and then we can meet again.'

Helen squeezed her eyes together tightly. If you are still alive, she thought. If you haven't met someone else. Some brave Resistance girl.

'Come back with me to Sussex on the train,' he said suddenly, pulling back. 'At least then we will have a little time to talk. I can't bear to say goodbye to you here.'

Helen looked up at him with watering eyes. 'You won't try to persuade me?'

He touched his heart. 'I promise,' he said. 'I just want to be with you. For as long as possible.'

The Compleat Angler was everything Louise could have wished for in a honeymoon hotel. Quaint and low beamed, it had a wonderfully romantic atmosphere and the staff treated them like royalty as they ate a beautifully cooked dinner of trout and apple pie in the candlelit dining-room. Their bedroom on the first floor looked out over beautiful gardens and at the end of the lawn the River Thames glinted in the moonlight. They had walked along the towpath earlier, before changing for dinner.

That had been romantic too, strolling hand in hand, stopping sometimes to watch the ducks sailing past in little flotillas, the regal swans, or once or twice to have a little kiss and cuddle, but only if nobody was looking. Even though they were now married, Jack still seemed shy at touching her in public. For her part Louise would have preferred to do the kissing and cuddling in the privacy of their bedroom as soon as they arrived in the hotel, and a bit more than kissing and cuddling too, but as soon as he had unpacked, Jack had ordered tea for them on the terrace and afterwards he had seemed keen to get some fresh air.

'That's if you're not too tired,' he added solicitously. 'It's been a long day.'

For a second Louise had toyed with tempting him to the bedroom by saying she was tired, but even though her hip was aching a bit after all the standing, she shook her head.

'Oh no, let's go for a walk,' she had said brightly. After all, there would be plenty of time later for sex. Sex. Louise had hugged herself as she followed Jack down to the river. She had fancied him so much today she could barely contain herself. Once or twice at the reception she had almost suggested that they sneak away upstairs for a few minutes, but now she was glad she had restrained herself. Jack obviously wanted to do everything by the book, and he certainly would have been shocked by any suggestion of pre-emptive lovemaking at Cedars House.

He was her husband whom she had vowed to honour and obey. Her husband. Louise could still hardly believe it. She was married. Married at last. To a handsome, gallant young naval officer. She had felt so proud today, showing him off to her friends and relations. Seeing him smiling and chatting in his easy, charming way. Even her parents liked him. For once she had even managed to please them.

And now as she lay between the crisp white sheets in the honeymoon bed and waited for Jack to finish in the bathroom, she was very much looking forward to the moment when he would please her.

The pub was just closing when Helen came in. Katy looked up from stacking bottles. It had been a busy evening. News of Mick Carter's presence seemed to have spread around the neighbouring streets and a lot of extra trade had come in to hear his Atlantic war stories. Molly had had to go back to the hospital and Jen, despite her husky voice, had gone to the theatre, so with only Jacob to help her Katy had been rushed off her feet.

'He's gone,' Helen said before Katy could ask. 'I said I wouldn't go with him.'

Katy stared at her, amazed by the lack of emotion in her voice. She seemed very steady, pale but controlled as she delved in her bag and brought out a five-pound note.

Smoothing it out she laid it carefully on the counter and glanced at Katy. 'How much alcohol can I get for that?'

Katy blinked. 'Helen, I don't think you ought …'

'Katy, please …' For a second Helen's composure wavered, but she squared her shoulders determinedly. 'Please. Help me. I want to get drunk. Very drunk.'

'Oh Helen,' Katy said helplessly. She wanted to say more but her voice suddenly felt choked, and then, before she could even reach for the bottle, to her horror she started to cry.

It was a long time since Katy had cried, and now once she had started she couldn't stop. All her grief and anxiety bubbled to the surface like some long-dormant volcano of emotion. There was suddenly too much of it to hold back. So much pain. So many worries. Ward, Malcolm, her mother, the pub, Jen and now Helen too. As her tears dripped unheeded on to the bar she was aware of Helen coming round, heard the glug of liquid, the chink of glasses and then a drink was pressed into her hand.

'I'm sorry,' Katy mumbled. 'It's you who should be crying, not me.'

'I'm not going to cry,' Helen said grimly. 'It's my own fault if I'm upset. I could have gone. I could have gone if I had the guts, but I didn't and that's all there is to it.'

Katy gulped for air. She didn't know what to say. How to console her. Blindly she swallowed her drink and felt the welcome rush of heat as it coursed down her throat. Helen was already reaching for the bottle again. She was aware that Helen had downed at least two glasses, and they weren't by any means small measures.

Katy shook her head. 'It's bad for you to drink too much,' she said.

Helen shrugged as she sloshed the whisky into the glass. 'Bad for me?' Her eyes glittered. 'What do I care? I don't care if it kills me. Just now I'd be glad if it did.'

'Helen, don't say that.' Katy was shocked.

'Why not?' Helen looked up from her drink. 'That's how you felt when Ward went missing that first time.'

It was true. Katy had gone to pieces over the news that Ward had been left alone and injured at the mercy of the Germans. So much had happened since then that she had almost forgotten that utter, knife-to-the-heart agony. Now when she thought of Ward, it was more like picking a scab, whereas Helen's wound was raw and bleeding.

'André's not missing,' she said, but she knew, as Helen did, that André's position in France would be even more dangerous than Ward's. At least Ward had been a serving officer and therefore had the tenets of the Geneva Convention behind him. André, as a civilian, had no such backing and could legitimately be shot on sight if suspected of terrorist activity.

'I'll never see him again,' Helen said. 'I know it.'

Katy wanted to deny it, but she knew only too well from her own experience how little comfort other people's reassurances gave. Silently she reached for the bottle and poured them each another drink. There was no doubt that the whisky had the effect of numbing pain.

Helen was looking at her. 'You know how I feel, don't you? You don't think you are going to see Ward again either, do you?'

'No,' Katy said. 'I don't think I am.'

They stared at each other, then Katy smiled faintly and lifted her glass. 'Cheers,' she said. 'At least we are in the same boat.'

It was as they chinked glasses that Jen walked in.

'Good God!' she said. 'What's going on here?'

'We're commiserating,' Katy said. Or she thought that was what she said. She could tell from Jen's startled expression it hadn't come out quite right. So she tried again. 'We're drowning our sparrows.' She frowned. That didn't sound quite right either.

'It's all right,' Jen said dryly. 'I get the message.'

Helen picked up the bottle and offered it to her. 'Have one,' she said. 'I'm paying.'

'It's good for the goat,' Katy said.

Jen giggled. 'What goat?'

'Throat,' Katy said. 'I said it's good for the throat.'

'Bloody throat,' Jen said. She glanced at the whisky dubiously then pulled up a chair. 'I sang like a dog tonight.' She watched Helen pouring the drink with a surprisingly steady hand and raised her eyebrows. 'So what's caused this sudden bout of alcoholism?'

'André's gone,' Katy said.

'And Ward's gone,' Helen added.

Jen stiffened. 'Gone? What do you mean gone?'

'Gone to France,' Katy said blearily. 'Gone away. He's left me.'

Jen stared at her. 'You're worse than I thought.' She shrugged. 'If you put it like that, then Sean's gone too.'

'I don't know Sean,' Helen said.

'Sean was Jen's love,' Katy explained. 'He was Scottish.'

'Irish,' Jen said. She sipped her drink. 'Bloody men,' she added. 'Bloody war. Bloody Hitler. It's all his fault.'

'All our men have gone,' Helen said.

Katy thought about it. 'All except Louise's,' she said. 'Louise has got her man.'

Jen sniffed. 'Bloody Louise,' she said. 'Why does she have all the luck?'

'Bloody Louise,' Katy said.

Helen nodded. 'Bloody Louise,' she agreed.

And then they started to laugh.

* * *

Coming in from the bathroom Jack looked uneasily at the moonlight filtering in through the window.

'Should I draw the curtains?'

'No, leave it,' Louise said. 'I want to see you.'

He looked rather taken aback, but stripping off his dressing-gown to reveal a pair of blue and white striped pyjamas he climbed into bed.

'What do you want me to do?' Louise murmured as he drew her in his arms.

He stroked her hair tenderly as he dropped a gentle kiss on her cheek. 'Nothing. Just relax, darling. It'll be all right.'

But it wasn't all right. It was all wrong. Jack just kept kissing her. She wanted his hands on her, she wanted him to touch her. More than anything she wanted to touch him, but she didn't want to annoy him – sometimes Stefan had got annoyed if she didn't do as she was told – so she lay there, waiting, wishing he'd get on with it. And then finally, abruptly, he reached down and pulled her night-gown up round her hips and climbed on top of her.

Tentatively Louise eased open her legs. She wanted him inside her, but despite his efforts it just didn't seem to happen. He just kept rubbing up against her. Again and again. His face was buried in her neck. She could feel his pyjamas rucking up against her thighs. She couldn't understand why he didn't take them off. She couldn't understand why he didn't use his hand.

'Jack, I ...' she began but he quickly shushed her.

It surprised her that he didn't want to talk. Stefan had always been so communicative in bed, with his murmured endearments and instructions about what to do next and which limbs to move where.

As he began to push again, Louise carefully adjusted her position under him, lifting her hips accommodatingly, and finally, suddenly he was inside her. At last. She sighed deeply expecting some change of rhythm, some long slow thrusts, even a pause to savour the sensation, but Jack didn't falter. Apart from a catch in his breath he didn't pause for a moment.

It was over quickly. Far too quickly. Louise had barely got into the swing of it before Jack was gasping out her name and collapsing on top of her.

A moment later he rolled off her and lay on his back panting. Then rather shyly he took her hand. 'Oh darling,' he whispered. 'That was wonderful.'

She wanted to say the same but she just couldn't. She had waited so long for this and now he had left her unsatisfied. Whatever bad things she could say about Stefan, he never left her unsatisfied.

'Was it all right for you?' he added nervously.

'Well, yes,' she said, 'but …'

'I hope it wasn't too sore?' he said awkwardly. 'They say it gets better.'

She certainly hoped so.

He turned on his side and she suddenly had a nasty feeling that he was intending to go to sleep. Certainly he was breathing deeply, and for the first time his limbs seemed relaxed and heavy. She couldn't have that. He couldn't leave her like this, all hot and bothered and aching for release. It wasn't fair.

'Can we do it again?' she whispered.

'Well, I …' He lifted his head. 'It doesn't really work like that, darling. I need time …'

But she was desperate. She couldn't wait for the natural course of events. She wanted him again now. 'I can help you,' she said.

'What do you mean?'

Kneeling up, she stripped off her nightgown and leaned over him, letting her breasts brush his face. Carefully, she trailed her nipple along his lips.

Jack's eyes widened in alarm. 'Louise, really. I don't …'

'It's all right,' she said. 'You can kiss it if you want.'

His whole body stiffened.

Reaching down through the gap in the pyjama flies she squeezed him gently, just as Stefan had taught her.

Jack jumped as though she had stung him. He pulled away and sat up. Louise giggled as he tried to cover the sudden bulge in his pyjamas.

'Oh dear, have I shocked you? Aren't nice girls meant to do that? Don't you like it?'

He was blushing. 'Well, yes, no … I meant …' he stammered. 'But I …'

'It's all right, you know,' she said, reaching for him again. 'It won't hurt. I've done it before.'

'Before?' For a second Jack watched her hand in rigid fascination, then suddenly, painfully, he grabbed her wrist. 'What? You mean that wasn't the first time for you?'

'Well, no,' she admitted. 'Was it for you?'

'Yes, of course it was,' he said, then stopped abruptly. 'No? What do you mean "no"? Was it just once? One mistake? Or how many times … ?'

Louise looked away. Why had she said that? Why had she got carried away with her expertise? Why hadn't she just kept her mouth shut? Now she had upset Jack and that was the last thing she wanted to do.

'It was this man,' she said, withdrawing her hand and pulling the sheet up over her breast. 'He was a Polish count. He was very attractive. Very sexy. I thought he loved me, but he was married …'

'Married!' Jack was appalled. 'Louise, how could you?'

'I didn't know,' Louise said. 'Honestly. I didn't know until I bumped into his wife. And then he left me. They went to America.'

Glancing at him to see how he was taking it, she thought she detected a hint of sympathy in his quick agonised glance and decided to get the whole thing out in the open while she had the chance. The whole sordid business. There was no point in holding it back now.

She looked at Jack through her lashes. 'The worst thing was he left me pregnant. But …'

'What?' Jack could hardly speak. 'You've had a baby?' He stared rather wildly round the room. 'But where … ?'

'No.' She almost giggled at the thought she might have a baby concealed somewhere in her honeymoon luggage. 'Don't worry. I didn't have it. I was going to have an abortion but actually I lost it in that bomb at Balham. The same time I damaged my hip. It was awful. Really frightening. Masses of people died. It's lucky I'm alive at all …'

She tailed off, realising that Jack had lost all the colour from his face. For an awful moment she thought he might be going to be sick. Or cry. She didn't know which would be worse. Hastily she took his hand. 'Jack, it doesn't matter, it's all over now.'

He stared at her incredulously for a moment. 'It does matter,' he said hoarsely. 'It makes you a different person.' Jerking his hand away he closed his eyes as though he could hardly bare to touch her, let alone look at her.

After a moment he took a long shuddering breath. 'I don't know what to say. I thought … I hoped we would learn together. Oh God …' He put his hands to his face, then abruptly he pushed back the bedding and swung his feet on to the floor.

'Jack, don't!' Louise realised she had made a grave mistake. As Jack dragged his trousers on over his pyjamas, she started crying. Crying for real. Everything was going wrong. Crawling across the bed, she clutched at his arm, clinging to him as he leaned down to tie his shoelaces. 'Jack, where are you going? Don't leave me. Don't be like this.'

But he shook her off and stood up. 'I don't know how else to be. I don't know what to think.'

Quickly, with stiff jerky movements he pulled on a sweater, then he opened the door and walked out into the night.

Chapter Nineteen

Jack didn't come back into the room until the early hours of the morning. By that time, Louise's mood had turned from tearful self-pity to indignation to an awful restless unease which had prevented her from sleeping even though she was dog tired after the rigours of the day. Once she got up to stare out of the window hoping she might see him pacing the gardens. She would have gone to him then. Pleaded with him, thrown herself on the ground at his feet if necessary, abjecting herself for her fall from grace.

She realised she would do anything to get him back. Anything to have him sitting next to her at breakfast tomorrow morning. The prospect of having to go into the dining-room on her own was unbearable. Her mind jumped ahead in total horror to the thought of returning to Lavender Road already estranged from her husband.

When he did eventually come back his first words were conciliatory. 'I'm sorry,' he said stiffly as he closed the door and came into the room. 'I shouldn't have left you like that. It was unforgivable.'

'It's all right,' Louise stammered. 'It's me who should apologise. I had no idea you'd be so upset. I would have told you before, but—'

Jack cut her off sharply. 'I don't want to talk about it.'

Startled by his abrupt coldness, Louise blinked and to her dismay felt tears prickling her eyes. Jack had never spoken like that to her before. Never. He was always so courteous, so warm.

'Look,' he said grittily. 'I know you're upset. Well, so am I, but I am going to try and make the best of it. It's not easy, but I will try not to mind about … about what happened …'

He stopped and moved away, clearly unable to think about it without horror.

He took off his sweater and trousers, and getting into bed in heavy silence he turned away from her and lay as close to the edge as he could without falling out.

It was already getting light outside and even without touching him Louise could see he was tense. His shoulders under the striped pyjamas were rigid. His breathing was shallow. He had his elbow over the top of the sheet and below it his fist was clenched. She felt a wave of despair wash over her. This was her husband. Her lovely, handsome husband. Too angry and upset with her even to look at her on her wedding night.

'Why do you mind so much?' she asked suddenly. 'I'm not the only girl in the world who has gone astray.'

He didn't answer at once and she thought he wasn't going to answer at all, but then suddenly he spoke. His voice was low and tight. 'I suppose I feel cheated,' he said. 'I feel such a fool. Everyone knows. Your parents. Your friends.' He moved impatiently. 'I should have known. I saw you flirting with that man at the pub, but I thought that was a game. I thought you were pure. Mine. I had no idea.'

Louise frowned. 'Not everyone knows. Only my parents and Katy Frazer actually.' She didn't feel it would be quite wise to admit that Aaref Hoch knew too. 'And I am yours,' she went on quickly. 'It was only a game with Aaref Hoch. I've never even kissed him. Not properly. And I've certainly never been to bed with him.' She glanced at his head on the pillow, longing to run her fingers through the short spiky hair at the back of his neck. 'I know what I did with Stefan was bad, but I honestly can't see why you're *so* upset.'

He sat up angrily. 'Well, I am. It's just not the same. Someone has been there before. And a baby.' He closed his eyes. 'You've conceived someone else's baby.'

'You'd never have known if I hadn't said.'

He stared at her. 'But I do know, and I can't just forget it now. It's changed everything.'

Louise felt a stab of irritation. 'Oh, for heaven's sake,' she said. 'It hasn't changed anything. Honestly, I had no idea you'd be so prudish. I'd never have married you if I'd thought you'd make such a fuss.' She saw him flinch and tossed her head. 'Well, it's not fair. I've been longing to go to bed with you ever since I met you. You should be pleased that I fancy you. Okay, I made a mistake with Stefan. I was young. Naïve. It was a mistake. Can't you understand that?'

'It didn't sound like a mistake,' Jack said. 'You obviously enjoyed it.'

Louise glared at him. 'Yes, I did enjoy it. Is that wrong?'

Jack flushed. The defiant challenge had startled him. He looked away. 'Well, no, of course not, but you didn't enjoy it with me, did you?' Suddenly he got out of bed and stood facing her angrily. 'That's what you're saying, isn't it? It was a disappointment with me after your previous lover?'

Momentarily dismayed by his angry sarcasm, it slowly dawned on Louise that behind his bitterness there lurked a ray of hope.

'Goodness,' she said. 'You can't expect wonders the first time.' She looked up at him, suddenly hopeful. 'Oh, come on, Jack. Let bygones be bygones. We're married, for goodness' sake. We might as well make the most of it. Come back to bed.'

Jack stood his ground. 'No,' he said. 'I can't. It's too soon.' He turned away abruptly, walking to the window, staring out blindly at the rapidly lightening sky. 'I just don't feel the same as I did.'

'Then let me make you feel the same.' Quickly she got out of bed, stripped off her nightgown, and went up to him and put her arms round him from behind. Slowly, languidly she rubbed her breasts against his back.

'Go on, Jack,' she murmured. 'Please …'

He broke away from her, pushing her away quite roughly. 'No, Louise really.' He walked round to his side of the bed. 'I can't. Anyway it's almost light now.'

But Louise wasn't fooled, she had felt his response. 'Is something wrong with you?' she asked. 'Something you don't want me to see?'

He looked at her, appalled. 'No, of course not.'

'Then for goodness' sake take off those blasted pyjamas and lie down.'

Given the same command, Stefan would have removed his pyjamas slowly and languorously and then lain down spreadeagled on his back waiting with lazy complacence for whatever she had in store for him. Jack, after a moment's final hesitation, took his off quickly and furtively, with his back to her, then pulled back the bedcovers and wriggled hastily underneath.

Louise didn't mind. As far as she was concerned, the fact that she had got him back to bed at all was a miracle. Smiling to herself she slid in beside him and gently pulled him over on to his back. His shoulders were cool to the touch. For a moment as he turned over Louise allowed herself to admire the muscled smoothness of his upper arms, the well-shaped collarbones, the strong tanned neck.

'I'm going to kiss you all over,' she said. 'Just to show you how much I love you. Even though you are so square.'

Jack clutched the sheet across his loins. 'Louise, you can't.'

'I can,' she said, prising the sheet out of his fingers and running her lips down his broad chest with its scattering of curly ginger hair. 'And then you are going to do the same for me.'

Katy woke to the sound of Malcolm's screams. Groping for the light on her bedside table her fingers only found air, and it was quite a long time before she realised she wasn't in bed at all but slumped over one of the bar tables. Straightening up was not only painful but difficult because her hair had stuck to some beer spilt on the table and the act of lifting her head ripped half of it out of her scalp.

While her head pounded as though she had been run over by a bus, the rest of her body felt unnervingly numb. It occurred to her momentarily that perhaps she *had* been run over by a bus, but then she realised that the chances of getting run over by a bus in the Flag and Garter public bar were quite remote.

It was only when her eyes lighted painfully on the empty bottle of whisky that she began to recall the events of the previous evening, and then she noticed the two bodies on the floor. Jen Carter and Helen de Burrel. Lying one each side of the table, completely still, limbs splayed as though dropped there from a great height, and glinting around them in the bar lights like a handful of diamonds was the remnants of a broken glass.

For a terrible moment Katy thought they must be dead. Then she saw they were breathing, albeit slowly, and realised that if anyone was close to death it was her.

Getting up the stairs and leaning over into the cot to pick Malcolm up was an act of supreme courage, and for a nasty moment as the room roared around her she was convinced she was going to be sick all over him. Somehow she staggered to a chair and opened her shirt, sliding her bra up over her breast as Malcolm reached eagerly for the nipple.

To Katy's relief Malcolm went straight back to sleep after his feed. It was only later that she realised she had probably filled him up with enough alcohol to addle his brain for ever.

Now, as she leaned weakly on the side of his cot, Katy eyed her own bed longingly. The thought of struggling back downstairs to rouse Jen and Helen was not appealing.

If they felt anything like as bad as her they would probably not thank her for it anyway.

They might as well stay where they are, she thought. As she lay down she glanced at the clock. Six o'clock. Thank God, she thought, closing her eyes. I can have at least another couple of hours' sleep. And then she was violently and copiously sick.

Jack Delmaine was fit, and young. Much younger and fitter than Stefan had been. He was also naturally sensitive, which made Louise's job much easier. Not that making love to him was any hardship. Just looking at his long naked limbs sprawled on the bed made Louise's heart kick in her chest. She even found his shyness quite arousing, and once he had got over his initial self-consciousness he became an avid pupil.

The first time he caused Louise to spasm convulsively was a moment of immense gratification for them both. The fact that she screamed his name at the same time, although slightly embarrassing as regards the chambermaid whom Jack could hear counting sheets in the passage outside, was a moment of triumph far exceeding any previous demonstration of prowess either in school exams or on the sporting field. Even the spectacular winning try he had scored in the Berkshire schoolboys' Rugby sevens tournament paled into insignificance in comparison.

Having always assumed that the desire for a physical relationship between men and women was one sided and therefore potentially rather awkward, he hadn't realised how addictive lovemaking could become, and as the honeymoon moved almost unnoticed through its second night into the third day, Jack found he just could not get enough of Louise's naked body.

Louise felt the same. With Stefan the second and third times had been a bit of a chore sometimes, but with Jack she was just as eager as he to start again. And unlike Stefan, who always needed a short sleep to recoup his drive, Jack's powers of recovery were such that there was barely time for the sweat to dry before they were off again.

Once they got up for a meal and had to leave it half uneaten in their urgent desire to get back to bed. After that, to the discreet amusement of the hotel staff, they gave up on any pretence at normality and had their meals sent up to their room. Occasionally they emerged for a walk along the towpath, or to take tea in the garden. One gloriously sunny day Jack hired a boat and rowed Louise upriver towards Henley, and overcome by lust they moored the boat and made love in the bottom of the boat, to the wide-eyed, blushing astonishment of a small group of passing ramblers. Later they swam naked in the river to cool off.

'I bet you can't do it now,' Louise teased him. 'Not in this cold water.'

'I bet I can,' he replied.

And to her astonishment he could. Making love in the water was the sexiest, most daring thing she had ever done. Afterwards as Jack clung to the boat, panting and utterly spent, he stared at her with glazed wonder-filled eyes. 'I had no idea it could be like this.'

She giggled. 'There. Aren't you glad now you didn't marry a virgin?'

For a second when Jack didn't respond she thought she had pushed her luck one step too far, but then, slowly, thoughtfully, he smiled. 'Darling Louise. At this precise moment, if your Polish count walked past, I'd shake him by the hand.'

20 July 1942

Dear Mum,

Thought you'd like a letter from sunny Egypt. Sunny's the word and all. It blazes down all the time. Voyage was hell. Hot and crowded but it's even worse here. You've never seen so many flies. They're bloody everywhere. God knows what we are meant to be fighting for either. All there is is sand and more bloody sand. Nobody knows what they're doing. Most of the equipment we're meant to have got lost in the last retreat. Half the officers are back in Cairo. Most of the time we play cards. Everyone is browned off. We feel like sitting ducks just waiting for Jerry to attack. And the food's bloody awful too.

Love, Bob.

21 July 1942

Dear Mater and Pater,

Just to say that I arrived safely and have now joined my unit. The other officers are reasonable chaps but the men seem a bit demoralised after the recent withdrawal which seems to have been a bit of a shambles. Quite a few of the regiment were lost and everyone seems to have lost confidence in the commanders. Conditions are pretty poor. Quite a few of the men are suffering from sunstroke and there seems to be quite a bit of disease too.

I'm hoping to get a chance to go back to Cairo next weekend. I've always wanted to see the pyramids. Hope the wedding goes well. I'm sure Sis will be very happy.

Yours, Bertie.

P.S. Have just heard that we are moving up to the front.

It took Helen, Jen and Katy three days to get over their hangovers. Three difficult days during which Jen's voice failed to improve and Helen learned that André had been dropped successfully in a field not far from Toulon with a large amount of equipment.

So that was it. André had gone and she had not.

As well as worrying about André, Helen was concerned about little George. Although on the surface he seemed to be back to normal, since running away on the morning of the wedding he hadn't once mentioned the baby. It was as though Pam's swelling stomach simply did not exist. When Mick Carter called by for a chat with Alan and made the mistake of congratulating Pam on the forthcoming arrival, George got off his chair where he had been sitting listening wide eyed to Mick's stories and went upstairs.

And of course there was still no news of Ward.

'It's been a bad week,' Helen said as she and Katy and Jen lay out on the common in the sun with baby Malcolm the following Sunday. She watched Malcolm reaching for the giraffe that the Miss Taylors had sent. How nice it must be to have as your only worry in life the whereabouts of your favourite toy.

Despite Mr Churchill's bulldog optimism there was no doubt that the war was going badly too. The Axis forces were devastating merchant shipping and now there was news that four hundred new U-boats were shortly to enter service. After the mauling the British and Commonwealth troops had suffered in the Western Desert, the appointment of the new commanders, Generals Alexander and Montgomery, seemed like a desperate measure. And in Russia, the Germans were now so close to Stalingrad that it was virtually under siege.

Katy sighed heavily. 'I reckon this is about as bad as it gets. Surely it can't get much worse than this.'

Jen sat up. 'Don't say that,' she said searching hastily for a piece of wood to touch.

Flat on her back, Helen opened her eyes and stared up at the blue sky. There were swallows everywhere, darting and swooping like little black arrows in the hot still air. Watching them idly, Helen found she envied them their carefree freedom. The war didn't touch them.

Then something else caught her eye. High above the swallows some kind of bird of prey, a kestrel perhaps, was circling lazily. For a second as it drifted effortlessly across the sky, its shadow crossed her face. Helen frowned and closed her eyes. Jen was right to be superstitious, she thought. There were a million ways things could get worse, and somehow, even though the ground was warm on her back and the sun hot on her face, Helen felt a cold shiver run up her spine.

The only person in high spirits was Mick Carter. Revelling in his newfound popularity and full of increasingly farfetched stories of life on the ocean wave, his standing was further enhanced by the arrival of a telegram instructing him to rejoin his ship two days earlier than expected.

'They can't manage without me, you see,' he grinned, showing the telegram round proudly in the pub.

'I've never known anything like it,' Joyce told Celia Rutherford in the café the following morning. 'He always used to be such a sulky little bugger, but this navy lark has been the making of him. You'd think he sailed the ship singlehanded the way he goes on, poking his nose into everyone's business.'

She frowned as she made the tea. 'Pete's all keen to go to sea now and all. Mick reckons he should sign up as an apprentice engineer. He even asked Miss Philips if she'd coach him in his maths to get him through the test. I wouldn't be surprised if she doesn't join up too. I overheard Mick telling her he'd seen plenty of Wrens with limps.'

She didn't tell Celia Rutherford that Mick had poked his nose into her own affairs too, suggesting of all things that she should think about getting a divorce. A divorce. She could hardly believe her ears. She shook her head now, thinking how crestfallen he had been when she had told him to mind his own business.

'I'm only trying to help,' he had said. 'I only want you to be happy, and Dad didn't exactly make you happy, did he, the way he went on?'

She didn't want to talk about it. It was humiliating to think that anyone, even her children, knew about the dreadful beatings and cruelty she had suffered at Stanley's hands.

I can't get divorced, she thought now as she began spreading the sandwiches. Divorce is for toffs. Filmstars and that. Rich people what can afford it. Not for the likes of me. People like me are expected to stand by their husbands when they are in jail. Not divorce them. Anyway, she thought, if I so much as mentioned the word divorce to Stanley he would send someone round to kill me.

Lifting the sandwiches carefully on to a plate she carried them through to the counter, then she glanced round the little café, checking automatically that the tables were ready. She could see there were people already outside.

'Are we ready, Mrs Rutherford?' she called. 'Shall I let them in?'

'Oh yes,' Celia called back heartily from the kitchen. 'Chocks away.'

Smiling, Joyce unlocked the door and flipped the closed sign to open. Another day. More eager customers. And since Mr Lorenz had taught them how to cost the food there seemed to be more cash in the till.

Suddenly a divorce seemed rather appealing. I'll think about it, she thought to herself. There's no rush.

Louise and Jack came back from their honeymoon on 16 August. When they came into the pub halfway through the usual Sunday American night, Katy was hard pressed not to laugh. It wasn't difficult to see that the honeymoon had been a success. Louise was quite simply glowing, and Jack looked happy but exhausted. Neither of them seemed able to stop smiling, sometimes at other people but mostly at each other. Nor did they seem able to stop touching each other. At first they held hands surreptitiously under the table, but as the evening progressed their display of affection quickly grew more blatant.

'It's disgusting,' Jen muttered to Katy behind the bar.

'Look at them. She's got her hand in his pocket now. You ought to say something. They'll give the pub a bad name.'

Katy giggled. 'They're no worse than your Americans,' she said, glancing around the noisy bar at the numerous flirting couples. Jen's American night had taken off in a big way. Every Sunday the pub was full of girls looking to meet a handsome Yank soldier. At first Katy had been rather dismayed by the transformation of the pub into a kind of dating parlour, but it brought in good business, and so far nobody had complained.

'At least my Americans have the grace to go outside into the alley,' Jen said. 'If you're not careful Louise and Jack will be making love right there in the corner.'

Katy laughed. 'Nobody else seems to have noticed,' she said, but then as she glanced around again she realised she was wrong.

Aaref Hoch had noticed. He was standing by the bar with a group of off-duty nurses, and although he appeared to be smiling along with their giggly conversation Katy could see that his eyes flicked repeatedly towards the corner where Louise was now virtually sitting on Jack's knee.

Poor Aaref, she thought. Then aware suddenly that Molly was standing behind her, she jerked her eyes away quickly, but it was too late. Molly had already seen the direction of her gaze.

Molly was less sympathetic. 'Serves him right,' she said with grim satisfaction. 'Now perhaps at last he'll be a bit nicer to me,' but behind the brave façade Katy knew Molly was hurt.

Later when she had a chance she spoke to Aaref. 'I know it's hard for you,' she said. 'Louise being married and that. But try not to take it out on Molly.' She hesitated. 'If you don't want her you should tell her. It's cruel to string her along.'

'I'm not stringing her along,' he said. 'I like Molly. I really do. But you know how I feel about Louise.'

Katy looked at him steadily, wishing he had used the past tense. 'I do know,' she said, 'but Louise is married now, Aaref, happily married, and that's the finish of it.'

After the anonymity of the hotel, Louise found being back at her parents' house extremely inhibiting. Sleeping in single beds in the guest room was bad enough, but knowing that her parents could hear every giggle and shriek put a definite dampener on their lovemaking.

'I can't wait to get a place of our own,' Louise whispered. 'I'll start looking as soon as I've put you on the train tomorrow.'

To her surprise Jack was less keen. 'But darling, your parents will look after you. After all, I'll be away for long periods of time. You'd be lonely on your own. In any case, flats are so difficult to find, and so expensive. Don't you think it would be more fun to save up for a house later? Somewhere of our own?'

'No, I don't,' Louise said crossly. 'I don't care about saving, and I don't want somewhere later. I want it now. Even if it's a tiny place.' She saw his frown and quickly changed her tack. 'Please, darling, darling Jack.' She leaned over and nuzzled his ear. 'Don't make me stay at home. Please tell Daddy I can't. Think how much fun your leaves will be if we have our own little flat.'

Jack closed his eyes in despair. He knew he could deny her nothing. He was enthralled by her. By her hands and her tongue. 'Well, all right,' he agreed reluctantly, pushing her away. 'I suppose there's no harm in looking for somewhere. I'll mention it to your father. But it must be cheap, Louise. If I come back and find you've taken on some fancy place in Knightsbridge, I'll be really cross.'

The joy in having thus gained freedom from her parents carried Louise through the potentially upsetting preparations for Jack's departure. Sitting on the bed while he carefully packed his two suitcases and put on his uniform for the first time for two weeks, she could barely wait for him to be gone so she could start looking in the property-to-rent section of the local papers.

It was only as they stood on the platform at Euston waiting for the Liverpool train to come in that the reality of the situation sank in. She was losing him. Her wonderful, handsome husband. For he was not only going to Liverpool, he was going to sea. Lieutenant Jack Delmaine, newly appointed first officer of the corvette HMS *Penelope*. And if the Germans had their way, he would not come back. Weeping, she clung to him as the train came in.

'Oh Jack. I can't bear it.'

He kissed her hair. 'Don't, darling. Don't cry. Be brave, or you'll make me cry too.'

Even in her distress that made her smile. The thought of Jack crying was so clearly absurd. He might go quiet, or sulk or grit his teeth manfully, but he would never cry. Not brave, steady Jack with his stiff upper lip and public-school reserve. Only in bed did he ever truly let his hair down, and burying her head in his chest, Louise realised perhaps for the first time how lucky she had been to find a man who was on the one hand a thoroughly eligible, true blue, upper-crust Englishman, someone she could really respect and admire, and on the other a passionate, sexy, uninhibited lover.

'I'll miss you, darling,' he said now. 'I can't tell you how happy you've made me.'

It was only as the train pulled out in a cloud of steam that she remembered that she hadn't told him she loved him. She stared after the train appalled. Perhaps if she rushed home and wrote to him he would get the letter before he sailed.

'I love my husband,' she said out loud as she ran back to the ticket barrier clutching her platform ticket. 'I love him to bits.'

A large woman in a pink hat was waiting at the barrier.

She laughed. 'That's nice for you, ducks,' she said. 'I can't stand the sight of mine.'

'What the hell's going on?' Angus McNaughton threw down the signal and banged his fist on Helen's desk causing a pile of files to slip and fall to the floor, scattering their contents all over the government issue lino. Then he straightened up and lit a cigarette.

'What is it? What's happened?' Helen asked nervously. She could see the signal was from Lucien, which she knew was the codename for Paul in Marseilles.

'I don't know what's happened,' Angus snapped. 'That's the whole point. One minute it's all hunky-dory down there, everything going to plan, cover stories in place, lines of communication set up, and the next minute this.' He stabbed his cigarette at the flimsy sheet of paper. 'A puzzled note from Paul saying that your man has completely disappeared.'

'My man?' Helen stared at him. 'André? You're saying that André Cabillard has disappeared?'

'Who else would I be talking about?' Angus said irritably. 'What I want to know is—'

'Disappeared?' Helen said again, more urgently this time. She could feel the blood draining out of her head. 'Angus, please? What sort of disappeared?' She put her hand to her throat, hardly able to say the words. 'Do you mean … do you mean the Germans have got him?'

Angus blew out smoke. 'Paul says not. Says he would have heard if they'd picked anyone up. He's got a good line on what's going on in the Vichy camp.'

'So what *does* Paul know?' Helen asked angrily. 'He must know something.'

Angus shrugged. 'All he knows is that they were due to meet in Toulon to arrange the handover of some equipment, and bloody Cabillard didn't show up.'

'Perhaps he was being followed or something,' Helen said, 'and he didn't want to compromise Paul. Or perhaps he thought Paul was being watched.' She swallowed hard. 'There's bound to be some explanation. Surely?'

They both knew she was clutching at straws. They both knew any other explanation would be a major disaster.

'I hope so,' Angus said. He looked at her. 'All I can say is that he'd better bloody get back in touch with Paul soon or there will be trouble.'

Chapter Twenty

Louise's misery at Jack's departure was compounded by the arrival home of her brother Douglas from some school corps training camp in the Brecon Beacons. Douglas had always got on her nerves even as a young child. Now at just seventeen, captain of cricket, a school prefect, and full of his own importance, he was even more unbearable than ever.

'You know when the Ruskies were defending Sebastopol they had to wear gasmasks,' he would remark suddenly over breakfast, 'because of the stench of decomposing bodies. I reckon it will be like that in Stalingrad soon if they don't pull their fingers out and make a decent stand at the Don.'

He seemed to know everything about the progress of the war. He'd got maps and charts and military lists and God only knew what else. He'd brought them back from school and his bedroom was like some general's operations room. He even claimed to have worked out to about one square mile exactly where Bertie's regiment was positioned. 'Right on the front line at Alam Halfa Ridge. Lucky devil. If Montgomery orders a push Bertie will be right at the front.'

At first Louise had found it mildly interesting, but alone in the house with him all day long her patience rapidly began to pall, and when he began bombarding her with information about the success of the German U-boats she began to reach the end of her tether.

'In June alone one of our ships was going down every four hours,' Douglas said, unaware of her dangerously heightened colour. 'And if Admiral Doenitz gets his grubby little hands on the French fleet too, we'll be really sunk.'

That was all she needed. Slamming down the book she was reading she screamed at him to shut up. 'I don't want to know! Do you understand? I simply don't want to know.'

'Goodness,' Douglas said. 'Keep your hair on. Oh sorry. I forgot about Hubby out there in the Atlantic. Don't worry, it's mainly merchant ships going down of course, although the Germans are meant to be getting a new—'

'Douglas, please!' Louise stood up abruptly and headed for the door. 'Just shut up.'

'Oh, what a squeamish girlie,' he taunted her. 'Where are you going anyway?'

Grabbing her straw boater off the hook in the hall she picked up the local newspaper and headed for the front door. 'I'm going to find somewhere else to live.'

Of course it wasn't quite as easy as that. It hadn't taken Louise long to discover that decent flats were like gold dust at the moment, nor that tramping round looking for them was tiring, depressing work. If only someone could have gone with her it might have been more fun, but Katy was always so busy in the pub and Helen was always at work. In any case, Helen and Katy were not particularly good company at the moment and she wouldn't dream of asking that awful Jen Carter.

That was another thing that depressed her. She had so longed to be able to gloat a little bit about Jack, but with Katy so worried about Ward and Helen so worried about André she didn't really feel she could.

All in all Louise felt aggrieved. She missed Jack badly. It was a letdown coming back to Lavender Road. She was bored and frustrated. She had persuaded Mr Gregg to give her a month off when she married, so she would have time to set up a home for her and Jack, but now all that had happened was that every flat or house was taken before she got there to see it, or was damp or had an unpleasant landlord. In one of them she even found a dead mouse on the sitting-room floor. Even when she began to look up a grade at more expensive places she got tired dragging round to see them only to find they were too far away, or already taken.

So when on her way back from visiting a dingy place in Glycena Road she saw Aaref Hoch on the other side of Lavender Hill she waved eagerly.

'Louise.' He smiled as he crossed over to join her. 'Or perhaps I should say Mrs Delmaine?'

Louise laughed, pleased. 'Oh, Louise will do,' she said graciously. 'After all, we're old friends, aren't we?' She couldn't help slanting him a coy smile. 'Even if you didn't come and say hello in the pub the other night.'

If she thought she would embarrass Aaref that easily she was wrong. He merely inclined his head regretfully. 'I would have come over,' he said. 'I wanted to congratulate you, of course, but you seemed, how shall I say, a little bit too occupied with your handsome new husband.'

'Oh.' To her dismay Louise found it was she who was embarrassed. Then she giggled. 'Don't be naughty, Aaref,' she said. 'You're making me blush. Anyway,' she pouted provocatively, 'I know you're only saying that because you were a teensy weensy bit jealous.'

'Yes,' he said. 'Of course I am jealous. You are a very beautiful and lovely girl and your husband is a very lucky man. I have never made a secret of how I felt about you.' He lifted his shoulders slightly. 'But you have made your choice. I hope you will be happy with it.'

Slightly taken aback Louise stared at him. Having expected him to be upset or confused by her question, his steady declaration rather took the wind out of her sails.

'Aaref, do you ever hear of houses or flats to rent?' she

asked as they began to walk back to Lavender Road. 'You know. Round here, I mean. Somewhere nice, not too expensive?'

He shrugged. 'Occasionally, although accommodation isn't easy to find just now. Too many places were bombed. Too many people now want to be in London. Why? Who wants one?'

'Me.'

'You?'

'Well, me and Jack.'

'But Jack is at sea, no? You don't want to stay at home with your parents?'

'No, I don't,' Louise said violently. 'I hate being at home. Douglas is driving me mad, and Daddy has been like a bear with a sore head since the wedding.' She nodded across the road. 'And Mummy spends all her time at the stupid café.'

Aaref followed her glance. 'It is good, your mother's café. Quite often I take my lunch there.'

'Do you?' Louise blinked. 'I've hardly ever been in there. Anyway, who cares about the blasted café? I can't live there, can I?'

'No.' He smiled. 'I don't think it would be very comfortable for you among the tea urns and sandwiches.'

'I don't need comfort,' Louise said. 'I just need somewhere of my own. Even if it's tiny. I don't care.'

Aaref was silent for a moment as they walked on and then he glanced at her. 'I do have a suggestion.'

Louise looked at him eagerly. 'Do you? You mean you know somewhere that might do?'

'Possibly,' he said. He looked on down the road to Mrs d'Arcy Billière's house on the corner opposite the Rutherfords', where he had lived since coming to England. 'We have some empty rooms on the top floor,' he said. 'Like a little attic apartment. Nothing special, but Mrs d'Arcy Billière has talked once or twice of making it usable.'

'Really?' For a second Louise felt a stab of excitement,

but then she hesitated. She had never felt very comfortable in Mrs d'Arcy Billière's house. It was, after all, where she had met Count Stefan Pininski, and Lael d'Arcy Billière herself was by any standard a rather strange woman with her extraordinary robe-like dresses and strappy flat sandals. It also occurred to her that Jack might not feel that a flat in the same house as Aaref Hoch was exactly what they were looking for. On the other hand surely anything was better than living with her parents.

'If you want you could come and see it now,' Aaref said diffidently. 'Lael is up in town today but I know she wouldn't mind.'

Of course the rooms were perfect, or they would be when Aaref had arranged for them to have a coat of paint. Tucked up under the eaves of the house, with slanted ceilings and awkward corners, they had obviously once been used as servants' quarters. There was even a little scullery with a sink and a small Belling cooker. The wooden floors could easily be polished up and Louise was certain she could find a bit of material somewhere to make up some curtains to soften the bleak, rather dirty little windows. They would need blackout too, but Aaref said he could get blackout material for her and a lightbulb for the central overhead light. The lack of furniture was more of a problem but Aaref was sure Mrs d'Arcy Billière would have some spare bits and pieces, and they agreed that they could make some hanging space by banging some nails into the walls.

'You'd have to share the bathroom,' Aaref said.

Louise nodded. 'That's okay,' she said. In the price range she was looking in, she had never expected to find somewhere with its own bathroom.

'So what do you think?' Aaref asked.

Louise smiled. 'I think it's wonderful,' she said. Already she could feel a mounting excitement at the thought of turning these bare, oddly shaped rooms into her own little home. Yes, there was quite a bit of work to do, but once it was done then it would be her place. Somewhere special and private for her and Jack when he came off leave. Leading into the scullery there was even a fire escape they could use if they didn't want to go in and out through the house.

She looked round eagerly. Jack would like it. She was sure he would. There would be no rigid breakfast times here, no parents to worry about. They could stay in bed as long as they liked.

As she momentarily relived some of those wonderful nights in Marlow she suddenly realised there was one crucial item of furniture Aaref hadn't mentioned.

'What about a bed?' she asked urgently. 'We haven't discussed a bed.'

'No,' Aaref agreed. 'We haven't discussed a bed.' He was silent for a moment then shrugged. 'I suppose I thought you might be able to bring one over from your parents'.'

She shook her head. 'I don't think they'd let me. Anyway, they've only got singles. We must have a double.' She giggled. 'It's not at all the same in a single bed. You get a bit carried away and the next thing you find you're on the floor.'

Aaref, however, was already heading for the stairs. 'I'll ask Lael,' he said over his shoulder. 'Of course, I don't know for certain that she'll agree to you having the rooms at all.'

Louise ran after him. 'Oh, she must,' she said. 'It's so perfect.' She clutched at his arm, aware that she had annoyed him with her bed talk. 'Aaref, please, you must persuade her. I'll die if she says no.'

Aaref shook his head. 'I doubt that,' he said.

Louise frowned. 'Why do you say it like that?'

He lifted his shoulders. 'Because it's true. You won't die. You might think you will but you won't. You'll be sad for a couple of days and then you'll bounce back like you always do. You're a survivor, Louise. You always have been and you always will be.'

Louise looked at him. There was something in his voice she didn't quite understand. Something hard, almost bitter, which puzzled her. 'But that's good, isn't it?' she said. 'To be a survivor?'

For a moment she thought he was going to say no, then he shook his head and smiled. 'Yes, it's good,' he said. 'It means that nothing will ever really hurt you.'

The following morning Louise received a note from Mrs d'Arcy Billière:

> My dear Louise,
> I'd love you to have the use of my attic rooms. We'll do what we can to tidy them up for you, of course, and I have a wonderful Chinese dressing table in the cellar that you might like. I've never found anywhere very satisfactory to put it. Regarding your sleeping arrangements, it occurs to me that it might be rather difficult to get an entire bed up those small stairs but perhaps a mattress on the floor might do the trick, or would that be too bohemian for you? If so, we'll think again. Why don't you pop over this evening and we'll arrange the money and so on. I was thinking of about ten shillings a week or is that too much?
> Lael.

Louise was utterly thrilled. If nothing else, ten shillings was less than half what she had been prepared to spend. But when she ran down to the pub to tell Katy later that morning, Katy was less than enthusiastic.

'What, you mean live in the same house as Aaref? Are you sure that's wise?'

Louise shrugged. 'I don't see why not. It's not as though Aaref doesn't know that I'm married. Anyway, he's just a friend now. That's all. And Katy, honestly, the rooms will be brilliant once we've done them up a bit. Jack will love them.'

'Well, yes,' Katy said, 'but …' About to re-express her concerns she saw Louise's face fall and suddenly decided against it. After all, it was none of her business really, and perhaps Louise was right. Perhaps she and Aaref could be just friends now.

Molly heard the news with less equanimity. 'Bloody Louise. She always spoils things. Just when Aaref was beginning to ask me out again.'

It seemed after a few weeks, however, that Louise was right. While Aaref helped her get the little flat cleaned and painted, Louise saw quite a bit of him, but once she was installed among Mrs d'Arcy Billière's rather exotic furniture, with her double mattress and the bits and pieces she'd been given as wedding presents, he made a point of leaving her alone. In any case she was back on day shifts at Gregg Bros. by then and as most of Aaref's nefarious activities apparently took place in the evenings it was true that they overlapped quite rarely.

For her part Louise was clearly utterly delighted with her new accommodation and seemed so happy to spend the weekends hemming curtains and combing the local shops for cooking ingredients it did indeed seem that Katy's fears were unfounded. As Aaref was once again spending quite a bit of time with Molly, Katy even began to believe that his infatuation with Louise was finally over.

In any case Katy was too busy to worry too much about Louise. Jacob had taken two weeks off to study for his exams and unfortunately his absence coincided with Malcolm's first tooth coming through. If only Katy could have dumped him off with Pam Nelson by day things might have been easier, but Pam coudn't have him any more. At thirty-six she was considered very old to be having a first baby, and the health visitor was insistent that she put her feet up as much as possible. Malcolm was just beginning to crawl and so was most unhappy about being kept penned up in his playpen for large chunks of the day.

Jen rescued him as often as she could. 'You're training him for a life behind bars,' she said one morning as she came downstairs after her usual prolonged gargling session. Gargling seemed to be the only thing that kept her voice going at all. She now had a very definite problem with the higher notes. 'He'll probably end up as a jailbird.'

Katy looked up from polishing glasses. 'Or a prisoner-of-war,' she said. She glanced at the child grimly. 'At least *he* can't escape.'

Pulling Malcolm out of the playpen Jen wished she hadn't spoken. Quickly she loaded Malcolm into his pram and headed for the door. Outside she glared at the baby. 'Your bloody father,' she said violently. 'Why couldn't he just stay put instead of trying to be some bloody hero and worrying everyone to death?' Malcolm looked at her uncertainly and she groaned. 'Don't look at me like that. You remind me of him when you look like that.' She glanced up and down the empty street, then lowered her voice anyway. 'And I don't want to be reminded, because I have a horrible feeling that none of us is ever going to see him again.'

Jen wasn't the only one who had given up hope of Ward Frazer. Helen too had been forced to acknowledge that they should have heard something by now. After all, they were well into August and he had been on the run since the end of March; by any standard odds on his survival were low. For all they knew, he had been injured in the break-out from the train and had been lying dead under some bush or in some deserted barn ever since. And for all she knew, the same fate might have befallen André.

Ever since Paul had reported André's disappearance Helen had berated herself bitterly for not going over with him. She knew that if something had gone wrong, some harm had come to him, she would never forgive herself for her cowardliness. She also knew that it was only the support of Katy and Jen and the Nelsons that got her through those first anxious weeks.

It helped too that Helen was frantically busy at work. The biggest assault yet on Hitler's fortress Europe had been planned. It was to take place at Dieppe and would involve British, Canadian, American and Free French troops and was designed not as an invasion but as a test of German resistance.

'It's a mistake,' Jean-Claude Monet said. '*Le Général* is not happy about it. We believe Dieppe is by no means unprotected.' But in the absence of conclusive evidence, Free French warnings were overruled by Admiral Lord Louis Mountbatten at Combined Operations HQ and the attack went ahead on 19 August.

As it turned out, German resistance was strong. Fierce fighting developed. Allied casualties were heavy. One and a half thousand prisoners were taken by the Germans, and in an air battle of proportions unseen since the Battle of Britain at least ninety-five Allied planes were lost.

The main repercussion of the Dieppe raid was that it focused attention on the importance of an effective intelligence network in France. Once again André's disappearance was on everyone's lips. Once again all anyone knew was a series of bland little messages from Paul in Marseilles saying that all enquiries had drawn a blank on the new arrival.

The war too seemed to be at an impasse, and when the popular Duke of Kent was killed in an air accident in Scotland, a gloom spread over London. Apart from the continuing blanket-bombing of German cities, nothing seemed to be happening towards winning the war. There was silence from the desert, and in Russia the Germans had finally crossed the Don, the last obstacle to an all-out assault on Stalingrad.

And then instead of getting better, things got worse.

News began to come in that there had been a devastating U-boat attack on one of the Allied Atlantic convoys, and the following day Rommel launched a sudden assault on General Montgomery's defensive line at Alam Halfa Ridge in North Africa.

As news filtered through of rapidly mounting casualties, the nation reeled in shock, and suddenly Helen and Katy weren't the only ones hoping for news of loved ones.

Having never worried before, Joyce Carter found herself in the position of having two sons unaccounted for: Mick, whose ship, the *Topaz*, was one of the vessels reported sunk, and Bob in Africa.

Celia Rutherford was of course concerned about Bertie, who according to Douglas was actually stationed on Alam Halfa Ridge, and Louise, having learned that HMS *Penelope*, the escort frigate for the ravaged convoy, had definitely been hit in the attack on the convoy, was beside herself with worry about Jack.

As August gave way to September with a flurry of rain showers and continual grey skies, virtually everyone in Lavender Road found themselves waiting for news. Any news. Ministry of War telegrams were what everyone dreaded most.

As it turned out, Helen was the first to hear.

It was 10 September. A beautiful day. The day the RAF dropped ten thousand bombs on Düsseldorf in under an hour. Helen had travelled into town in the company of Jen who was on her way to an audition for a leading soprano role in an ENSA concert party.

'Well, good luck,' Helen said awkwardly as they parted at Victoria. 'I hope your voice holds out.'

'So do I,' Jen said. 'Otherwise I might have to take up spying.'

Helen smiled, but behind Jen's blasé unconcern she could sense a deep, debilitating fear that her voice would let her down.

Letting herself into her office Helen had barely sat down at her desk when Angus McNaughton appeared in the doorway.

'Helen,' he said stiffly. 'I'm glad you're in early. Can you come into the conference room please? We need to talk to you.'

Helen knew at once something was wrong. It wasn't just Angus's awkward silence as he led her along the passage, it was the very summons itself. If anyone needed to talk to her why didn't they just come to her office? And who exactly was the ominous we?

André's dead, she said to herself. They're going to tell me André's dead. They are going to be sympathetic, concerned. They are going to tell me that he died for a good cause. That the struggle must go on.

However, as Angus pushed open the conference room door and ushered her inside, the faces that greeted her were not at all sympathetic. On the contrary, there was an atmosphere of carefully controlled anger. Anger and an unpleasant sensation of suspicion.

'Helen.' It was Maurice Buckmaster, Head of French Section, who spoke. His voice was cool. 'Please sit down.'

Helen sat obediently in the chair Angus pulled out for her at the end of the table. They were all there, she realised. All the bigwigs. Whatever they wanted to talk to her about was obviously important. Very important. She racked her brains wondering what she might have done wrong. What terrible mistake she might have made. It was a moment before she realised that Maurice Buckmaster was speaking again. Speaking about André.

At first all she took in was that André was alive. Alive. Relief coursed through her, weakening her limbs like rich wine. It was a further moment before she began to absorb the terrible import of what Maurice Buckmaster was saying.

'Your friend André Cabillard, codename *Renard*, has

finally been located by our agent *Lucien*, whom you of course know as well.'

Helen nodded. 'Paul,' she said.

'Indeed.' Maurice Buckmaster inclined his head. 'As you know, André Cabillard disappeared shortly after arriving in France. For several weeks we have had no idea what had happened to him, or why he had apparently evaded our people on the ground. The report Paul has now sent us gives us grounds for extreme concern.'

He shuffled a few papers in front of him and then looked up again. 'Paul came across *Renard* quite by chance while on a surveillance mission in Toulon. He saw him in a café.'

'A café?' Helen blinked. 'What's wrong with that?'

'Nothing is wrong with it, per se,' Maurice Buckmaster said. 'The problem, my dear Helen, was that the man with whom your friend André Cabillard was dining, on apparently convivial terms, was a senior officer of the German SS.'

The silence that followed this revelation was intense. The whole room was focused on Helen. All she could think of was André's face. His strong, hard face. And the extraordinary intensity of his eyes.

It was the faint squeak of a leather sole on the wooden floor that brought her to her senses.

'No!' She stood up abruptly, tipping the chair over with a crash behind her. She could feel the blood rushing to her head. 'It's impossible. I can't believe it.'

Maurice Buckmaster cleared his throat. 'Nobody wants to believe it,' he said quietly, 'but we have little choice. And I'm afraid, Helen, we are going to have to ask you some very serious questions. We need to know how much he knew about the organisation. How much you told him.'

Helen stared at him appalled. She couldn't speak. She couldn't breathe. They thought André was a traitor, and now she was under suspicion.

Then as the room began to spin and her vision blurred,

she suddenly knew that they could ask all they liked, but just now they wouldn't get any answers. For, at that moment, her limbs gave way and she sank gracefully to the floor.

Chapter Twenty-One

The Drury Lane Theatre was dark and cold after the bright sunlight outside. Jen could feel the goosebumps on her arms as she sang her first number to the three shadowy figures sitting together in the stalls. She had chosen to give them 'Deep Purple' first. It was an easy song, its main advantage as far as Jen was concerned being that it wasn't too high. She sang it well and followed it up with 'The White Cliffs of Dover'. At the end there was the usual silence while the audition panel made notes.

Jen had forgotten how unnerving that silence could be. In a show, even in a rehearsal, there was always some reaction at the end of a song, but in an audition there was nothing, and as she stood there, alone in the middle of the stage, waiting to be thanked and dismissed, she realised perhaps for the first time how much she loved applause. Needed applause. She needed people to think she was good. It wasn't enough that she knew she had given a good performance, it was the clapping, feet stamping and cheers that gave her the thrill and made the whole exhausting business worthwhile.

That was why she was putting herself through this ordeal. Even the nagging problem with her throat wasn't going to stop her ambition. Nor was the war. She wanted bigger parts, more applause, better audiences, more money. She wanted her name in lights. She wanted to be a star. And on good days she knew she could do it.

She could hear a low-voiced discussion now and,

knowing she had performed well, she was faintly surprised to sense that there was some disagreement among the selectors.

One of them leaned forward and addressed her. 'We are looking for something more lively, Miss Carter. We see you have "Funiculi Funicula" in your repertoire. Would you sing that for us, please?'

'Yes, of course,' Jen said, smiling grittily to cover the sudden nervous tremor that flicked through her. 'Funiculi Funicula' was lively all right. It also contained a top C. It came at the penultimate note. A final dramatic climax which audiences loved. Jen had learned the song on tour with ENSA the previous year, but she hadn't sung it recently, and now as the pianist struck up the introduction she quickly ran through the ridiculous rat-e-ti-tat words in her head. Fixing a bright confident smile on her face she squared her shoulders and breathed deeply.

She came in well and the first verse was excellent. Then as the refrain came round she had her first moment of anxiety. For a second she sensed the telltale weakening in her voice, but thankfully the high note this time round was only an A and she sang it true and clear. Reassured, she embarked on the second verse, but as the dreaded top C finale approached she felt the huskiness again. Even as she continued to smile brightly she felt ice forming in her stomach. There was a cop-out option, of course, which was to take the A again. Some singers did, but Jen knew the selectors were waiting for that C. She could feel them watching her.

'Fu-nic-u-li,' she sang confidently. 'Fu-nic—' At exactly the right moment she reached for the top C, but to her utter horror, nothing happened. Nothing. No sound at all. Not even a squeak. Just a soft grating somewhere in her larynx and then, professional that she was, the final, anticlimactic 'la!'

The silence this time had a different quality about it.

'I'm so sorry,' she said, putting a hand to her throat. 'I've got a touch of the flu.'

They didn't believe her of course. Even if they did, nobody wanted a soprano with a tendency to lose the high notes, touch of flu or not, but they thanked her anyway as she left the stage.

Picking up her bag from the wings she avoided the gleeful glances of two other waiting sopranos and hurried quickly out into the street.

Wanting to get far enough away from the theatre as possible before she allowed herself to scream or cry or both, she was startled to hear rapid footsteps coming up behind her and feel a hand close on her arm.

'Miss Carter? Jennifer? May I have a word?'

Glaring at her accoster, she was about to jerk her arm away when she realised that there was something familiar about that distinguished, rather angular face, the glossy well-cut hair, those cool assessing eyes, the air of authority.

The man dropped her arm of his own accord and smiled. 'Henry Keller,' he reminded her courteously.

'Oh yes.' Jen flushed. 'Mr Keller, I'm sorry. I was miles away.' She recognised him now. She hadn't really needed the prompt. Henry Keller was a friend of Ward Frazer. He was also the producer who had helped her to get into ENSA two years ago. She was about to return his smile when it occurred to her that this was no chance encounter.

'You were in there,' she said, 'Weren't you? Just now? You were on the panel.' When he nodded she groaned. 'So you saw me fluff the top C.'

He didn't deny it. He just frowned and put his hands in his pockets. 'What happened?' he asked. 'You were so good. Really good. And then …' His eyes narrowed slightly as he looked at her closely. 'I don't remember you having problems with the high notes.'

Jen shook her head and looked away. She didn't want to talk to him. She didn't want to talk to anyone. She just wanted to be left alone to her misery.

'I don't think it was really the flu, was it?' he went on. 'Because the rest of your voice would have been affected, and I only detected the faintest huskiness there in the earlier pieces.'

'Did you?' Jen turned back to him, aghast. She knew Henry Keller was a professional, one of the best producers in the business, but surely he would have needed the ears of a bat to detect any huskiness during her rendering of 'Deep Purple' or 'The White Cliffs'. And then a thought struck her. 'It was you?' she accused him. 'Wasn't it? You who insisted on that extra number. You were trying to catch me out.' She glared at him, eyes flashing angrily. 'How could you be so mean to me?'

'I was doing my job,' he said shortly. 'I knew there was something wrong.' He shrugged slightly as he gave her a faint rueful smile. 'It's not my fault that I still retain such a vivid memory of the purity of your voice two years ago.'

To her dismay Jen felt herself colouring. Then to her complete horror she felt her eyes fill with tears. Furious with herself she searched her handbag for a handkerchief and blew her nose, wishing he would take his low cultured voice and civilised concern elsewhere.

Henry Keller was watching her. 'There is something wrong, isn't there?' he said. 'What I can't quite work out is whether it's physical or psychological.'

Jen felt a stab of annoyance. What was he suggesting? That she had somehow bottled out? That she hadn't got the guts for a top C? 'It's physical,' she said crossly. 'I've got some problem with my throat, that's all.'

But he wouldn't leave it. 'What sort of problem? Have you seen a doctor?'

'No,' Jen snapped. 'I haven't.'

'Well, you should,' he said. 'And once you've got it sorted out I'd like you to sing for me again.' He glanced at his watch. 'Now I must get back. We've still got several people to hear.'

As he turned away, Jen closed her eyes. She had been so

rude. So incredibly rude. And yet he was still prepared to give her another chance. 'Oh God,' she muttered to herself, before racing after him as he strode away back towards the theatre.

'Mr Keller,' she called.

Stopping at once he waited for her to catch him up. When she did, she looked into his cool, faintly quizzical eyes and realised she didn't have a clue what to say.

'I'm sorry,' she said humbly at last. 'And I will go to a doctor ... I suppose I've been too scared it might be something awful.' She made a comical, half apologetic, half pleading face. 'And, well, thank you ... for what you said back there. For being kind.'

To her relief he smiled again. Just a slight enigmatic curve of his lips. 'Not kind,' he said dryly. 'Merely self-interested. You have a bright future, Jennifer, and I have half a mind to be part of it.'

By mid afternoon Helen was exhausted. She had come round from her faint to find herself propped in her chair with her head between her knees. Her interrogators barely gave her time to sip at a glass of water before starting their grilling. They had been on at her all morning, forcing her to tell them everything about her relationship with André, in particular to remember what she had told him about the SOE.

The truth was that she had told him far too much. She had been indiscreet. Especially on that last day when she went back with him on the train to Brockenhurst.

It was that afternoon as they had sat alone in a carriage already suffering the anticipated pain of separation that he had specifically asked her to tell him about the organisation.

'I shouldn't really,' she had said. 'It's dangerous for you to know.'

'It's dangerous for me not to know,' he had replied. 'There have been too many mistakes. Too many betrayals.

I need to know where I stand. Who I am working for. Who is in control.'

Helen had still hesitated, but to be honest it had been a relief to have something to talk about. Something other than how much she would miss him. So she had told him what she knew.

And now she had told her interrogators.

It had been a humiliating experience. They clearly believed André had pulled the wool over her eyes. Had been pulling it from the start. She had been used. Duped. And it still wasn't over.

'André Cabillard is a handsome man,' someone asked now. 'Did you have sexual intercourse with him?'

Helen gritted her teeth. It was like being back in that awful windowless interrogation room in Scotland all over again. Except this time it was for real, and it wasn't just André who was on trial, it was her. They needed to know whether she had introduced André into the organisation and given away SOE secrets on purpose. Out of some misguided sympathy for the enemy. For money. Or for sexual favours.

'No,' she said. 'I didn't have sexual intercourse with him.'

Some time during the morning they had brought in the same psychologist who had interviewed her all those weeks ago for her selection. It was he who had now taken over the questioning.

'But you wanted to?'

Helen felt her colour rise, and it was impossible to deny it. 'Sometimes,' she said.

'But he didn't take advantage of that desire?'

'No.'

'Did he kiss you?'

'Yes.'

'That was all?'

'Yes.'

'I see.' The psychologist leaned back in his chair. 'It

never occurred to you that he was holding back for a purpose? To make you more eager? To make you give him the information he wanted? I believe that was his game, but it went wrong. When his departure was advanced there were still things he needed to know. That was why he had to come and say goodbye to you.'

Helen shook her head. 'No,' she said steadily. 'I don't believe that was what happened.'

'No?' Angus McNaughton leaned forward suddenly. 'Then what do you think happened?'

Helen turned slightly to look at him. Angus had never liked the idea of André. Had never wanted him in the organisation. Now, behind his professional concern, there was a definite hint of smugness that he was being proved right.

'I think he fell in love with me,' she said. She ignored their expressions of incredulity. 'He didn't come to say goodbye, he came to ask me to go to France with him. Why would he do that if he was intending to betray the organisation?'

'Perhaps because he knew you could tell the Germans even more than he could,' Angus McNaughton said dryly.

'No!' Helen snapped back angrily. 'André knew perfectly well I would never tell the Germans anything.'

A small silence followed this outburst. They all knew that under duress she probably would have told the Germans everything they wanted to know.

'But you didn't go, did you?' the psychologist continued mildly. 'Why not? Didn't you love him enough? Or didn't you trust him?'

'I was scared of the parachute jump,' Helen said, but as she saw their scepticism she wondered what really had held her back. Was it really the parachute jump? The fear of getting caught? Or were they right? Had she too had some slight underlying mistrust of André?

They worked on that hint of doubt of course. They seemed to know her insecurities. They pressed home her lack of judgement. Her inability to face up to the truth. They wore her down. Made her admit that it was entirely possible that André had intended to betray the organisation all along. And then they sent her home.

She was suspended from work until further notice.

For ten days she doggedly refused to believe in André's defection. Then in the middle of September she was called back into the office.

Another SOE radio operator had been picked up by the Gestapo. André was being blamed for the betrayal. He had apparently been in touch with the agent soon after he had arrived back in France.

The same day Helen heard that a girl agent, codename *Denise*, had successfully parachuted into France. The first girl to do so. Everyone was talking about it.

Helen knew it was the final blow. She didn't cry. She was beyond crying. She was beyond everything.

In any case she wasn't the only one suffering.

There was still no news of Bertie Rutherford, nor of Bob and Mick Carter. Nor of Ward Frazer of course. And Louise was absolutely frantic for news about Jack.

Ever since a bad experience with an infected splinter in her foot as a child, Jen had been wary of the medical profession. It had always been a mystery to her why Katy had wanted to take up nursing. Nurses were bad enough but doctors had always struck her as arrogant and dismissive, and as luck would have it the doctor in Northcote Road whom she consulted about her throat didn't give her any reason to change her mind.

She could tell from the look on his face when she walked into his surgery that he wasn't going to like her. It was obvious from the start that he thought she was a timewaster, because he didn't really bother to listen to her. He just told her to stick her tongue out and glanced down her throat for about two seconds.

'Clear as a bell,' he said, turning away to wash his hands with ostentatious thoroughness. 'I'm afraid you'll have to think up something better than this if you want to get a few days off.'

Jen stared at him incredulously. 'I don't want time off. That's the whole point. Don't you understand? Singing is my career. I'm good. I want to be better. But there's something wrong. Something affecting my voice.'

He shook his head. 'There's nothing the matter with you. You just need to pull yourself together. You've probably just had a bit of a cold, that's all. You're lucky to be in a safe job, young lady. Lots of girls are risking their lives in this war, you know.'

Thinking about it later, Jen was amazed she kept her temper. If he only knew what it had been like last year, performing in armament factories night after night. Keeping the workers in Birmingham and Coventry happy while the sirens wailed outside and the fire-watchers banked up sandbags at the doors. Looking at his long, complacent face she longed to ask what he had done during the blitz, but she didn't. She just put on her gloves and walked out.

While her mother and Mrs Carter reacted to the lack of news about Bertie, Bob and Mick with a kind of stoic reserve, Louise had sublimated her anxiety about Jack into a complete and utter hatred of the Admiralty.

They were so slow with information. She had rung them up every day from the public call box outside the factory asking for news of Jack's ship. Each time it took her hours to get through, but even when she did they were so grudging with information that she wanted to scream, and frequently did. Eventually a woman told her that radio contact with the HMS *Penelope* had been broken. She would have to wait for news until the scattered remains of the convoy limped into harbour.

'But when will that be?' Louise screamed. 'When am I likely to know?'

'I'm afraid I can't tell you that. The position of the ships at this time is classified information.'

'But my husband was on one of the ships.'

'A lot of people's husbands were on those ships.'

The woman's tone was reproving and Louise slammed the receiver down. She didn't want to feel guilty. She didn't want to feel anything except anger. Anything else was too painful.

The telegram came a week later on 10 October. Her mother brought it round to Mrs d'Arcy Billière's at nine o'clock in the evening and waited while she opened it with shaking fingers.

It was from Jack. It was short to the point of curtness but Louise didn't mind that. Jack was alive and that was all that mattered. 'Back in harbour. Have been given leave. Arriving Clapham tomorrow.'

Louise looked up. 'Mummy, he's safe,' she said. 'He's all right.' And then her eyes filled with tears.

In the absence of anything else to do, Helen took on the task of looking after Malcolm. If the weather was nice she spent her time with him on the common trying to teach him to walk, otherwise she pushed him for miles around Clapham and Wandsworth in the pram. Once she even found herself in Wimbledon and had to take a series of buses in order to get him home in time for his tea.

Wandering around with the baby she felt numb and detached from the real world. Oddly calm. Even the news passed her by. She was only vaguely aware of the reported build-up of Allied strength in the desert, the desperate Russian defence of Stalingrad, house by house, as the Germans closed inexorably on the beleaguered city.

Whereas once Helen would have been gripped to the wireless and the newspapers, now she let it all drift by. Sleep was her great escape, but in order to sleep she had to drink, and as Katy had obstinately refused to sell her a bottle of whisky for private consumption, drinking meant going down to the pub.

Normally she sat at the end of the bar, exchanged a quick word with Katy, drank her whisky and left, but tonight was a Saturday and the pub was busy. Most of the clientele were laughing over a questionnaire that someone had received, asking what help they would be prepared to offer in the event of a winter invasion. Katy was busy keeping their glasses topped up and Helen found it hard not to listen to the lively banter. She even found herself smiling at some of the irreverent suggestions people came up with.

'You could offer to set your mother-in-law on them, Ginger,' someone called.

'Or your wife,' someone else shouted across. 'I reckon as she'd keep the whole bleedin' Third Reich at bay.'

It was as Helen glanced round to see which one the henpecked Ginger was, that someone touched her arm.

'Miss de Burrel?'

Turning back, Helen stared blankly at the young man at her side, and then suddenly, with a jolt she realised it was the cipher clerk from Baker Street. Seeing her startled look, he flushed slightly.

'Look, I'm sorry to turn up like this. I know it's late and that, but I've just come off duty. I hope you don't mind. I got your address from one of the secretaries at work. I only live in Balham so I thought I'd drop by on the way home. Your landlady said she thought you'd be in here—' He stopped abruptly and peered at her through the smoky haze. 'Are you all right?'

Helen was aware of a strange sensation in her chest as though her heart was shaking. 'Yes,' she said quickly. 'I'm fine. What exactly was it you wanted to tell me?'

The radio operator glanced around uneasily. 'Well,' he said, 'it's about that chap you knew. That agent.'

Helen gripped the bar. 'André?'

'Who?' The operator frowned. 'No, it's that other fellow. Ward Frazer. The one you were asking about months ago.'

Helen stared at him. Then, glancing round, she saw to her relief that Katy was busy collecting up empty glasses. Turning back to her informant, Helen grasped his arm. 'Tell me quickly. What's happened? Is he dead?'

'No.' The man looked surprised. 'Alive. He's in the South of France. There was a message from that *Lucien* in Marseilles.' He was flushing again. 'I know it's classified info and that. You won't get me into trouble, will you? But you know how funny they can be in that place. I didn't know if anyone else would tell you. I knew you was off sick, you see, and I thought you'd like to know.'

'Oh my God.' Helen could hardly believe it. After all this time, Ward Frazer was alive. Not out of danger of course, but alive.

Aware that the operator was watching her anxiously, Helen roused herself sufficiently to thank him. Nobody knew better than she how funny 'they' could be. 'Of course I won't get you into trouble,' she said. 'On the contrary, I'll buy you a drink.' She called down to Molly who was at the other end of the bar. 'Give this man whatever he wants, Molly. It's on me.' Then she slipped off her stool and on rather shaky legs walked over to the small kitchen where Katy was rinsing glasses.

As she approached, Katy looked up and smiled wearily. 'Are you off?'

'No,' Helen said. She edged further into the small galley space. 'Katy,' she said carefully, 'I've got something to tell you about Ward, but I want you to sit down first.'

Immediately what small amount of colour there was in Katy's pale face disappeared. 'No,' she whispered. Then her voice rose. 'No! Don't tell me. I can't bear it. I don't want to know.'

'You do want to know,' Helen said quickly as Katy tried to push past her. 'Believe me, you do.' She grabbed her arm, shook her slightly. 'Katy, listen. He's alive. He's been seen in the South of France.'

At once Katy stopped struggling. For a second she was still. Rigid. Then she pulled her arm away and stared at Helen suspiciously. 'You've been sitting in here for the last hour,' she said grittily. 'How come you suddenly know this?'

Helen blinked. 'One of the SOE clerks came to tell me,' she said. 'He's over there at the bar. The chap who looks like a ferret.'

There was a long pause, then Katy put a hand to her face. 'Oh Helen,' she said. 'Oh Helen!' Then she began to smile and then laugh and then cry, and then she mopped herself up and clapped her hands together. 'That's it,' she said. 'Drinks on the house.'

'Katy, is that wise?' Helen murmured. 'He's not completely out of danger yet, and there's a lot of people in tonight.'

'I know,' Katy said. She ripped off her apron and rolled up her sleeves. 'I don't care. I want to celebrate while I have the chance, and I'm going to start by giving Mr Ferret at the bar a smacking kiss on the lips.'

An hour later the cipher clerk was still at the bar looking rather stunned.

'This is a jolly nice place,' he remarked rather blearily. 'I might come here again.'

7 September 1942 (delayed at sea)

Dear Mater and Pater,

Thought you might be interested to know that I saw my first bit of action yesterday and survived. Jerry attacked the ridge where we were positioned and we had a devil of a job to defend our gun. But we held firm and stood our ground. General Montgomery visited our position this morning, shook us all by the hand, and said he was very proud of us. He's definitely a good man. Morale has improved considerably since he took command. I'm sure we'll soon have Rommel on the run.

Yours, Bertie.

7 September 1942 (delayed at sea)

Dear Mum,

Sorry I haven't written for a bit but we're on the go twenty-four hours a day now that this Monty bloke is in charge, what with training and that. It's exhausting but at least we'll have a better chance if Jerry has a go at us. Although why he wants all this sand God only knows. There was a bit of action up the line yesterday but it didn't affect us. Some of the lads was disappointed but I don't know. I reckon I'm happy to wait my turn.

Love, Bob.

P.S. The food's better now and all.

Jack got back late on the evening of Saturday, 10 October. At first when he didn't immediately express enthusiasm for the new flat Louise thought it was because of the proximity of Aaref Hoch downstairs. Certainly his face was drawn and tense as he swung his kitbag off his shoulder, and his eyes seemed blank and strangely unfocused as he looked around. But he was handsome as ever and, in fact, as always Louise found his reserve rather appealing.

In any case, she knew exactly how to take his mind off whatever was worrying him.

Kicking the door closed behind them she entwined herself into his arms, then giggling, pushed him back so they fell in a sprawl of limbs on to the mattress on the floor.

'Darling Jack,' she murmured as she opened his jacket and untucked his shirt and vest. 'Darling, darling Jack.' She ran a trail of kisses down his flat stomach. 'I can't tell you how much I've missed you.'

But he was still and unresponsive under her caresses and

she sat up pouting crossly. 'Jack? What is it? What's the matter?'

He didn't answer, although she was relieved when a moment later he rolled over and held her tight in his arms. But that was all he seemed to want to do.

Louise wanted more, much more than that, and slowly, gradually, she began to move against him, squirming gently against his groin in the way he had been unable to resist on their honeymoon.

At first he seemed to like it, but when her fingers began to probe again he pulled away. 'Louise, don't. Please don't,' he said gruffly. 'Not yet.'

Louise frowned. 'Why not?' she asked. 'Don't you like me any more?'

He sat up then and leaned his elbows on his knees, his head bowed. Louise could see that he was breathing deeply. His hands were clenched.

'It's not you,' he said at last. 'It's me.'

'You.' Louise knelt beside him on the mattress, puzzled. 'What do you mean?'

He looked up at her then, and she was shocked by the bleak expression in his eyes, then suddenly, to her dismay, he seemed to crumple. 'I'm sorry, Louise.' His head was in his hands. 'I'm so sorry.'

Louise stared at his bowed head. As far as she was concerned there was only one thing he could possibly have done that would make him apologise so abjectly. 'Is there someone else?' she whispered in horror. 'Have you been with someone else?'

He looked up then. 'No, of course not,' he said. He was silent for a moment, clearly trying to pull himself together. 'Louise, you obviously have no idea what I've been through.' He swallowed hard. 'Our convoy was attacked.'

Louise felt a rush of relief. So that was what was upsetting him. Just the stupid convoy. 'I do know,' she said eagerly. 'It was all over the newspapers. I was worried to death.' She was going to say more, but the look he gave her stopped her in her tracks. She had never seen such emptiness in anyone's eyes ever before. She tried to take his arm, but he pushed her away, staring at the wall.

'The first ship that went down was so quick,' he said. His voice was distant. 'It was gone before we could get back to it. But the second and third were slow. There were so many men in the water.' He stopped and closed his eyes for a moment. 'Thrashing around, trying to escape the burning oil. So much burning oil.' Suddenly he was shaking as though he was freezing cold, but it wasn't cold – Louise had got Aaref to light the fire for her earlier, specially for Jack's return.

'We knew the sub was just there,' he said. 'Right under us. It had to be.'

'Jack, don't,' Louise said. 'Try not to think about it.'

He didn't seem to hear her. 'All those faces,' he went on doggedly. 'You could see them clearly. You could even hear them shouting. Waving. They thought we were going to pick them up, you see. And then the captain ordered the depth charge …' He stopped again and put his head in his hands again.

'Well, you're home now,' Louise said. 'Safe and sound. That's the important thing.'

'They were like toys,' he said. 'The blast blew them out of the water. Like dolls. And afterwards they were still there, but floating, not swimming. Bobbing on the surface. Until the fire got to them of course. You could smell it then. The burning flesh. Even over the oil …'

Louise jumped to her feet. 'For God's sake, Jack!' she shouted. 'Stop it!' Glaring at him angrily she shuddered violently. 'Anyway,' she added more calmly, 'you can forget it now.'

Whether he forgot it or not, she certainly didn't want to know about it. She felt sorry about it too, of course she did, but there was a limit. 'I'll make a cup of tea,' she said. 'That'll make you feel better.'

Jack shook his head. 'Louise, you don't understand,' he

said. 'I can't forget about it. I don't think I'll ever be able to forget. The submarine was never there anyway. Even as we ploughed through those bodies it struck again. And again.'

To her horror she realised he was crying. Crying. Her strong, handsome Jack. *Crying*. Sobbing like Katy's baby sobbed when he hurt himself falling over trying to walk.

As she stood, shocked and helpless in the doorway, all Louise found she could do was hope that nobody else in the house could hear.

It was a dark night. So dark out in the blacked-out street that Joyce could barely make out one house from the next. She didn't like firewatch duty, but war was war and you had to do your bit. So when Alan Nelson had come round asking for volunteers for the street's fire-watch rota a couple of weeks ago, Joyce had agreed to be put down.

It was only four hours once a week, after all, and you didn't have to be outside all the time. Just a short patrol once an hour unless you heard planes. Then you had to hotfoot it out into the darkness to watch out for dropped incendiaries.

That was why she was outside now. She had heard planes, but as Pete was still in the pub and Miss Philips was away for the weekend at some Wrens selection board, she had no means of knowing if they were ours or theirs.

However, there was no sign of any incendiaries and the only noise she could hear now was coming out of the Flag and Garter where it sounded as though they were having a right old knees-up. Surprised that the pub was still open when it was already well after closing time, she wondered idly what they were celebrating. There wasn't much to celebrate these days, after all.

By the look of him when he passed by earlier, that young man of Louise Rutherford's wasn't in a mood to celebrate neither. She'd wanted to stop him. To ask him if he knew anything about Mick's ship. She knew it had gone down of course. She'd had a telegram to tell her that. But nobody had told her how quickly it had sunk or whether young Mick might have had a chance. Might have found a lifeboat or been picked up by another vessel.

Squaring her shoulders determinedly she looked up again at the sky and was wondering whether to go back indoors when the pub door opened and Mr Lorenz emerged, bringing with him a brief blast of noise and laughter.

'Ah, Mrs Carter,' he said, raising his hat courteously. 'I thought you might be out here. I was bringing you a little fortifying tipple on my way home.'

Joyce was touched. 'You're very good to me, you know,' she said as she accepted the glass of Guinness.

'Not at all,' he said mildly.

'So what's going on in there?' Joyce nodded to the pub. 'Someone won on the races? Or is it war news? Something good for once?'

'It is good news,' Lorenz said gravely. 'It's Katy Frazer's husband. Apparently word has come that he is in France. Still on the run of course, but alive.'

It was the last thing Joyce expected to hear. To be honest, she had given poor Ward Frazer up for dead months ago. Not that she ever would have said so, mind. Not when poor young Katy was trying so hard to keep her hopes up. Oddly enough Joyce had been there when Ward had proposed to Katy. It was at Stonehenge. It had taken him long enough but she'd never seen anything like it when he brought Katy back to the car. The love in their eyes. The love and the fear. It had made her feel quite choked. She felt choked now just thinking about it. More than choked. A bit tearful in fact.

She was starting to feel embarrassed when Lorenz took the Guinness gently out of her hand and replaced it with a handkerchief, a crisp white handkerchief that smelt as though it had come straight from the laundry. A moment later she felt his arm come rather tentatively round her shoulder.

It was the first time he had ever shown any desire to touch her and Joyce stiffened nervously. At once he withdrew his arm and stood back.

'I'm sorry,' he said. 'I didn't mean to upset you.'

'I'm not upset,' Joyce said quickly. 'I'm happy. I just hope he manages to get home, that's all.'

'I'm sure he will,' Lorenz said. 'Ward Frazer always seemed to be a most competent and resourceful young man.'

Joyce nodded. She felt guilty now for rejecting Lorenz's offer of comfort. 'You'd better get home and all,' she said gruffly. 'You're taking over from me, aren't you? You'd best get some sleep. I'll give you a knock at two.'

Without demur Lorenz handed her back the Guinness. 'I'll see you later, then,' he said.

'Sleep well,' Joyce called after him. 'Oh, and thanks again for the Guinness.'

He stopped by his gate and turned round. Even in the darkness she could see the small inclination of his head. 'It's my pleasure,' he said.

Or she thought that was what he said, because his words were lost in a cry of shock as two large men materialised out of the shadows of his front garden and grabbed him by the arms.

Chapter Twenty-Two

'Hey, are you sick?' Dirk asked when he met Jen at the stage door. 'You sounded real husky tonight.'

'I'm just tired,' Jen said, but she couldn't conceal her dismay from the sharp-eyed American boys. They were most concerned to see her so brought down.

'I guess it sounded more sexy than husky,' Dirk amended quickly and the others nodded, quickly reassuring her that husky or not she was still the best thing in the show.

They were kind. In the pub they plied her with drinks, everyone insisting that another small one would be just the thing to put her back on her feet, and when the pub closed Dirk even paid for her to have a taxi back to Lavender Road.

As the taxi pulled away from Shaftesbury Avenue, leaving him standing on the kerb, waving, Jen realised that she was genuinely fond of Dirk. She was fond of them all. Her posse of Yankee fans.

And soon they would go. Already they were talking of new kit issues, and desert survival training. There was a restlessness about them. A hint of excitement. They wanted to go. Apart from Jen's show and Sunday nights at the Flag and Garter, London bored them. What they wanted was 'to go win the war' and then get back to Mom in America as soon as possible.

Well, that was fine by Jen. The sooner the bloody war

was over the better. She just hoped their departure wouldn't have too much effect on Katy's trade.

As soon as the taxi pulled up outside the Flag and Garter Jen heard the laughter and singing inside and her heart sank. The last thing she wanted was to have to join in some rowdy Saturday night session at the bar.

And then she heard the other noise and, blinking through the darkness, she saw that a little bit further up the road there was some kind of fight going on.

There was often the odd brawl in the street around closing time. Katy had become a dab hand at getting any likely contenders outside before anything got broken. Katy now took it in her stride, but Jen hated it. Having lived all her life with a father all too ready with his fists, Jen had been left with a bitter hatred of any kind of violence, and even now hearing the dull thud of flesh on flesh she shivered convulsively and drew her coat round her. Bloody men, she thought, no wonder they enjoyed wars so much.

Then she heard her mother's voice, shrill and frightened. 'Leave him alone. For God's sake, leave him alone.'

Jen's hand froze on the pub door.

Another voice, a grunting, breathy, typical South London voice. 'You shut your face or you'll get it and all. Your husband don't like you messing with this Jew.'

Jen didn't even stop to think. Turning, she ran silently up the road towards the voices. It was a clear night and already she could see her mother struggling with one man while another repeatedly punched Mr Lorenz in the stomach.

Quickly Jen crouched down and took off her shoes. Then clutching one in each hand she ran forward and slammed the heel of her shoe as hard as she could into the elbow of the man holding Lorenz.

'You bloody men,' she screamed. 'I hate you. Let him go, you bullying bastards.'

Caught unawares, the man let go his grip with a grunt of pain and reeled back clutching his arm.

Lorenz fell into his front hedge and Jen at once turned to the other man, battering his chest and face with the shoes until, swearing furiously, he caught her flailing wrists in an iron grasp. She could feel the pressure as he tried to twist the shoes out of her hands, but Jen hadn't been brought up with four brothers for nothing, and even as she smelt the cheap oil of his hair and the sharp goaty tang of sweat, she balanced herself on one bare foot, leaned in towards him and brought the other knee sharply up between his legs.

As he screamed and fell back on the road, she yelled at him. 'Serve you right, you stinking oaf. You smell. Did you know that? You bloody stink.' Then as he lay on the ground, she wished she had her shoes on her feet because there was nothing she wanted more than to give him a good kicking. Perhaps aware of her intentions he scrambled up, clutching himself and moaning.

The other man was still nursing his arm. 'You've broken my bloody arm,' he shouted at her, backing off as she approached again.

'Good,' Jen hissed at him, her voice rasping in her throat. 'I wish I'd broken your bloody neck. 'Now bugger off or we'll get the police on to you. And if you ever, ever, show your faces round here again you're dead. All right?'

The men didn't say whether it was all right or not. They just ran.

Jen stared after them for a moment then she turned slowly. Joyce was leaning over Lorenz.

'Is he all right?' Jen asked abruptly.

Joyce nodded. 'I think so,' she said.

Jen could see her mother was shaking. For a second she felt sorry for her. 'Dad sent them, didn't he?' she said. 'Well, I doubt they'll be back.'

Joyce shrugged. 'Those two might not, but there's plenty more where they came from,' she said.

It sounded ungrateful and Jen flared up at once. 'Well,

I'm sorry I bothered to intervene, then. I might as well have left them to do their business.'

'No,' Joyce said at once. 'I didn't mean that.'

There was a catch in her voice, but Jen ignored it. She didn't want to get involved in her mother's problems anyway. Why should she?

Mr Lorenz was struggling to his feet. 'Thank you, Miss Carter,' he said. 'I am so sorry to have caused you trouble.'

Jen brushed off his thanks. Suddenly she was feeling tearful and rather shaky. To her astonishment she felt Joyce's hand on her arm.

'Jen, love, are you all right?'

It was the first time her mother had ever seemed to care about her. Certainly the first time in her entire life she had called Jen 'love'. Pushing her away Jen bent to put on her shoes. 'Of course I'm all right,' she said shortly. Straightening up she nodded at Lorenz who was now again leaning against the gate. 'I just hope he is. I reckon he needs a doctor.'

'I'll see to him,' Joyce said. 'And, well … thanks, Jen. They might have killed him if it hadn't been for you. I felt pretty scared and all.'

Jen didn't want her gratitude. She didn't want anything from her mother. Or from Lorenz. 'Serves you right for messing around with him in the first place,' she said and walked back to the pub.

After three days of long silences, intense gloom and several more abortive attempts at lovemaking, Jack went back to his parents.

When Louise told Katy that Jack had popped home for a few days Katy was surprised Louise hadn't gone too.

'I have to work,' Louise said. 'I'll probably go down at the weekend.'

Katy looked at her. 'Is everything all right?' she asked.

'Oh yes,' Louise said, and flushed. 'Of course. Why do you ask?'

'Well,' Katy put down the glass she was polishing, 'we haven't seen much of you, that's all.'

'Goodness, Katy. We're only just married. We've got other things to do.'

'They obviously spend the whole time in bed,' Jen said to Katy later.

Katy smiled. 'She certainly looked tired.'

'That'll be you soon,' Jen said. 'You who's in bed all the time with your sexy husband. How do you feel about that after all this time?'

'I don't know,' Katy said. 'It's an odd thought, isn't it?' She shook her head slightly. After the initial euphoria she had experienced on hearing news of Ward, she had been aware of a new tension growing in her.

So much had changed since he had married her. She was no longer the pampered little daughter of overprotective parents. Her father had died. Her mother had gone off to the country and showed no sign of coming back. Katy didn't mind. She was a different person now. Much more self-sufficient. But the thought of a big handsome stranger marching into the pub and expecting to carry on where they had left off on the honeymoon was daunting to say the least.

'To be honest I'm trying not to think about it,' she said. 'Anyway, he's not back yet. He still might not make it.'

'If he's survived this long, he's bound to survive long enough to get home somehow,' Jen said. 'And then you'll be all lovey-dovey again and I'll be out of a home.'

'Don't be ridiculous!' Katy said hotly. 'You can stay as long as you like.'

Jen shook her head. 'I wouldn't stay if Ward was back. It wouldn't be fair.'

Katy was horrified. The thought of losing Jen was almost as bad as the thought of regaining Ward Frazer.

'But I don't want you to go,' she said. 'I've got used to you being here. Anyway, where would you go?'

'I might join up,' Jen said.

Katy almost choked. 'Join up?'

'I might have to. There's not much else I can do without a voice, is there?'

Katy could hardly believe her ears. The thought of Jen subjecting herself to military discipline was laughable, and as for the uniform … But then she saw the tension around Jen's pretty mouth and suddenly she felt guilty for not taking Jen's concerns seriously enough. Jen was always over dramatic, but this was the first time she had mentioned the possibility of giving up singing. Singing was her life. She couldn't possibly give it up.

'Jen, don't be ridiculous,' she said. 'You're brilliant. Didn't that Henry Keller producer chap say so the other day? You just need to see a proper doctor. That's all. Someone good.'

'There's no point,' Jen said. 'He'll only tell me I'm trying to skive …' And to Katy's horror, Jen, who never cried, burst into tears.

15 Oct '42

Dear Joyce,

So now you know what happens to people who mess about with other people's wives. I hope you've learned your lesson. It's lucky for you my blokes got seen off because they wasn't happy to find you out in the street in the middle of the night with that Jew. Not happy at all and it would of served you right if they'd had a go at you and all.

Still, no hard feelings. You've always been a sensible woman and I reckon you'll watch your step now. If not, you'll pay. And you'll pay hard. After all, it's under a year now till I'll be out. I tell you, I can't wait to be out of this place. I don't know if it's the food or what but I've been feeling pretty rough the last few weeks. Pains in my stomach and that. The doctor gave me some pills but they don't do any good.

Your loving husband, Stanley.

On Katy's behalf, having heard no word from the SOE regarding Ward, a couple of days later Helen forced herself to summon the courage to telephone Angus McNaughton from the public call box on Lavender Hill, but she found that he had no more news about Ward Frazer's whereabouts or condition than she did. Clearly stunned that she knew so much, he was annoyed when she refused to tell him how she had come by her information, but she was damned if she was going to get the cipher clerk into trouble.

'I know I am *persona non grata* at the moment,' she said, 'but I would be grateful if you would let me know if you hear any more. If nothing else, I believe Ward's wife is entitled to the information.' And with that she put the phone down with a sharp satisfying click.

Her satisfaction was short lived, because she had just pushed Malcolm's pram back up Lavender Road and was about to cross over on to the common when Greville Rutherford's car drew up alongside her. Her first thought was to flee but already he had turned off the engine and was getting out.

'My dear Helen,' he said. 'What a nice surprise. I thought you would be hard at work behind your office typewriter.'

'I'm not working at the moment,' Helen said stiffly.

'Oh dear,' he said. 'That's the trouble with you girls. No staying power.' He nodded at little Malcolm in the pram. 'Still, I expect you are enjoying a bit of nannying. A much more suitable occupation, if you don't mind me saying so.'

Helen did mind him saying so. She minded even more what came next.

'I hear your Frenchman has run off,' he said. 'Well, I'm not entirely surprised about that. I've always said you can't trust the French. Still, you're a pretty girl. I'm sure you'll find someone else.' He laughed and reached forward to squeeze her hand. 'I'd marry you myself if I could.'

It was as much as Helen could do to remain civil. For weeks now she had been suppressing her pain and anger under a veneer of blank disinterest, but a veneer was all it was. Underneath was a seething mass of unexpressed fury. Fury with André. Fury with Angus McNaughton and the SOE bosses. And most of all fury with herself. It was poor old Greville Rutherford who got the full blast of it.

'Oh really?' she said, snatching her hand away. 'And what on earth makes you think I would want to marry a pompous arse like you? I want to marry someone I can respect and admire, not someone who makes a fool of himself over a girl half his age.'

He pretended to laugh it off but she could tell that she had riled him. She was right. 'Oh, come now, Helen,' he said grittily, grabbing her arm and pulling her up against him. 'You weren't so fussy a few months back, were you? Before you met your so-called boyfriend?'

'I was always fussy,' she shouted at him. 'I never wanted your attentions. I just didn't know how to avoid them. And if you don't let me go this second I won't be responsible for my actions.'

He didn't let her go. Instead he tried to kiss her. Jerking her head out of the way Helen was on the verge of kneeing him in the crutch when over his shoulder she caught sight of Celia standing only feet away at the end of the Cedars House driveway. She was dressed in a tweedy coat, grey felt hat and sensible shoes and her eyes were so wide it was surprising her eyeballs didn't pop out on to the pavement.

'Greville,' she gasped. 'What are you doing? What are you thinking of?'

At the sound of his wife's voice Greville Rutherford's arms dropped away as though he'd been shot. 'Celia …' He swung round, but he didn't say any more. After all, what could he say? It was perfectly obvious what he had been thinking of.

It was also obvious that Celia was not having too much difficulty in putting two and two together. 'Helen,' she said stiffly. 'I am so sorry.'

Helen had never felt so embarrassed in all her life. 'It's all right,' she said, impressed by Mrs Rutherford's restraint. The poor woman must be deeply distressed, but she wasn't allowing it to show. On the contrary, as she turned to face Greville, she seemed stronger and more controlled than Helen had ever seen her.

'I think an apology to Lady Helen is in order, Greville,' she said coldly.

'No, no,' Helen said. 'Honestly. It's all right.' She swung the pram round so quickly that Malcolm nearly flew out on to the bonnet of the car. 'Look, I'd better go. Malcolm's getting restless.'

As she swiftly crossed the road she heard Greville's blustering voice behind her. 'My dear, I can explain everything, I—'

And then Celia's cold dismissive response. 'I haven't time to listen to your excuses now, Greville. I'm on my way to the café. I'm late as it is.'

When Helen glanced back a moment later, Celia had already turned the corner into Lavender Road and Greville was standing alone on the street by the Rover, rather red about the neck, staring blankly after her.

The solicitor's office on Northcote Road was dark and forbidding, so dark and forbidding that it was several minutes before Joyce could bring herself to press the bell. In fact it was only the small brass plaque by the door announcing the presence of the optimistic-sounding Mr Martin Hope inside that gave her the courage to proceed at all.

However, when she was eventually shown into Mr Hope's office by an elderly, painfully stooped clerk she knew at once that, as so often with names, Mr Hope's was distinctly misleading. Much older than she had expected and wearing a sombre suit and black tie, and an expression to match, Mr Hope looked more like a funeral director than a solicitor, and his stern glance over heavy-framed spectacles as he rose slowly to his feet behind his enormous wooden desk was almost enough to make Joyce run for the door. Bravely she sat down and folded her trembling fingers in her lap.

'Now, madam,' he said heavily. 'What can I do for you?'

Joyce had hoped they might exchange a few pleasantries before getting down to business, but it was clear that Mr Hope wouldn't recognise a pleasantry if it jumped up and hit him on the nose. So taking a deep breath in a vain attempt to control her shaking nerves she plunged straight in. 'I want to know how much it would cost to divorce my husband.'

As soon as the words were out of her mouth she wished she had wrapped it up a bit, because you could have cut the silence that greeted her announcement with a knife.

Mr Hope looked at her over the spectacles. 'I am sure you are aware, madam, that divorce is a very serious matter. It is not something to be taken lightly. It is not something that either society or the Church condone. To be quite frank it is not something that I myself condone except in exceptional circumstances. Do you understand what I'm saying?'

'Yes, I think so,' Joyce said. Actually she wasn't all that sure what condone meant but she got the gist of it.

'And you still wish to proceed?'

She nodded again.

'So you don't mind what people say? You don't care about the stigma attached to the notion of divorce? Particularly to a divorced woman.'

Joyce frowned. 'Well, of course I mind, but—'

Mr Hope was in his stride now. 'And how does you husband feel about this?'

'He doesn't know,' Joyce said. 'He's in jail.'

Mr Hope's brows rose sharply. 'For how long?'

'Another year.'

'I see.' Mr Hope leaned forward, his eyes piercing hers. 'So because your husband is temporarily incarcerated you wish to absolve yourself of your responsibilities relating to him? Is that it, madam? Is that what you are implying?'

He had lost her completely now. She didn't know what he was on about with all those long words. She didn't know whether she was implying it or not. It didn't seem to matter, though, because he didn't wait for her response anyway.

'You married your husband for better or worse. What are you saying now? That because he's in jail those vows didn't mean anything?'

She understood that. 'It's not because he's in jail,' she stammered, flushing in embarrassment. 'It's because he used to hit me.'

Mr Hope's eyes narrowed slightly. 'Why did he hit you?'

'Well, he was drunk, wasn't he?' Joyce said.

'Was that the only reason?'

'He said I answered back.'

Mr Hope shrugged. 'He's your husband, madam. He is entitled to some respect.'

'That's as may be, but I reckon as I'm entitled to some respect too,' Joyce said, and for the first time Mr Hope looked startled.

'I don't think you understand, madam. Under the law of our land a man is master in his own home. How he chooses to act within that capacity is his business, and it is not the business of the law to intervene.'

Joyce was silent. So that was it. As far as the law was concerned Stanley could do what he liked.

'Where would you live if you left your husband?' Mr Hope asked.

'I wouldn't leave,' she said. 'I'd stop where I was.'

His brows rose once again. 'Is your house rented?'

'Yes, of course.'

'And it's your name on the rental agreement?'

'Well, no,' Joyce admitted. 'It's Stanley's of course. They don't generally let women sign things like that.'

Mr Hope nodded. 'Exactly, madam. Women don't sign things like that. Therefore the house in effect belongs to your husband. Which means that in the event of a separation, you would be obliged to make alternative arrangements, which for a woman in your position might be difficult. Landlords are understandably reluctant to let to divorced women, for obvious reasons ...'

Joyce didn't want to hear any more. She had heard more than enough as it was. She didn't want to hear that divorced women were considered loose, just because they refused to put up with regular beatings from their husbands. The law was made by men. She should have known that. She had known. But somehow she had convinced herself she was a special case. Well, she obviously wasn't. In society's eyes she was just a run-of-the-mill working-class wife who had a few problems with her old man on a Saturday night, and she had no right to expect any help from the law.

She stood up abruptly. 'Thank you,' she said. 'I'm so glad I came to see you.'

Mr Hope frowned. 'I wouldn't be doing my job if I didn't point out the potential problems. You need to know where you stand.'

'Oh, I know where I stand all right,' Joyce said, turning at the door. 'And I hope you'll be standing at my graveside when he beats me to death this time next year.'

As she stepped out into the lobby and slammed the door behind her, the old clerk shuffled out from behind his desk. 'Is everything all right, madam?' he asked.

'Oh yes,' Joyce said. 'Mr Hope was very helpful.'

The old man looked surprised. 'Oh, that wasn't Mr Hope that you saw,' he said. 'Mr Hope is a much younger man. Mr Hope has joined up and is serving in Egypt.'

Joyce stared at him. 'Who was that, then?' she asked.

The clerk glanced nervously at the closed door. 'Oh, that was Mr Truelove,' he said. 'He's come out of retirement to stand in for Mr Hope while he's away ...'

But Joyce was already out in the street. Mr Truelove, she thought. Mr bloody Truelove. If she hadn't been so utterly depressed she would have laughed. Wasn't it just her bloody luck to end up consulting a man called Mr Truelove about a divorce.

5 October 1942

My dear Helen,

I am so sorry I haven't written for so long but life over here really is awfully hectic and I never was much of a correspondent at the best of times. But I do feel guilty, because your last letter seemed rather low, which isn't like you at all. I'm quite sure, knowing you, that you will have bounced back by now, but if not, don't forget you can always jump on a ship and come over. I would love to see you. The apartment is plenty big enough for two, and the marvellous West Indian couple who look after it (and me) would be thrilled to meet you.

I bumped into old Busby Watson the other day in the Willard and he was asking about you. He said he thought he'd seen you with some rather handsome Frenchman at a reception at the Russian embassy. (Was that right? If so I hope you told old Maisky how terribly impressed we all are with the Russian resistance to the Hun?) Anyway, I told Busby that you were in the FANYs now and were frightfully busy dealing with some Inter-Services liaison project. He looked rather startled. I think he expected you to be rolling bandages for the Red Cross or something 'ladylike' like that. You know how stuffy these War Office chaps are. Not my daughter, I said. She likes to be in the thick of it!

Anyway, Poppet, I must run, as they say over here, I'm due at the White House for coffee and doughnuts.

With all my love,

Daddy.

P.S. Who is the Frenchman? Is he worthy of you? If so you have my blessing!

Louise went down to see Jack at his parents' on Sunday. His mother had sent her a note asking her to come, and even though Louise was scared about what might be awaiting her down there she replied by return to say she would go.

It was an awful journey involving a train to East Croydon and a long wait for two different, geriatric buses and Louise couldn't help remembering that wonderful day all those months ago when Jack had driven her down in a borrowed car and had stopped the car to kiss her before roaring up the drive to introduce her to his parents. Jack had been so happy that day, and his parents had been so welcoming, so charming, so delighted to meet his new fiancée.

Now as she limped up the long drive Louise looked nervously ahead at the long low house nestling in the wooded countryside, and wondered how when everything had seemed to be going so well, it could so suddenly go so badly wrong. She knew it was going to be a difficult day, and she was right.

Jack was listless and preoccupied and made it embarrassingly clear that he didn't want to be alone with her.

Mrs Delmaine tried to explain. 'Jack has suffered a terrible experience,' she said. 'All he can think about is those men dying in front of him, and he can't understand why everyone doesn't feel the way he does. That's why he finds it hard to talk about other things, it's completely knocked him off balance.'

'But what can we do?' Louise asked. 'It's so awful when he's like this.'

'Well,' Mrs Delmaine said, 'on Friday he will go back to the ship. We've been told he must try to get this out of his system. Face it again.'

What about me? Louise wanted to shout. When's he going to face me again?

'I know it's hard for you, Louise,' Mrs Delmaine said gently, 'but perhaps you can find it in yourself to be patient. Jack loves you deeply. Part of his trouble is that he can't bear for you to see him like this.'

Slightly mollified, Louise frowned. 'So you think going back to sea will help?'

Mrs Delmaine hesitated for a moment. 'I hope so,' she said. 'If not Jack may have to have some treatment.'

'What sort of treatment?'

'Well, I think some sort of psychiatric treatment probably.'

Louise gaped at her in utter horror. 'You mean a mental hospital? You mean Jack might have gone mad?'

'No, Louise,' Mrs Delmaine said firmly. 'I don't mean that at all. I just mean that there are people specially trained to deal with cases of severe shock.'

Louise was not convinced. Jack's gone mad, she whispered to herself as she made the laborious journey back to Clapham Junction. I've married a madman.

To Katy's delight Jacob won a full scholarship to Emanuel College in Wandsworth. He came in to tell her the news on the morning of 23 October, the same day that, after months of seeming inaction, General Montgomery opened a major offensive along the coast at El Alamein in Egypt.

'Don't order any beer for Sunday night,' Jen said, coming downstairs in her silk dressing-gown, 'because the Americans have gone.'

'Gone?' Katy asked blankly. 'Gone where?'

'To North Africa, I suppose,' Jen said. 'All I know is that the theatre was empty last night.'

'Oh, what a shame,' Katy said. 'I never said goodbye.' She glanced at her watch and then at Jen who was stirring salt into water for her morning gargle. 'Um … do you think you ought maybe to get dressed?'

Jen looked up. 'Why?' She grinned. 'I'm sure Jacob doesn't mind my *déshabillé.*'

'Well, no,' Katy said, 'but Sister Morris said she might pop in this—'

She was too late. The pub door had swung open and Sister Morris was already marching in purposefully.

At once Katy leaped to her feet, but it was the sight of Jen, standing, frozen with one foot on the first step of the stairs, the dressing-gown gaping prettily over her thigh, that stopped Sister Morris in her tracks. For a second her mouth opened and shut in shock, then pushing Katy peremptorily out of the way she drew herself up to her full impressive height and glared at Jen.

'My goodness, girl,' she barked. 'What do you think you are doing? Parading around with next to nothing on. In front of this young man as well. I have never seen anything like it in all my life.'

Katy quailed but Jen just flexed her bare ankle provocatively and winked at Jacob. 'Oh, Jacob doesn't mind, do you, darling?'

Certain that Sister Morris would have a heart attack at such insubordinate effrontery Katy closed her eyes, but not for the first time, she had underestimated her old mentor. Instead of flying off the handle Sister Morris merely turned to Jacob who was still sitting, scarlet faced, at the table. 'Don't take any notice of her,' she said briskly. 'She's only trying to show off.' Sister Morris stripped off her gloves. 'Now, young lady,' she said to Jen. 'I hear you have a problem with your throat. Is it your tonsils, do you think?'

Jen shook her head. 'No,' she said grudgingly. 'My

throat doesn't really hurt. It's just that I don't always seem to be able to reach the high notes any more.'

'Hmm.' Sister Morris frowned. 'Then it's probably something to do with the larynx, or the vocal cords themselves.'

Jen's eyes widened. 'You mean you actually believe me?'

Sister Morris looked at her. 'I have no reason not to. You have a lot of faults but you're not one to make a fuss unnecessarily.' She paused to clear her throat. 'So I had a word with Mr Goodacre in ENT at the Wilhelmina and, as a special favour, he will see you on the sixth of November at ten o'clock.'

The silence that followed this announcement was intense. Katy felt deeply touched. Glancing nervously at Jen's tense face she just prayed her friend would rise to the occasion and give Sister Morris the thanks she deserved, but Jen, being Jen, did better than that. Spreading her arms in a gesture of delight she ran forward and kissed Sister Morris on both cheeks. 'Sister Morris, you're an angel. Behind all that starch and stuffiness you have a heart of pure gold.'

To Katy's amusement, Sister Morris flushed. 'That's quite enough of that,' she said. Straightening her uniform crossly she glared at Jen. 'Now, I suggest you go upstairs and get yourself properly dressed. There is a war on, you know.'

Two days later, to the delight of the entire nation, news came that Montgomery's forces, after fierce fighting, had punched deep into Rommel's position. A few days later again and they had broken through, and by the end of the month it was reported that Rommel was in full retreat.

It wasn't long before the cinemas started running newsreels showing the Air Force harrying the German retreat, breaking up columns and sending men scurrying sideways into the sand. The audience clapped and cheered.

'Have we won the war?' George whispered to Helen.

She shook her head. 'Not yet,' she said. It was 5 November and she had taken George to see *Pinocchio*. In any normal year they would have been celebrating fireworks night, although tonight there were enough fireworks on screen for anyone. 'But it looks as if we've made a start.'

Actually the newsreel shocked her. The war had moved on so much since she had last taken real interest in it. Now as she looked at the map on the screen and saw the crosses marking the new American landings in Morocco and Algeria, she saw how vulnerable the Germans were soon going to feel in Europe. If this goes on, the Germans are bound to occupy the rest of France, she thought. They won't be able to run the risk of an Allied invasion of the south coast from North Africa.

For a second she allowed herself to imagine André eating a companionable meal with some jackbooted SS officer and then she jerked her thoughts away and stood up abruptly.

'Come on, George,' she said. 'Let's go and get some fish and chips.'

> To Carter: 6 Nov 42. I regret to inform you that during recent action Private Robert Carter was taken prisoner by the enemy. War Office.

> Dear Mrs Carter,
>
> 5 November 1942
>
> I am pleased to report that your son Michael Carter, formerly reported missing presumed dead, has now been located in Iceland where he is recovering from injuries sustained during the sinking of his ship. I am also delighted to tell you that due to his courage during the attack in attempting to rescue fellow sailors trapped

in the burning vessel, he is being awarded the British Empire Medal.

I remain, madam, your faithful servant,
Humphrey Bottomley, P & O.

Dear Mr and Mrs Rutherford,

2 November 1942

I very much regret having to tell you that your son Bertram was killed in action during the assault on German positions at El Alamein. Bertram Rutherford was a fine officer and I would like you to know that he died bravely. He will be buried with full military honours.

Yours sincerely,
Marcus Ogilvy, Commanding Officer

'Oh, Mrs Rutherford, I'm so sorry,' Joyce said. 'I really am. He was a nice boy. Look, why don't you take a couple of days off?'

'Thank you, Mrs Carter, but I'm all right. Really. Life must go on.'

Pam was washing up the breakfast when she heard the knock on the door. 'George,' she called. 'Could you see who's at the door?'

Only another week or so of this, she thought, drying her hands, and then I'll be in the country at the maternity unit. She didn't really want to go but the health visitor had insisted. 'It's essential for an older woman like you to have all the facilities at hand. In any case,' she added briskly as Pam paled, 'it's less upsetting for the little boy. Much better that he's presented with a fait accompli.'

As George still refused to acknowledge the baby's imminent arrival it was hard to know what he would prefer. Thank God for Helen, Pam thought. Whatever happened when the baby was born, at least Helen would be on hand to help with George. She smiled to herself as she heard him run down the stairs. She'd be happy to bet that there weren't many expecting mothers who had a titled lady on tap to help out.

She heard George open the front door. 'Who is it, darling?' she called.

There was a short exchange and then George's voice came clearly down the passage. 'It's a man called Agnes McNaughton,' he shouted. 'He wants to talk to Helen.'

Biting back a smile, Pam rubbed her hands on her apron, but before she could call, Helen appeared suddenly at the top of the stairs, pale but composed.

'What's happened?' she said. 'Tell me what's happened.'

'Nothing's happened,' the man replied, but even Pam, who had never seen him in her life before, could tell he looked a bit shifty.

Helen was staring at him coldly. 'Then why are you here?'

Angus McNaughton glanced uncomfortably at Pam and George who were both standing goggle eyed in the passage. 'Look, I'm sorry to disturb you,' he said awkwardly, 'but is there somewhere private we can go?'

'You can use the front room,' Pam said hastily, pushing the door open for him. 'It's a bit cold, I'm afraid. I haven't lit the fire yet …'

She tried not to listen. She really did. But when a minute later she heard Helen's voice raised in most unHelenlike anger it was impossible not to overhear.

'I don't want to know what's going on in France, Angus,' she was shouting. 'I don't care what the Germans do. They can have the entire French navy for all I care. It's nothing to do with me any more. Nothing.' Then a moment later, slightly less stridently, 'What do you mean? What are you saying? For God's sake, Angus, spit it out.'

And the man's angry response: 'I'm saying that we need you, Helen. We need you to go over there. There's nobody else who can do this job.'

Chapter Twenty-Three

Angus McNaughton's voice was low and intense. 'We simply cannot afford to have the French navy fall into German hands,' he said. He lit a cigarette and narrowed his eyes at Helen through the blue smoke. 'You know as well as I do that half the French fleet is moored up in Toulon harbour. You did the research. There's close on a hundred ships there, and submarines. We *must* get them away. What we need is someone to deliver a personal message from Winston Churchill to Admiral de Laborde.'

Helen stared at him in disbelief. It wasn't the actual request that shocked her so much as the sheer gall of his asking. How dare he treat her like dirt for the last couple of months and then come crawling up to her to ask a favour like that? It was unbelievable.

'De Laborde is fiercely anti-British,' she said. 'I put that in my report. It will take more than a letter from Winston Churchill to get him to hand over his ships.'

For a second Angus was silent then he nodded. 'I know,' he said. 'We'd be sending explosives too. Just in case. That's why we need someone like you who knows the situation and can decide the best route to take.'

Helen could barely believe her ears. 'And what makes you think I wouldn't take a route straight to the nearest SS officer and tell him everything?' she asked grittily.

Angus had the grace to look embarrassed. 'Your integrity was never in doubt.'

'Oh no?' Helen raised her eyebrows. 'What was that interrogation about, then? Why have I been laid off?'

Angus was silent.

She felt her temper rising and for once she didn't see why she should hide it. 'Because someone had to take the blame and I was the easiest person,' she said heatedly. 'Okay, I was wrong about André, but so were a lot of other people. You needed a scapegoat, didn't you? Someone to take the rap.'

Angus frowned. 'Now come on, Helen, that's not true, although you must admit you were somewhat indiscreet.'

Helen shrugged. 'André had gone through your fool-proof training programme by then. I naturally assumed he was one of us.'

Angus sniffed.

'Oh, I know you never liked him,' Helen said. 'I suppose that puts you in the clear. I suppose that makes you think you were blameless?'

'Well, I did have my reservations,' Angus said, faintly complacent, 'but we're getting off the point here.'

'No, we're not,' Helen said angrily. 'If you're so incredibly marvellous, with such perfect judgement, why don't you go and see Admiral bloody de Laborde yourself?'

'My French isn't good enough. We need someone who was brought up in the South of France.'

'I wasn't brought up in Toulon docks.'

He shrugged. 'You are as close as we can get without using a native, and we have no one else available. There have been so many agents lost. We have been sending replacements over as quickly as we can, and now we need someone urgently there is nobody suitable left. It was Paul in Marseilles who suggested you.'

'Why can't Paul do it?'

'Paul has too much on his plate. He needs help. Someone to work alongside him.'

Helen swallowed hard. 'How is this someone going to get to France?'

Angus hesitated. 'By parachute,' he said flatly. 'There's too much equipment for a plane small enough to land. Look,' he added resignedly, 'I can see how you feel, Helen. I really am sorry for asking. I knew it would be hopeless.' He glanced at his watch and leaned down to stub out his cigarette in the grate. Straightening up he glanced at her and spread his hands. 'So, what do you think?'

Helen didn't know what to think. Dimly, against the sudden silence she heard Pam hustling George down the passage and out of the front door. She walked to the window and saw them going through the gate. George was asking Pam something eagerly. Pam looked flustered, leaning back to support her protruding stomach as she hurried the little boy away from the house. Helen felt her heart twist. She realised suddenly how fond she had grown of the Nelsons over the six months she had been with them. In all that time, through all her upsets, their quiet affection for her had never wavered, and that meant a lot.

Turning away from the window abruptly she found Angus watching her sceptically, and she felt a strange sense of freedom as she faced him. She didn't care what he thought of her. Her anger had liberated her. For the first time in weeks she felt strong. She might be the last possible person the SOE could ask for help but they had still asked. Despite everything they still thought she was up to it.

'Yes,' she said quietly. 'Yes, all right. I'll go.'

Angus was so surprised that for a moment he just stared at her, then without further ado he galvanised himself into action. 'Right,' he said briskly. 'In that case you'll need to come with me now. There's a hell of a lot to do. Briefing. Preparation. Cover story. So why don't you fetch anything you need for the next couple of days and then we'll go. I've got a taxi waiting outside.'

Helen shook her head. 'Oh no,' she said coolly. 'I'm sorry, Angus, but if I go, I go under my own terms, and that includes saying goodbye to my friends. You take the taxi. I'll come up to the office later. When I'm ready.'

She expected him to argue, but then he just shrugged. 'Okay,' he said.

She thought that was it, but at the door he stopped and turned. 'You're not doing this to get to see Cabillard, are you?' he asked quietly.

Helen met his gaze squarely. 'No,' she said. 'Of course not.'

Angus frowned. 'Because it would be tantamount to suicide to make contact. I can't be more blunt than that.'

'You don't have to be,' Helen said coldly. 'I know the risks as well as you do.'

The goodbyes were hard, and both Jen and Katy cried.

Pam Nelson was stoical. 'I have to admit that I overheard,' she said when Helen told her she had got to go away for a while. 'Not everything of course, but I know where you are going, and some of what you'll be doing there.'

'Oh.'

'I won't tell anyone of course, but I just want to say that I think you're very brave.'

'Pam, don't,' Helen said quickly. 'Don't talk about it. I'm not brave at all. If only you knew. And I feel awful about leaving just as the baby's due.'

'Don't worry about that,' Pam said bravely. 'We'll cope somehow. You've done enough for us as it is.'

Helen shook her head. 'It's you who's done it for me. I would never have survived the last few months without you all.'

It was true. She felt she owed them so much. If only there was a way to repay them, she thought as she hastily packed up her things, and then she realised that there was. Two very small ways that just might help.

The first involved writing a note to Mrs Rutherford.

The second involved calling at the school on her way down Lavender Road.

George was startled to be brought out of his lesson, but when he saw Helen sitting on a bench in the playground he came running over. Helen hugged him. He smelt clean and fresh and faintly of ink.

'I've got to go away for a while, sweetheart,' she said. 'I've come to say goodbye.'

'Where?' he said. 'Where are you going? Are you going to France to rescue the ships like that Agnes man said who came to see you this morning?'

Helen groaned inwardly. So much for SOE security. 'Something like that,' she said, 'but it's a secret, darling, so you mustn't tell anyone.'

'All right,' he said. He nodded seriously. 'Mum said it was a secret too.'

Helen smiled and put her hands on his thin little shoulders so she could look him straight in the face. 'And will you be very grown up when the baby comes? And look after Mum for me?'

He wrinkled his nose. 'I'll try,' he said reluctantly.

Feeling tears in her eyes she held him closer. 'I'll miss you.'

'Perhaps I could come with you.'

Helen smiled. 'I wish you could, but I don't think they make parachute harnesses small enough for children.'

His eyes widened. 'Are you going to parachute? Really? Out of an aeroplane?'

Kicking herself, Helen hastily put her finger to her lips. 'Shh,' she said as she stood up. 'That's a secret too. Our secret.'

Mr Goodacre, the ENT consultant at the Wilhelmina, wasn't at all what Jen had expected. For some reason she had imagined that he would be of a similar type to Sister Morris. Without the enormous bosoms of course, but with the same gruff manner and old-fashioned attitudes. However, Mr Goodacre bore no resemblance to Sister Morris at all. He was short and fat and very jolly. What's more he seemed delighted to have his expertise called upon.

'Right then,' he said. 'Miss Morris tells me you are having difficulty with the high notes, Miss Carter. Now, tell me, when did this first begin to cause you problems?'

Briefly Jen explained about the couple of colds she had had and how afterwards her voice never fully recovered. How sometimes she could get those top notes and other times for no apparent reason she couldn't.

'I see.' Mr Goodacre stood up briskly. 'Well, I think the best thing is for me to take a peek.' He pulled up a chair next to hers. 'Now if you turn to face me,' he said brandishing some lethal-looking instruments. 'A little closer. Perhaps if you put your arms on my shoulders? That's it. Now, open wide. I'm going to pull your tongue forward to see if I can get a glimpse of your cords and then I'd like you to run up a scale for me.'

A moment later Jen found herself in the most extraordinary position, with her knees pressed firmly into Mr Goodacre's groin, her arms round his neck and her tongue pulled so far out of her head that it made her eyes water. How he expected her to sing in such a state, God only knew, but she did her best with a strangled gurgle and heard his grunt of satisfaction.

'Hah, there's the little blighter. Just what I thought.'

Then, just as she hoped he might let her go, he grasped her tongue even more firmly and sticking his head and his mirror even further down her throat, called out, 'Once more, please, Miss Carter. As high as you can.'

Releasing her a minute later he retreated behind his desk.

'You have a nodule,' he said. 'On one of your vocal cords.'

Jen had never heard of a nodule. 'Is that bad?' she asked anxiously.

'Not life threatening, but bad enough to cause problems in the high notes.'

'Will it go away?'

He shook his head. 'Not on its own. The only way to get rid of it is to have it taken off under general anaesthetic. It's a tricky operation but not impossible.' He hesitated, tapping his pen gently on the desk. 'There is one problem though, I ought to point out. Under current wartime restrictions such an operation would not be considered essential, which means the only way to get it done would be to pay for it.'

'Oh,' Jen said blankly. 'And how much would it be?'

For the first time since she had walked in he frowned. 'I would hazard a guess that for an operation like that you would be looking at something in the region of two hundred pounds.'

Jen's eyes widened. 'Two hundred pounds!' Two hundred pounds just to get some 'nodule' off her vocal cord? Two hundred pounds was well over half her wages for the year, and what with giving Katy rent, and travelling, and clothes and that, she spent everything she earned. It would take her years to save up that much. For a moment she stared at him indignantly and then suddenly her shoulders slumped. Well, that was that, then. The end of her career. She would have to find another job. There was no way in the world she'd be able to find two hundred pounds. It was out of the question.

Aware of her despair Mr Goodacre leaned forward with a kindly smile. 'Don't look so down, Miss Carter. I'm sure you will be able to find the money somewhere. Where there's a will there's a way.'

As she walked on down to Clapham Junction to take the train into town for her matinee shows, Jen could not for the life of her see a way.

On arriving at SOE headquarters, Helen was immediately

dispatched by car to a graceful country house in Buckinghamshire. Like many other stately homes, Roughwood Park had been 'borrowed' from its owners by the government and was now used by the SOE as a training establishment. Generally referred to as Chorleywood because of the nearby railway station of that name, Roughwood Park was one of the Group 'C' schools where skills were honed, cover stories perfected and agents kept in semi-isolation waiting for their opportunity to depart for foreign lands.

Partly as a security measure and partly to give moral support, all agents were allocated a 'conducting officer' prior to departure and, perhaps in respect of her sex, Maurice Buckmaster had sent his assistant Miss Atkins not only to accompany Helen to Buckinghamshire but to co-ordinate her briefing as well.

Miss Atkins was an officer in the WAAF, and although her manner was friendly, it was clear from the start that she wasn't going to waste time on small talk. 'Your SOE codename is *Danielle*,' she said as they drove out of London along the Marylebone Road, 'But as far as everyone else is concerned you are Marie Dubois. You work as a representative from a fictitious couture house in Paris. You are in the South of France on business, presenting new styles to the fashionable shops on the Riviera. In a couple of days we will have ration cards, permits and an identity card ready for you. These documents are not foolproof of course. You should endeavour to avoid any checks but they should get you through a cursory examination if necessary.'

Aware of her quick sideways glance, Helen nodded. She didn't quite trust herself to speak. It was all happening so fast.

'Paul's going to try to find an officer close to de Laborde,' Maurice Buckmaster had told her only minutes before she and Miss Atkins had left. 'Someone with leanings towards the Allies. It may already be too late for the ships to get away. The harbour entrance is almost certainly mined. We don't know about the fuelling situation. Scuttling may turn out to be the only option.'

Once at Chorleywood, the pressure hotted up even more. They had arranged for the best SOE instructors to come and brief her. They called her *Danielle.* If any of them knew who she really was they made no sign of it. One kept her abreast of the political situation right up to her departure, another took her through the maps. She learned grid references of possible landing fields, contours, approaches to the harbour, street names. She studied a series of hazy sepia photographs of Admiral de Laborde, grey and balding, virtually indistinguishable from the other officers in the frame.

That first evening she tried to memorise maps of Toulon harbour. Tried to get her mind around the variety of ships moored there. Tried to remember the names of the crucial ones: the great battleships *Provence, Dunkerque* and *Strasbourg* ... the predatory destroyers *Lynx*, *Tigre*, *Lion*, *Panthère* ... and the romantic-sounding submarines *Casabianca*, *Glorieux*, *Venus*, *Iris* ... As she tried to get to sleep that night the names churned round and round in her mind in an endless, repetitive litany.

The following morning a small man with a beard ran her through the explosives she would be taking with her. 'This is 808,' he said, showing her a pale reddish-brown rubbery substance that smelt of rancid marzipan. He smiled at her distaste. 'Ironically, it was invented by Alfred Nobel,' he said, 'creator of the Nobel Peace Prize. Keep it as cool as you can. If it sweats it's dangerous.'

Helen eyed it nervously. 'What do I do with it?' she said. 'How do you make it explode?'

'Oh, you don't need to worry about that,' he said. 'I gather Paul is meeting you. He will know. But you will need to tell him about these new pencil detonators. See the coloured safety strip? Red is thirty minutes. Blue is twenty-four hours. Okay? Oh, and there's the limpet mines of course. Two dozen is all we can manage.'

Helen was hardly listening. Paul, she thought. Thank God for Paul. At least she wasn't going to be completely on her own.

'Are you all right, Helen?' Miss Atkins asked suddenly. 'Do you need a few minutes' break?'

'No,' Helen said. 'I'm fine.'

'Right then.' Miss Atkins walked to the door to usher in the next batch of instructors. 'In that case we'll move straight on to tradecraft.'

Tradecraft was what they called the skills and techniques of espionage, the tricks of the trade that enabled operatives to go about their business effectively without being caught themselves. Helen had learned the basics up in Scotland. Now they reminded her about hairs across doorways, leaves in locks, talcum powder on steps. They ran through the procedures to use if she thought she was being watched or followed; they talked about shops with two entrances, parallel streets, the cover given by crowds; they advised her always to carry a scarf in case she needed to change her appearance, always to check for escape routes, never to run, and never to take the first cab in a rank.

Mostly Helen listened in silence. On the occasions when she asked a question she did so coldly and abruptly. It was as though her emotions had deserted her and with them her manners. She didn't care that the instructors glanced at each other uneasily nor that Miss Atkins was looking concerned.

If they wanted her to do the job, she had to do it in her own way, and as each day turned inexorably into the next she knew with increasing certainty that her only chance was to put her real character and emotions into cold storage. She simply would not be able to do the job otherwise. She could not afford to be sensitive. She could not afford to care if people didn't like her. She had to turn herself into a completely different person, a tough, unemotional, professional person. A person called *Danielle.*

'Is she going to be carrying a sidearm?' one of the instructors asked Miss Atkins quietly.

Miss Atkins shook her head. 'No,' she said. 'We don't really think—'

'Yes,' Helen interrupted. 'I want a gun. I'm not going without a gun.' Shooting had after all been one of the things she had been good at in Scotland.

'A gun is so incriminating,' Miss Atkins said gently. 'If you are searched.'

Helen looked at her. 'No more incriminating than a letter written by Winston Churchill,' she said coldly.

So they gave her a gun. The standard .38 was too heavy and cumbersome for a coat pocket so she opted for the more compact .32 Colt which weighed only one and a half pounds. Even that felt heavy but it was better than nothing.

'Don't shoot if you don't have to,' the weapons instructor warned her, 'but if you need to shoot, shoot. And shoot to kill. Two fast shots between crutch and head. Don't fart around. Just get on and do it. And do it well.'

That night Miss Atkins came to her room. 'I didn't know if you might like a chat,' she said tentatively as Helen opened the door. 'You seemed very quiet at dinner.'

Helen didn't want a chat. She wanted to have a bath and go to bed. 'I'm fine,' she said. 'I'm just a bit tired.'

Miss Atkins looked at her closely. 'You must say if you have cold feet,' she said gently. 'It's not too late to turn back. You are entitled to change your mind. You would not be the first. I have every respect for the man or woman who admits frankly to not feeling up to it. For me there is only one crime; to go out there and let your comrades down.'

Meeting the other woman's gaze steadily, Helen squared her shoulders. 'Thank you for your concern,' she said, 'but I am not going to change my mind, and I would be grateful if you didn't mention it again.'

Louise felt very alone. Very isolated. Bertie's death had shocked her badly. At one time she and Bertie had been very close, and now she would never see him again. It was sad, terribly sad, but there was nothing she could do about it. Bertie was dead. Whereas her unhappiness over Jack was ongoing.

The only person she had told about Jack's so-called breakdown was Aaref Hoch, and that was only because he kept finding her crying.

If it hadn't been for Bertie's death Louise might have sought support from her parents, but there was something odd going on with her parents. The loss of their son seemed to have affected them in a very peculiar way. Her father had been unusually subdued and her mother had become very brisk and efficient. The whole balance of power between them seemed to have changed. It was most unsettling. When Louise tried to ask her mother about it when she called in there one evening she got more than she bargained for in response.

'I don't know what you're talking about,' Celia said.

'But Daddy's so odd,' Louise said. 'So quiet. Is it to do with Bertie or has something gone wrong at the brewery? Has someone found a rat in the beer or something?'

'Don't be flippant, Louise,' Celia snapped. 'There's nothing wrong with your father, and if there was it would be none of your business. More to the point,' she went on, walking over to push the door to, 'what's the matter with you?'

'With me?' Louise blinked. There was something rather ominous about the closed door. 'What do you mean?'

'I mean that you hardly spent five minutes with Jack when he was home on leave and twice already this week I have seen you hanging around with that Aaref Hoch.'

Her mother's eyes were cold. To her dismay Louise felt

herself blushing. She shrugged to cover it up. 'Aaref's a friend,' she said, 'and he just happens to live in the same house as me. There's nothing in it.'

Celia stood very still. 'There had better not be,' she said. 'Marriage is a serious matter, Louise. I think it's about time you began to realise that.'

'I do realise it,' Louise said crossly.

Celia was silent for a moment, then she crossed her arms over her chest. 'When is Jack next due home?' she asked quietly.

Louise frowned. 'I don't know,' she said sulkily. Suddenly she felt a wave of self-pity wash over her. She had thought marriage would be so wonderful. So easy. And it wasn't. It was horrid and difficult. Nobody had told her how difficult it would be. 'He didn't tell me,' she said, and was annoyed that her voice sounded choked. 'He was too upset about that stupid convoy.' She looked up at her mother with tears in her eyes. She wanted sympathy. She wanted it so badly. And yet she couldn't bring herself to say the word breakdown. It was just too shocking. 'It was awful, Mummy,' she said instead. 'He would hardly talk to me at all, and now I don't know what to do ...'

Sniffing pitifully as the tears began to trickle, Louise was shocked when her mother's expression hardened. 'What you need to do is pull yourself together,' she said crisply. 'Jack is your husband for better or worse, and if he needs your support it is your job to give it to him. It is not your job to collapse into snivelling self-pity the first time things get tough. In marriage you have to take the rough with the smooth, and if things don't go your way you put a good face on it.'

'Jack didn't put on a good face over that convoy,' Louise said. 'Even that beastly Mick Carter managed to get a medal out of it. All Jack did was cry—'

'Louise!'

Louise stopped abruptly, shocked by her mother's tone. In all her life she had never seen her mother look so angry, and as Celia flung the door open and pointed out to the front door, Louise felt a chill of fear crawl up her spine.

'Get out!'

'What?'

'You heard,' Celia hissed. 'I said get out. I don't want to hear another word out of you. I am disgusted by your attitude and ashamed to call you my daughter. You are behaving like a child of ten, not a twenty-year-old married woman. For goodness' sake, Louise, your brother died last week and all you can think about is yourself.' She took a sharp breath. 'As for Jack, he is a fine young man. It must have taken immense courage for him to return to his ship, more than you could possibly imagine, and I won't stand here listening to your self-centred whining. You asked me what you should do. Well, I'll tell you. You can go back to your "flat" and stay there. I certainly don't want to see you in this house again.'

By 8 November, everyone at Chorleywood knew they were involved in a race against time. All eyes were on the international news. Rommel had retreated into Libya, and American troops were pouring into North Africa. Tons of leaflets had been dropped telling the population not to resist, that the Allies did not want territory, merely to rid the continent of the evil Axis forces.

On the tenth Algeria signed an armistice with the Allies, and by the following evening all North Africa except Tunisia had surrendered. In a triumphant speech in Parliament Winston Churchill reported that the enemy had lost fifty-nine thousand men, and for the first time during the war church bells were to be rung on Sunday to celebrate the victory.

Helen knew she would not hear those bells. The news of the North African capitulation was barely out before German and Italian troops began to enter the vulnerable southern part of France.

Miss Atkins knocked on Helen's door. She caught

Helen's quick glance. 'Weather permitting, we're on for tomorrow night,' she said. She smiled ruefully. 'I hope you're not superstitious.'

'Why?' Helen asked, as her stomach clenched painfully.

Miss Atkins shrugged. 'Tomorrow is Friday the thirteenth,' she said.

As always Mr Lorenz was one of the first customers in the café. Usually he was waiting at the door when Joyce unlocked it. Today he came in just as she was checking the urn was hot for the morning rush on teas. As he always looked exactly the same, with his carefully pressed dark suit, a freshly laundered, crisp button-collared shirt, sober tie and neatly oiled and trimmed moustache, Joyce sometimes couldn't help wondering what small variation it was in his morning routine that occasionally delayed him for a couple of minutes.

This morning she nodded to him and waited for him to make his usual opening remark about the weather. It was always either the weather or the war. Lorenz was always studiously formal in the café, very careful not to embarrass her by any show of friendship. He was much more relaxed when he came to the house for Sunday lunch. Only last weekend he had made Pete and Miss Philips laugh out loud at some wry tale he told them about a customer bringing him in a tortoise to pawn, and they'd all laughed even more when Joyce admitted she had a soft spot for tortoises.

'I always wanted one as a child,' she had said, 'but of course I never got one.'

Now though, instead of remarking on the amazing breakthrough in Africa, or the terrible newsreel scenes from Russia where women were having to soak themselves in water in order to fight the fires in Stalingrad, to her astonishment he started talking about Jen.

Joyce stared at him blankly. 'What's she done now? Got herself up the duff with one of them Yanks?'

Lorenz looked shocked. 'Not at all. Not at all,' he said. 'It's just that I heard in the pub last night that she has been told that she has some kind of growth in her throat.'

'A growth?' Joyce was surprised to feel a slight maternal twinge. She didn't rate Jen, but she didn't want her to have a growth. 'Can it be treated?' she asked.

Lorenz leaned forward slightly. 'Well, that's the point,' he said. 'The surgeon has offered to operate, but at a price. A price she can't afford.'

'It can't be that bad, then,' Joyce said. 'If it was bad they'd do it anyway. There's usually funds for emergencies. Even for run-of-the-mill people like us.' Typical Jen, she thought sourly, obviously making a fuss about nothing as usual. Assuming that was the end of the conversation, she was reaching for a teapot when Lorenz spoke again.

'It's her career that's at stake,' he said.

'Well, that's her problem,' Joyce said. 'There's nothing I can do about it.' She'd never thought much of Jen's choice of career anyway. 'I haven't got any spare money.'

Lorenz coughed. 'But you wouldn't object if someone else helped her out, would you?' As Joyce looked up sharply he cleared his throat and went on quickly, 'I know you've had your differences in the past, Mrs Carter, but she's really not a bad girl. She's worked hard at her career. It would be a shame for it all to go to waste.'

Staring at him incredulously Joyce was surprised by a sharp stab of jealousy. Why should Jen have his money, she thought. Bloody little Jen. Why should she get everything on a plate? And then even as she frowned Joyce noticed the faint colour staining Lorenz's cheeks and felt a sudden wash of affection for him. He was a kind man, and a surprisingly generous one too, even though people thought because he was a Jew he was tight-fisted. It was just that he had a different way of being generous than most people. She was also touched that he felt it necessary to ask her permission.

Turning away she shoved the teapot under the urn's

tap. 'You do what you want,' she said gruffly. 'It's nothing to do with me.'

The weather did permit. In England the night of Friday, 13 November was clear, cold and moonlit. The forecast for France was for broken cloud, light winds and occasional drizzle.

'Enough light to see, but not enough to get seen,' Miss Atkins remarked with some satisfaction as she pulled up at the well-guarded gates of the airfield. 'Perfect conditions for a covert parachute descent.'

Tempsford aerodrome near the village of Everton in Bedfordshire was the base for nearly all clandestine airborne operations. The building assigned to the secret services was a dilapidated old barn known as Gibraltar Farm.

It was to this building, tucked away at the corner of the airfield, that Miss Atkins drove now, and the closer they got, the more peculiar Helen began to feel. All day she had been feeling extraordinarily calm. So calm in fact that it had occurred to her that they might have put some sort of tranquilliser in her food. Miss Atkins had been shocked by the suggestion.

'Goodness me, no,' she had said. 'I'm afraid it's just the calm before the storm. It's quite natural. The nerves will come, and you must be ready for them when they do.'

She was right. The nerves were coming now, all right. Coming with a vengeance as though making up for lost time. As Miss Atkins bumped the car slowly past the rows of silent planes, unwieldy grey shapes against the low dark sky, Helen could feel the sweat prickling on her palms and in her armpits. Her heart was beating a low rapid tattoo in her chest and she began to wish she hadn't eaten a huge portion of cottage pie just before she left Roughwood Park.

'What are you doing?' she had asked, when the mess sergeant presented her with the plate of food. 'Fattening me up for the kill?'

'Not at all, ma'am,' he had replied. 'I just thought as you'd like a decent square meal before you went. Where you're going all you'll get is frogs' legs and garlic.'

Now as Helen stepped out of the car on shaking knees, the thought of frogs' legs and garlic was almost enough to turn her stomach. Leaning back against the car she breathed in a good lungful of the damp marshy scent of the airfield and closed her eyes.

The airfield was eerily silent, there was no noise at all from the building behind them, but in the distance she could hear the faint murmur of traffic from the Great North Road. What am I doing, she thought. What the hell am I doing?

And then Miss Atkins spoke. 'Are you all right, Helen? Is there anything you want to ask before we go in?'

Helen swallowed hard. 'Yes,' she said. 'There is one thing.' She put her hand in her pocket and drew out two envelopes. 'I've addressed these to my father and to my friend Katy Frazer. If … if anything should happen to me, will you make sure they get them?'

Miss Atkins nodded. 'Yes, of course,' she said quietly. 'Of course I will.'

Part Five

Chapter Twenty-Four

It was cold in the plane, cold and cramped. Even with the old sleeping bag that the sergeant dispatcher had given her, Helen found it hard to get warm, and, trussed up like a butcher's chicken in the overlarge flying suit and parachute harness, comfort was out of the question. At least there was no flak, and with a convenient layer of low cloud over France the plane juddered on steadily through the night. Time passed agonisingly slowly.

At some stage the dispatcher had manoeuvred the long cylindrical containers nearer to the hatch. He had stowed them at the front of the plane for the take-off but now he was clipping their static lines to the fuselage so their parachutes would open automatically when he shoved them out of the plane.

Helen knew he would be shoving her too when the moment came. She wondered if anyone had told him about her failure to jump at Ringway.

At four hundred feet it only takes twenty seconds to hit the ground, she told herself firmly. Twenty seconds. That was all.

The dispatcher was brewing tea now, hunched over a tiny Gaz stove. 'Here, love,' he shouted. 'Get this down you. It's not far now.' Accepting the hot metal mug, Helen pulled up her knees, hugged them hard against her chest and tried to think beyond the next couple of hours.

She had a week. A week. Seven days, in which time, she had to find a way of getting the letter discreetly to Admiral de Laborde, and if that failed or if he ignored it, she and Paul had to find some means to scuttle the fleet.

It was a tall order, and the only light on the horizon was that on the seventh night, whether she had succeeded or not, a tiny, single-engined, low-flying Lysander from 161 Squadron would be touching down briefly in a remote field in Provence to pick her up and take her back to England. The grid reference of that field was engraved on her brain.

Suddenly she heard the tinny voice of the pilot in the dispatcher's headphones, and tensed. 'We're approaching the jump site,' he shouted. 'They've lit the fires.'

'Oh God,' Helen muttered as he hauled her to her feet. 'Oh God.'

'Are you all right?' he asked urgently. 'Do you want us to circle?'

Helen shook her head. She knew as well as he did that any delay was asking for trouble. If the Germans were tracking the plane, circling was a surefire way of giving away the position of the jump. The last thing she wanted was a reception committee of SS.

'No,' she said. 'I'm all right.'

For a second he stared at her, then he clamped his mouthpiece over his mouth. 'She's going,' he said.

At once she felt the pilot throttling back, losing height. Her stomach lurched and she staggered to one side, engaging the dispatcher in a brief ungainly waltz, but the sergeant was not in a dancing mood. Pulling away abruptly, he picked up the cloche jump helmet and handed it to her, then he was urging her forward, checking her harness, clipping her static line to the fuselage.

'First the cylinders, then you,' he shouted, reaching down to open the hatch. 'Okay?'

Helen frowned, surprised by the jump order. Normally the crates went last. And then, as the fresh, cold air rushed into the plane she understood. They *had* told him about the fiasco at Ringway, and he was going to make damn sure Paul got his equipment, even if, when the moment came, she refused to jump.

There was no time to worry about it. Already the green light was flaring, and the dispatcher grunted as he shoved the two cylinders out, quickly, one after the other. Helen saw the lines snaking out after them, and then, somehow, she was sitting with her legs dangling out of the hatch. She could feel the air dragging at her feet, see the ground flashing past below, some dark trees, the silver snake of a tarmacked road, and then, before she could scream, before she could panic, before she could do anything, the dispatcher yelled, 'Go!' and slapped her hard on the back.

Swept back in the slipstream, the sensation of falling was less than she had feared, and almost before she had become aware of the rush of wind in her face, she heard the crack of the chute catching the air above her.

One sudden jerk, then she was swinging and turning, and all around her the distant curving line where the dark land met the paler sky swung and turned too. Above her the enormous canopy whispered and flapped gently.

The plane was already far away and she could see for miles over the moonlit countryside. The patchwork of tiny fields, the dark lines of trees edging a distant road, a steep hill terraced with vines, or perhaps they were olive trees. It was hard to tell. Either way, it was definitely France and to her surprise she felt a thrill of recognition.

Below her the cylinders had landed, and already two dark figures were running forward, gathering up the billowing waves of silk. In the silence she heard a truck's engine start up with a roar.

Then she saw the fire rushing towards her. Oh God, she thought, Oh God! I'm going to land in the fire, but she didn't. The flames flashed past beneath her. Seconds later her supply bag hit the ground, warning her that it was her turn next.

'Feet together,' she murmured. 'Bend the knees. Bend the . . . Aaghff!'

With a jarring impact, she was pitched forward on the wet grass and the breath kicked out of her.

Lying there in shock, it took a moment for feeling to return and then a tremor of excitement ran through her. She had done it. She had landed. She was alive. She was in France.

A moment later she was hauled to her feet and, desperately trying to unclip the quick release on her harness at the same time as pulling the awful cloche hat off her head, she found herself face to face with Paul.

She recognised him at once, even with a bushy moustache and hair much longer than she recalled, slicked back under the navy peasant's beret. There were so many emotions she could have felt on seeing him again – relief, nervousness, embarrassment – but to her amazement what she actually felt was shy.

'Hello,' she said.

He smiled. 'Welcome to France,' he said. 'Better late than never.'

Paul was efficient. Within minutes the cylinders had been loaded on to the lorry and the chutes had disappeared. The fires were stamped out and dug over and her flying suit had been buried. Paul's helpers were shabbily dressed but they reacted quickly and silently to his low-voiced commands.

Standing at the edge of the field in her smart French-style suit and high-heeled shoes, with a handbag on her arm and a small leather suitcase at her feet, Helen felt absurdly conspicuous. It didn't help that one of the men was staring at her quite openly. She turned away, not liking the faint leer on his face, and was glad when Paul came back.

'Oh la la, quel chic!' he said, raising his eyebrows. 'I might have known you wouldn't be dressed as a peasant.' He

peered at her more closely. 'But what's happened to your hair?'

'They told me to dye it,' Helen said. She fingered her new brown locks. 'In case I bumped into someone I knew. Does it look awful?'

'On the contrary,' he said. 'I prefer it. It makes you look warmer. Less of the ice maiden.'

Helen felt herself blush, but before she could speak one of the Frenchmen called across. *'Lucien? C'est prêt. On y va?'*

Paul nodded. *'Merci. A bientôt.'* And with a grind of gears, the lorry pulled away.

'Where are they taking the stuff?' Helen asked.

Paul tapped the side of his nose. 'Need to know,' he said, then he smiled. 'Seriously, we've got to be very careful. The Gestapo are everywhere. The safest way is not to tell anyone anything they don't need to know.' He glanced along the track and lowered his voice. 'Now listen up, we haven't got much time.' He reeled off an address. 'This is where you're staying. It's near the fish market. It's a hotel. A small place. The room was booked by telephone in the name of Marie Dubois.'

'How will I get there?'

'I've brought a bicycle for you. When you hit the main road, turn right, and right again when you hit Mourillon.'

Helen followed his gaze to a small tree. There was just one bicycle propped up against it. She blinked and turned back to him. 'Aren't you coming with me?'

'Sadly not,' Paul said. 'It's too risky, but I'll contact you in a couple of days.'

'A couple of days?' Helen felt a stab of fear. 'What shall I do until then?'

'Get to know the town,' he said. 'Walk about, get the feel of the place, but try to avoid checkpoints until we're absolutely sure your papers are in order. And be careful not to let anyone get their hands on old Winnie's letter.'

He spoke quickly, clearly eager to be on the move, but

before he went there were two questions Helen had to ask even though she dreaded the answers.

'Paul, I mean … *Lucien*, wait. You mentioned in one of your reports that an escaped prisoner-of-war was in the area. A man called Ward Frazer … ?'

'That's right,' Paul said. 'He made contact with another cell, further north. They sent him on down here, but he hasn't made contact with me.'

'Why not?'

'I don't know,' he said. 'He's a slippery devil by all accounts. Maybe he's found his own way of getting home.'

'I hope so,' Helen said. She hesitated. 'There was another agent they sent in,' she said. '*Renard*. Do you know what's happened to him?'

Paul grimaced. 'I know what ought to happen to him,' he said grimly. He stopped abruptly as a thought occurred to him. 'Do you know him?' Helen nodded and Paul swore. '*Merde!*' He closed his eyes for a moment. When he opened them again he looked serious. Deadly serious. '*Renard* is bad news,' he said. 'If you see him, tell me, but for God's sake don't let him see you.'

'There's a letter for you,' Katy called up to Jen.

Jen was still in bed. It was Saturday morning, dark and cold, and the last thing Jen wanted to do was get out of bed. Instead she yawned and stretched, wishing she could close her eyes and sleep for ever. Life was so much easier when you were asleep. 'Who's it from?' she called back eventually. 'What's the postmark?'

'I don't know,' Katy said. 'It must have been delivered by hand, there's no stamp. Old-fashioned copperplate writing.'

Puzzled, Jen pulled on her dressing-gown and ran lightly down the narrow stairs.

Taking the envelope from Katy she opened it and unfolded the single sheet of flimsy war-quality paper inside.

'Good God!' she said.

'What?' Katy asked urgently. 'What's happened? Is it bad?'

Jen looked up. 'No,' she said. 'It's not bad, but it is rather awful. That old bastard Lorenz has offered to pay for my operation.'

Helen found the hotel with little difficulty. As Paul had said, it was quite close to the fish market, indeed the smell of fish seemed to permeate the whole place. Nevertheless it was clearly a respectable lodging house: the steps leading to the door were recently swept, the flagged entrance hall was clean and neat, the white walls were freshly painted, and an elegant curving staircase with an ornate wrought-iron banister rail led to the upper floors.

The small front desk was guarded by an old crone of a woman wearing a voluminous black dress with her hair pulled up in a tight bun. She seemed faintly surprised to find someone wanting to check in to their room so early in the day, but thankfully she asked no questions and, having swiftly relieved Helen of a hundred francs, she took a large key off a hook behind her.

'*Numéro trois,*' she said, handing it over. 'At the top of the stairs.'

Helen was glad to reach the comparative safety of her room. The bicycle ride from the landing site had taken her two hours, and round every corner, every turn in the road, she had expected to find a road block. But nobody had stopped her. In fact nobody had paid her any attention at all.

Now, despite her weariness, she quickly checked the hotel for escape routes and found that in an emergency her best chance would be out of the bathroom window. She taped Winston Churchill's letter to the underside of a heavy dresser which stood in the corridor outside her room, and then she closed her door and let out her pent-up tension in a long sigh.

The room itself was not at all bad. It was clean and spacious. There was a brightly coloured Moroccan rug on the boarded floor, the single bed was a fantasy of wrought iron and the light coming through the slatted shutters made attractive horizontal stripes on the white walls. The only thing Helen didn't like about the room was a heavy crucifix on the wall above the bed, which depicted Christ in such a contortion of agony that she almost toyed with taking it down.

Instead she quickly unpacked her things, washed thoroughly in the tiny porcelain sink, slid her pistol back into the pocket of her coat, took a deep, steadying breath and sortied out into the streets of Toulon.

It was strange being back in France, and even stranger being in a town she had never visited before but whose layout and street names she knew so well. Her researches had led her to expect a dull, dirty industrial town with all the disadvantages associated with a large naval port. But actually, tucked neatly between the green slopes of Mont Faron and the sea, with its tall, flat-fronted buildings along the front and the quaint jumble of the *vieille ville* behind, the city had a certain shabby charm.

There was no doubt that the fleet was in harbour, however. The streets were teeming with sailors, distinctive in their flared trousers, striped, Breton-style undershirts and red-bobbled berets. Passing the town hall she spotted two French fleet officers in more formal navy suits, double breasted with gold buttons and smart peaked caps, and then a moment later she caught sight of two senior German Wehrmacht officers, distinctive in high boots and belted greatcoats with black and gold Swastikas at the collar.

It was Helen's first glimpse of the enemy, and pausing behind a kiosk, she watched them stroll along arrogantly, laughing loudly, as though they owned the place. Which of course, to all intents and purposes, they did. Or soon would.

Turning away she glanced at the headlines of the newspapers on the racked display and learned that the German and Italian occupation troops were moving steadily southwards to 'protect France' against the imperialist British and the greedy Americans. Helen frowned. Surely nobody believed such nonsense, but it seemed that someone did, because a moment later she saw that on the wall of the kiosk someone had stuck a cartoon depicting General de Gaulle as a ridiculous French poodle licking the bottom of a British bulldog.

It was a timely reminder. A reminder that despite the feeling of coming home, despite the nostalgic smells – the aroma of coffee, the tangy scent of garlic and shellfish – despite the familiar sight of old men playing boules in the shade of palm trees, or draughts outside a café, she was to all intents and purposes in an enemy country.

The following day she walked a bit further to try to get a glimpse of the docks. However, although she occasionally was able to catch sight of the superstructures of the larger ships, it quickly became clear that the entire port area was very much off limits. Fences and checkpoints controlled every access to the ships and to the depots and warehouses. It was also much rougher down here. There were a lot of men hanging about rather threateningly at the street corners, and the acrid, all-pervading odour of decaying fish, oil and urine was quite enough to make her retrace her steps.

In any case she had seen enough. The task was enormous. Impossible. The docks covered several square miles and they were still full of ships. The idea that she and Paul could sabotage the fleet and put the docks out of use with the small amount of explosive at their disposal was simply ludicrous.

Clearly Admiral de Laborde was their only hope. She wondered what steps Paul was taking towards getting an entrée to the admiral's office and felt a stab of frustration. After his apparent interest in her in England it was oddly galling that Paul was keeping her so much in the dark. She wanted to get on with it. She wanted to do what she could. She wanted a task. And more than anything she wanted to keep her mind off the nasty fact that somewhere in this town, possibly even now strolling along the street towards her, or lurking round the next corner, was a man who would recognise her. André Cabillard. A man she thought she had loved. A man who would almost certainly betray her.

With a faint shiver, she pulled her coat closer round her and headed quickly back to the hotel, carefully skirting a police checkpoint on avenue de la République.

It was that evening that she heard the bells. Just faintly, as though far away. Church bells, ringing out in peel after joyful peel, such as Helen had not heard since before the war. At first she thought it must be a nearby wedding and then she heard a crackle of static and realised the sound must be coming from a wireless somewhere. Somewhere close by. Tiptoeing out on to the landing, she leaned over the banister, and sure enough, there was Madame and another old lady hunched over an ancient set in the little back office.

Just at that moment Madame glanced up, and when she saw Helen her wrinkled face paled so rapidly that, for a second, Helen thought the poor old thing was going to faint. Leaping into action, the other old lady clawed at the dial with arthritic fingers.

'Don't turn it off,' Helen said. 'It's lovely. What is it?'

Madame looked stricken. *'C'est les Anglais,'* she muttered. 'They are celebrating their victory in North Africa.'

Even as she spoke, the bells faded and an English commentator's voice spoke strongly through the static. 'Those were the bells of Coventry Cathedral, where despite repeated German bombing, the bell tower still remains standing. Did you hear that in occupied Europe? Did you hear that in Germany … ?'

Madame swung round in panic. 'Turn it off,' she hissed at the other old lady. 'If anyone hears …'

The sound clicked off abruptly.

'Alors, mademoiselle,' Madame said, smoothing her heavy black dress. 'I am sorry to disturb you. I thought you were out, otherwise …'

For a moment their eyes met and Helen was shocked by the terrible fear she saw there. More than anything, that made her realise the atmosphere of the town. The constant fear, fear of the Gestapo, of informers.

'You didn't disturb me,' she said carefully. 'I like music. I didn't hear anything else.'

The old lady hesitated. 'Nor did we,' she said, 'but the music was pleasant.'

Helen smiled. 'Very pleasant,' she agreed and went back upstairs.

The following morning she was just about to go out when Madame called her to the telephone. 'Meet me this afternoon,' Paul said. 'Outside the town hall. Two o'clock.'

Jen was admitted to the private wing of the Wilhelmina on Monday, 16 November.

She had had no idea the operation would be so soon but Mr Goodacre had been keen to get on with it. 'We might as well strike while the iron is hot,' he said happily. 'What do you say?'

Jen wanted to say that she thought his choice of expression was somewhat inappropriate but actually she was far too scared to say anything at all. The thought of Mr Goodacre plunging down her throat and yanking some growth off her vocal cords had haunted her dreams even before Mr Lorenz had come up with the money.

Lorenz. For a moment her thoughts jumped back to the embarrassing meeting she had had with Lorenz after receiving his letter.

'He's only trying to bribe me,' she had said to Katy before setting off. 'He's only trying to get round me so I won't run to Dad if he knocks off my mother.'

'That's a beastly thing to say,' Katy had protested, 'and I'm sure it's not true. Lorenz is an extremely kind man. He's only trying to help you out of a jam. Anyway,' she added stiffly, 'if you really feel that way, you shouldn't accept the money.'

Jen had flounced out then, but when she was admitted by buzzer to Lorenz's grim little shop on Northcote Road half an hour later and saw his solemn, almost shy face on the other side of the counter, she couldn't help wondering if Katy was right. Perhaps she had misjudged Lorenz.

'I couldn't possibly take the money,' she had stammered suddenly. 'It's not right. I don't deserve it. And it would take me years to pay you back.'

'But I don't want you to pay me back,' he said. 'It's a gift. A gift with no obligation of any kind.' He saw her guilty flinch and lowered his eyes. After a moment he had looked up again. 'If you don't want to accept it from me as a gift,' he said gently, 'perhaps you could think of it as sponsorship of the arts?' And Jen had felt like the lowest kind of worm.

Now, as she lay in bed waiting to go under Mr Goodacre's knife and listening to the nurses flirting with the anaesthetist, Jen wished she had turned him down after all. I'm going to die, she muttered to herself. Either I'll haemorrhage and drown in my own blood or I'll never wake up from the anaesthetic.

Helen didn't meet Paul in front of the town hall, she met him in a dark alley on the way, and it wasn't a pleasant experience. One minute she had been walking along rue d'Alger minding her own business and the next her arm was nearly jerked out of its socket and a hand was clamped over her mouth.

Unable to breathe she felt the panic gripping her

muscles. She smelt the aroma of Caporal tobacco, tasted it on the hard fingers, and then she heard Paul's voice in her ear. 'What the hell are you doing? I've been following you for ten minutes and you never even looked over your shoulder.'

Shaken, Helen immediately started to apologise. 'Oh God,' she mumbled through his hand. 'I'm sorry. I'm really sorry.'

Letting her go, Paul flicked ash off his roll-up cigarette with an impatient gesture. 'Well, keep your eyes open next time. I don't want to find you've brought me a tail.'

Recovering her equilibrium, Helen glared at him. He was right to reprimand her, but suddenly she felt annoyed with him for deliberately scaring her. And she would have checked, when she got nearer to the rendezvous. Of course she would.

'I would have come quietly,' she said. 'You didn't have to break my blasted arm off—' She stopped abruptly as she noticed that Paul was holding her pistol.

Seeing her expression he laughed, a slightly sour laugh, and weighed it in his hand. 'Don't worry, I'm not going to seduce you at gunpoint. I just wanted to check your pockets.' He tossed it back to her. 'So where do you keep old Winnie's letter, then? In your handbag?'

'I didn't bring it with me,' she said. 'I thought it was safer not to.'

'Safer?' He raised his eyebrows. 'What? To leave it lying around in your room?'

'It's not in my room,' she said, irritated by his sarcasm. 'It's hidden somewhere else. I thought it was safer not to carry it around Toulon until I knew what I was going to do with it.'

'Where's it hidden?'

Helen frowned. 'I'm not telling you that.'

He smiled and she realised he had been testing her.

'What did you want me for, anyway?' she asked crossly. As soon as the question was out of her mouth she regretted its phrasing. For a second as his eyes flickered she thought he was going to make some suggestive response but, glancing at his watch, he took a last draw on his cigarette, dropped it on the road and ground it with his heel.

Using the diversion, he glanced casually up and down the alley and lowered his voice. 'Wednesday,' he said. 'An officer will come to the Café aux Trois Dauphins in rue Hoche. Meet him there at two exactly, wearing your blue headscarf. He is a lieutenant commander and he will carry yellow roses for you. He is an aide to Admiral de Laborde. He believes France should join the Allied cause. He should deliver the letter anonymously.' His eyes narrowed as his gaze swung back to her. 'Do you understand?'

'Yes,' Helen said steadily. 'Yes, I think so.'

Paul nodded. 'Good,' he said. 'Then good luck.' And with a brief smile he turned on his heel and walked away.

Helen stared after him. Even though she was piqued by his faintly condescending attitude, she couldn't help being impressed by his competence. He made it all seem so easy. Leaning back against the cold alley wall she closed her eyes briefly. So this was it. Wednesday. The day after tomorrow. Suddenly she realised she could hardly wait. Just two more days and she would have done her duty. And then, thank God, she could go home.

Chapter Twenty-Five

In the event Jen's operation was delayed until the Tuesday morning, so she was still unconscious when Joyce called tentatively at the private-block reception to ask how she was.

It was an odd thing, but ever since Lorenz had offered to pay for Jen's surgery, Joyce had been absolutely convinced that something was going to go wrong. She wasn't a fey woman. In the normal course of events she would have poo-pooed anyone who claimed to be able to see into the future, but all weekend she had this peculiar feeling that someone was going to die. And as Jen was in hospital, she was the obvious candidate. So when the private-block duty sister told her that Jen still hadn't come round from the anaesthetic Joyce feared the worst.

'Perhaps you would like to sit with her for a while,' the nurse suggested kindly.

Joyce shook her head. 'Oh no,' she said quickly, and then she thought, why not? It had been quiet in the café when she left, and she was Jen's mother after all. If something did happen she didn't want people saying that she had refused even to see her daughter before she died.

She realised suddenly, as she crept into the quiet room and saw the small pale figure in the crisp white bed, that she quite badly didn't want Jen to die.

It was a long time since Joyce had looked at Jen. Really looked at her. For so long they had argued every time they met, she had preferred not to look at her, and she realised that she had forgotten how pretty her daughter was. So delicate. As she stood at the end of the bed Joyce wondered where Jen had got that delicate prettiness. Neither she nor Stanley were delicate.

Turning away Joyce glanced at the three vases of flowers on the windowsill and the little cards that someone had laid out alongside them. The largest bouquet was from the cast of Jen's show. 'Come back as soon as you can,' it read. 'We miss you, darling.' The next was from 'All of the regulars at the Flag and Garter. Get well soon,' it said, followed by a mass of signatures. The final offering was a small bunch of white roses from Mr Lorenz which had a card next to it saying meekly, 'With best wishes from Albert Lorenz.'

To her surprise, Joyce felt sudden tears prickle her eyes. She didn't know why but the thought of people liking Jen, of people wanting to take collections for her, wanting to help her, made her feel ridiculously emotional. She was just dabbing away the tears when to her horror the door opened and a small jolly-looking man in a white coat came marching in.

'Oh.' For a moment he looked disconcerted to find anyone there and then he smiled. 'Ah yes, you must be Mrs Carter?' He thrust out his hand. 'My name's Jeremy Goodacre. I performed your daughter's operation. I gather she hasn't come round yet. Now let me see.' He quickly took Jen's pulse and flicked up one of her eyelids to peer inside. 'Ah, yes,' he said. 'She's obviously reacted a bit heavily to the anaesthetic. Still,' he straightened up, beaming reassuringly, 'nothing to worry about yet.'

'I'd better go,' Joyce mumbled. She wasn't used to being treated with such jovial familiarity by important doctors. By anyone, come to that.

Mr Goodacre looked dismayed. 'Oh, don't let me drive you away, Mrs Carter. I'm sure she'll want to see you when she comes round.'

Joyce glanced at the still, pale figure in the bed. Good

God, she thought. I'm the last person she'll want to see. Then, realising that Mr Goodacre was heading for the door, she hurried after him. 'She will be all right, won't she?' she asked. 'She's not going to die or anything?'

'Die?' Mr Goodacre looked astonished. 'Goodness me, no.' He chuckled happily. 'She'll be right as rain now, although I'm afraid she won't be very chatty for a day or two.'

The Café aux Trois Dauphins was situated on a corner of the busy rue Hoche. It had grubby green awnings and it was clear that on fine days the tables spilled out on to the pavement. Today, though, everything was closed up against the cold wind blowing up from the front, and the steamed-up windows prevented Helen from seeing inside.

Damn, she thought, but she didn't go in. She was too early anyway. Deliberately so. She wanted to check the lie of the land. So she walked on past.

It was only as she reached Place Puget and saw the statue at its centre that she realised where the café got its name. There, covered in some kind of chalky deposit which gave it a curious whitish appearance, was a fountain depicting the three cavorting dolphins. Fingering the blue scarf in her handbag, she circled the statue and began to walk slowly back down rue Hoche.

She was perhaps a hundred yards away when she noticed the man. Why, she asked herself, if a man wanted to read a newspaper, would he stand uncomfortably hunched and cold in a dark, draughty doorway when there was a perfectly good café only yards away on the other side of the street?

The answer to that question made her move casually into the cover of a fruit stall. And then she noticed the car. A black sedan, parked round the corner from the café, with two men sitting inside. It might mean nothing, but it might mean something.

Just as she began to wonder what to do about it, she saw

a naval officer armed with a bunch of yellow flowers stop outside the café, look up at the name on the awning and then, after a moment's hesitation, step inside.

Quickly Helen looked back at the newspaper reader, but either he was well trained or it wasn't the naval officer he was watching for, because he evinced no evident interest in the café's new customer.

So who was he waiting for? she wondered. Probably someone completely different, a friend or a lover, but she was damned if she was going to take any unnecessary risks.

'Can I help you?'

Helen jumped but it was the fruit stall owner, obviously keen to make a sale. She glanced at his stall. There wasn't much fruit. Just a few bunches of grapes, some rather dry-looking apples, and a pile of fresh field mushrooms. She wondered how long she could spin out a purchase. 'I haven't got much money,' she said.

The man shrugged. 'You'd better get what you can. Once the Germans get here there won't be anything left for the likes of us. It's bad enough already.'

In the end she bought two apples. Just as she paid, at exactly five past two, the young lieutenant emerged from the café and set off quickly back towards avenue de la République still clutching his roses. At the same moment Helen saw the man on the corner fold his newspaper and cross the road into the café.

For a second she hesitated, but then as nobody appeared to follow the officer, she walked swiftly down a nearby side street, then turned and ran along a narrow alley parallel to the rue Hoche, thus neatly avoiding passing the café. At the next junction she stopped on the corner and was pleased to see the young officer still heading towards the front and the docks. Letting him pass, she watched the people behind him carefully. There appeared to be nobody following him. Or her.

She caught him up on the avenue de la République. 'The flowers are pretty,' she murmured in French. 'I like the colour.' Then, as he swung round to face her, she added sharply, 'Turn right at the next corner and keep walking.'

Dropping back she watched to see that he did as he was told and then caught him up again in a small square in the *vieille ville*.

'You were not at the café,' he said accusingly.

He was pale and clearly very tense, younger than she had thought before. On the face of it he seemed an odd person for Paul to have selected for this potentially dangerous task, but perhaps there had not been much choice.

'The café was being watched,' she said.

At once he paled even more and glanced over his shoulder.

'It's all right,' she said. 'We are not being followed, but we don't have much time. I gather you want to help us?'

The young officer nodded.

'And you currently work for Admiral de Laborde?'

'Well, yes,' he muttered, 'but if something goes wrong … what about my career?' Ten anxious minutes alone in the Café aux Trois Dauphins had clearly been enough to give him second thoughts. Helen couldn't help being sorry for him but this was no time to be soft.

'Would you prefer to be working for Admiral Doenitz of the German navy?' she asked.

'Well, no, of course …'

'Because that's what will happen if you don't help us. Your ships will fall into German hands and you will effectively be under Doenitz's command.'

'Yes,' he muttered. 'I understand that. Others are concerned too.'

'Good,' Helen said. 'Then please make sure Admiral de Laborde receives this letter. He and he only. Be sure he cannot trace the delivery to you. And tell no one. No one at all. Not even fellow sympathisers. Do you understand?'

Taking the envelope with some reluctance, he nodded. 'I think so.'

'We need to know Admiral de Laborde's reaction to the letter,' she said. 'If there is any news you should come to the square in front of the cathedral. Come at exactly ten o'clock any morning and wait for five minutes only.' He nodded nervously and she held his gaze steadily. 'And of course it is important to do everything you can to get the ships to sail. You can be sure that wherever they go they will be well received by the Allies.'

He shrugged helplessly. 'I have no influence ...'

'Do what you can,' she said, then she touched his arm briefly and smiled. *'Au revoir,'* she said. '*Et merci.* It's a brave thing you are doing. We are very grateful.'

Jen had never felt so ill in all her life. If she had known how awful she would feel, she never would have had the operation done. On coming round she had immediately been violently sick and the pain as the vomit passed her wounded throat had almost made her pass out again. The nurses had tried to reassure her that nausea was quite normal after an anaesthetic, but now twenty-four hours later she still felt absolutely dreadful. As well as the terrible ongoing sickness and agonising pain in her throat she was under strict orders not to try to speak, not even to whisper, nothing. That, more than anything, had convinced her that something had gone wrong, but because she couldn't speak she couldn't ask.

Eventually in desperation she wrote down the question, and the more the nurses tried to reassure her with hearty good humour the more she mistrusted them.

She even mistrusted Mr Goodacre, especially when he told her how concerned her mother had been about her. Jen knew perfectly well that Joyce had never been concerned about her in her entire life. She was amazed that she had even bothered find out that she was still alive.

She obviously wasn't so concerned that she felt the need to come again, though.

Even Katy lied to her. 'It'll be the painkillers that are making you feel sick,' she said knowledgeably when Jen gave a graphic mime of her nausea. Jen knew that she was lying, because if they were really giving her painkillers why the hell was she still in such excruciating pain?

The final confirmation was when Sister Morris dropped in to see her. That was bizarre enough in its own right. She and Sister Morris were hardly close buddies. And when Sister Morris called by again only hours later, Jen began to smell a pretty large rat.

To test her out Jen grimly held up her 'Will I ever sing again' sign.

'Look at that,' Sister Morris chortled to Mr Goodacre who happened to be in the room at the same time. 'Some people have no faith, do they?'

Jen eyed them suspiciously and picked up her pen. 'Are you sure he hasn't left one of his instruments down my throat?' she scrawled balefully. Surely that would get the old dragon back on her customary high horse.

Sister Morris just smiled fondly. 'My dear girl,' she said, patting her arm reassuringly, 'don't you realise you have been treated by one of the most eminent ENT surgeons in the country?'

That's it, Jen thought in despair. Now I know for sure she's lying. Either that or she fancies me. Either way I'm clearly doomed.

3 November 1942

Hi Jen and Katy,

We thought you'd like to know we got here safely. What a weird place. All the guys wear dresses and the women won't show their faces, let alone their bodies (not like round the back of the Flag and Garter!). But generally they seem pretty friendly and the kids are cute, especially when they think they might get some

American gum! We haven't seen any Germans yet but it sounds as though your boys in the west are giving them a good hammering. Hope they leave a few for us …

So there you go, that's the news. We miss you girls and we want to tell you how much we appreciated your hospitality and friendship during our stay in London. We were a long way from home and you made it one hell of a lot easier for us. Now we are looking forward to doing our bit for you.

With all our love always,

Dirk, Hank, Tod, Steve, Walt and the other boys from the US of A.

11 November 1942

Dear Katy,

Just a short note to see how you are and to ask you if you could possibly do us a little favour and get some flowers for poor Jen on our behalf.

We will reimburse you when we come up next week for the café party. Isn't it marvellous that Mrs Carter and Mrs Rutherford have done so well with their little venture? We are so touched they thought to invite us. We are looking forward to seeing you, and little Malcolm too.

We have been thinking about Ward a lot recently too. We both feel very positively about him, which must be a good sign.

With love,

Your old friends, Esme and Thelma Taylor.

P.S. Mrs Rutherford has kindly asked us to stay at Cedars House the night of the party, but we are hoping that it will be all right for your mother to stay at the pub with you?

The first letter made Katy cry. The second made her feel rather uneasy. 'Of course Mummy must stay with me,'

Katy wrote back. So long as she doesn't want to stay too long, she added to herself. She loved her mother dearly, and she was looking forward to seeing her, but the thought of having her flustering around the pub on a long term basis was not appealing.

It was on her way back to the hotel after the successful handover of Winston Churchill's letter that Helen's concentration slipped and, suddenly, for the first time since she had arrived in Toulon, she found herself approaching a group of hard-eyed Vichy policemen who were stopping people at the corner of Lafayette and asking to see their ID.

There was nowhere she could go, no way of avoiding the checkpoint without drawing attention to herself, so, as calmly as she could, she opened her handbag and handed over the fake identity card and the papers that Miss Atkins had given her only four days before.

'May I look in your handbag?'

Silently Helen handed that over too.

Not my pockets, she prayed. Please God, don't let them ask to check my pockets. Even as she stood there, she could feel the weight of the gun in her pocket pulling her coat down slightly on the right-hand side. She could also feel the prickle of sweat in her armpits.

'You are from Paris?'

'Yes.' She nodded and was about to launch into her cover story when she recalled the SOE instructor telling her never to say more than she had to.

He was right. A moment later, without further questions, the policeman handed her back the papers and the bag.

It was at that precise moment that the door of a nearby restaurant opened and she caught a glimpse of a group of German SS officers sitting at a white-clothed table just inside the door. It was only a glimpse – a very short glimpse, just the time it took for two women to leave the restaurant – but it made Helen's heart stop with a jerk.

There was another man sitting with those officers. A civilian dressed in a navy blazer over a thin roll-necked jersey. A civilian who was leaning back in his chair and smiling at something one of the officers had just said. Even as she looked, his eyes flicked up and, for an awful numbing instant just as the door swung shut, he seemed to be staring straight at her.

André, she thought. It's André. The shock was total and it hit her like a punch in the stomach.

'Is everything all right, mademoiselle?' one of the policemen spoke behind her.

Helen turned back to him slowly. For a second she was so disoriented that she almost answered him in English.

'Oui,' she said. '*Merci.* Everything is quite all right, thank you.'

Everything wasn't all right, though. Everything was horribly, horribly wrong, and she wanted to close her eyes and run. But she couldn't possibly run, not without drawing even more attention to herself, so she had to walk. To walk and think and try to control the emotion that was surging through her like an electric current.

She was sure he hadn't recognised her. After all she was a brunette now. It was for this exact scenario they had made her dye her hair. Even if he had, she was sure he wouldn't come after her. Or would he?

At the corner, she risked a quick glance back and saw the restaurant door open. A man emerged. She didn't know if it was him or not. She didn't want to know. Forgetting all her training, she turned on her heel and ran.

Katy was halfway through a stocktake when Louise tapped on the door and her heart sank. Louise was not her favourite person at the moment. Only last night Louise had come into the pub looking for Aaref and, with hardly a glance of apology at poor Molly who was standing right next to him, Aaref had abandoned his drink and disappeared with Louise for two hours.

'Two hours,' Katy had ranted at him later when he finally reappeared. 'You were gone two hours. And now you are surprised that poor Molly has gone back to the hospital. If she's got any sense she will never speak to you again.'

'Louise is upset about Jack,' Aaref had said mildly. 'She needs help and support.'

'Oh yes,' Katy had said angrily. 'Funny how she needs it from you and not from anyone else.'

But now, as she opened the door, Louise did indeed look to be in quite a bad way. There was definite strain around her eyes and her chin was wobbling slightly.

'I've got to talk to you,' Louise said.

'I'm rather busy,' Katy said.

'Oh Katy, please.' Louise's face crumpled with sudden desperation. 'Everything has gone wrong, and everyone is being so horrid to me.' And then to Katy's dismay it all poured out. Bertie's death. The German attack on the convoy. Jack's breakdown, his inability to make love, the way he had run to his mother instead of her, her own mother's angry response that she should stand by her man regardless.

Katy felt awful. She had had no idea that Louise was so unhappy. Pouring out a whisky, Katy handed it to her. 'What about Aaref?' she asked.

'Aaref has been so kind,' Louise said, sipping the drink gratefully. 'All right, I admit I wanted him to fancy me. I needed someone to, as Jack obviously didn't any more. But Aaref wouldn't do anything. He says it's not fair to Jack. I know what everyone is thinking and it's not fair that everyone should think badly of him because of me.'

Feeling guilty, Katy rapidly revised her estimate of Aaref, who had obviously behaved most honourably throughout. 'Oh Louise, I'm so sorry,' she said. 'I've been so wrapped up in my own problems I hadn't noticed yours. You should have said something earlier.'

But sympathy was not enough. 'What shall I do?' Louise wailed.

'Do you still love Jack?' Katy asked.

Louise blinked. 'Well, yes, of course I do. It's just that I realise now I don't really know him. We've had so little time together. I suppose I married him because he was handsome and strong and well-to-do.' She bit her lip as tears welled in her eyes. 'I didn't know he was suddenly going to start crying ...'

Katy leaned over and put an arm round her shoulders. 'I think your mother is right. You do have to take the rough with the smooth. But Jack's a lovely man. I think he's worth waiting for.'

'Do you? You really think he's nice?'

'Of course he's nice,' Katy said. 'He's absolutely gorgeous. Everyone thinks so.'

Louise seemed pleased with that. 'All right, then,' she said, standing up decisively. 'I'll write to him now and tell him I love him.' At the door she turned and gave Katy a watery smile. 'Why is everything so difficult?'

At that moment Malcolm started crying. He was teething and had already kept Katy awake most of the night. Katy groaned. 'Why indeed?' she said. After all, Malcolm and Louise weren't the only ones with problems. She thought of Molly Coogan, distraught over Aaref's apparent defection to Louise. Jen, convinced that she would never speak again. Pam, terrified that George would start behaving badly again when the baby was born. Helen, probably scared to death in France, and God only knew what might have happened to Ward.

'Oh baby,' Katy murmured wearily as she picked up the tearful Malcolm and hugged him to her chest. 'Will anything ever be normal and nice again?'

Helen didn't run far, but she ran far enough to get lost.

Certainly far enough to lose a tail. So when she heard footsteps running lightly up to a corner she had just turned she could hardly believe her ears. She didn't know if it was André after her or not. It might just as well have been the police, or the Gestapo. Whoever it was, she had to lose them.

Crossing the road, she slipped silently into a dark, narrow alleyway. Halfway along it she realised her mistake. It was a dead end. Already, ahead of her she could see the walls of the surrounding buildings closing in. There was just one door, a back door to a shop surrounded by crates. She knew it would be locked. It was. There was nowhere to go. No exit. She was well and truly trapped.

For a moment she stood there, waiting for the bullet, but there was no shot. There was no noise at all. Putting her hand in her pocket she pulled out her gun and turned round slowly.

At first she thought there was nobody there, and then she saw him. Halfway up the alley. Leaning against the wall. He looked thin and tired. His hair was long and rather unkempt. There was some growth of beard on his face. More than anything he looked like some dirty old tramp, but Helen would have recognised that firm chin and those cool grey eyes anywhere, and her mouth fell open.

It wasn't André at all. It wasn't the Vichy police or an SS officer. Or Paul. It was Ward Frazer.

Ward Frazer. Her old boss. Katy's husband. Escaped prisoner-of-war. She could not believe it. It was like a gift from heaven.

He straightened up as she approached, and, under the stubble and grime, he was smiling that faint wry smile she remembered so well.

He spoke in English. 'Well, hello,' he said. 'So it is you under those copper curls. Thank God for that. I thought I must be going mad.'

It was the same voice. The soft Canadian accent. And even in those few words she heard that steady unshakeable confidence he had in himself and the same unswerving faith he had always had in her.

'Oh Ward,' she whispered, and then she took a step forward and fell into his arms.

It didn't take Helen long to realise that Ward Frazer was in a bad way. Half a dozen times he had narrowly evaded capture even when so-called friends were helping him. Consequently he had lost all faith in the escape networks. He had no papers, no ID and very little money. He looked like death and there was no doubt his leg was giving him pain.

'How on earth have you survived this long?' Helen asked.

'Burglary mostly,' he said. 'I'm a dab hand at drainpipes. I've got most of my clothes and food that way. I've even managed the odd ID, although you can't use them long because they quickly get reported.' He shook his head. 'But now my time's running out,' he said. 'One police check and I've had it.'

Helen looked at him. He was clearly close to the end of his tether. He had been on the run too long.

'Where are you living?' she asked him.

'I spent last night in a cave on Mont Faron.'

'A cave?' No wonder he looked so unkempt.

He shrugged. 'I was staying with some Jewish shopkeepers in Mourillon but it got too risky for them. The whole place is riddled with informers. In any case, now the Germans are so close the Jews are trying to leave too. It's not going to be any place for Jews soon.'

Nor for escaped prisoners-of-war, Helen thought. Nor for anyone come to that.

'Ward, listen,' she said. 'There's a plane coming on Friday night to pick me up. It's only a Lysander but I'm sure they can squeeze you in too. You can hide in my hotel room until then.'

He shook his head. 'It's too dangerous. I've got a price on my head. Every damn Nazi-paid crook in the South of France is on the lookout for me, let alone the police. If they connect you to me, then you've had it too.'

Already he was looking around, watching the people passing the end of the alley. He knew as well as she did that they'd been there too long.

'Ward, you must. It's your best chance. Nobody need know you were there.' Quickly she gave him the address of the hotel. 'There's a roof adjacent to the yard. You can jump across to the bathroom window. I'll leave a towel hanging out if it's safe.'

He still didn't look convinced.

'Ward, please,' she said. 'If you won't do it for yourself, do it for Katy.'

He blinked. It was as if the mention of Katy opened up another part of his mind, and Helen realised that he had only survived by closing off his emotions, just as she had tried to do.

'Helen, about Katy,' he whispered. 'Is she all right?'

'Yes,' Helen said. 'She's okay. She's fine, apart from being worried about you.'

He hesitated. 'And what about the baby? I'm sorry, Helen, but I have to know.'

'He's fine too.'

He stared at her. 'Oh God,' he muttered, then suddenly he closed his eyes. When he opened them again he put a hand to his head. 'I'm sorry,' he said. 'It's just that, well, to be honest, I'd convinced myself he'd died.'

Helen looked at him in concern. 'Ward, listen,' she said urgently. 'You're in a bad way. You must do as I say. You must come tonight. As soon as it's dark.'

He nodded. 'All right,' he said. 'I'll try. And thank you. You don't have to do this, I know.'

'Of course I have to,' Helen said. 'That's what friends are for.'

Chapter Twenty-Six

'It's a most peculiar thing,' Alan Nelson said to Pam, 'but old man Rutherford told me this morning that if I wanted to I could work short hours while you're down in the country having the baby so that I could look after George. I nearly fell off my chair. What do you think has come over him?'

Pam looked up from her packing in delight. 'It must be something to do with Helen,' she said. 'She mentioned something about it before she left. I can't think how on earth she managed it, mind, unless she sent a carrier pigeon from France.'

'I hope she's all right,' Alan said. 'I heard on the wireless earlier there are Germans tanks pouring into Vichy France now and they're heading south fast.'

Pam shuddered. 'Don't think about it,' she said. 'There's nothing we can do after all except keep our fingers crossed.' She lowered her voice. 'Do you think you'll manage George all right? He still refuses to acknowledge that the baby is coming.'

'I find it quite hard to believe myself,' Alan said. 'It'll be pretty odd saying goodbye on Friday and then getting you back a month later with a sproglet in tow. I wish you were staying here.'

'So do I,' Pam said. 'I can't think of anything worse than sitting in some awful maternity hospital with a hundred other pregnant mothers.'

'Good God, what a thought,' Alan said, 'but it's

probably for the best. At least you'll be calm and relaxed for the birth, knowing that they've got doctors there and all the specialist equipment right on hand.'

One minute Helen had convinced herself Ward wasn't coming, the next he was sliding through the window. His silent speed and agility even with the bad leg was incredible, and even though she had seen him do it Helen could hardly believe he was standing next to her in the bathroom.

'Remind me to lock up my jewellery when I get back to London,' she whispered, and he grinned.

'I'll be able to keep Katy in furs and diamonds for the rest of her life.'

She was glad to see him more relaxed. He had made some attempt to shave and he looked calmer than he had earlier. The prospect of escape had obviously done him good.

Tiptoeing across to the bedroom he glanced at the narrow iron bed. 'I'll sleep on the floor,' he murmured.

'No,' Helen said. 'You're the one who needs decent rest.' She saw he was going to demur. 'Okay. We'll take it in turns, but you first. In any case, I think we shouldn't both sleep at once. Just in case.'

In fact Ward slept so soundly that Helen hadn't the heart to shift him out for her turn. It was probably the first decent sleep he had had since his escape from the prisoner-of-war camp, she realised. No wonder his nerves were frayed.

The following morning Helen asked Madame at reception if she would mind not cleaning her room for the next couple of days because she had some dress patterns laid out and she didn't want them disturbed, then she walked down to the cathedral to see if the young lieutenant commander was going to turn up.

He didn't, but she wasn't altogether surprised. He

would have been lucky to have had a chance to get the letter to de Laborde overnight.

On the way back she bought a couple of bags of cooked *moules* from a shellfish stall and some bread and wine from a small store nearby to go with them. Seeing Madame eyeing her suspiciously as she re-entered the hotel she smiled and brandished the wine. 'To help me work.'

'Of course,' Madame nodded. 'Provençal wine is very beneficial. It is good for the blood. And Cabillard wine too, I see. The very best.'

Helen looked at the bottle. She hadn't noticed. She genuinely hadn't noticed. But there it was printed on the label. '*Vin supérieur des caves Cabillard.*'

'The Cabillard vineyards are not so far from here,' Madame said.

'No,' Helen said faintly. 'So I understand.'

'Drink it while you can, mademoiselle,' the old lady whispered. 'The Boches will be here soon and there will be none left for the likes of us then.'

No, Helen thought bitterly. In fact she was surprised André wasn't shipping it all off to Berlin already.

Ward ate the *moules* as though they were going out of fashion, then with an apologetic groan he lay back on the bed and immediately went back to sleep again.

Poor man, Helen thought, as she stared pensively out of the window. God only knew what he had been through for the last few months.

When he woke she would tell him where the plane was landing, she decided, in case something happened to her, and then he could go anyway.

It's not long now, she thought, as she once again surveyed the empty street below. Just a couple more days and they would be on the way home. She just prayed the lieutenant commander would come tomorrow with some good news, and then she would be able to leave with a clear conscience.

* * *

At the cathedral the following day, however, there was no sign of the lieutenant commander.

It was as she headed back to the hotel that Helen noticed a bicycle leaning up against a wall outside a café. She stopped. She was going to need another bicycle on Friday night to get Ward to the plane, and here was one. She didn't even think twice.

I've just stolen a bicycle, she thought, as she hitched up her skirts and rode it away. Who would ever have thought the day would come when Lady Helen de Burrel was forced to steal a bicycle?

Having hidden the bike round the back of the hotel with the one Paul had given her, Helen hurried indoors, eager to tell Ward that she had procured transport for him, but Madame stopped her in the hallway. 'A man called for you earlier,' she said. 'He wouldn't leave his name.'

'A man?' She was hard pushed not to show her shock. 'What sort of man?'

The old lady shrugged as though all men were one and the same to her, as indeed perhaps they were. After all, Helen thought suddenly, when you were as heavily wrinkled and grey as she was, the slight differences in appearance and manner between one young man and another were probably somewhat irrelevant.

Evidently she was wrong, because to Helen's utter astonishment Madame's mouth widened and she gave a sudden, somewhat alarming cackle. 'Quite a handsome man.'

Helen's heart jumped anxiously.

'He had a fine moustache,' Madame added helpfully.

So it was Paul, then, Helen thought in relief. Of course it was. Who else could it have been, after all? Even if he had seen her and recognised her with her newly dyed hair, André could not possibly have tracked her back to the hotel. 'Thank you,' she said. 'Thank you for telling me.'

'He said he would come again later,' Madame said as

Helen headed for the stairs. 'I didn't tell him about the other man.'

Helen stopped abruptly in her tracks. 'The other man?'

The old lady winked. 'The one in your room. I didn't mention him.'

Helen stared at her. 'Thank you,' she said weakly. 'Thank you, madame.'

'It is not my business,' the old lady said. Then she smiled and touched her chest. 'I am too old to interfere in the affairs of the heart.'

George was organising his conkers on his bedroom rug when he heard the noise downstairs. He half listened for a moment and then when it didn't immediately come again he carried on with his task, determined to get them all laid out in exactly the right ascending order of merit. It wasn't easy because some of them were nicer than others, more shiny or stronger looking somehow, even if they were fractionally smaller. He was just in the process of puzzling out what to do with two of the ones that he thought of as twins, which came together beautifully shiny, but each with one side completely flat, when he heard the noise again. This time he decided to investigate.

From the landing at the top of the stairs he heard the noise again. It was coming from the kitchen. A kind of groaning roar. Exactly, George realised with some dismay, the sort of noise monsters made.

'Mum,' he called out. 'Are you there?'

The only response was another roar and for a moment he toyed with going back into his room, but it occurred to him that it wouldn't take the monster long to find him there, so instead he decided to creep downstairs and out of the front door.

This was a course of action he had taken on more than one occasion before and he knew how to do it quietly. It was only as he reached the bottom of the staircase that he began to wonder if he ought not at least to take a glimpse of what was going on in the kitchen. After all, the monster might just have Pam pinned up in a corner. It might not have eaten her yet and he didn't want to run away if there was any chance of saving her.

Tensing himself in case he had to flee, he crept along the passage, pushed the kitchen door open and froze.

There was no monster, although there had clearly been one there moments before, and it had left Pam lying in a pool of blood on the floor. At first as he stared in utter horror George thought the monster had killed her, and then he saw her hands clenching so hard her knuckles went white. Her whole body heaved and she let out that same terrible roar.

George nearly leaped out of his skin, and then, without further ado, he turned and ran.

'I'm thinking of applying for a job down in Surrey,' Molly Coogan told Katy. 'At the sector maternity hospital. I don't want to leave London but maybe it would be better for me to go away. It's obvious that Louise is never going to leave Aaref alone, and much as I love him I'm sick of being left with the crumbs of his affection.' She stopped suddenly. 'What? What are you looking at me like that for?' She put a hand to her face. 'Have I got a bogey on me or something?'

'No,' Katy said. 'No, of course you haven't. It's just that, well, Aaref hasn't told you, has he?'

'Told me what? What do you mean?' Molly's voice shook. 'He's not going to tell me it's all over, is he?'

'No, no,' Katy said. 'Nothing like that.' She looked at Molly's anxious face. 'These bloody men,' she muttered. 'Why can't they just behave like human beings occasionally instead of rushing about being honourable and stoic all over the place?'

'What are you talking about?' Molly wailed. 'Katy, please, if it's something horrid, please at least put me out of my misery.'

'It's not horrid,' Katy said. 'At least not as far as you are concerned. It's pretty horrid for Louise. I can't really say what it is, but I promise you that there's nothing going on between her and Aaref.' She saw Molly's scepticism and shrugged. 'I know, I thought there was too, but it seems Aaref is just being kind, helping her over a bad patch.'

It took Molly a few moments to decide if she really believed what Katy had said, then she sighed. 'Well,' she said, 'I suppose that makes me feel a bit better, but I still don't know if there's any future in going on seeing him, or whether I should go for this job in Surrey and turn into a bitter old spinster nurse instead.'

Katy smiled then. 'You'll never be a spinster, Molly. You're far too lovely. Your problem is that you don't realise it. You know, maybe what you should do is ...'

She stopped because at that moment the door opened and George rushed in as though wolves were after him.

'George!' Katy said. 'Whatever are you—'

'Mum,' he gasped. 'It's Mum. She's dying. I think a monster got her. And there's blood everywhere ...'

'Oh my God,' Katy whispered, then she turned to Molly. 'It must be the baby,' she said. 'We'll have to go.'

'I'll go,' Molly said, grabbing her coat. 'I'm more up on gynae than you. You go and phone the doctor.'

For a second Katy hesitated then she hauled Malcolm out of his playpen and thrust him into the pram. Seeing that George was about to follow Molly, she quickly grabbed his arm. 'You'd better come with me,' she said.

Paul didn't come to the hotel later but his helper did. It was the man Helen had seen with him at the parachute drop site. As soon as she saw him she ran downstairs and met him in the street.

'Where's *Lucien*?' she asked.

'Busy,' he said. 'More to the point, where were you the other day? You didn't show at the café. What went wrong?'

'The café was being watched,' Helen said. 'I thought it was too risky to go in.'

The man frowned. 'So what have you done with the letter?'

Helen hesitated. She didn't like this man. She didn't like the way he looked at her. Mainly she didn't like the way he smelt. On the other hand, he was clearly one of Paul's trustees.

'I gave it to the officer later,' she said. 'Somewhere else.'

For a second he looked taken aback, then he smiled. Not a friendly smile. 'Clever, aren't you?'

Helen shrugged. 'I asked him to tell me de Laborde's reaction, but so far he hasn't shown up at the meeting place.' She glanced at the man. 'If he doesn't come before I leave, *Lucien* will have to deal with it.'

'When do you leave?' he asked. 'We'll need to help you bring in the plane. Where are they landing?'

Helen was just about to give him the grid reference when something stopped her. It occurred to her that if this man didn't already know from London the details of her departure, there was no reason for her to tell him. 'Don't tell anyone anything they don't need to know,' Miss Aitkens had said.

Quickly she worked out the options. The man was right. It took more than one person to bring in a Lysander, but she already had two torches and now she also had Ward.

She couldn't tell the man that of course. She had promised Ward she would tell nobody of his existence.

So she lied. 'Oh, it's not until Sunday,' she said. 'I can't remember the grid reference off hand.'

'Paul thought it would be Friday,' he said. 'When the moon's good.'

'Oh no,' Helen said, 'definitely Sunday.' Damn, she thought. I forgot about the moon. 'If I don't see Paul before then I'll leave him a note at the café,' she added. 'With all the details.'

He didn't like it. She could see that, but she didn't care.

She was damned if she was going to put her life in this man's hands. She wished he didn't know where she lived.

'Was there anything else?' she asked.

'Yes,' he said with a slight leer. 'Paul sends his love.'

Helen nodded coolly. 'Then please send mine back.'

By the time Katy got back to Pam's house she was absolutely exhausted. The phone box on Lavender Hill had been out of order, so in the end she had run all the way to the Wilhelmina, dragging George and pushing the pram.

There she had poured out the story to the startled casualty sister who promised to send a doctor and an ambulance as soon as she could. She also agreed to ring the Rutherford & Berry brewery to tell Alan that his wife had gone into premature labour.

It was at that point that Katy had the brainwave of leaving Malcolm and a rather reluctant George at the café in the care of Mrs Carter while she herself hurried back to Pam's house.

She was expecting the worst. She was also, after all the effort she had expended, expecting to find some medical rescue activity going on. But the house, when she cautiously pushed open the front door, was ominously quiet.

At first she assumed that the ambulance had been and gone, taking everyone with it, but then she heard a faint noise from upstairs and saw Molly beckoning her up. It was dark on the landing and she couldn't see the expression on Molly's face. Heart thumping, she ran up the stairs and then jerked to a halt as Molly put her finger to her lips.

Oh no, she thought. She's dead. We're respecting the dead. So when Molly pushed open the bedroom door a second later she could hardly believe her eyes.

There, in bed, all neat and clean, pale and dozing, but very much alive, was Pam Nelson, and in the crook of her arm, wrapped in a stripey towel, was a tiny red-faced infant.

'It's a girl,' Molly said.

'I don't believe it,' Katy whispered, thinking back to her own prolonged and agonising labour. She turned to Molly open mouthed, but before she could say any more Pam opened her eyes.

'Is George all right?' she asked weakly. 'It must have been so awful for him finding me like that …'

The doorbell rang. 'Don't worry about George,' Katy said reassuringly as Molly went to answer it. 'I'll look after him for a day or two until you're back on your feet.'

'Goodness me.' A white-coated doctor strode into the room. 'It seems I've missed the boat, but perhaps I'd better have a quick check to see that everything is tickety-boo with you and the baby.'

As he approached the bed purposefully, Katy and Molly withdrew.

'How did you manage that?' Katy whispered as they went downstairs.

'I'm not sure,' Molly said. 'I think the baby was upside down or inside out or something. Whatever it was, Pam was fading fast and it was obvious I had to do something pretty sharpish. So I rolled up my sleeves, plunged in and kind of hoicked it out.'

'Oh my God!' Katy said. 'Thank heaven I chose to do the phoning.'

'I know,' Molly grinned. 'Won't Sister Morris be proud of me? I'll definitely get that gynae job in Surrey now!'

'*I'm* proud of you,' Katy said faintly.

Molly giggled. 'You look a bit pale, Katy. Come into the kitchen. Unfortunately I haven't had time to clear up, but if we're careful where we tread I could make you a cup of tea.'

The alley was dark, dark and narrow, and the man following her was getting closer and closer. Then she saw the light at the end of the alley and in the light was a plane. She could see its propellers turning as it taxied round, and she knew if she could only reach it she would be safe. But the man behind her was catching up. She could hear his footsteps closing on her as she ran. She knew it was André, but when he grabbed her arm and swung her round, it was Paul. He was kissing her and she was struggling against him, but he was so strong, too strong … And the plane was going, she could hear its engines revving for take-off. André was calling her name – 'Helen, Helen, for God's sake' – and someone was shaking her. She was screaming for André to help her, but he wouldn't help her, he just kept shaking her, hurting her. And then, belatedly, she realised he was trying to kill her.

But it wasn't André, it was Ward, and he was trying to wake her up, not kill her.

'Helen, for goodness' sake,' he was hissing. 'You're shouting the house down, and in English.'

Helen was shaking all over. The bed was drenched in her sweat. Sitting up, she stared around wildly, unable to shake off the dream, then when she realised there was nobody in the room other than her and Ward she put her face in her hands. 'Oh God.'

Ward's arm was round her shoulders. 'Do you want to tell me about it?' he asked gently.

She could feel the warmth of him, the strong wall of his chest, and it was so tempting, so, so tempting, to confide in him, but she knew she couldn't. It wasn't safe. And it wasn't fair. Just now he needed her more than she needed him.

Sitting up straighter, she shook her head. 'I'm sorry,' she said. 'This secret life must be getting to me. I try to pretend it isn't, but deep down I find it awfully scary.'

'It's a scary life,' Ward said. 'You wouldn't be human if you didn't find it scary. But you're going home tomorrow. So long as you've done what you came for, that's all that matters.'

But I haven't, Helen thought, closing her eyes. That's part of the problem. Oh yes, she had delivered the letter all right, but that was all. Any Tom, Dick or Harry could have done that. She had done nothing about meeting senior officers. Nothing to persuade anyone to put pressure on de Laborde, or to take unilateral action. If only Paul was more communicative. If only she hadn't seen André ...

When she opened her eyes Ward was looking at her. 'Go with your instincts,' he said softly. 'That's the only advice I can give.'

He got up then and poured her a glass of wine. As he handed it to her silently, Helen couldn't help thinking of Ward's repeated visits to enemy-held France before he was captured. Of the havoc he had inflicted on the German occupiers, the gallant men and women he had recruited to the Resistance. She had gathered something over the last couple of days of the awful time he had spent in interrogation, his leg broken, the Germans refusing treatment until he told them what he knew. But he had told them nothing and so eventually they had been forced under the Geneva Convention to treat him as a prisoner-of-war and not a spy. On top of that he had escaped and made his way injured and unassisted the whole way from Germany to the South of France. All in all it made her attempt at undercover work seem distinctly pathetic.

Oh God, she prayed finishing her glass and trying once again to sleep. Please let that blasted lieutenant commander come to the cathedral with good news tomorrow.

The blasted lieutenant commander didn't come up with good news, however. Instead he came to confess that he had been unable to deliver the letter at all.

'The admiral has been away,' he said nervously. 'In Vichy.' He saw Helen's face fall and went on quickly, 'But I have not been idle. I have found several other officers,

officers of the fleet, who feel as I do, but they are unsure. To sail without orders is not easy. They need help to act. Perhaps, mademoiselle, if you could meet them? You could persuade them …'

Oh no, Helen thought. Oh no, not this. Please not this.

He was looking at her eagerly, keen to make amends for his failure over the letter. He didn't know she was leaving that very night. He didn't know that the thought of meeting a group of dubiously patriotic French officers filled her with horror. He was just trying to do his duty for his country. For La France.

She knew if she let him down now, she would be letting down the whole effort. He and his friends would lose heart. The opportunity for effective action would be lost. Even as she stood there in front of Toulon Cathedral, she felt the fate of the French fleet swaying in the balance. She had to say something. She had to give him hope.

'Come here tomorrow,' she said. 'At the same time. Someone will be here to meet you. To make arrangements.'

'Someone?' He looked wary. 'Who? Why not you, mademoiselle? It is you I have spoken of to my colleagues. It is you they want to meet.'

Helen groaned inwardly. It was getting worse and worse. 'It may not be possible for me to come,' she said, 'but my colleague *Lucien* will arrange things just as well.'

But will he? she thought as she walked away. Paul hadn't shown much interest in this mission so far. Go with your instincts, Ward had said. Just now her instincts were to pack her bags and run as fast as she could for that plane.

It was a long day. Ward slept for most of it while Helen sat at the window, thinking. Then as dusk approached she slipped outside to check the bicycles.

When she came back in Ward looked at her questioningly. 'Aren't you going to pack?' he asked.

Helen swallowed. This was it. This was the moment she

had been dreading. She met his gaze steadily. 'I'm not going,' she said. 'I'm going to stay on. I'll come with you to the plane, but then I'll come back here. There's so much more I can do.'

Ward stared at her. 'Helen,' he said softly. 'You know what that means?'

She knew very well what it meant. It meant she was alone in France with the Germans approaching rapidly, and only the elusive Paul in a position to help her get out.

It was obvious to Katy that George was fretting. Ever since she had picked him up from the café yesterday afternoon he had been cross. He had adamantly refused to set foot in Pam and Alan's house even when Alan came over specially to try to persuade him. This morning he had seemed almost pleased to go to school. Now, though, he wouldn't settle at anything and refused to eat his tea.

'I'm not hungry,' he said, pushing the toasted fingers away.

'Right.' Katy stood up abruptly and picked up her coat. 'In that case we'll go over and see Mum and the baby.'

'I don't want to see the baby.'

'I don't care what you want,' Katy said. 'Your mum will be very sad if you don't go soon. Or do you want to make her sad? Is that what you want?'

He looked away. 'No,' he whispered. 'That's not what I want.'

'Good,' Katy said briskly. 'In that case, let's go.'

Pam was still in bed. The baby was asleep on a couple of towels in Pam's suitcase, which was serving as a makeshift cot.

As soon as she saw them Pam sat up. 'Sweetheart,' she said warmly. 'Are you all right? You were so brave running for help. If it wasn't for you the baby and I might have died.'

George was looking as though he rather wished the

baby had died. He just stood there, silently by the door, his little arms rigid at his sides.

Pam didn't press the point. Instead she nodded towards the suitcase. 'What do you think we should call her?' she asked. 'We thought you might like to choose her name.'

Feeling suddenly choked, Katy glanced down quickly at the tense little boy beside her.

He shrugged with studied indifference. 'I don't know,' he said.

Katy wanted to shake him, but Pam and Alan just glanced at each other.

'We thought of calling her Helen,' Pam said tentatively. 'What do you think about that?'

Katy had to bite her lip hard to stop herself from crying. Oh God, she thought, please let him say yes, please let him smile, please let this work out, even if nothing else does.

George was clearly thinking about it. Thinking hard. And while he thought, the three adults watched him, hardly daring to breathe. The nameless baby slept on regardless.

Then George looked up at Katy. 'Do you think the real Helen would mind?' he asked.

'I think she would be very pleased,' Katy said.

George looked dubious. He scuffed his foot on the fringe of the bedroom carpet. 'I wish she was here so we could ask her,' he said.

'So do we,' Pam said, 'but hopefully she'll be back very soon. Perhaps we could kind of borrow her name for the baby until then?'

George seemed happy with that. Immediately some of the tension went out of his little shoulders and he nodded. 'All right, then.' He glanced at the suitcase. 'Perhaps if it's got the same name the baby will grow up really brave like the real Helen.'

Startled, Katy glanced at Pam and saw her flush slightly as she mumbled a noncommittal reply.

Once again they all waited in silence willing George to

take the next step, and then finally curiosity overcame him and he peered into the suitcase. 'Hello, baby Helen,' he whispered, then suddenly self-conscious, he looked up at Katy accusingly. 'You said she was pretty,' he said. 'I think she looks like a walnut.'

Katy blinked hastily to clear her swimming eyes. 'Well, yes,' she admitted with an apologetic glance at Pam. 'She does a bit, but a very sweet walnut.'

It was as George giggled suddenly and looked back at the baby, that they heard the grumble of a heavy engine as a vehicle pulled up outside. A moment later someone knocked on the front door.

Katy ran quickly downstairs. Opening the door she stared in amazement at the enormous coach parked on the street outside. It was remarkable that it was there at all, but what was particularly odd about it was that it seemed to be absolutely crammed full of very large women.

A rather flustered-looking nurse was standing on the step. 'We've come for Mrs Nelson,' she said briskly. 'We're running a little bit late so I hope she's ready.'

Oh God, Katy thought. In all the panic and worry about George, nobody had remembered to cancel Pam's place at the Surrey maternity hospital. Suddenly Katy started laughing. 'I'm afraid you are more than a little bit late,' she said. 'Mrs Nelson had her baby yesterday afternoon.'

The field was exactly as the RAF instructor had described. At least a mile from the nearest habitation, it was flat, long and grassy and protected by a ring of trees from any prying eyes. Glancing at each other in relief, Helen and Ward left their bicycles hidden in a ditch and settled down under the hedge to wait.

The Lysander came in on the dot of midnight. By the light of their torches it landed perfectly. As it taxied round ready for take-off, and came to a halt, Helen ran forward.

The navigator reached out to help her in. 'No,' she

shouted up at him over the noise of the propeller. 'I'm sending someone else back. A man.'

As she beckoned Ward forward the navigator grabbed her arm. 'I was told to take a girl,' he shouted. 'Nobody mentioned a man.'

'For God's sake,' Helen hissed at him. 'What does it matter who you take?'

He shrugged. 'You know best.'

Helen looked at him, surprised at his rapid capitulation. I hope I do, she thought. Oh God, I hope I do.

'Well, make it snappy, whoever it is,' the navigator called down, and she realised that his desire for a speedy exit outweighed any other qualms. 'We don't want to hang around here all night.'

'Helen.' Ward spoke quietly behind her. 'It's not too late.'

Helen looked at him. Dear Ward. She was going to be lost without him. Earlier he had offered to stay and help her and she had been awfully tempted to accept, but she knew it wasn't fair. Either to him or to Katy. Now she reached up and gave him a short fierce hug. 'Give everyone my love,' she said, pushing him towards the plane. 'Tell them I miss them.'

The hardest thing she had ever done in her life was watch that plane take off.

'So that's it,' she whispered to herself as the noise of the engine receded. Then she brushed the tears from her eyes and walked quickly back to her bicycle.

It was a long lonely bicycle ride from the field back to Toulon, and it was with weary legs that Helen wheeled the bicycle quietly into the hotel yard.

She had told Madame that she was going to be out late, and the old lady had promised to leave the front door on the latch for her. Thankfully she hadn't forgotten.

Locking it behind her, Helen crept silently up the stairs.

Checking that the hair was still stuck across the jamb of

the bedroom door where she had left it, she turned the key as quietly as she could and quickly slipped inside.

At once a shadow detached itself from the wall. She knew who it was. She could see the gun glint in his hand.

Helen stood rigid in shock. There was no point reaching for her pistol. Even if she beat him to the draw, which was doubtful, she knew she couldn't kill him. In any case her hands were shaking far too much to pull the trigger.

'André,' she whispered.

'Yes, Hélène,' he replied coldly. 'It's me. I'm so glad you remember my name.'

Chapter Twenty-Seven

The edges of the room were dark, but outside the sky was clear and a thin waning moon cast an eerie glow across the Moroccan rug on the floor.

'Of course I remember your name,' Helen said. 'How could I forget?'

'How indeed.' His eyebrows rose slightly but the pistol didn't waver. 'So tell me,' he went on. 'Who was the man you've had sharing your room?'

'That was Ward Frazer,' Helen said. 'Katy's husband. He was in danger from your German friends, so I kept him here until I could get him out of the country.'

'Which you have now done?'

'Yes,' she said. 'I knew there was a Lysander coming tonight. I put him on it.'

She felt quite calm. Calm and oddly detached. She realised that if she was going to be shot, she would rather be shot by André Cabillard than anyone else in the world. He was a worthy assassin.

Standing there by the window in the half light of the moon with the pistol in his hand, he looked hard and cold and heartshakingly desirable. She wondered what he was going to do with her. She also wondered how on earth he had found her.

'Please take off your coat, Hélène.'

André's voice was abrupt, and despite what she had been thinking a moment before, she felt a flicker of unease. 'Why?'

'Because you have a gun in your pocket and it occurs to me that they might have sent you over here to kill me.'

'They didn't actually,' Helen said, but she took off her coat obediently and dropped it on the floor in front of her. 'Although I expect they would be pleased if I did.'

'I'm sure they would,' André said coldly. He walked towards her and pushed the coat out of the way with his foot, then he raised his eyebrows and moved his pistol slightly. 'Tell me, Hélène, before I put this away, have you got any other weapons concealed about your person?'

'No,' she said. 'No, I haven't.'

'Good.' He slipped the pistol casually into his pocket. 'Because I want very badly to kiss you and I don't want you stabbing me in the back while I do it.'

He also wanted to use two hands. One to slide round the back of her head, the other to cup her chin so he could rub his thumb over her lips. 'Why did you dye your hair?' he murmured.

She swallowed. 'So you wouldn't recognise me.'

'Well, it didn't work, did it?'

He smiled then, but behind the long, thick lashes, his eyes glittered dangerously, hard as diamonds.

'No,' she whispered. 'André, please, no.'

But it was too late. His kiss was angry, deep and passionate, and, used to his former gentleness, it took Helen completely by surprise. She felt her own anger rise. Felt the tension and agony of the last few months swelling up in her. How dare he? How dare he treat her like this? Like some cheap tart. And yet, even as she kicked and struggled, she became uneasily aware that her body was longing to respond. Shocked, it occurred to her that danger must act as an aphrodisiac and she wondered why Miss Atkins hadn't warned her of that.

Then the nature of his kiss changed slightly and suddenly she wasn't fighting any more. When he pushed her back on to the bed she found it impossible to resist the exploration of his hands on her body, or to prevent her own hands creeping up over his shoulders into his short thick hair, and when he lifted his head and began unbuttoning her blouse she could hardly wait for the closer intimacy. In any case, she thought, there was nothing else she could do, was there? He was the one with a gun, after all.

But after three buttons he stopped abruptly and drew back. 'Goodness me, Hélène,' he said. 'So you are prepared to make love to a traitor, when you weren't prepared to make love to a patriot? What has come over you? Are you trying to lull me into a false sense of security until you can slip your suicide pill into my wine?'

'No,' Helen said. 'I haven't got a suicide pill. They offered me one but I refused.'

'How very British,' he said, 'but how very stupid. Don't you know what the Gestapo would do to you if they got their hands on you?'

'I don't want to know,' Helen said, but something in his tone, in his angry words, made her look at him. Look at him properly for perhaps the first time. 'Anyway,' she said slowly, 'you're not, are you?'

'Not what?'

'Not a traitor.'

Suddenly she was sure, although it wasn't his angry lovemaking that had made her say it. It was something else. Something deeper. Something much more fundamental. Go with your instinct, Ward had said, and just now her instinct was shouting that André was innocent.

She looked at him expectantly, but to her dismay, he stood up and walked to the window. Thrusting his hands in his pockets he glanced up the street both ways then he turned back to face her. 'What makes you suddenly say that?' he asked.

'I just know. Now I'm with you I can just tell.'

'I'm flattered,' he said dryly, 'but, *chérie*, look at the evidence. Agents whom I have met have been betrayed to the Germans. You, yourself, have seen me dining with officers of the SS.'

'I don't care about the SS officers,' she said. 'I'm sure you have your own reasons for that.' She thought quickly, working out the implications. 'But you're right about the other agents. There obviously is a traitor, but it's not you. So who is it? Surely not *Lucien*? It must be his helper, the man who smells?' She stopped as another thought hit her. 'God, it's not someone at SOE HQ, is it? In London?'

André didn't answer. Instead he turned round and once again peered out into the road. Angry now, Helen glanced down at her coat which still lay on the floor with the pistol still in the pocket. Maybe if she moved very carefully she could get the truth out of him at gunpoint.

Before she had even eased her legs off the bed, he had swung round. 'Don't even think about it, sweetheart,' he said.

'Then tell me,' she hissed. 'Tell me what's going on.'

'No,' he snapped back, equally angry. 'You tell me. You're the one who has been sitting comfortably in London, happy to write me off as a traitor while I've been running around here trying to stay alive. So you tell me what's going on, Hélène. You tell me why you are suddenly prepared to come to France and put your trust in a bastard like *Lucien* when you wouldn't put it in me.'

His anger was genuine. Helen felt her heart wrench. But more than the bitterness in his tone she was shocked by the enormity of what he said. '*Lucien*,' she said. 'No. It can't be.' But it could. Suddenly she knew it could. Paul. *Lucien*. The top of the class. The man with initiative.

'Oh my God,' she said.

'He's been working for the Germans ever since he got here,' André said. 'I guessed almost straight away what was going on, but without *Lucien* I had no means of getting word to London. When I tried to contact another agent, he had him killed and used me as a scapegoat. Of course by then he realised I was on to him, so rather than attempt to carry on with my cover story I decided to resume my old life. At least it meant I had somewhere to live, and people to watch my back. And thank God, as yet Paul doesn't seem to know who I really am.'

But he knows who I am, Helen thought. And where I am too.

André caught her expression. 'Yes, you've been lucky,' he said. He was calmer now. Calm and cold. 'Very lucky.'

Helen stared at him. 'Oh God,' she whispered. 'What am I going to do? I've no means of getting back to England now the plane has gone.'

For the first time André looked startled. 'What? You mean you were meant to be on that plane yourself?'

Helen nodded.

'So why did you stay on?'

'There isn't really room for more than one passenger on a Lysander,' she said. 'I wasn't sure that they'd take both of us. Anyway, I hadn't finished the task I came to do.' Quickly she told him about Churchill's letter and the lieutenant commander. How he wanted her to arrange a meeting with other sympathisers. How, if necessary, the ships and the docks were to be blown up before the Germans came.

There was a slight pause when she had finished, then André looked at his watch. 'Right,' he said. 'In that case we'd better get moving. You'll have to come and stay with me until we've dealt with the ships. Don't worry,' he added caustically, catching her start of surprise. 'My father will chaperone.'

'I'm not worried about that,' Helen said. 'I'm worried about *Lucien*.'

'What about him?'

'He's got all the equipment. The explosives. New timer detonators. Limpet mines.'

André frowned. 'Where?'

'I don't know,' Helen said. 'That's the problem.'

André swore softly. 'I have explosives too,' he said, 'but

to blow up the whole damn harbour we'll need everything we can lay our hands on.' He stopped and looked at her. 'Does he know you're still here? Does he know you didn't take the plane?'

'He doesn't even know there was a plane,' Helen said. 'As far as he's concerned I'm leaving on Sunday.'

'Good,' André said. He glanced around the room. 'In that case you'd better leave some things here. Enough to make it look as though you are still living here. We don't want to make anyone suspicious. I'll arrange for Madame downstairs to corroborate the lie. Then maybe we can somehow trick your friend *Lucien* into telling us where the explosives are.'

'He's not my friend,' Helen muttered, but she obediently packed up her few essentials. Whatever she did or did not want to do, staying here was clearly out of the question.

Already André was at the door, but before stepping out he slid his hand into his pocket and waited in silence for a moment, listening. Then he turned back to her. '*Ça va*?'

She nodded. '*Ça va*.' He was good. She had to give him that. He was quick and careful.

It was as she crept after him into the passage that she remembered what had been puzzling her earlier. 'How did you get in without disturbing that hair I'd left?' she whispered.

He shrugged. 'I got Madame to put it back for me.'

'Madame downstairs?' she said, amazed. 'How on earth did you persuade her to do that? Do you know her?'

He glanced back at her and smiled. 'I've never met her before in my life,' he said, 'but most people round here would do anything for a Cabillard.'

Helen had forgotten the power of that smile, but he was right, she realised as she followed him silently down the curving staircase. If he smiled like that again she would do anything for him. Anything.

* * *

Katy was in the middle of changing Malcolm's nappy when the postgirl knocked on the door. Running down to open it, Katy almost snatched the telegram out of her hand.

The postgirl looked surprised. People weren't generally awfully keen on telegrams these days. 'Expecting good news, then?' she said.

'Yes,' Katy said. She was certain that it was from Helen. She had promised to telegram the moment she set foot back in the country, and her week was up today. Bringing the telegram back inside she slit it open quickly.

'Ward Frazer returned safely,' it read. 'Arriving Clapham tomorrow.'

Whoever had sent it had not been overly generous with words, but it still took Katy a minute to take it in. Realising that her legs were about to give way, she pulled up a chair and sat down hastily. Ward was coming home.

Malcolm was crawling around under the bar tables. 'Ugh,' he said indignantly as a chair blocked his path.

Katy looked at him and then around the public bar. This was hers. All hers. It had been a struggle but she had done it. It worked. She had a routine. She had good customers and healthy accounts, and now things were going to change.

It was early afternoon and raining when Helen finally got to see André's home. Despite the less than flattering weather, she fell in love with it the moment they turned in through the pillared gates and first saw it through the hazy drizzle at the end of an avenue of poplars. Long fronted and low with the typical pink roof and creeper-covered stone walls, it was a classic Provençal sixteenth-century *manoir*. Set on a hill in wide landscaped lawns, sheltered by some magnificent old trees, it overlooked the vine-covered countryside in all directions. To one side of the main house was a small chapel, and between it and the vineyard buildings an arch in the high stone wall led into a wide cobbled courtyard.

Turning in through the arch, André parked the van alongside two enormous old crumbling wooden vats. 'Welcome to Domaine St-Jean,' he said. Seeing her look at the vats he shrugged. 'Don't worry. Our wine is a little more hygienic nowadays. These are waiting to be used as firewood.'

Indoors the house was warm and comfortably informal. The wide stone-flagged floors of the main hallway were strewn with faded Persian rugs, two kind-faced mongrel dogs rose, wagging their tails lazily, from in front of the enormous fireplace, and even the portraits of André's ancestors which hung on the walls in gilded frames seemed remarkably relaxed. Some were even smiling.

She wished André was more relaxed. He was courteous, calm and extremely efficient, but he definitely was not relaxed. At least not with her. She had tried to apologise again for misjudging him. She knew he felt she had let him down.

'André, I'm sorry,' she had said. 'I tried to believe in you. I really did. But they made my life hell. The evidence was so conclusive. And then I saw you with those SS officers ...'

It was a mistake. She saw his expression harden.

'They want to commandeer our house for their officers' mess,' he said coldly. 'My father and I had little choice but to agree. In any case, we realised it was a good way of finding out what they were doing, providing we could continue to live there too. The day you saw me I was negotiating them down to one wing of the house.'

Now, as he led her quickly up the wide curving staircase of that very same house, she wondered what she could do to make him smile again. If only she could talk to him, explain more fully the attitude of Angus McNaughton and Maurice Buckmaster. How she had been interrogated and then laid off ...

André didn't give her the chance. Opening the door into a spacious guest bedroom with its own adjoining bathroom, he checked the bed was made up, and pulled the long pale yellow velvet curtains. 'You look tired,' he said. 'You should try to sleep for a couple of hours,' and then he left her to do exactly that.

She was tired, but she was too strung up to sleep. Instead she lay on her back, closed her eyes and allowed the events of the day to churn through her brain.

There had been no surprise in the Café aux Trois Dauphins when she asked to leave a message for *Lucien*. 'Ask him to meet me in Place Puget by the fountain at six o'clock tonight,' she had told the waiter, who had agreed without comment to pass the message on.

She and André had then made their way to the cathedral for her tête-à-tête with the lieutenant commander at ten.

'Ask him to bring his friends to the restaurant I was in with the Germans,' André had said. 'It is safe there. The owner is a friend. Make it Monday night. We'll know by then if we have the equipment.' So she had imparted this information to the young officer and he had seemed pleased to hear it, pleased also that she would be there herself.

'We will come,' he said. 'As many as I can find.'

Now as she lay in the warm feather bed, Helen could hear the rain pattering against the windowpanes. She longed to sleep, but more than that she longed for André to come to her. She desperately wanted to clear the air between them. More than anything she wanted to feel his arms round her.

But when he woke her it was because it was time to go back to Toulon to meet Paul.

'Tomorrow?' Jen's husky exclamation of delight was the loudest noise she had achieved since the operation. 'Oh Katy!' She sat up. 'I bet you can hardly wait.'

'*He* obviously can,' Katy said. 'If he arrived this morning he's hardly hurrying to get home, is he?'

'I expect they want to debrief him first,' Jen whispered, then she giggled. 'Which I dare say is exactly what you'll want to do too.'

Katy thought of Louise and poor agonised Jack. 'He may not want to,' she said. 'I may not want to.'

Jen's eyes widened. 'Don't you?'

'I don't know,' Katy said helplessly. 'It's been such a long time.'

'Good God,' Jen said. 'Don't forget it's Ward Frazer we're talking about here. Of course you'll blasted want to. Damn,' she sighed. 'That means I'd better start looking for a new home.'

'I don't want you to move out,' Katy said. 'Honestly, Jen, you don't have to.'

'Ward won't want me hanging around all the time.'

'I don't care what Ward wants,' Katy said crossly.

Jen stared at her reprovingly. 'Katy,' she said. 'He's your husband, don't forget. He does have a say.'

Katy frowned. She had made the decisions for so long, it was hard to imagine bowing to someone else's wishes. 'Well, he'd better not start throwing his weight around,' she said.

To her surprise Jen just laughed. 'Ward Frazer has never thrown his weight around in his life,' she said. She leaned back on her pillow and shook her head. 'Katy, relax. Honestly, it will be fine.'

'Will it?' Katy said. She wasn't so sure.

Nor was Jen actually, despite her show of confidence. She didn't want to move out of the pub. It hadn't always been easy there, but it felt like home, and despite the anxieties about Malcolm and Ward it had been fun. The thought of living on her own in some bleak lodging house was distinctly depressing.

Sunk in gloom she barely looked up when a probationer nurse came in carrying a plant wrapped in brown paper.

'This has come for you, Miss Carter,' she said.

It was a miniature rose with tiny, exquisite red buds.

'Oh, how romantic.' The nurse smiled shyly. 'Is it from your boyfriend?'

'No,' Jen whispered. 'I haven't got a boyfriend.' She opened the note that came with the plant.

'Dear Jennifer, I was pleased to hear on the grapevine that you had taken my advice. I hope everything went well and that you will soon be back in fine voice. I look forward to seeing you then. Yours, Henry Keller.'

'Well?' The little nurse was watching her eagerly, and to her dismay Jen felt herself blush slightly.

'It's from a producer,' she said. 'Someone who wants me to work for them.'

'Oh.' The nurse looked disappointed. 'Is that all? What a shame.'

'Oh, I don't know,' Jen said. 'At least I might get a job out of it.'

But when the nurse had gone, Jen couldn't help reading the note again. After all, Henry Keller didn't have to send her roses, did he? He didn't have to send her anything at all. He knew that she would get in touch when she was recovered. If she recovered. Just now, it didn't seem all that likely.

'I will recover,' Jen muttered to herself. 'I'll recover so well that I'll blast him with that top C so hard he'll never forget it.'

Helen did not want to meet Paul. Not one bit. She and André and his two henchmen, Jules and Raoul, had discussed it at length, but eventually they had agreed there was no other way of getting their hands on his explosives. It was a risk. A major risk. For all they knew, Paul might already have been in communication with London and would therefore know that Helen's plane had been and gone. Their only hope was that his radio equipment was at his base in Marseilles and he had not been back during the week.

Place Puget was a good place to meet. A wide square, easy to watch. André's men spread out discreetly. André himself waited in a borrowed Citroën hidden down an adjacent side street.

Helen saw Paul at once. He seemed to be alone, sauntering quite casually through the traffic towards her as she stood at the fountain.

'So *Danielle,*' he said. 'What's the news? Has your officer organised a rebellion?'

'No,' she said. 'I haven't seen him again. I think he must have got cold feet.' She tried not to search his face too obviously. She realised she had never really liked him. Never really trusted him. But even now, knowing what she did, it was hard to believe he was a traitor.

He lit a cigarette. 'So what have you been up to?'

'Oh, this and that,' she said. 'Waiting mostly, and even that's pretty nerve-racking. To be honest, I won't be sorry to go home. I've brought the grid reference of the landing field for tomorrow night.' She handed him a slip of paper. 'I know I shouldn't really write it down but I didn't want to get it wrong. It's quite a way away, I'm afraid. The plane is coming in at midnight. It's probably safest if we meet there, isn't it?'

Paul glanced at the paper. 'Okay,' he said. 'We'll meet there at eleven.'

'It's not an easy landing,' she said. 'Especially with so little moon. Do you think you'll be able to bring some men with you? It would be awful if the plane couldn't land.' She wanted as many of Paul's men as possible out of the way.

Paul laughed. 'Don't worry, sweetheart,' he said. 'The plane will land all right.' Something in his voice made Helen shiver. Suddenly she suspected that he was intending to hand her over to the Germans on Sunday night. Not only her, but also the crew of the Lysander.

'So you'll have to deal with the ships,' she said. 'I hope there'll be enough explosives.'

'We'll do what we can.'

'Talking of which,' she went on blandly, 'I forgot to tell you before. Those new timer fuses I brought out must be stored upright and in very cool conditions otherwise there's a danger they can go off. I don't know where you've got them hidden but maybe you ought to check they're okay. It would be awful if the whole lot went up unexpectedly.'

It sounded so fake, and Paul was no fool, but when she looked at him, she was pleased to see that he looked rattled. More than rattled actually. 'Good God,' he said angrily. 'You might have told me before.'

'I know,' Helen said. 'I'm sorry. I meant to mention it to your colleague the other day but he annoyed me so I forgot.'

'Simon? Got a bit fresh with you, did he? I don't blame him. You're a pretty girl, *Danielle.* I wish I could have seen more of you myself.' He winked. 'Still, we'll have time for a nice fond farewell tomorrow night, won't we?'

Somehow Helen mustered a smile. 'I can't wait,' she said. Even to her ears it sounded sarcastic, but Paul didn't seem to notice. He was clearly keen to be off. She hoped he was rushing off to check the fuses. 'See you there, then,' he said. 'At the field.'

Oh no you won't, Helen thought even as she nodded agreement. What's more, with any luck she would never have to see him again.

While André and his cohorts stayed in Toulon, poised ready to follow Paul, one of André's estate workers took her back to the manor, a kindly old man who drove the van with immense care and a lot of gear grinding.

Back at the house she found André's father waiting for her. 'My dear girl,' he greeted her warmly, kissing her firmly on both cheeks. 'I have heard so much about you.

May I call you Hélène? I do apologise for not being here when you arrived. I had business today in Marseilles but André has left me a note explaining everything.' He raised his eyebrows as he poured her a glass of some absolutely delicious red wine. 'I hope your meeting went satisfactorily this afternoon?'

Helen nodded. 'I think so.'

Monsieur Cabillard was a distinguished-looking man, perhaps not quite as tall as André but just as broad shouldered. His face was craggier than André's, the skin more lined. His eyes were blue too, although not that extraordinary deep midnight blue of André's, but they were just as shrewd, and he had the same thick dark hair, albeit slightly silver at the temples, and the same wry smile.

'So now we hope your man will lead André to his cache of explosives?'

'How long do you think it will take?' she asked.

Monsieur Cabillard lifted his shoulders in a negligent gesture so similar to André's that Helen almost smiled. 'Who can tell?' he said. 'But André said you shouldn't wait up for him. There is no danger. They will not attack tonight. So perhaps we will eat something and then you can get some sleep?'

Over a dinner of succulent roast pork and home-grown vegetables served by a plump smiling lady from the kitchen, he talked about the war, the hopeful signs of a turnaround in Stalingrad where relief columns were finally enabling the Russians to fight back, the Allied successes of North Africa and the less good news of the arrival of the German Panzers in Provence.

'There were tanks already in Marseilles,' he said. 'Soon they will be here.' For a moment she saw the deep anger in his eyes then he leaned back in his chair and smiled. 'But you will be glad to know, Hélène, that I have taken the precaution of hiding my best wines. The Boches officers will only be served *vin de table.* From bottles with reserve labels of course.' His eyes twinkled. 'They will not know any better.'

Helen liked him. Even more than she liked his wines. He could not have been more charming nor more courteous, but he was absolutely adamant that she should get to bed in good time.

'The days ahead will not be easy,' he said. 'We must all take our rest while we can.'

But although she took his advice and went to bed she couldn't sleep, and when just before midnight she heard a vehicle pull up outside, she leaped out of bed and ran to the window. She was too late to see André, but she heard him pat the car on the roof and call a low goodbye to the driver.

Back in bed she waited tensely for his footsteps in the passage. Surely he would come to her now, if only to tell her what had happened?

'No, Malcolm, no!' Katy cried, rushing across the bar. 'Leave that! It's dirty.' But she was too late. Malcolm had already plunged his hands into the coal scuttle and selected two pieces of coal. As she advanced on him, he clutched them to his chest protectively, covering his clean pale blue cardigan with ugly black smears. And then even worse, under the impression that she couldn't see him if he hid behind his hands, he dropped the coal and put his filthy hands to his face.

Any other day she might have found it funny, but today she wasn't in the mood for pranks. She had wanted Malcolm to look his best when Ward came home. She had wanted everything to look its best, and to that end she had been working like a slave since the early hours, cleaning and scrubbing the flat and the bars. And now, just as she wanted to stop for a well-deserved cup of tea, not only was Malcolm black from head to toe but he had spread a trail of coaldust all over the clean damp floor.

For an awful second she thought she was going to cry,

and then she heard a movement behind her, a low laugh, a voice …

'I thought the British had banned the use of child chimney sweeps years ago,' it said and Katy felt her heart stop. Once that voice had sent shivers up her spine. Now it froze her into an awful kind of rigor mortis.

She couldn't move. She couldn't turn round. She couldn't do anything. That's it, she thought wildly. I'm stuck here for ever. A gruesome, mummified statue to remind people that this was once my pub.

She saw Ward walk over to the fireplace. 'I guess you're Malcolm,' he said. 'In which case I'm your dad.'

Unfortunately Malcolm chose this moment to uncover his stripy face, and the shock of finding a strange man crouching in front of him caused him to open his mouth and scream blue murder.

'Oh dear.' Ward glanced at Katy. 'I'm sorry …'

At once Katy leaped into action. 'Malcolm. Stop it,' she said as still screaming Malcolm squirmed out of sight under a nearby table. 'It's all right. Malcolm, it's all right.'

'Katy, please.' Ward spoke behind her. 'It doesn't matter. He'll get used to me in time.'

If Katy had wanted to cry before, now she wanted to die. She could hear the disappointment in Ward's voice and it cut her to the quick. Everything was going wrong. Everything.

Ward stepped forward and the next minute she was in his arms, but that wasn't right either. She felt edgy and tense and Malcolm was still bawling under the table.

He tried to kiss her, but agonised by her lack of response she pulled away.

'I'm sorry,' she muttered as his arms dropped to his sides. 'I'm so sorry. It's just such a shock.'

'Didn't you get the telegram?'

'Yes, yes,' Katy said. 'I got it. But even so …' She glanced round wildly and her eyes lighted on the dresser.

'Perhaps a drink?' she suggested. 'Perhaps a drink would help.'

He smiled then, a small wry smile. 'A drink? Helen told me you'd changed but she didn't say you'd taken to the bottle.'

'Helen?' The whisky bottle almost dropped from Katy's hand. 'You've seen Helen?'

He nodded. 'It's thanks to Helen that I'm here. She sent me back in the plane she was meant to take.'

'What? You mean you left her behind?'

Ward flinched. 'I didn't want to, but she insisted. Katy. It was her choice.'

'But how will she get home now?' Katy asked.

'I don't know.'

Katy looked at him and then swung away in despair. He had only been back twenty minutes and she was falling out with him already. And still Malcolm was crying.

As her own tears began to fall she felt Ward take her arm and sit her down at one of the bar tables with a small whisky in her hand.

A moment later after a brief struggle he hauled Malcolm out from under the table. 'You're cute,' he muttered, 'but you're sure as hell noisy,' and dumped him unceremoniously in Katy's lap.

He waited until Malcolm had stopped crying and she had finished the whisky and then he leaned over and took her hand, forcing her to look at him.

'Katy, listen,' he said. 'I know you've changed. Of course you have.' He glanced round the bar. 'You've worked wonders with this place, and you've had to cope with Malcolm all on your own. I can't tell you how much I regret that. But I still think you are the most wonderful person I have ever met. I just have to add admiration to all the other things I feel about you. I am deeply sorry I have caused you additional anxiety. I can't promise I never will again, but I will try. So please don't fight me.'

It was a moving speech. Not only did it take the wind

right out of Katy's sails but it also touched her deeply. As she stared into his face properly for the first time, she saw the tension on his beautiful mouth, the sincerity in his grey eyes and she felt her heart twist. It wasn't easy for her, but it wasn't easy for him either. Suddenly she saw how tired he was, the dark shadows under his eyes, the lines of strain, and she felt guilty for making it harder than it need be.

And then he smiled, a slow, infinitely appealing smile that curled round her heart and squeezed it tight.

'Oh Ward,' Katy whispered. 'Jen was right. She said it would be all right.'

'That Jen's always been a clever girl.'

Having lain awake for a long time hoping André was going to tap on the door, Helen overslept and it was close to eleven when she eventually made her way downstairs.

She found André reading the newspaper with a cup of coffee on a Louis XIV table at his elbow.

'How did it go last night?' she asked.

He stood up at once and went to a sideboard to pour her a cup of coffee. 'It was very satisfactory. Paul led us straight to a farm near Ollioules. We had to leave the car at some distance, but we were able to approach on foot and we saw quite clearly where the equipment is stored, in a building right under the house. No wonder he was concerned it might blow up.' He smiled as he handed her the cup. 'Altogether a good evening's work.'

'You might have let me know you'd got home safely,' Helen said.

'I thought you would be asleep. I told my father to send you to bed early.'

'He did, but I would still have liked to have known what happened.'

He shrugged. 'I didn't want to disturb you.'

She wished he would smile. She wished he would look at her. Look at her the way he used to. With warmth in his eyes.

'So tonight we get the stuff out?' she asked.

He looked at her then. 'Tonight *we* get the stuff out,' he corrected, tapping his chest.

'But—'

'No, Hélène,' he said. 'It's too risky. We need you alive to talk to the officers on Monday. That is more important than anything. In any case, there won't be any problems. My men are well trained. It will be a matter of moments to load the truck.'

It was another long day. Helen felt she had spent her whole time in France waiting, and André's presence didn't make it any easier. Oh, he was polite enough, almost too polite, the perfect host in fact, showing her round the estate, making sure she had enough food and drink, but he wasn't the André she had known in England. That André had been warm, open and utterly charming. This one was cool. Still charming of course, but entirely uninterested. He'd either lost his feelings for her entirely or he had them well hidden behind a bland, faintly antagonistic reserve. She even wondered if he didn't fancy her any more now she was a brunette.

The only time she felt a spark of hope was when she tried to make him promise to come and wake her to tell her what happened.

'Only if you are prepared to take the consequences,' he said, and for a second she saw a glimmer of dangerous light in his eyes.

'I think so.' She couldn't make her feelings clearer than that.

To her dismay he just laughed lightly. 'We will see. When the moment comes.'

He refused to take anything seriously. Even as he shrugged on a thick dark coat after dinner and slid his revolver into the pocket, he was smiling about a derogatory remark his father had said about Adolf Hitler.

'He seems so calm,' Helen said as she and his father stood on the step watching him get into the van.

'That is because he is not afraid,' Monsieur Cabillard said.

'But he must be,' Helen said. Her own nerves were jumping all over the place and she wasn't even going on the raid.

Monsieur Cabillard shook his head. 'André has nerves of steel,' he said. 'He has always been the same, even as a child. Nothing scares him.' He raised his hand briefly as the car pulled away. 'Except the thought of losing the woman he loves.'

Helen stared at him. 'But he doesn't seem to care,' she said slowly as a blush crept into her cheeks. 'Not any more.'

'Oh, he cares all right,' Monsieur Cabillard said dryly, ushering her back indoors. 'He's been like a cat on hot bricks all week since he saw you outside that restaurant. He was hurt when you ran away. Very hurt. He knew what it meant. It was an act of faith that he tried to find you.'

'How did he find me?' Helen asked.

He shrugged. 'I believe there was a police checkpoint?'

She nodded.

'*Alors*, you are a pretty girl. They were happy to give André your name.'

'But even so …'

'The policeman remembered seeing a hotel key in your handbag.' He smiled. 'So André and his men checked every hotel and guest house in Toulon until they found you.' He hesitated. 'But unfortunately you were with another man.'

'That was a prisoner-of-war,' Helen said. 'A friend. Not a lover.'

Monsieur Cabillard nodded. 'But of course André didn't know that,' he said. 'To him it seemed like one more betrayal. He is a proud, passionate man, Hélène. He does not want to make a fool of himself.'

* * *

The first Helen knew of André's return was when she felt a hand gently stroking her hair. For a moment she thought she must be dreaming, but then she smelt the cold fresh air of outdoors, a hint of eucalyptus and lime mixed with a faint tang of tobacco, and with some difficulty she opened her eyes. The room was very dark but she could just make out a shape sitting on the edge of the bed beside her.

'André,' she said sleepily. 'I didn't hear the car. I must have dozed off.'

'So you don't care so much for my safety after all?'

'André, I do.'

'It's okay. Don't wake up. I just came to say it all went as planned and the chapel vaults are now full of gelignite, timer fuses and limpet mines.'

She didn't answer for a moment and she felt his weight lift from the bed. At once her lethargy left her. 'No, André, please, don't go.'

He was very still for a second. 'Hélène, I warned you.' His voice was low.

'I know,' she said. 'But one of us might get shot tomorrow.'

She heard his low exhaled breath and a muttered expletive and then he was taking off his coat. 'If you regret this in the morning it's not my fault,' he said grimly.

'I won't regret it,' she said, but she was somewhat daunted when he didn't stop at his coat and proceeded to take off everything he wore.

Having invited him into her bed Helen suddenly felt desperately shy. It was one thing to fancy him but another to find herself tangled up in his long cold limbs.

'You probably ought to know that I've never done this before.'

'It's all right,' he said. 'I have. I know what to do.'

He was right, although to give him his due he didn't do it straight away. Expecting him to carry on where he left off in the hotel, she was surprised when he seemed prepared to take things slowly. Even his kisses were gentle now, gentle and infinitely sensual. Gradually her whole body began to react. She could feel his hands on her back, her hip, the long curve of her thigh, and all the time his mouth was seducing hers. By the time her nightdress was discarded, she was swept too far along on a tide of desire to worry what his fingers were doing and which limb was where.

But André knew. He seemed to know instinctively what would excite her. Which portion of her anatomy he should next select for his lazy, seductive caresses. Even when she began to get seriously heated, he was calm, languid almost, refusing to hurry, although she couldn't help urging him on to some unknown but extraordinarily appealing destination. It was only towards the end, when she felt the hard glorious strength of him inside her and she found herself writhing under him like a mad thing, that she felt the sudden tension in his shoulders, the low groan in his throat, the clenching of the muscles in his jaw.

And then suddenly, shockingly, a wave of liquid fulfilment broke deep inside her, and at the same moment his whole body froze and she felt the pulsing heat of him, the sweat on his back before he murmured her name and sank on top of her.

For a terrible moment she thought he had died, but his heart was thumping wildly and she smiled to herself. So André wasn't quite as cool as he made out, after all.

But then he levered himself off her abruptly and rolled on to his back at the side of the bed. Dismayed by his abrupt withdrawal, Helen waited for him to speak. She badly wanted him to say something but he didn't. There was silence in the dark room. Complete silence. She could hardly even hear him breathe. Helen felt suddenly desperately emotional. Had something gone wrong? Had he not enjoyed it as much as she had? Did he now regret succumbing to her invitation?

Then he moved and she felt his fingers close on her wrist. She didn't know what she had expected him to say, but what he did say almost made her fall out of bed. His voice was low, but the words quite precise.

'Will you marry me, Hélène?'

Chapter Twenty-Eight

Even after the intimacy they had just shared it was unexpected.

'Are you going to refuse me, Hélène?' he asked softly into the silence. 'I hope not.'

Turning on to her side she levered herself up on one elbow and peered at him through the darkness. 'I … André, you know you don't have to propose to me just because of what happened just now.'

Putting a hand each side of her face he drew her down and kissed her gently on the mouth. 'I am proposing to you because I want you to be my wife,' he said. 'I am proposing to you because I am selfish. I love you and I want you to be mine.'

Helen closed her eyes. He made it seem so easy. If the world had not been at war perhaps it would have been easy, but the truth was that they were both living on borrowed time. By now Paul would know he had been tricked. By tomorrow morning, if not already, the Vichy police and probably the Gestapo too would be searching for her. For Marie Dubois. She had no other papers. No other identity. One road block and she was doomed. And as soon as Paul found out André's real identity, so was he.

'We should have killed Paul yesterday,' she said.

'Is that a yes?' André asked.

Helen groaned. 'André, I would love to say yes,' she said. 'I would love it more than anything in the world, but what's the point?'

'The point,' he said fiercely, 'is that I want you to stay here with me. We will find a way. It's dangerous, I know, but at least we will be together ...'

'Oh André ...' But she didn't get any further. His kiss was hard and passionate and immediately Helen felt her whole body fire up again in response, but to her dismay he drew back.

'I want a verbal answer,' he said. 'Not a physical one.'

'All right,' she said. 'I'll marry you. But when? And how? I've got no papers ...'

'When and how doesn't matter,' he said, pulling her into his arms. 'The intent is all I'm concerned about. Anyway,' he added calmly after a moment, 'we couldn't kill Paul yesterday because we needed him to lead us to the explosives, and we didn't want to arouse suspicion until we had got them safely away. But rest assured he will be dealt with as soon as possible.'

Helen held him tight. That's assuming he doesn't deal with us first, she thought grimly.

'I can't believe it's a year,' Joyce remarked to Celia Rutherford as they ran through their guest list for the café's first anniversary party. 'It doesn't seem five minutes since we first hung that "open" sign up on the door.'

'It is though,' Celia said. She glanced round the room at the eight neat little tables already set for Tuesday's breakfast. 'I don't think we've done too badly, have we?'

Something in her voice made Joyce look up sharply. 'You've got the figures, haven't you? Lorenz must have brought them in while I was at the bank.'

Celia laughed. 'You're too sharp for your own good,' she said.

'Are they all right?' Joyce asked, although she knew they were. She could tell from Celia's carefully controlled excitement that they were all right.

'We've made a profit of one hundred and twenty pounds,' Celia said. Joyce gaped. It was Celia's money of course. It was she who had put in the original investment, she who had paid for the redecoration, the kitchen equipment and the furniture. But Joyce didn't care about that. All she wanted was a job, and if the café was making money, her job was all the more secure.

'It's mostly thanks to old Lorenz,' Joyce said. 'It was him who put us on the straight and narrow.'

Celia disagreed. 'It's mostly thanks to you,' she said. 'I've talked it over with Mr Lorenz and he thinks it's fair if I give you fifty pounds now as a kind of bonus, then next year we'll raise your wages. And we can definitely afford a girl to help with the washing-up and the dirty jobs.'

Fifty pounds. Joyce had never had fifty pounds in her entire life. She didn't know what to say.

'Perhaps that'll mean you won't need a lodger now,' Celia said. She knew Joyce was worried about replacing Miss Philips, who was leaving that evening having been accepted into the Wrens. The teacher had been a perfect lodger, quiet and neat. She had also helped Pete get through his navy engineer selection exams. He'd come in earlier brandishing a letter to say that he had passed, so he'd be leaving home soon too.

Joyce slowly came back down to earth. 'I don't know,' she said. 'It would be odd being there all on my own after all these years.'

Celia hesitated for a moment then glanced back at the guest list. 'Have you asked Jen to the party?' she asked.

Joyce frowned. 'Have you asked Louise?'

'Well, no,' Celia admitted, flushing slightly.

They were both silent for a moment then Celia looked up and, catching her expression, Joyce grimaced. 'We're neither of us much good with our daughters, are we?'

'Well, it's their fault,' Celia said crossly. 'Girls these days think they can have everything their own way. They don't realise in life you have to make concessions, compromise. Take the rough with the smooth.'

Joyce nodded. She wasn't too hot on the smooth but she

reckoned she knew everything there was to know about the rough. With that ghastly, tight-fisted husband of hers, Celia probably did too, although Joyce had to admit that Greville Rutherford had been a lot more obliging recently. At first Joyce had thought it was something to do with the death of their son, but now she wasn't so sure. Something in Celia's manner made her wonder if there wasn't a bit more to it than that. Whatever it was, it had had a dramatic effect, because Greville Rutherford had even agreed to provide the drink for the party, an arrangement which had nearly caused Joyce to drop the teapot she was holding when Celia had told her casually the other day.

'But they're not bad girls deep down, are they?' Celia went on now. 'And let's face it, life hasn't been easy on either of them—'

She stopped abruptly as someone tapped on the door. It was an odd time for anyone to call at the café. Wondering if it was Lorenz come over for a bit of a celebration, Joyce went to the door. Turning off the light she pushed back the blackout curtain and peered out into the November dusk.

The postgirl peered back at her. 'Telegram, Mrs Carter. There was nobody at home so I brought it round here for you. I hope it's not bad news.'

'So do I,' Joyce said. Quickly she ran through her children: Bob safe in a prisoner-of-war camp; Jen safe in hospital; Mick safe in Iceland; Paul and Angie safe in the country. And Pete was at home having his tea.

Feeling slightly reassured she switched the light back on and slit open the envelope: 'I regret to inform you that your husband Mr Stanley Robert Carter passed away this morning at ten o'clock after suffering a ruptured appendix. Please notify re funeral arrangements.'

Joyce stared at it and then sank into a chair.

Through a dim haze she heard Mrs Rutherford's anxious voice. Felt her hand on her arm. 'What is it? Mrs Carter, what's happened?'

'Stanley,' she said. 'Stanley's dead.'

'Dead?' Celia blinked. 'Oh, Mrs Carter. How dreadful. I am sorry.'

'He's dead,' Joyce said. Her voice was a monotone. 'He's dead. I can't believe it. I can't believe it.'

Celia was looking at her in concern. 'We'll cancel the party,' she said. 'You'll want a funeral.'

'I don't want to cancel it.'

'Well, we'll delay it, then. Put it off a week or two.'

Joyce shook her head. 'No.' She tested her emotions to see how she felt really. The numb shock and flash of guilt that had hit her when she read the telegram were already passing off, leaving an extraordinary sense of relief. That's what she felt. Relief. *Relief.*

Feeling Celia's hand on her arm she looked up. 'No,' she said. 'I don't want to organise a funeral. Why should I? Let the prison do it. We'll have the party, and we'll enjoy it. I've let that bugger spoil enough of my life already. I'm damned if he's going to carry on doing it from beyond the grave.'

Twelve French naval officers came to Helen's meeting. It wasn't many, but it was better than nothing, and the young lieutenant commander assured her that there were more sitting on the fence who might be persuaded once the first meeting had taken place. They came in dribs and drabs, and as soon as they entered the restaurant they were ushered through to a private room at the back where Raoul and Jules frisked them quickly before handing them on to André's friend, the *maître d'*, who placated them with wine and canapés.

Helen herself arrived in the Cabillard delivery truck, hidden among two dozen crates of wine. As the German occupation force got ever closer, preceded by fleeing Jews, deserters and other 'undesirables', the Toulon police were getting increasingly jumpy and André was not prepared to risk her being asked for her papers if the truck was stopped.

Being bumped along in pitch darkness in the back of the truck was nerve-racking enough, but it was nothing compared with walking into a room full of uniformed men and having to try to persuade them to disobey orders and join the Allied cause.

She told them that the whole world's eyes were on them. That to a certain extent the whole outcome of the war lay in their hands. That their actions would influence how France was viewed internationally in years to come. They could strike a blow now, she told them steadily, for the freedom of the country or they could hand themselves over with their ships as toadies to the Germans.

The officers sat impassively. It was hard to gauge their reaction. They were clearly nervous and seemed reluctant to meet each others' eyes let alone hers. It was hardly surprising. They knew they were putting themselves on the line: one dissenter among them could ruin the careers and lives of them all.

When Helen had finished, André spoke to them about the explosives he now had available. Whatever happened to the ships, he said, he would ensure that the munition dumps, the oil tanks, and all the equipment and stores of value in the naval arsenal would be blown up, along with the coastal gun batteries.

'We don't have enough explosive to take care of the ships,' he said. 'They remain your responsibility. We are still hoping they can sail to join the Allies.'

'The harbour entrance is mined.' One of the more senior officers spoke for the first time. He hadn't introduced himself, nobody had, but Helen recognised him from the pictures she had studied at her SOE briefing as Captain Meynier, the commander of one of the submarines. *Glorieux*, she thought. Or it might have been *Casabianca*. Either way he looked as though he knew what he was talking about. 'So it is unlikely the larger ships could get out safely in any case,' he said.

Helen glanced at André. This was an unexpected blow,

but André took it in his stride. In fact he almost looked pleased, and she realised that the comment had at least shown a definite commitment to the cause.

'It is a risk,' he said, 'but I believe it is a risk that would be worth taking. France is a proud country. We are proud of our fleet, but for the greater good of our country, for our national pride, for our standing in the world of the future, I believe we must all be prepared to make sacrifices.' His voice lowered slightly as he went on. 'Many of our countrymen have already given their lives for the sake of freedom. I hope we would be prepared to do the same.'

I love him, Helen thought as a lump of emotion formed in her throat. I love him and respect him and admire him so much that at this precise moment I would be prepared to die for him. From the wide-eyed look on the officers' faces and the sudden squaring of their shoulders as he shook their hands, thanked them and left the room, she surmised that they felt much the same.

'How long have we got?' the young lieutenant commander asked as she too headed for the door.

Helen looked at him. A new fervour shone in his eyes. 'I honestly don't know,' she said. The German tanks were already at Aix. 'A few days. Probably not longer than a week?'

'Tomorrow I will give the letter to the admiral,' he said grittily. 'Even if I have to hand it to him myself.'

Helen smiled. 'Thank you,' she said. 'It will be much easier if de Laborde is on our side. And now I will leave you. There may be things you want to discuss among yourselves. I will ask the *maitre d'* to bring in some more wine.'

Leaving the room, Helen found André standing at the café's long zinc bar nursing a Pernod. As she approached he turned to face her and she was shocked by the grim expression in his eyes as he held out his hand to her.

'What is it?' she said. 'What's the matter? Didn't you think it went well?'

He pulled her close to him. ‘I think it went very well,’ he said, ‘and you were wonderful. But something else has happened … *Lucien* and his friends have been to your hotel.’

‘So they’re looking for me,’ she said. ‘Well, we knew it would happen.’

André nodded. ‘Yes, but it’s rather worse than that,’ he said. ‘They interviewed Madame as to your whereabouts.’ He saw her expression. ‘She didn’t tell them anything,’ he said. He hesitated. ‘Although I’m afraid they took measures to make her.’

‘What?’ Helen whispered. She could see the pain in his eyes. ‘What measures? What did they do?’

‘They systematically broke the fingers of her right hand.’

‘Oh André.’

He put his arm round her. ‘I know,’ he said. ‘It’s horrible. But she is being looked after. She is getting the best possible medical treatment.’ He shook his head. ‘She is a tough old lady. I gather she is proud to have done her bit.’ He hesitated. ‘And knowing what the enemy is capable of, it could have been worse.’

Hardly, Helen thought, but she could not speak. She had put that poor old lady in danger. Put her through terrible pain. It was awful. Completely awful.

André was holding her close against him. ‘Don’t take it too hard,’ he murmured into her hair. ‘If nothing else it proves that what we are doing is right.’

Katy was delighted with how easily Ward fitted into the life of the pub. He didn’t interfere with her systems and habits although he did raise his eyebrows when she admitted that her finances and accounts were handled by a fifteen-year-old boy. For her part she was worried about his leg, which obviously gave him some pain, but when she tried to talk to him about it he said it was perfectly all right.

'You look like the cat that got the cream,' Molly Coogan murmured wistfully to Katy. 'Not that you don't deserve it of course.'

Following Molly's gaze over to where Ward was chatting to Mr Lorenz in the corner, Katy smiled. She was lucky. She knew it. She also knew she couldn't wait for the pub to close so she and Ward could go to bed. Last night had been the most perfect reawakening she could have possibly imagined. She knew she was glowing and she didn't care if people noticed it.

'Everyone deserves a bit of luck now and again,' she said now, 'and a bit of happiness. Even you, Molly.'

Molly made a face. 'Maybe I'll find it down in Surrey,' she said.

Katy made a sympathetic face. 'You're definitely going, then?'

'I reckon so,' Molly said. 'If I'm not going to get married and have fifteen children, I'll have to put some effort into my career instead.' She sighed gloomily. 'Being a spinster's not the end of the world. Old Sister Morris seems happy enough with her lot.'

'Oh, I don't know,' Katy said. 'Jen reckons Sister Morris has a soft spot for that surgeon, Mr Goodacre, who operated on her throat.'

'Really?' Molly's eyes widened to saucers. 'Poor Mr Goodacre, imagine being assaulted by all that starch. Do you think he meets her standards of godliness and hygiene?'

'She'd probably pop him in the steriliser first,' Katy giggled.

Katy was glad to see Molly laughing, but when Louise came in with Aaref a few minutes later the smile soon faded from her lips.

'Ward!' Louise cried. 'I heard you were back,' and rushing across the bar she flung herself into his arms.

'There,' Molly hissed at Katy. 'How do you feel now?'

'Amused,' Katy said, catching Ward's desperate expression over Louise's head.

'Fancy a drink, Molly?' Aaref asked casually.

'No, thank you,' Molly said, shrugging on her hospital cloak over her uniform. 'I was just on my way out. I've got masses to do before I go on Saturday.'

'Go?' Aaref looked startled. 'Where are you going?'

'To Surrey,' Molly said shortly. 'I've been offered a maternity job there. I did tell you the other day, but you obviously weren't listening.'

Katy was pleased to see that Aaref looked rather taken aback, but before he could say anything Louise was dragging Ward up to the bar.

'Oh Katy,' she cooed. 'Isn't it simply wonderful to see Ward again?'

'Yes,' Katy said. 'It is.'

Ward smiled. 'I hear you have a wonderful husband of your own now, Louise?'

Actually he had heard rather more than that from Katy as she lay gossiping happily in his arms last night, but you wouldn't have known it from his blandly congratulatory expression.

'Well, yes,' Louise said rather less exuberantly. 'Jack. You'll probably meet him actually, because he's coming back on Thursday.'

'Oh Louise,' Katy said. 'How lovely for you. You must be so pleased.'

Louise smiled a slightly wobbly smile. 'I am.'

'I look forward to meeting him,' Ward said. 'Katy says he's a really great guy.'

Louise looked at her fingernails. 'Well, Mummy's asked us to the café party on Friday evening, so if all goes well you'll meet him then. You are going, aren't you?'

'Oh yes,' Katy said. 'Molly's promised to hold the fort here.' She glanced thoughtfully at Aaref. 'Perhaps you wouldn't mind popping in as well, Aaref? I don't like to think of her here all on her own. She's not as tough as she makes out.'

Jen was eating her dinner when Joyce came in, although 'eating' was perhaps a slightly over-optimistic term to use. What she was actually doing was staring at a large piece of grey ox liver floating in a plateful of thin gravy and wondering how on earth she was ever going to get it down her throat without her tastebuds noticing.

As the door opened she looked up eagerly hoping for a reprieve. When she saw her mother standing there, her face stiffened. For a moment neither of them spoke and then Joyce came in and closed the door.

'Goodness,' Jen said sarcastically. 'A visit from my mother. What an honour. And I've only been here a week.'

Joyce ignored her. 'I've got some bad news for you,' she said. 'Your father's dead.'

'What?' Suddenly all Jen's self-righteous indignation faded. 'How? When? He's in prison. People don't die in prison.'

Joyce handed her the telegram. 'Well, he has,' she said.

Jen read it in silence, wishing she felt more upset. She had never got on with him, of course. He had always been too ready with his fist. Particularly when he was in his cups, which was most of the time. Still, he was her dad and he was dead.

'Poor old Dad,' she said, pushing the telegram back towards Joyce.

Joyce picked it up and put it in her handbag impassively.

Jen stared at her. 'You don't care, do you?' she said, attacking her mother for the very lack of emotion she had a moment before recognised in herself. 'I reckon you're pleased.'

She thought Joyce would deny it, but to her surprise, she just shrugged. 'I'm not pleased,' she said, 'but I'm not sorry either. He wasn't too bad in his younger days, but you know as well as I do that over the last few years he has caused me a lot of trouble and a lot of physical pain. More than anything I feel relief. Now at least I can get on and live my own life.'

Jen was astonished by her composure. She also realised that her mother was looking remarkably clean and tidy in a smart belted coat and a small felt hat over her recently permed hair. Even the handbag was new.

'I suppose that means marrying old Lorenz?' she said.

Once again her mother surprised her. 'I'm not sure,' Joyce said. 'I don't reckon I'm ready for that, but it is possible, I suppose. In time.' She hesitated and glanced at Jen. 'Would you mind?'

Startled by the question, Jen shook her head. 'No, not particularly,' she said. 'For a Jew, he's not a bad bloke.' She could hardly object now, could she? Not after Lorenz had paid for the operation and for the private room. Whatever he had said about no strings. She rallied slightly. 'Anyway, what do you care whether I mind or not?'

Joyce glanced across at the flowers on the windowsill, then she took a deep breath and sat down on the edge of Jen's bed. 'Well, it might sound odd,' she said, 'but I do care. I know I haven't been much of a mother to you, what with one thing and another.' She glanced up quickly and then away again. 'You was always so pretty and bright. I reckon I always felt you were going to escape and leave me with no money and no hopes for anything other than avoiding a black eye on a Saturday night.'

Joyce paused for a moment and then went on. 'Since I've had the café I understand a bit more now. About you wanting to do your own thing and that. And I'm pleased that you've done so well with your singing. Anyway,' she was rushing a bit now, keen to get the words out before she changed her mind, 'I wondered, what with Ward Frazer coming back, and Pete going, and Miss Philips joining the

Wrens, whether you might want to move back into the house when you come out of hospital?'

Once the offer was out Joyce stopped abruptly. Jen knew her mother had her pride, and she knew how much it must have cost her to have said what she had. Even now she could also tell from Joyce's braced shoulders that she was preparing herself for a scornful refusal.

It was a poignant moment, and only by sitting rigidly still could Jen control the choking feeling at the back of her throat. She certainly couldn't trust herself to speak.

When she didn't answer, Joyce looked away. 'It's only a thought,' she said gruffly, picking up her handbag and sliding it on to her arm. She stood up. 'It might not work out. You don't have to say yes or no now, but at least think about it.'

She was already at the door when Jen managed to speak. 'All right,' she mumbled. 'I'll think about it.' It was more of a husky croak than a gracious acceptance but it was the best she could do and Joyce looked quite pleased.

'I'll send you over a bit of food tomorrow and all,' she said, nodding at the plate of now congealed liver still sitting on the tray on Jen's lap. 'You can't eat that muck. You need building up after what you've been through. You're much too thin.'

It was one concession too many. To her horror Jen found her eyes were suddenly swimming with tears. She looked up at the door in panic, but thank God Joyce had gone. It would be mortifying to be caught blubbing just because Joyce had shown a bit of motherly interest for the first time in twenty years.

By Wednesday, 26 November 1942 two German Panzer divisions had almost encircled the Toulon area. That afternoon half a dozen SS officers took up residence in the east wing of the Domaine St Jean.

'Ah yes,' André murmured as the flagged staff cars came

roaring up the long drive. 'I must remember to sharpen some stones. Nails in the tyres would be too obvious.'

Helen smiled. 'You're wicked,' she said.

'Oh, I'm wicked now, am I?' André said as he prepared to go out to meet them. 'And yet in bed this morning you thought I was so lovely.'

'You are,' Helen said. 'Very lovely.'

He was. He was more than lovely. He was wonderful. For the last three days he had offered her a glimpse of heaven. Never had she imagined finding such total fulfilment. The fact that they spent much of the time together preparing the explosives, briefing their team and agonising over plans of the harbour, was irrelevant. They were together and that was all that mattered. She was glad now that André had asked her to marry him. Their engagement was like a seal. A seal of faith. Whatever happened, they were bonded together.

It wasn't just the days. It was the nights too. The times they spent in bed were times of intense joy. And the colour of her hair in no way detracted from André's desire for her. He was amazed when she mentioned her earlier fear.

'Good God,' he said. 'It wasn't your hair I was worried about. It was you. After that awful scene in the hotel, I thought if I touched you again, I'd scare you off forever.'

Helen smiled, 'You couldn't scare me off if you tried.'

On the contrary, the passion, tenderness, the excitement and the very fact of lying in André's arms were like a culmination, an expression of all the pleasure she felt in his company. In a strange stirring way it was like coming home. A sensation of harmony and safety, detached from the real world. A perfect dream. She knew that André felt it too.

But they both also knew that dreams couldn't last. That evening, lying entwined under the covers as the euphoria of their abandonment faded into a mellow contentment, Helen could tell that André was tense. She knew he was worried that the Germans would move forward unexpectedly. The last thing he wanted was for them suddenly to close the gap between the house and Toulon. It would be impossible to get a truckload of explosives through the German lines. On the other hand there was no point in taking the stuff to the harbour until it was needed, because there was nowhere to hide it. It was a fine balance and she knew it was preying on his mind.

'If only blasted de Laborde would give the order to scuttle,' Helen whispered into the darkness, 'then we could get on with it.' She knew that it was already too late for the ships to sail. One hint of them putting to sea and the Germans would be blasting through the streets of Toulon like there was no tomorrow.

'I know,' André said. 'But—'

Before he could go on they both heard the creak of a footstep in the passage outside the door. André was out of the bed and at the door, gun in hand, before Helen had even reached for her dressing-gown.

There was a light tap on the door and they heard Raoul's low voice. 'Monsieur André, I'm sorry to disturb you, but a message has come.' A moment later a scrawled note was pushed under the door. The sudden glare of light as André switched on the lamp made Helen blink. Quickly she made her way to his elbow. In silence he held out the note: 'Germans preparing to move in.'

'This is it,' he said.

Dropping the note on the bed Helen looked at him and felt her heart shake. She was glad when he took her in his arms.

'We'd better get dressed,' she said unsteadily after a moment.

André didn't let her go. He took a slow breath and spoke into her hair. 'I don't want you to come.'

'But you need me,' she said, pulling back to look at him. 'I've got the plan, I know the layout. We've planned it all so carefully.'

'I know,' he said, 'but I don't want to lose you.' He closed his eyes and when he opened them again his expression was agonised. 'I lost you once and I don't think I could bear it a second time.'

Helen knew what he meant. She was scared for him too. Desperately scared. God only knew what lay ahead of them in Toulon but it certainly was not going to be a picnic. Ranged against the combined might of the Germans and the Vichy police and much of the French navy, their small band of rebels seemed pitifully inadequate. It would be a miracle if any of them got out alive.

Taking a deep breath, she kissed André on the chest. She could feel his heart beating strongly under her trembling lips. A moment later she looked up at him and smiled. 'You won't lose me,' she said. 'From now on I'm sticking right by your side. I'm not going to get lost again.'

24 November 1942

Dear Mum,

Thanks for the toad-in-the-hole. It was the best food I've eaten in months. And thanks too for offering me my room back. Mr Goodacre told me this morning that I should be ready to leave here by Friday, so if it's still all right I'd like to accept your offer of a room. I know we haven't seen eye to eye in the past but maybe we've both changed a bit now. Anyway, if I get on your nerves again you must say and I'll find somewhere else.

Yours, Jen.

P.S. You must tell me how much you want me to give you for keep and that.

25 November 1942

Dear Jen,

Thanks for the note. I'll get your room ready for Friday. We'd best wait until you are working again to discuss keep. I don't know if you'll feel up to it, but Mrs Rutherford and I are having a little party that night to celebrate a year at the café. Katy and Ward are coming and your old friends the Miss Taylors and Mrs Frost, and I've also taken the liberty of inviting Mr Goodacre who I bumped into on my way out yesterday. If there's anyone else you'd particularly like to be there do ask them.

Love, Mum.

P. S. I thought you might like a slice of apple pie to go with the lamb casserole.

26 November 1942

Dear Sister Morris,

My mother has asked me to invite you to a little party she is having at her café tomorrow evening. I do hope you will be able to come.

Yours sincerely,

Jennifer Carter.

Chapter Twenty-Nine

The late evening wireless news on 26 November was ecstatic. Or as ecstatic as the deliberately deadpan BBC radio newsreaders could get.

The defeated Axis forces were in full retreat across Libya. American forces were poised to trap them at the Tunisian border. In Stalingrad the Soviet troops had smashed comprehensively through the German lines and seventy-seven thousand German soldiers had been killed or taken prisoner.

Hoping for news of events in France, Ward was lying on the bed with his hands behind his head watching Katy giving Malcolm his last feed when they heard a man shouting her name outside.

'Who on earth … ?' Ward reached over to turn off the wireless. 'Is this some ardent lover you forgot to tell me about?'

'Of course it's not,' Katy said. She peered out of the window. 'Goodness, it's Jack. Louise's Jack.' Louise had been hanging around all day waiting for Jack, but he hadn't come and eventually she had given up and gone sadly back to her flat on her own.

Jack shouted up again. 'Oh dear,' Katy said. 'His words are rather slurred.'

Ward groaned. 'Shall I get a bucket of water?'

Katy giggled. 'I'll have to go down. I think Malcolm's had enough anyway. I'll put him in his cot.'

Resignedly Ward got up and pulled on his trousers. 'I'll

come with you. I'm not having you getting assaulted by some drunken lout.'

'Jack Delmaine is far too much of a gentleman to assault anyone,' Katy said.

But Jack Delmaine was looking far from gentlemanly as he staggered into the pub a minute later. His uniform was in complete disarray. His face was blotchy and his hair looked as though he'd dunked it in beer. From the smell of him he probably had.

'Jack?' Katy gasped, pulling out a chair and steering him on to it. 'What's happened?'

Jack seemed to have some difficulty in explaining what had happened.

'What's happened is that he's had far too much to drink,' Ward said and Jack nearly jumped out of his skin.

'Glood Glod,' he shouted. 'Who's that?'

'That's my husband,' Katy said, biting back a giggle as Jack's eyes goggled in astonishment. She grimaced at Ward. 'We'll have to get him sobered up. Louise will die if he turns up like this.'

'I love Louise,' Jack announced, the first really coherent words he had uttered.

'Well, that's something,' Katy said. She rolled her eyes. 'You know, I think that bucket of water might come in handy after all.'

'I love Louise,' Jack said again, this time to Ward.

Ward nodded. 'Good. I'm glad, and I'm sure she loves you too,' he said, 'but I want to go to bed with my wife and so you'd better sober up pretty sharpish.'

It took them an hour, by the end of which Jack, damp haired and repentant, was dressed in a set of the clothes Ward had bought himself only that morning at Arding & Hobbs with a couple of Katy's spare coupons and a wad of cash out of the till. All his old clothes had been lost when his aunts' house was bombed last year.

'I'm really grateful,' Jack said to Katy now. 'I knew you

would help me. It's just that I feel so worried about seeing her after what happened …'

'Good God, there's no need to be worried.' Ward slapped him on the shoulder bracingly as he steered him inexorably towards the door. 'She's only a woman, after all. You don't have to put up with any nonsense from them. Anyway, they respect you more if you're tough with them. I hadn't seen Katy for over a year and I soon sorted her out.'

Not altogether pleased by this homily, Katy made a rude face at him but Jack looked distinctly impressed.

'Righto,' he said, squaring his shoulders. 'I'll remember that.' Then realising he might have slightly outstayed his welcome he nodded awkwardly. 'Well, I'll be off, then. Goodnight.'

'Nice guy,' Ward said as they closed the door behind him.

Katy stared at him incredulously, then she leaned back against the door and started laughing. 'I love you,' she said. 'Only you could spend half the night helping someone vomit and then say they were a nice guy.'

He laughed too. 'And only you, my darling, would have let him in in the first place, so I reckon we're quits. And I love you too.'

Driving without lights André threaded the truck cautiously through the dark streets of Toulon towards the harbour. Before setting off he had splashed a coat of paint over the vineyard logo on the sides of the truck to give them some anonymity. Squashed up against him Helen wished the smell of the paint didn't make her feel so nauseous. Wedged between her and the door were two of André's men, submachine-guns on their laps. Two spare belts of ammunition slithered back and forth on the dashboard. Three more men were sharing the back with the explosives.

Nobody said much. They were all tense, staring fixedly

out of the dusty windscreen. Even from within the vehicle they could sense the strange waiting atmosphere in the darkened city. Some of the streets were deserted, but in the centre people were hurrying about, heading home to their loved ones, or to friends. Others, hanging about on the street corners or huddled in groups under the palm trees, clearly had nowhere to go. These were the dispossessed, who having been driven like fleeing animals ahead of the German advance, were now trapped in Toulon and knew their time was running out. Over the last few days their numbers had swelled. Some were deserters from the German army, others innocent victims of the advance, driven out of their homes by the Germans' need for accommodation and food. Mostly, of course, they were Jews.

'Poor buggers,' André muttered. 'We'll have to do something about them next.'

Helen glanced at his hard profile. 'Oh André,' she said. She knew he would too. He'd probably end up with a couple of dozen of them living in the chapel crypt right under the SS officers' noses. 'But how … ?'

As the words left her mouth she saw the road block ahead. At the same moment André slammed his foot on the brake and the truck skidded to a violent halt.

Flinging his arm across to stop her going through the windscreen, André slammed into reverse. 'Get down!' he shouted, and as one, Helen and the two men dived into the footwell. The tyres screamed. The truck swerved backwards then swung round in a fog of exhaust fumes. Trying not to lurch against André's legs Helen forced herself not to mind that her face was pressed hard up against Raoul's buttocks.

André swore as they bumped a parked car. There was a shriek of metal tearing, the smell of burning rubber, and then they were roaring away, screeching round a corner, even as a spatter of police bullets hit the side of the truck. The window broke with an explosion of flying glass.

'Is everyone all right?' André shouted over the crashing of gears.

There was a murmur of assent as the three of them eased themselves gingerly up off the floor. Helen glanced through the tiny slit of a window into the back of the truck. The three men there were looking shaken but alive. One of them gave her a thumbs-up. She smiled. On the whole she would prefer her nose to be pressed up against someone's buttocks than against a box of sweating gelignite.

'We're not going to get through,' André said a minute later, pulling up in a dark alley and switching off the engine. 'We can't afford to get shot at or the whole bloody lot will go up.' Quickly he briefed the men. 'We'll have to separate and go in on foot. You know the weakest points in the defences and you know what targets you've each been allocated. Prepare them but don't let anything go up until I give the signal, or until the Germans are right on the dock. We must give the ship captains as much time as possible. *Eh bien.*' He grinned and shook hands with each man. '*Bonne chance.* And for God's sake don't get caught.'

'He's not going to come,' Louise wailed. 'I was going to try so hard to be good this time, and now he's not going to come. Oh Aaref, what am I going to do?'

They were sitting on the edge of Louise's mattress, where they'd been ever since Aaref had found her sobbing on the stairs. The tears were over now but her despair had not abated. Aaref put his arm round her shoulders and squeezed her tight.

'He'll come tomorrow,' he said. 'I'm sure he will. I expect the trains—' He stopped abruptly, hearing a clink on the fire escape outside. A moment later the door burst open, the blackout curtain was pushed to one side and Jack came in.

For a moment he stood blinking myopically at the sudden light, and then he took in the scene on the bed and his face darkened. 'What the hell are you doing in here?' He took a step forward and Aaref scrambled hastily to his feet.

'Jack, it's not what you think,' Louise cried, getting up too and trying to catch Jack's arm.

Jack brushed her off, his eyes fixed on Aaref. 'She's my wife and I'm sick of seeing you pawing her about,' he said. Then as Aaref raised his hands placatingly and began to speak, Jack lost his cool. 'I've had enough of you,' he muttered and punched him on the nose.

'Jack!' Louise screamed as Aaref fell back on the bed. A second later blood began to trickle over his lips. White with shock, Louise stared in horror from one to the other.

Jack was rubbing his knuckles. 'Leave him alone,' he snapped as Louise went to kneel on the bed. Louise stopped in her tracks, and he barely glanced at her. 'It's your fault as well.'

Clearly dazed, holding a hand to his pouring nose, Aaref slowly got to his feet and headed for the door.

Jack opened it for him. 'I say, I'm awfully sorry,' he said.

'It's all right,' Aaref mumbled.

Louise stared in amazement as they shook hands, then she rounded on Jack. 'It's not all right,' she shouted. 'You can't come in here punching my friends.'

Jack closed the door. For a second he stood with his back to her, then slowly he turned round. 'I can,' he said grittily. 'I'm your husband and I can do what I damn well like. And you'd better remember it, my flirty little wife. I'm not going to put up with your high jinks any more.'

Louise gaped. He had never spoken to her like that before. Never. Nor had he ever looked so angry. So powerful. 'Oh Jack …' she breathed.

His eyes narrowed. 'Don't "oh Jack" me,' he snapped. 'Just get your kit off and lie down.'

There was a strange atmosphere in the port. A kind of

dark ominous hush, broken only by the occasional roar of planes overhead. Junkers, Helen thought, listening to their engines rattling unevenly in the darkness while André clipped a hole through the perimeter fence.

A moment later they were climbing through, dragging the boxes of explosives after them.

As they straightened up on the other side, André touched her arm. *Ça va?*'

She nodded. '*Oui, ça va.*'

Flitting from shadow to shadow, avoiding the armed guards, the port personnel, the odd hurrying sailor, Helen and André located their allocated targets – five ammunition depots, two oil silos and two towering cranes – and carefully positioned the strips of gelignite. Later the fuses would need igniting, but for now they needed to ensure the explosive was fixed at the most vulnerable point of each target. It wasn't easy and several times they were forced to crouch in silence, as footsteps approached, praying that they would not be discovered. With André's strength and Helen's deft fingers they made a good team. They worked quickly and efficiently.

Suddenly there was a commotion high up on the enormous superstructure of one of the nearby ships. It was one of the great battleships, the *Colbert*, moored right next to the mighty *Strasbourg*, lead ship of the fleet. Pulling out André's binoculars Helen squinted up. Some sailors had stormed the bridge. Even as she watched, one of them grabbed a loudspeaker and suddenly a voice rang out. '*Vive de Gaulle! Vive la France libre!* Let us sail for Algeria now!'

Everyone was staring. Beside her André straightened up. 'Good God,' he said, but even as he spoke the sailors were overpowered and removed. They could see the tension among the crews on other ships as they waited for a command, any command.

Then, just as Helen and André were about to withdraw back into the shadows, they saw a group of officers walking briskly along the quay towards the *Strasbourg*.

'Look,' Helen said. 'It's the lieutenant commander. I must go and speak to him.'

'No.' André pulled her back. 'It's too dangerous.'

'André, I must …'

'Hélène, please …' but it was too late. She was already out in the light, running along the quay.

She caught them up at the gangplank to the *Strasbourg*.

The lieutenant commander recognised her at once and drew her quickly to one side. 'I gave Admiral de Laborde the letter,' he said, 'and I told him about the meeting. I wanted him to know that I am not the only officer who wishes to prevent the fleet falling into German hands.'

'What did he say?'

'He said he has Hitler's word that provided the French fleet does not take action against German forces, it will remain neutral and under French command.'

'Hitler's word?' Helen said angrily. 'Since when did Hitler ever keep his word?'

The lieutenant commander shrugged helplessly. 'The admiral is an honourable man. He will not break that trust unless the Germans do.'

'And then it will be too late,' Helen said bitterly. She looked up at the towering grey flank of the great battleship behind them. 'The Germans will overrun the port, the officers will be ordered off, and all these gallant ships will become theirs.'

The lieutenant commander lifted his chin and Helen saw the pride flash in his eyes. 'I don't think the officers will leave their ships,' he said. 'Not without a fight. Word of resistance has spread. You heard just now the attitude of the matelots. I think most of the captains will hold fast until the end.'

It was what she wanted to hear. She wondered why it made her feel so choked. She smiled as she held out her hand. 'Then all I can say now is good luck, and thank you. We are all in your debt.'

He inclined his head as he shook hands, then to her

surprise he came to attention and saluted her. 'The debt is ours,' he said. 'You have given us hope, and courage. I doubt whether that can ever be repaid.'

Feeling even more choked, Helen ran back to the spot where she had left André, but there was no sign of him and she felt a shiver of anxiety. Where was he? Making her way quickly along the dock, peering into every alley and shadow, Helen suddenly heard a strange distant rumbling and stopped abruptly in her tracks.

Tanks, she thought. It could only be tanks. German tanks in the streets of Toulon.

Suddenly people were running all over the place. Somewhere behind her by the Arsenal Maritime a shrill police whistle pierced the night air.

'Oh God,' she muttered. 'Where are you, André?'

And then she saw him, backed up against a dark wall. He looked unnaturally still. His hands wide and stiff. There was clearly something very wrong, and then she saw what it was.

A few yards away from him, deep in the shadows, was another man. Paul. And in his hand was a gun. A gun trained on André. His finger was tense on the trigger, but, being Paul, he wasn't so intent on his aim that he failed to notice someone creeping up on his flank. His shouted order was perfectly clear. 'Stay where you are or he dies.'

'Drop your gun,' Helen called back.

'Ah, my dear *Danielle*.' Paul relaxed slightly. 'I heard there was a girl running about. It had to be you. Now let me see if I can guess what you are doing here. A little attempted sabotage, perhaps, with your stolen explosives?'

Slowly, discreetly, Helen drew her gun out of her pocket.

'You're too far away,' Paul said. 'You'll never hit me at that range. Not with a .32.' He chuckled. 'Actually he dies anyway, but there's no reason why we can't have a chat first. So where've you been, Helen?' He waved his gun slightly. 'Shacked up with *Renard* somewhere? I hope he gave you a good time. Upper-class girls like a good ride, don't they? Although I must admit I'm surprised, because I always thought you were a frigid little bitch.'

'Don't answer him, Hélène,' André said. 'Just go. Go as quickly as you can.'

There was no way Helen could go. In any case, Paul was speaking again. 'Oh, how touching,' he said. 'What a gentleman.' His voice hardened. 'You pulled the wool over my eyes, Helen. You made me look a fool and your boyfriend is about to pay the price. Where shall I shoot him? You can choose. The head or the heart? Or shall I make it linger? Perhaps you'd like to hear him scream.' When Helen didn't reply, he laughed. 'Oh, don't worry. I won't kill you. I've got much more enjoyable plans for you. And afterwards I'll sell you on. I know plenty of nice Gestapo officers who will pay good money for a lovely SOE office girl like you.'

Suddenly someone else was running towards them. It was Paul's helper, Simon, the one who smelt. He too had a gun in his hand. Quickly glancing back at Paul, Helen realised that from where he stood Paul couldn't see who it was, nor was he going to take a risk. Helen saw him steady his aim on André, saw his hand tense, and, holding her breath, before she could even think what she was doing, she pulled the trigger on her own gun.

Twice. Always fire twice. At the vulnerable area between the head and the crutch. It was automatic. Without even pausing for a moment she steadied her aim and fired again. The gun jumped violently in her hand. The shots echoed violently round the confined space. Lowering her arm in shock, Helen saw that Paul was on the ground.

André was jumping to one side and running, low and fast, towards him. 'Get down,' he shouted. 'Get down.'

Helen realised she could no longer see the other man, and then she heard another shot, a jolt, and the gun dropped from her hand, clattering on the concrete. For a startled second she thought something had hit her but she felt no pain. More shots were echoing round the buildings. She could smell the cordite. It reminded her of Scotland all those months ago. She had liked the smell then. Now she knew it was the smell of death.

A moment later she saw André kneeling beside Paul, then he ran over to the other man, who she could now see sprawled at the corner a few yards away, and then he was at her side. Pale but uninjured.

'Both dead,' he said. 'Good shooting. Actually, incredible shooting.' Raising a hand to her face he touched her gently. 'Thanks, darling.'

Helen stared at him. He looked fuzzy at the edges. She realised she felt very odd. Numb and very cold. Almost as if she wanted to laugh. Is this what killing does, she wondered, it makes you light headed? And then André pulled her into his arms and suddenly, like an exploding dream, she felt the pain. Pain such as she had never felt before. Pain that welled up like a ball of fire in her throat and emerged in a scream that almost took her head off.

André jerked back. 'Oh my God, you've been hit.' His face was white. White and fuzzy and reeling in front of her. 'Where? Hélène, where?'

She didn't know where. All she knew was that her fingers were wet. Wet and red and dripping where she was holding her chest. Suddenly the ground began to tilt alarmingly. Through a dark blur she was aware of André helping her to a dark corner and wrapping his jacket around her as he lowered her on to the cold hard concrete.

Only yards away Paul's body lay sprawled in a dark pool of blood. 'I killed him,' Helen whispered, or she thought that was what she said, but André either didn't hear or didn't understand.

'Oh no, please no,' he muttered and his voice was agonised. She felt his fingers hot on her ice-cold face. 'I ought to try and get help but I don't want to leave you.'

Help? Helen thought. What on earth sort of help could he get on a night like this?

Please don't leave me, she whispered. Please don't leave me to bleed to death like a stuck pig. But the words didn't come. Just a bubbling hiss of breath.

'Oh God.' She heard André's muffled oath from a long way away. 'I love you, darling,' he said. 'Be strong.'

Katy couldn't sleep. She had woken with a jerk several minutes before and now she couldn't go back to sleep.

'Are you all right, darling?' Ward asked.

'I can't get to sleep,' Katy said. 'I'm worried about Helen. I think she's in difficulties.'

Ward hugged her close. 'You're only saying that because of what I said earlier.' He had been to the SOE that day, where he had found everyone in a state of disarray. A message had apparently just come in from an operative in Lyons casting some doubt about Helen's contact, *Lucien*. There had been some sharp words exchanged, and one man in particular, Helen's former boss, Angus McNaughton, had looked very uncomfortable about it.

'André,' Katy had whispered. 'That must mean André is on our side after all. Oh, I do hope Helen realises that.'

Ward had shrugged. He had heard all about André Cabillard by now. 'I think that's what the SOE are coming round to thinking,' he said. 'And if that's the case, this Angus McNaughton fellow is apparently going to have to eat a very large portion of humble pie.'

Now, thinking about the conversation again, Katy shifted uneasily in the bed, wishing she wasn't conscious of a vague sense of panic, and felt Ward's hand reach for hers. 'Talk to me,' she said. 'Tell me something nice. Something to keep my mind off it.'

Ward drew her close to him. 'Okay,' he said. 'I'll tell you something I forgot to tell you earlier, which is that I bumped into Henry Keller in town. He was asking all about Jen's operation.'

Katy nodded. 'He wants her to work for him.'

'That's what he said,' Ward agreed, 'but, well, you know, I thought there was a bit more than professional interest there. He seemed awfully keen to know when she was coming out of hospital.' He hesitated. 'So I took the liberty of asking him to the party tomorrow night. I know, I know,' he went on quickly as Katy started to object. 'It's okay. I checked with Mrs Carter and she said it was fine. She seemed quite excited about it actually. I think she's really pleased that Jen's moving back in. And secretly so is Jen.' He smiled and kissed her hair gently. 'It's funny how things work out, isn't it?'

Katy felt tears prickle her eyes. 'Oh Ward,' she whispered. 'I'm so glad you're back.'

'Not half as glad as I am.' Gently, he eased her on to the pillow. 'Now go to sleep, darling. I have every confidence in Helen, I always have done. Those German occupation forces are no match for her.'

'I hope you're right,' Katy murmured. 'I do so hope you're right.'

Helen was drifting out of consciousness when through the dock fence she heard the hard insistent rhythm of marching feet. The vibration of heavy vehicles. Guttural German commands. So it's too late, she thought. The Germans are here. Then she heard the shrill squawk of a loudspeaker and the rattle of small arms. Opening her eyes she saw that sailors were suddenly pouring off the nearest ships.

André was cradling her in her arms, and she felt him tense. 'What's happening?' she asked. 'What's going on?'

'The Germans are here,' he said, 'and de Laborde has given the order to scuttle. All inessential personnel have been sent off the ships. I just hope to God there's time …'

Even as he spoke the ground seemed to heave under

them, and a great thunderclap of sound rent the air. André looked up, startled, and then as another thunderclap followed the first, behind them, far behind them, they heard a distant thumping explosion.

'Good God,' he said in awe. 'The battleships are firing on the German tanks.'

'You must go and light the fuses,' Helen whispered.

He shook his head. 'How are you feeling? I think I ought to look at your wound. You're losing a hell of a lot of blood.'

'No.' She tried to push him away. She knew if he saw the wound he would never go. 'Go. Go and blow the fuses. I'm all right.'

'You're far from all right,' he said, 'and the Germans—'

'André, go,' she said. 'You must. We've come so far. We can't let everyone down now.'

There was a long silence, then he kissed her gently. She closed her eyes. She couldn't look at him. When she opened them again he had gone.

It was only minutes before she heard the first explosions. Shouting. Pounding feet. She saw the flames rising high into the lightening sky, the smoke. She tasted the burning oil on her tongue. And all the time, the deep, deafening, thunking roar of the great battleship guns.

As consciousness slipped again, her thoughts became a strange jumble of memories. One minute she was a child running into the sea, screaming as the waves crashed over her head, the next she was in the shooting gallery in Scotland, killing all the cardboard cut-outs, even the women and children.

She had no idea how long she had been there. All she knew was that she felt stiff and cold and very tired, and the memories began again.

This time it was her father standing in the hallway of the Mayfair house, telling her he never worried about her; Katy, serving drinks with Malcolm in her arms; Madame and her old friend hunched over the wireless listening to the bells of Coventry Cathedral; Ward haggard and exhausted but offering to stay on. Then there was little George, Pam, Alan, Jen, Mrs Carter, Louise …

The thought of never seeing any of them again brought tears to Helen's eyes. She realised suddenly that it was because of them that she was here. It was for them, and all the millions of people like them, that the Germans had to be defeated.

Please let everything work out for them, she whispered. Please let them all be happy. Just as I've been happy for the last few days. Happier than I'd ever believed possible.

The pain was now a hard throbbing ache, but the bleeding seemed to have stopped. Either that or the pressure of her fingers was holding the wound closely. If only Katy was here, she thought. Katy would know what to do.

There André was back, kneeling beside her, calling her name urgently. 'Hélène! Open your eyes. Darling. Listen to me. The submarines are leaving. Captain Meynier has agreed to take you. He's got a medic on board.'

For a moment she didn't understand, and then she realised what he meant. He was sending her away. To safety. It was the ultimate sacrifice. The ultimate sign of his love.

'No,' she whispered. 'I don't want to go. I want to stay with you to the end.'

'It's your only chance,' he said. 'We'll never be able to get medical help for you here, not now.'

He picked her up, apologising as the pain swept over her. He seemed to run for ever, and every step jolted through her. She could barely keep consciousness. She could feel the bones, or what was left of them, in her chest and shoulder jarring together.

Just once he rested, and while he recovered his breath he drew a notebook out of his pocket. 'I'm sorry, sweetheart,' he muttered. 'I must just write something down.'

Slumped against the wall Helen stared at him, but the relief of being still was such that she didn't question him. In any case she would not have been heard. The noise was intense now. The whole dock was milling with sailors. Their voices were high with fear and excitement. They were battling to get away from the fires, or the Germans. Or were they were preparing to fight? It was hard to tell which in the swirling smoke. The smell of it was harsh at the back of her throat. Somewhere near by a massive crane crashed into the water, sparks flew. Helen closed her eyes. Tried to breathe.

She was in André's arms again. She felt the wool of his highnecked jersey rough against her cheek. The warm smell of him. Her arm felt as though he was trying to twist it off. Then he stumbled over a railway line and everything mercifully disappeared.

The next thing she heard was André's voice. '*Permission de monter à bord?*'

'*Accordé.*'

The clump of feet on wood, then on metal. The sinister long grey shape low in the water. The metal nameplate, *Glorieux*, glinted on the rail.

'André, don't leave me.' Helen clutched his jacket as he lowered her to the ground.

He prised her fingers off. 'I must,' he said. 'There are soldiers right behind us.'

Even as he spoke, Helen could hear an order barked in German through a megaphone.

Raising his own megaphone, Captain Meynier gave a rude reply. A bullet came zinging past. Everyone ducked. Meynier fired back.

At the next mooring *Casabianca* was pulling away. A third submarine, *Marsouin* perhaps, was already moving slowly across the harbour. There were planes overhead. Helen hadn't noticed them before, but now in this quieter part of the dock she could hear the erratic beat of the engines, the dull vibration as they swooped low over the two departing submarines.

'Go!' Meynier shouted to André. 'I'll look after her. But for God's sake go, or they'll be on board.'

Clutching the cold rail, Helen took a last look at the man she loved. Wild haired, with her blood on his cheek, he looked back. She could see the fires reflected in his eyes.

'Hélène,' he said. His voice was raw. Then he kissed her hard on the lips and was gone.

A second later someone was carrying her down a spiral metal staircase, feet clanging on the metal rungs, and then she was in some kind of mess room. The walls were panelled in wood, and on the walls were pictures of senior officers, their cuffs and hats thick with gold braid. Silver trophies sparkled in a glass cabinet, and an aged flag was furled in the corner.

The officer helped her to a heavy wooden chair. 'Here,' he said. 'You can sit here. We will find a cabin for you later.'

André, she thought. Oh André. I can't bear it.

Slowly, carefully, she pulled her gun out of her pocket and put it on the long polished table. Already the submarine was moving. She could feel the vibration.

She felt reality slip again, and then, just as she was closing her eyes, there was a violent explosion and the submarine seemed to leap to the side. Helen screamed as her arm bashed the table. The lights flickered alarmingly. Immediately some kind of whistling siren went off, and two men ran past the door.

'What's happened?' she shouted, clutching her arm as the pain rocketed through her.

'We've hit a mine,' they shouted back.

This is it! Helen thought, and she hoped André could not see from wherever he was, but the engines continued to judder and the low hum that pervaded the ship continued.

She heard a distant shout of '*Plongez!*', a klaxon sounded and a moment later the whole ship tipped forward. The boardroom door clanged shut. Helen's gun fell off the table and slithered across the metal floor.

The dive seemed to last for ever. We're sinking, Helen thought, clutching the table for dear life. Something's damaged and we're going straight to the bottom.

She expected water to come gushing through the door at any moment, but the only liquid on the floor was blood, and slowly, agonisingly slowly, the vessel righted itself to horizontal. Again the timbre of the engines changed.

As a semblance of peace returned, Helen leaned weakly on the table. When the door opened she barely noticed.

'We are clear of the harbour,' Captain Meynier said. 'We have been slightly damaged. I intend to put into Valencia for repairs, and then we will sail to join the Fighting French at Oran.' He was gone again before she could even thank him.

A bearded officer came in carrying a leather case. '*Le capitaine* has sent me. I am a medic. I will do what I can.' Quickly he brought out a knife and began to cut her sweater at the shoulder. He paled when he saw the wound. '*Sacré bleu*,' he muttered, and produced a swab. 'Hold tight, mademoiselle. I just need to see … I'm afraid it might hurt a little but …'

It hurt all right, but now, even though the blood still dripped steadily on to the boardroom carpet, the pain seemed to be more in her heart. 'I can't bear it,' she whispered. 'I can't bear the pain of not being with him.' And then he stuck a syringe in her arm and mercifully everything began to fade.

Chapter Thirty

'It's gone,' Katy said suddenly to Ward as they got ready for the café party.

He looked alarmed. 'What's gone?'

'The feeling,' she said. 'The feeling I had in the night. About Helen.'

Ward lowered his hands from his tie. 'Is that good or bad?' he asked.

'I don't know,' Katy said. 'I just know it's gone.'

'Are you sure it wasn't indigestion?'

Katy glared at him. 'Of course it wasn't,' she began, but then she stopped. 'Ward, um … is that what you're intending to wear to the party?'

'I haven't got any choice,' he said. 'You gave my only decent set of clothes to Louise's husband last night.' He glanced down at the ill-fitting trousers and jacket. 'Do I look really awful?'

'Terrible,' Katy said, 'but who cares? Everyone will be so delighted to see you home safely that they probably won't notice.'

She was right, although his aunts' delight unfortunately took the form of uncontrollable weeping. Even Winston their ancient little dachshund looked rather overcome as he blinked up anxiously at the two sobbing old ladies.

'We knew you'd come back safely,' Esme Taylor said, clutching Ward's arm. 'Didn't we, Thelma?'

Thelma Taylor dabbed her eyes with an inadequate lace-edged hanky. 'Oh, we did, we did,' she wailed.

'We knew you'd come home,' Esme sobbed.

'We did, we did.'

'It's like some awful Greek play,' Jen muttered to Katy.

Katy giggled, and catching Ward's please-come-and-rescue-me glance she shook her head. 'It serves you right,' she mouthed, shifting Malcolm from one hip to the other, 'for putting us all through such agony.'

'How's the Ward and Malcolm situation working out?' Jen asked.

Katy's smile faded. 'Ward's tried,' she said, 'he really has, but Malcolm won't have anything to do with him.' She sighed. It was the one thing that had been disappointing about Ward's return. Catching Celia Rutherford as she went past with a tray of drinks, she asked if she could put Malcolm down on the floor. 'I don't think he'll get under people's feet,' she said. 'Normally he just sits quietly under a table. It's just that he's getting a bit heavy.'

'Of course you can,' Celia said. 'I'm sure he'll be good as gold.'

'Heavy?' Jen remarked as Katy lowered him to the ground. 'Good God. I never thought I'd hear you say that.'

'I know,' Katy said. 'I can hardly believe it myself. And he's such a good baby now. So quiet and well behaved.'

'Yes,' Jen said dryly as Malcolm screamed in delight at his sudden freedom and crawled off at high speed in hot pursuit of the Miss Taylors' startled dachshund. 'So I see.'

When Molly appeared at the door a little later, Katy was convinced that some disaster must have occurred at the pub.

'It's all right,' Molly said hastily. 'I just thought I'd pop up to say everything is okay, in case you and Ward wanted to stay a bit longer than you thought.'

'Oh Molly,' Katy said. 'That's kind.' Then noticing a

strangely bright light in Molly's eyes she peered at her more closely. 'You haven't been on the bottle, have you, Molly?'

Molly giggled. 'Of course not,' she said. 'It's just that when I said everything was all right, I meant everything. You know, me and Aaref and that.'

'Oh Molly,' Katy said. 'How wonderful. I thought you were going to tell him to get lost.'

'Well, I was,' Molly said, 'but when he came in he'd got this terrible black eye and, well, I suppose I felt sorry for him. So …'

'A black eye? How did he get a black eye?'

Molly shrugged. 'He said he tripped on the stairs. I didn't really believe him, but he was so busy telling me how much he loves me, and pleading with me not to go to Surrey, I didn't press it.'

'So you won't be going to Surrey after all, then?'

'Oh no,' Molly said. 'I'm going all right. It's a really good job. If he wants to see me he'll just have to get a bike and come and see me there … Good God!' she added, gaping open mouthed across the room. 'Is that Sister Morris? I didn't recognise her for a minute. What's she done to her hair?'

Katy giggled. 'I think it's a new perm,' she said. 'I hope Mr Goodacre arrives soon or it will be wasted.'

An hour later Joyce looked around the room at everyone chatting away nineteen to the dozen and felt a warm feeling of satisfaction. The bell on the door had barely stopped clanging all evening as more and more people poured in. Everyone seemed pleased to be there. They were all so complimentary about the little finger snacks she and Mrs Rutherford had prepared so carefully, and they were certainly tucking into the booze that Mr Rutherford was handing round so courteously.

Mr Goodacre had indeed arrived and turned out to be the life and soul of the party. He had chatted to everyone and was now trapped in the corner by Sister Morris's mighty bosom. Jen had amused everyone by making a coy little speech of thanks to them both and presenting them with a pair of tickets to her show.

'And as another little thank you, I've got a pair for you and Mr Lorenz as well,' she had gone on, turning to Joyce. 'I thought it would be fun if you all came on the same night.'

Mr Lorenz had been delighted, almost as delighted as he had been when Joyce had stopped him in the street a couple of days ago to tell him that Stanley had copped it. Not that he had shown his delight then, of course. He had offered his condolences most correctly, but there was definitely a spring in his step as he walked away. Today, the first to arrive, he had brought a big bunch of carnations for Mrs Rutherford and a small wooden box with holes punched in the top for Joyce.

'What on earth is it?' Joyce had asked as he handed it to her solemnly.

'I hope you like it,' he had said. 'I know it's a strange gift, but you did say you wanted one.'

'Oh Mr Lorenz!' she cried. 'You haven't!'

But he had. Inside the box was a large, rather dazed-looking tortoise. 'Oh, he's beautiful,' Joyce had whispered, and impulsively she had leaned over and kissed Mr Lorenz on the cheek.

Mr Lorenz had been quite overcome at such a public display of affection and had been glugging back the wine ever since.

All in all, Joyce thought now, the party was passing off remarkably well. In fact it could hardly have been better.

Catching Mrs Rutherford's eye across the room a moment later she smiled and Celia smiled back. It was a moment of quiet triumph. It was their success. Theirs only. Two middle-aged women from totally different backgrounds coming together to make something work. Not just work either, but to make a profit too. Fifty pounds.

Joyce's smile widened. Perhaps she would use a bit of it to buy Mr Lorenz a little thankyou gift and all. And she'd sign the card Joyce, not Mrs Carter.

On the other side of the room Jen and Katy watched anxiously as Greville Rutherford topped up Ward's wine.

'Glad to see you back, Frazer,' he said heartily. 'I gather you gave Jerry the slip. Jolly good show. Well, I suppose you'll be taking over the reins at the Flag and Garter now. Good thing too. A pub needs a man at the helm.'

Ward's dark brows rose slightly. 'Really?' he said. 'I am surprised you should think that when it has clearly done so well under my wife's management. I had a look at the books yesterday and I really don't think anyone could hope for a more successful business. Frankly, I don't know how she's done it with so little support from the brewery, but she has, and I'm certainly not going to interfere unless she wants me to.'

'That's told him,' Jen whispered to Katy as Ward nodded politely and moved away. 'Poor old Groper, I've never seen him look so taken aback!'

A moment later Greville Rutherford had a further shock as the door clanged open once more and Louise and Jack came in hand in hand, looking distinctly dishevelled.

Louise was beaming from ear to ear. 'Hello, everyone,' she cooed. 'I'm so sorry we're late. We, er ... got a bit tied up.'

Unaware of her father's mouth opening and shutting like a startled goldfish, Louise took Ward's arm and pulled him round to meet Jack. 'This is Ward Frazer, Katy's husband,' she said, 'and this is Jack. Lieutenant Commander Jack Delmaine. My darling husband.'

'How nice to meet you,' Ward said gravely, shaking hands. 'I must say, Jack, I do like your shirt. I wouldn't mind one like that myself. And that jacket too, it reminds me—'

'Hello, Jack,' Katy interrupted quickly. 'Long time no

see. Oh, goodness me,' she added innocently, staring at his bruised knuckles. 'Whatever have you done to your hand?'

Jack flushed slightly. 'Oh, it's just a graze.'

Louise giggled. 'He was protecting my virtue,' she said. 'Rather manfully, I must say.'

'By the look of those love bites on her neck, that's not the only thing he was doing manfully,' Ward murmured dryly as Louise dragged Jack off to see her mother.

'Wow,' Jen rolled her eyes a moment later as Katy joined her by the drinks table. 'They certainly seem to have made up all right. I wonder how that came about?' Then glancing across the room as the bell on the door jangled once again, Jen felt her stomach turn a double somersault.

'Oh my God!' she hissed. 'What's he doing here?'

Katy followed her gaze and saw a tall distinguished-looking man in a sober but elegant grey suit shaking hands politely with Mrs Carter.

'Oh yes,' Katy said. 'That's Henry Keller, isn't it? Ward bumped into him in town yesterday, and for some reason he decided to invite him tonight.'

Jen was looking distinctly white about the gills. 'Oh, did he indeed?' she muttered grimly. 'Well, you'd better enjoy your dear Ward Frazer while you can, because when I get the chance I'm going to kill him.'

But she didn't get the chance just then, because Henry Keller was already approaching. 'So how is my favourite singer?' he asked easily as Katy melted tactfully away. 'Feeling better, I hope?'

'Yes, I am feeling better, thank you,' Jen muttered weakly.

'You don't sound it.'

'Don't I?' Jen cleared her throat and looked at him anxiously. 'What do you mean? How do I sound?'

'Well, rather husky, actually,' he said. 'And surprisingly flustered.'

Jen lowered her eyes. 'Well, that's your fault,' she said coyly. 'Nothing to do with the operation.'

He raised his eyebrows. 'My fault?' he asked. 'Why ever's that?'

Oh no, Jen thought. I've got it wrong. This was a nightmare. She was one step off making a total idiot of herself. Flattery, she said to herself. Flattery is my only hope. 'Because you're so important and it makes me feel nervous,' she said. 'I suppose I'm not used to chatting socially with eminent theatre producers.'

'Ah,' he said gravely. 'So that's the problem. Well, I wonder if it might help you feel less nervous if I took you out to dinner one evening next week?'

Jen blinked. A miniature rose was one thing. Dinner was quite another. 'Dinner?'

'Yes,' he said blithely. 'I always feel particularly uneminent at dinner. Especially when I am attempting to court the most extraordinarily desirable girl I have met in a long time.'

It took a second for his meaning to penetrate Jen's defences, but when it did she could not believe it. She realised that deep down it was what she had really wanted all along, but now it had happened she didn't know what to do. What to say. All her usual sparky retorts seemed to have deserted her. All she could do was stand there like a complete dope and let the hot flush creep up into her face.

A twittering noise behind her warned her that the Miss Taylors were approaching. 'Oh Mr Keller, we are such fans of your shows.' Esme Taylor grasped his hand reverently. 'We saw your production of *Dear Octopus* before the war. We used to be in the theatre ourselves, you know. And this is our dear friend Mrs Frost, Jen's old teacher ...'

With a faint smile at Jen, Henry Keller greeted them courteously. 'How lovely to meet you all. You must be so proud of your protégée.'

Grateful for the reprieve, Jen backed away and bumped straight into her mother.

'You're looking a bit flushed,' Joyce remarked. 'Although I don't reckon as it's the heat that's put the colour back in your cheeks.'

In the past Jen would have taken offence but now she was so out of her depth that she felt she needed moral support from any corner. Glancing over her shoulder she lowered her voice. 'What do you think of him?' she asked. 'Do you think he's all right?'

'I've hardly spoken to him,' Joyce said. 'Looks a nice enough fellow. Bit on the smart side for the likes of us.' She hesitated for a second. 'Although, of course, he's got one thing in his favour …'

'Oh?' Jen brightened. 'What's that?'

Joyce smirked. 'Well, he's Jewish, isn't he? Must be with a name like that.'

'I've just been talking to your mother,' Ward said to Katy. 'My aunts have asked her to stay on with them indefinitely, but she seems to be labouring under the impression that you want her to come back to live at the pub.'

Katy stared at him. 'Oh no. What did you say?'

'I said I thought my aunts would miss her terribly and it would be doing me an enormous favour if she would stay down there and look after them. And that of course we'd come down to see them all just as soon as possible.'

Katy felt a sense of relief wash over her. The last thing in the world she wanted to do was hurt her mother's feelings, but the thought of having her back in the pub …

Suddenly out of the corner of her eye she saw Sister Morris bearing down on them. 'Hello, Sister,' she said brightly. 'How are you? I love your new hairstyle …'

But Sister Morris wasn't interested in her. It was Ward she wanted to talk to. 'Glad to see you back, young man,' she barked. 'And about time too, if you don't mind me saying.'

Ward smiled. 'I came as quickly as I could.'

Sister Morris snorted. 'You'd have come a lot quicker if

you'd had that leg properly dealt with. It looks to me as though it needs resetting. I'll make an appointment for you to see the orthopaedic surgeon next week. Can't have a handsome man like you going around with a limp for the rest of your life.'

Once again Katy met Ward's eyes and once again she could barely control her laughter. Ignoring his terrified glance, she turned to Pam Nelson. 'How's motherhood?' she asked.

'Tiring,' she said, 'but Alan's being wonderful and George simply dotes on the baby.'

As though to bear out her words, a few minutes later, having inspected the tortoise and helped Malcolm chase Winston round a bit, George suddenly remembered that he was too old for such childish pursuits and decided to show off his little sister instead.

'She's called after our friend Helen who came to live with us,' he told Greville Rutherford proudly.

'Ah yes,' Greville Rutherford said. 'Lady Helen de Burrel.' He raised his glass to his lips and looked round vaguely. 'I wonder why she's not here tonight?'

George was surprised. 'Because she's in France,' he said.

'In France?' Greville almost choked on his wine. 'What are you talking about, child? She's not in France.'

Angry at having his word doubted, George's chin came up ominously. 'She is too,' he said. He raised his voice. 'Isn't she, Mum?'

Pam smiled across at him distractedly. 'What's that, darling?'

'Isn't Helen in France?'

The smile left Pam's face abruptly. Glancing round uneasily, she tried to steer him away. 'No, I don't think so, darling …'

'She is! She is!' George shouted, wriggling free. 'She told me. She parachuted in and she's going to blow up the ships in the harbour. She's the bravest person in the whole world.'

'Hear, hear.' Ward Frazer spoke dryly into the shocked silence that followed this outburst.

As he glared round defiantly, a stricken look crossed George's little face. Slowly he brought his hand up to his mouth. Tears welled in his eyes. 'Oh dear,' he whispered, hanging his head in a picture of dejection. 'It was a secret. And now I've said.'

'It doesn't matter, darling.' Pam crouched down quickly and drew him into her arms. 'I don't think Helen would mind people knowing. Most of us knew anyway, didn't we, Katy?'

'Oh yes,' Katy agreed. 'Most of us knew.'

'Well, I didn't know,' Greville Rutherford blurted out. He looked absolutely stunned. 'I had no idea. But she's only a girl, so pretty and delicate, she can't possibly … Oh my word,' he added, blenching slightly, 'that probably explains—'

Perhaps fortuitously, before he could tell everyone what it explained, he was swiftly interrupted by his wife. 'I think a toast might be in order,' Celia said crisply. 'To absent friends.'

Katy could hardly hold her glass for laughing as Greville Rutherford subsided abruptly, flushing as red as his wine. 'Yes, of course, dear,' he muttered, raising his glass obediently. 'Absolutely. To absent friends.'

It was as they drank the toast that Jen glanced at the clock. 'We're missing the news,' she screamed, running to the wireless. 'We must hear the news.'

She was just in time. The last chimes of Big Ben were fading away, and a second later the newsreader's voice filled the small café.

'Good news from France this morning,' he announced calmly. 'At dawn, just as German troops finally entered the great naval port of Toulon, the French fleet was scuttled in the harbour. Munition dumps, oil tanks and all stores of military value were blown up. Some of the warships fired on the Germans to gain time for the ships to be sunk. The captains of all the vessels stayed on their bridges until their ships went down. Many of these officers lost their lives. The destruction of the fleet has brought to an end the fear that it might fall into Axis hands and thus sway the balance of naval power.'

As the clipped BBC voice moved on to further successes in North Africa and in Russia, Jen and Katy fell into each other's arms.

'She's done it,' Jen screamed. 'She's done it.'

Katy only just had time to see the thunderstruck expression on Greville Rutherford's face before Pam gripped her arm. 'Katy, look,' she said. 'Look at Malcolm.'

Turning round slowly Katy felt her heart stop.

'You didn't tell me he could walk.'

'He can't,' Katy said, but he could. Having finally abandoned his pursuit of poor Winston, Malcolm had pushed himself off from a table leg and was now, wobbly step by wobbly step, advancing across the floor, and the person he was heading for was Ward.

Ward was too busy cheering to notice, however, and it was only as the whole room fell suddenly silent that he glanced round and saw what was happening. For a second he looked up and met Katy's eyes, and then just as Malcolm began to topple he caught him and swept him up into his arms. 'Hey,' he said. 'You're far too young to walk,' but he couldn't disguise the pride in his voice, and Katy saw the Miss Taylors once again scrabbling frantically for their damp hankies.

'Da-da-da,' Malcolm said, happily clapping his hands.

As she stood there watching the two of them, the same proud laughing expression in both pairs of eyes, Katy felt her own tears well up.

Suddenly once again everyone was clapping, and through the clapping Katy realised the voice on the wireless had changed. It was the Free French leader, General de Gaulle, who was speaking now, speaking with pride of the sailors who had finally seen through the odious veil of lies, and, caught by the emotion in the deep accented voice, she turned her head to hear.

'France heard the guns of Toulon,' he said, 'the explosions, the desperate shots fired in a last stand. And a tremor of pain, of pity, of rage shook the whole country.'

Suddenly everyone in the café was listening. Even the children seemed affected by the powerful, sonorous voice. When he paused for a moment, the silence was absolute. And then he spoke again, and his sudden rousing declaration sent shivers up Katy's spine.

'On to victory,' he cried. 'There is no other road.'

'To victory!' Jack Delmaine echoed suddenly, raising his glass. 'To victory and the freedom of France,' and everyone followed suit. Even Greville Rutherford.

'To victory …'

When Helen woke she was lying full length on a narrow bunk, with her arm splinted and her shoulder swathed in bandages. The medic must have given her something to make her sleep, she realised, wondering what time it was. It felt like night, but in a submarine there is no difference between day and night of course. The low hum of vibration and the artificial light go on and on regardless of time.

Glancing around the small cabin, she saw her jacket hung on a chair beside her, and reaching over tentatively with her good hand she fumbled in the pocket in the hope of finding her watch which was no longer on her wrist. But instead of her watch her fingers closed on a folded piece of paper.

Drawing it out with a frown, she realised it was the note André had written on the dock.

There were actually two sheets. The first sheet was printed in bold letters: 'Urgent and most secret. Whoever finds this should deliver it to Maurice Buckmaster c/o War Office, London.' It was short, succinct and unemotional. There were no recriminations. It merely stated coldly that

Paul was a traitor but now dead, then it listed the equipment and medical supplies André needed to carry on the struggle. Most urgent of all was a radio transmitter. He gave a grid reference and asked for a personal message, 'the fox is waiting' to be broadcast after the BBC overseas news the night of the drop. He also wanted to hear a message regarding Helen's condition: 'the girl loves the fox' if she survived the journey, and 'the girl says goodbye' if not.

Biting her lip, Helen turned to the second sheet, which was addressed to her.

> My darling Hélène, in haste. I think you know how much I hate to let you go, but it is for the best. You are badly hurt and I cannot guarantee getting medical help here. But it is not goodbye, it is farewell. We will be together again one day. I know it. And one day too the world will be free again. Until then my duty lies here. I wish it were otherwise. I will miss you. And long for you. Keep safe. And well. And happy.
>
> With all my love, always,
>
> André.

As the tears poured from her eyes, Helen felt the restorative power of his love flood through her, and then, hugging the note to her chest, she closed her eyes and slept.

also available from

THE ORION PUBLISHING GROUP

☐ **The Girl from Penvarris** *£5.99*
ROSEMARY AITKEN
0 75280 342 5

☐ **The Tinner's Daughter** *£5.99*
ROSEMARY AITKEN
0 75280 596 7

☐ **The Girl from the Back Streets** *£4.99*
JOYCE BELL
1 85797 418 2

☐ **Silk Town** *£5.99*
JOYCE BELL
0 75280 405 7

☐ **Lavender Road** *£5.99*
HELEN CAREY
0 75280 066 3

☐ **Some Sunny Day** *£5.99*
HELEN CAREY
0 75280 247 X

☐ **Dreams of Other Days** *£5.99*
ELAINE CROWLEY
0 75280 403 0

☐ **The Ways of Women** *£5.99*
ELAINE CROWLEY
1 85797 438 7

☐ **Goodbye Sweetheart** *£5.99*
LILIAN HARRY
1 85797 812 9

☐ **The Girls They Left Behind** *£4.99*
LILIAN HARRY
0 75280 333 6

☐ **Keep Smiling Through** *£5.99*
LILIAN HARRY
0 75280 407 3

☐ **Moonlight and Lovesongs** *£5.99*
LILIAN HARRY
0 75281 564 4

☐ **Lights out Liverpool** *£5.99*
MAUREEN LEE
0 75280 402 2

☐ **Put out the Fires** *£5.99*
MAUREEN LEE
0 75280 408 1

☐ **Stepping Stones** *£5.99*
MAUREEN LEE
0 75281 726 4

☐ **Through the Storm** *£5.99*
MAUREEN LEE
0 75281 628 4

☐ **Old Father Thames** *£4.99*
SALLY SPENCER
0 75280 313 1

☐ **Salt of the Earth** *£4.99*
SALLY SPENCER
1 85797 146 9

☐ **Those Golden Days** *£5.99*
SALLY SPENCER
0 75280 911 3

☐ **Up our Street** *£4.99*
SALLY SPENCER
1 85797 870 6

All Orion/Phoenix titles are available at your local bookshop or from the following address:

Littlehampton Book Services
Cash Sales Department L
14 Eldon Way, Lineside Industrial Estate
Littlehampton
West Sussex BN17 7HE
telephone 01903 721596, *facsimile* 01903 730914

Payment can either be made by credit card (Visa and Mastercard accepted) or by sending a cheque or postal order made payable to *Littlehampton Book Services*.

DO NOT SEND CASH OR CURRENCY.

Please add the following to cover postage and packing

UK and BFPO:
£1.50 for the first book, and 50P for each additional book to a maximum of £3.50

Overseas and Eire:
£2.50 for the first book plus £1.00 for the second book and 50p for each additional book ordered

---

BLOCK CAPITALS PLEASE

name of cardholder ....

address of cardholder ....

....

....

....

postcode ....

delivery address
(if different from cardholder)

....

....

....

....

postcode ....

☐ I enclose my remittance for £..............................

☐ please debit my Mastercard/Visa (delete as appropriate)

card number ☐☐☐☐☐☐☐☐☐☐☐☐☐☐☐☐

expiry date ☐☐☐☐

signature ....

prices and availability are subject to change without notice